THE BUMPER BOOK OF
CLASSIC STORIES

THE BUMPER BOOK OF
CLASSIC
STORIES

HAMLYN

**Illustrated by Harry Bishop,
except *Robinson Crusoe*, illustrated by John Berry.**

This collection of abridged stories first published 1987 by
Dean an imprint of The Hamlyn Publishing Group Limited,
Bridge House, 69 London Road, Twickenham, Middlesex TW1 3SB.
Copyright © Text and illustrations
The Hamlyn Publishing Group Limited 1983, 1985, 1987

ISBN 0 600 53149 X

Printed in Czechoslovakia.
52139

These abridged stories first appeared as individual titles
in *The Illustrated Classics series*,
published by Deans International Publishing,
an imprint of The Hamlyn Publishing Group Limited 1983, 1985.

CONTENTS

Note: These stories have been abridged and re-told

AROUND THE WORLD
IN EIGHTY DAYS

Phileas Fogg's New Servant

Mr Phileas Fogg was every inch an Englishman who lived, in 1872, at No. 7, Savile Row, Burlington Gardens, the house in which Sheridan died in 1814. He was one of the most noticeable members of the Reform Club, though he seemed always to avoid attracting attention; an enigmatical personage, about whom little was known, except that he was an undoubtedly rich and polished man of the world. He was the least communicative of men and few knew how he had come by his money. Phileas Fogg was a member of the Reform, and that was all.

The way in which he got admission to this exclusive club was simple enough. He was recommended by the Barings, with whom he had an open credit. His cheques were regularly paid at sight from his current account, which was always flush.

Mr Fogg was not lavish, nor, on the contrary, avaricious; for whenever he knew that money was needed for a noble, useful, or benevolent purpose he supplied it quietly and sometimes anonymously.

His sole pastimes were reading the papers and playing whist. He lived alone in his house in Savile Row, where a single domestic sufficed to serve him. He breakfasted and dined at the club, at hours mathematically fixed, in the same room, at the same table, never taking his meals with other members, and went home at exactly midnight.

The mansion in Savile Row, though not sumptuous, was exceedingly comfortable. The habits of its occupant were such as to demand but little from the sole domestic, but Phileas Fogg required him to be almost superhumanly prompt and regular.

On this very 2nd of October he had dismissed James Forster, because that luckless youth had brought him shaving-water at eighty-four degrees Fahrenheit instead of eighty-six; and he was awaiting his successor, who was due at the house between eleven and half-past.

Phileas Fogg was seated squarely in his armchair, his feet close together like those of a grenadier on parade, his hands resting on his knees, his body straight, his head erect; he was steadily watching a complicated clock which indicated the hours, the minutes, the seconds, the days, the months, and the years. At exactly half-past eleven Mr Fogg would, according to his daily habit, quit Savile Row, and repair to the Reform.

A rap at this moment sounded on the door of the cosy apartment where Phileas Fogg was seated, and James Forster, the dismissed servant, appeared.

"This is the new servant," said he.

A young man of thirty advanced and bowed.

"You are a Frenchman, I believe," asked Phileas Fogg, "and your name is John?"

"Jean, if monsieur pleases," replied the newcomer, "Jean Passepartout, a surname which has clung to me because I have a natural aptness for going out of one business into another. I believe I'm honest, monsieur, but, to be outspoken, I've had several trades."

"You are well recommended to me; I hear a good report of you. You know my conditions?" asked Mr Fogg.

"Yes, monsieur."

"Good. What time is it?"

"Twenty-two minutes after eleven," returned Passepartout, drawing an enormous silver watch from the depths of his pocket.

"You are too slow," said Mr Fogg.

"Pardon me, monsieur, it is impossible—"

"You are four minutes too slow. No matter; it's enough to mention the error. Now from this moment, twenty-six minutes after eleven, a.m., this Wednesday, October 2nd, you are in my service."

Phileas Fogg got up, took his hat in his left hand, put it on his head with an automatic motion, and went off without a word.

Passepartout heard the street door shut once; it was his new master going out. He heard it shut again; it was his predecessor, James Forster, departing in his turn. Passepartout remained alone in the house in Savile Row.

Passepartout Finds His Ideal Master

During his brief interview with Mr Fogg, Passepartout had been carefully observing him. He appeared to be a man about forty years of age, with fine, handsome features and a tall, well-shaped figure; his hair and whiskers were light, his forehead compact and unwrinkled, his face rather pale, his teeth magnificent.

As for Passepartout, he was a true Parisian of Paris. Since he had abandoned his own country for England, taking service as a valet, he had in vain searched for a master after his own heart. Passepartout was an honest fellow, with a pleasant face, lips a trifle protruding, soft-mannered and serviceable, with a good round head, such as one likes to see on the shoulders of a friend. His eyes were blue, his complexion rubicund, his figure almost portly and well-built, his body muscular, and his physical powers fully developed by the exercises of his younger days. His brown hair was somewhat tumbled.

It would be rash to predict how Passepartout's lively nature would agree with Mr Fogg. It was impossible to tell whether the new servant would turn out as absolutely methodical as his master required; experience alone could solve the question. Passepartout had been a sort of vagrant in his early years, and now yearned for repose; but so far he had failed to find it, though he had already served in ten English houses. But he could not take root in any of these.

At half-past eleven, then, Passepartout found himself alone in the house in Savile Row. He began his inspection without delay, scouring it from cellar to garret. So clean, well-arranged, solemn a mansion pleased him; it seemed to him like a snail's shell, lighted and warmed by gas, which sufficed for both these purposes. When Passepartout reached the second storey he recognized at once the room which he was to inhabit, and he was well satisfied with it. Electric bells and speaking-tubes afforded communication with the lower stories; while on the mantel stood an electric clock, precisely like that in Mr Fogg's bedchamber, both beating the same second at the same instant.

"That's good, that'll do," said Passepartout to himself.

He suddenly observed, hung over the clock, a card, which, upon inspection, proved to be a programme of the daily routine of the house. It comprised all that was required of the servant, from eight in the morning, exactly at which hour Phileas Fogg rose, till half-past eleven, when he left the house for the Reform Club—all the details of service, the tea and toast at twenty-three minutes past eight, the shaving-water at thirty-seven minutes past nine, and the toilet at twenty minutes before ten. Everything was regulated and foreseen that was to be done from half-past eleven a.m. till midnight, the hour at which the methodical gentleman retired.

Mr Fogg's wardrobe was amply supplied and in the best taste. Each pair of trousers, coat, and vest bore a number, indicating the time of year and season at which they were in turn to be laid out for wearing; and the same system was applied to the master's shoes. In short, the house in Savile Row, which must have been a very temple of disorder and unrest under the illustrious but dissipated Sheridan, was cosiness, comfort, and method idealized. There was no study, nor were there books, which would have been quite useless to Mr Fogg; for at the Reform two libraries, one of general literature and the other of law and politics, were at his service. A moderate-sized safe stood in his bedroom, constructed so as to defy fire as well as burglars; but Passepartout found neither arms nor hunting weapons anywhere; everything betrayed the most tranquil and peaceable habits.

Having scrutinized the house from top to bottom, he rubbed his hands, a broad smile overspread his features, and he said joyfully, "This is just what I wanted! Ah, we shall get on together, Mr Fogg and I! What a domestic and regular gentleman, a real machine! Well, I don't mind serving a machine."

A Wager

Mr Fogg had been at the Reform Club for most of the day, where he had been perusing the daily papers. After dining, he returned to the reading-room and at precisely twenty minutes before six, he sat down to the *Pall Mall*.

Half an hour later, several members of the Reform came in and drew up to the fireplace, where a coal fire was steadily burning. They were Mr Fogg's usual partners at whist: Andrew Stuart, an engineer; John Sullivan and Samuel Fallentin, bankers; Thomas Flanagan, a brewer; and Gauthier Ralph, one of the directors of the Bank of England—all rich and highly respectable personages, even in a club which comprises the princes of English trade and finance.

"Well, Ralph," said Thomas Flanagan, "what about that robbery?"

"Oh," replied Stuart, "the bank will lose the money."

"On the contrary," broke in Ralph, "I hope we may put our hands on the robber. Skilful detectives have been sent to all the principal ports of America and the continent, and he'll be a clever fellow if he slips through their fingers."

"But have you got the robber's description?" asked Stuart.

"In the first place, he is no robber at all," returned Ralph, positively.

"What? A fellow who makes off with fifty-five thousand pounds no robber?"

"No."

"Perhaps he's a manufacturer, then."

"The *Daily Telegraph*, however, says that he is a gentleman."

It was Phileas Fogg, whose head now emerged from behind his newspapers, who made this remark. He bowed to his friends, and entered into the conversation. The affair which formed its subject, and which was town talk, had occurred three days before at the Bank of England. A package of banknotes, to the value of fifty-five thousand pounds, had been taken from the principal cashier's table.

As soon as the robbery was discovered, picked detectives hastened off to Liverpool, Glasgow, Havre, Suez, Brindisi, New York, and other ports, inspired by the proffered reward of two thousand pounds, and five per cent on the sum that might be recovered. Detectives were also charged with narrowly watching those who arrived at or left London by rail, and a judicial examination was at once entered upon.

As they placed themselves at the whist table, the gentlemen continued to argue the matter. Stuart and Flanagan played together, while Phileas Fogg had Fallentin for his partner. As the game proceeded the conversation ceased, excepting between the rubbers, when it revived again.

"I maintain," said Stuart, "that the chances are in favour of the thief, who must be a shrewd fellow."

"Well, but where can he fly to?" said Ralph. "No country is safe for him."

"Pshaw!"

"Where could he go, then?"

"Oh, I don't know that. The world is big enough."

"It was once," said Phileas Fogg, in a low tone. "Cut, sir," he added, handing the cards to Thomas Flanagan.

The discussion fell during the rubber, after which Stuart took up its thread.

"What do you mean by 'once'? Has the world grown smaller?"

"Certainly," returned Ralph. "I agree with Mr Fogg. The world *has* grown smaller, since a man can now go round it ten times more quickly than a hundred years ago. And that is why the search for this thief will be more likely to succeed."

"And also why the thief can get away more easily."

"Be so good as to play, Mr Stuart," said Phileas Fogg.

But the incredulous Stuart was not convinced, and when the hand was finished, said eagerly: "You have a strange way, Ralph, of proving that the world has grown smaller. So, because you can go round it in three months—"

"In eighty days," interrupted Phileas Fogg.

"That is true, gentlemen," added John Sullivan; "only eighty days, now that the section between Rothal and Allahabad, on the Great Indian Peninsula Railway, has been opened. Here is the estimate made by the *Daily Telegraph*:

From London to Suez via Mont Cenis and Brindisi, by rail and steamboats	7 days
From Suez to Bombay, by steamer	13 „
From Bombay to Calcutta, by rail	3 „
From Calcutta to Hong Kong, by steamer	13 „
From Hong Kong to Yokohama (Japan), by steamer	6 „
From Yokohama to San Francisco, by steamer	22 „
From San Francisco to New York, by rail	7 „
From New York to London, by steamer and rail	9 „
Total	80 days."

"Yes, in eighty days!" exclaimed Stuart, who in his excitement made a false deal. "But that doesn't take into account bad weather, contrary winds, shipwrecks, railway accidents, and so on."

"All included," returned Phileas Fogg.

"But suppose the Hindoos or Indians pull up the rails," replied Stuart; "suppose they stop the trains, pillage the luggage vans, and scalp the passengers?"

"All included," calmly retorted Fogg; adding, as he threw down the cards, "Two trumps."

Stuart, whose turn it was to deal, gathered them up, and went on: "You are right, theoretically, Mr Fogg, but practically—"

"Practically also, Mr Stuart."

"I'd like to see you do it in eighty days."

"It depends on you. Shall we go?"

"Heaven preserve me! But I would wager four thousand pounds that such a journey, made under these conditions, is impossible."

"Quite possible, on the contrary," returned Mr Fogg.

"Well, make it, then!"

"The journey round the world in eighty days?"

"Yes."

"I should like nothing better."

"When?"

"At once. Only it will be at your expense."

"It's absurd!" cried Stuart, who was beginning to be annoyed at the persistency of his friend. "Come, let's get on with the game."

"Deal over again, then," said Phileas Fogg.

Stuart took up the pack with a feverish hand.

"Well, Mr Fogg," said he, "it shall be so: I will wager the four thousand on it."

"Calm yourself, my dear Stuart," said Fallentin. "It's only a joke."

"When I say I'll wager," returned Stuart, "I mean it."

"All right," said Mr Fogg; and turning to the others he continued: "I have a deposit of twenty thousand at Baring's, which I will willingly risk upon it."

"Twenty thousand pounds!" cried Sullivan. "Twenty thousand pounds, which you would lose by a single accidental delay!"

"The unforeseen does not exist," quietly replied Phileas Fogg.

"But, Mr Fogg, eighty days are only the estimate of the least possible time in which the journey can be made."

"A well-used minimum suffices for everything."

"But, in order not to exceed it, you must jump mathematically from the trains upon the steamers, and from the steamers upon the trains again."

"I will jump—mathematically."

"You are joking."

"A true Englishman doesn't joke when he is talking about so serious a thing as a wager," replied Phileas Fogg solemnly. "I will bet twenty thousand pounds against anyone who wishes that I will make the tour of the world in eighty days or less; in nineteen hundred and twenty hours, or a hundred and fifteen thousand two hundred minutes. Do you accept?"

"We accept," replied Messrs Stuart, Fallentin, Sullivan, Flanagan, and Ralph, after consulting each other.

"Good," said Mr Fogg. "The train leaves for Dover at a quarter before nine. I will take it."

"This very evening?" asked Stuart.

"This very evening," returned Phileas Fogg. He took out and consulted a pocket almanac, and added, "As today is Wednesday, the second of October, I shall be due in London, in this very room of the Reform Club, on Saturday, the twenty-first of December, at a quarter before 9 p.m.; or else the twenty thousand pounds, now deposited in my name at Baring's, will belong to you, in fact and in right, gentlemen. Here is a cheque for the amount."

A memorandum of the wager was at once drawn up and signed by the six parties, during which Phileas Fogg preserved a stoical composure. He certainly did not bet to win, and had only staked the twenty thousand pounds, half of his fortune, because he foresaw that he might have to expend the other half to carry out this difficult, not to say unattainable, project. As for his antagonists, they seemed much agitated, not so much by the value of their stake, as because they had some scruples about betting under conditions so difficult to their friend.

The clock struck seven, and the party offered to suspend the game so that Mr Fogg might make his preparations for departure.

"I am quite ready now," was his tranquil response. "Diamonds are trumps: be so good as to play, gentlemen."

Passepartout is Stupefied

Having won twenty guineas at whist, and taken leave of his friends, Phileas Fogg, at twenty-five minutes past seven, left the Reform Club.

Passepartout, who had conscientiously studied the programme of his duties, was more than surprised to see his master guilty of the inexactness of appearing at this unaccustomed hour; for, according to rule, he was not due in Savile Row until precisely midnight.

Mr Fogg repaired to his bedroom, and called out, "Passepartout!"

Passepartout did not reply. It could not be he who had called; it was not the right hour.

"Passepartout!" repeated Mr Fogg, without raising his voice.

Passepartout made his appearance.

"I've called you twice," observed his master.

"But it is not midnight," responded the other, showing his watch.

"I know it; I don't blame you. We start for Dover and Calais in ten minutes."

A puzzled grin overspread Passepartout's round face; clearly he had not comprehended his master.

"Monsieur is going to leave home?"

"Yes," returned Phileas Fogg. "We are going round the world."

Passepartout opened wide his eyes, raised his eyebrows, held up his hands, and seemed about to collapse, so overcome was he with stupefied astonishment.

"Round the world!" he murmured.

"In eighty days," responded Mr Fogg. "So we haven't a moment to lose."

"But the trunks," gasped Passepartout, unconsciously swaying his head from right to left.

"We'll have no trunks; only a carpet-bag, with two shirts and three pairs of stockings for me, and the same for you. We'll buy our clothes on the way. Bring down my mackintosh and travelling cloak, and some stout shoes, though we shall do little walking. Make haste!"

Passepartout tried to reply, but could not. He went out, mounted to his own room, fell into a chair, and muttered: "That's good, that is! And I, who wanted to remain quiet!"

By eight o'clock Passepartout had packed the modest carpet-bag, containing the wardrobe of his master and himself; then, still troubled in mind, he carefully shut the door of his room, and descended to Mr Fogg.

Mr Fogg was quite ready. Under his arm might have been observed a red-bound copy of *Bradshaw's Continental Railway Steam Transit and General Guide,* with its timetables showing the arrival and departure of steamers and railways. He took the carpet-bag, opened it, and slipped into it a goodly roll of Bank of England notes, which would pass wherever he might go.

"You have forgotten nothing?" asked he.

"Nothing, monsieur."

"My mackintosh and cloak?"

"Here they are."

"Good. Take this carpet-bag," handing it to Passepartout. "Take good care of it, for there are twenty thousand pounds in it."

Passepartout nearly dropped the bag, as if the twenty thousand pounds were in gold, and weighed him down.

Master and man then descended, the street-door was double locked, and at the end of Savile Row they took a cab and drove rapidly to Charing Cross. The cab stopped before the railway station at twenty minutes past eight. Passepartout jumped off the box and followed his master, who, after paying the cabman, was about to enter the station, when a poor beggar-woman, with a child in her arms, her naked feet smeared with mud, her head covered with a

wretched bonnet, from which hung a tattered feather, and her shoulders shrouded in a ragged shawl, approached, and mournfully asked for alms.

Mr Fogg took out the twenty guineas he had just won at whist, and handed them to the beggar, saying, "Here, my good woman. I'm glad that I met you"; and passed on.

Passepartout had a moist sensation about the eyes; his master's action touched his susceptible heart.

Two first-class tickets for Paris having been speedily purchased, Mr Fogg was crossing the station to the train when he perceived his five friends of the Reform.

"Well, gentlemen," said he, "I'm off, you see; and if you will examine my passport when I get back, you will be able to judge whether I have accomplished the journey agreed upon."

"Oh, that would be quite unnecessary, Mr Fogg," said Ralph politely. "We will trust your word, as a gentleman of honour."

Phileas Fogg and his servant seated themselves in a first-class carriage at twenty minutes before nine; five minutes later the whistle screamed, and the train slowly glided out of the station.

The night was dark, and a fine, steady rain was falling. Phileas Fogg, snugly ensconced in his corner, did not open his lips. Passepartout, not yet recovered from his stupefaction, clung mechanically to the carpet-bag, with its enormous treasure.

Detective Fix

The Commissioner of Police was sitting in his office at nine o'clock one evening, when the following telegraphic despatch was put into his hands:

Suez to London
ROWAN, COMMISSIONER OF POLICE, SCOTLAND YARD:
I've found the bank robber, Phileas Fogg. Send without delay warrant of arrest to Bombay.
Fix, *Detective.*

The effect of this despatch was instantaneous. The idea of Fogg as the polished gentleman, held at the Reform Club, disappeared to give place to the bank robber. His photograph, which was hung with those of the rest of the members at the Reform Club, was minutely examined, and it betrayed, feature by feature, the description of the robber which had been provided to the police. The mysterious habits of Phileas Fogg were recalled; his solitary ways, his sudden departure; and it seemed clear that, in undertaking a tour round the world on the pretext of a wager, he had had no other end in view than to elude the detectives and throw them off his track.

The circumstances under which this telegraphic despatch about Phileas Fogg was sent were as follows:

The steamer *Mongolia* was due at eleven o'clock a.m. on Wednesday, the 9th of October, at Suez, and Fix was there pacing up and down the wharves waiting for its arrival. Fix was a small, slight-built personage, with a nervous, intelligent face, and bright eyes peering out from under eyebrows which he was incessantly twitching. He was one of the detectives who had been despatched from England in search of the bank robber, and he was evidently inspired by the hope of obtaining the splendid reward which would be the prize of success, and so he awaited, with a feverish impatience, the arrival of the steamer.

Little by little the scene on the quay became more animated; sailors of various nations, merchants, shipbrokers, porters, fellahs, bustled to and fro as if the steamer were immediately expected. The weather was clear, and slightly chilly. The minarets of the town loomed above the houses in the pale rays of the sun. A jetty pier, some two thousand yards long, extended into the roadstead. A number of fishing-smacks and coasting boats, some retaining the fantastic fashion of ancient galleys, were discernible on the Red Sea.

As he passed among the busy crowd, Fix, according to habit, scrutinized the passers-by with a keen, rapid glance.

Then there sounded a succession of sharp whistles, which announced the arrival of the *Mongolia*. The porters and fellahs rushed down the quay, and a dozen boats pushed off from the shore to go and meet the steamer. Soon her gigantic hull appeared, passing along between the banks, and eleven o'clock struck as she anchored in the road. She brought an unusual number of passengers, some of whom remained on deck to scan the picturesque panorama of the town, while the greater part disembarked in the boats, and landed on the quay.

Fix took up a position, and carefully examined each face and figure which made its appearance. Presently, one of the passengers, after vigorously pushing his way through the importunate crowd of porters, came up to him and politely asked if he could point out the English consulate, at the same time showing a passport which he wished to have visaed. Fix instinctively took the passport, and with a rapid glance read the description of its bearer. An involuntary motion of surprise nearly escaped him, for the description in the passport was identical with that of the bank robber which he had received from Scotland Yard.

"Is this your passport?" asked he.

"No, it is my master's."

"And your master is——"

"He stayed on board."

"But he must go to the consulate in person, so as to establish his identity."

"Oh, is that necessary?"

"Quite indispensable."

"And where is the consulate?"

"There, on the corner of the square," said Fix, pointing to a house two hundred steps off.

"I'll go and fetch my master, who won't be much pleased to be disturbed."

The passenger bowed to Fix, and returned to the steamer.

A Visit to the Consul

The detective passed down the quay, and rapidly made his way to the consul's office, where he was at once admitted to the presence of that official.

"Consul," said he, without preamble, "I have strong reasons for believing that a man I am looking for on account of a robbery is a passenger on the *Mongolia*." And he narrated what had just passed concerning the passport.

"Well, Mr Fix," replied the consul, "I shall not be sorry to see the rascal's face; but perhaps he won't come here—that is, if he is the person you suppose him to be. A robber doesn't quite like to leave traces of his flight behind him; and besides, he is not obliged to have his passport countersigned."

"If he is as shrewd as I think he is, consul, he will come."

"To have his passport visaed?"

"Yes, and I must keep this man here until I can get a warrant to arrest him from London."

"Ah, that's your look-out. But I cannot——"

The consul did not finish his sentence, for as he spoke a knock was heard on the door, and two strangers entered, one of whom was the servant whom Fix had met on the quay. The other, who was his master, held out his passport with the request that the consul would do him the favour to visa it. The consul took the document and carefully read it, whilst Fix observed, or rather devoured, the stranger with his eyes from a corner of the room.

The consul proceeded to sign and date the passport, after which he added his official seal. Mr Fogg paid the customary fee, coldly bowed, and went out, followed by his servant.

Mr Fogg, after leaving the consulate, repaired to the quay, gave some orders to Passepartout, went off to the *Mongolia* in a boat, and descended to his cabin. He took up his notebook, which contained the following memoranda:

"Left London, Wednesday, October 2nd, at 8.45 p.m.

"Reached Paris, Thursday, October 3rd, at 7.30 a.m.

"Left Paris, Thursday, at 8.40 a.m.

"Reached Turin by Mont Cenis, Friday, October 4th, at 6.35 a.m.

"Left Turin, Friday, at 7.20 a.m.

"Arrived at Brindisi, Saturday, October 5th, at 4 p.m.

"Sailed on the *Mongolia*, Saturday, at 5 p.m.

"Reached Suez, Wednesday, October 9th, at 11 a.m.

"Total of hours spent, 158½: or, in days, six days and a half."

Fix Talks to Passepartout

Fix soon rejoined Passepartout, who was lounging and looking about on the quay, as if he did not feel that he, at least, was obliged not to see anything.

"Well, my friend," said the detective, coming up with him, "is your passport visaed?"

"Ah, it's you, is it, monsieur?" responded Passepartout. "Thanks, yes, the passport is all right, but we travel so fast that I seem to be journeying in a dream."

"Where is your master going?"

"Always straight ahead. He is going round the world."

"Round the world?" cried Fix.

"Yes, and in eighty days! He says it is on a wager; but, between us, I don't believe a word of it. That wouldn't be common sense. There's something else in the wind."

"Ah! Mr Fogg is a character, is he?"

"I should say he was."

"Is he rich?"

"No doubt, for he is carrying an enormous sum in brand-new banknotes with him. And he doesn't spare the money on the way, either: he has offered a large reward to the engineer of the *Mongolia* if he gets us to Bombay well in advance of time."

The effect of these replies upon the already suspicious and excited detective may be imagined.

"Is Bombay far from here?" asked Passepartout.

"Pretty far. It is ten days' voyage by sea."

Fix, now fully convinced he'd got his man, left Passepartout and hurried back to the consulate.

"Consul," said he, "I have no longer any doubt. I have spotted my man. He passes himself off as an odd stick who is going round the world in eighty days."

"But are you not mistaken?"

"I am not mistaken."

He reported in a few words the most important parts of his conversation with Passepartout.

"Well, what are you going to do?"

"Send a despatch to London for a warrant of arrest to be despatched instantly to Bombay, take passage on board the *Mongolia,* follow my rogue to India, and there, on English ground, arrest him politely, with my warrant in my hand, and my hand on his shoulder."

Having uttered these words with a cool, careless air, the detective took leave of the consul, and repaired to the telegraph office, whence he sent the despatch to the London police office. A quarter of an hour later found Fix, with a small bag in his hand, proceeding on board the *Mongolia.*

And ere many moments longer, the noble steamer at last rode out at full steam upon the waters of the Red Sea.

Passepartout Loses His Shoes

The *Mongolia* was due at Bombay on the 22nd; she

arrived on the 20th. This was a gain to Phileas Fogg of two days since his departure from London, and he calmly entered the fact in the itinerary, in the column of gains.

The passengers of the *Mongolia* went ashore at half-past four p.m.; at exactly eight the train would start for Calcutta.

Mr Fogg, after bidding goodbye to some whist partners, left the steamer, gave his servant several errands to do, urged it upon him to be at the station promptly at eight, and, with his regular step, which beat to the second, like an astronomical clock, directed his steps to the passport office. As for the wonders of Bombay—its famous city hall, its splendid library, its forts and docks, its bazaars, mosques, synagogues, its Armenian churches, and the noble pagoda on Malabar Hill with its two polygonal towers—he cared not a straw to see them.

Having transacted his business at the passport office, Phileas Fogg repaired quietly to the railway station, where he ordered dinner.

Fix had gone on shore shortly after Mr Fogg, and his first destination was the headquarters of the Bombay police. He made himself known as a London detective, told his business at Bombay, and the position of affairs relative to the supposed robber, and nervously asked if a warrant had arrived from London. It had not reached the office; indeed, there had not yet been time for it to arrive. Fix was sorely disappointed, and tried to obtain an order of arrest from the director of the Bombay police. This the director refused, as the matter concerned the London office, which alone could legally deliver the warrant.

Passepartout, having purchased the usual quota of shirts and shoes, took a leisurely promenade about the streets, where crowds of people of many nationalities were celebrating a sort of religious carnival, with processions and shows.

Unhappily for his master, as well as himself, his curiosity drew him unconsciously farther off than he intended to go. He was turning his steps towards the station, when he happened to espy the splendid pagoda on Malabar Hill, and was seized with an irresistible desire to see its interior. He was quite ignorant that it is forbidden for Christians to enter certain Indian temples and that even the faithful must not go in without first leaving their shoes outside the door. It may be said here that the wise policy of the British Government severely punishes a disregard of the practices of the native religions.

Passepartout, however, thinking no harm, went in like a simple tourist, and was soon lost in admiration of the splendid Brahmin ornamentation which everywhere met his eyes, when of a sudden he found himself sprawling on the sacred flagging. He looked up to behold three enraged priests, who forthwith fell upon him, tore off his shoes, and began to beat him with loud, savage exclamations. The agile Frenchman was soon upon his feet again, and lost no time in knocking down two of his long-gowned adversaries with his fists and a vigorous application of his toes; then, rushing out of the pagoda as fast as his legs could carry him, he soon escaped the third priest by mingling with the crowd in the street.

At five minutes before eight, Passepartout, hatless, shoeless, and having in the squabble lost his package of shirts and shoes, rushed breathlessly into the station.

Fix, who had followed Mr Fogg to the station, and saw that he was really going to leave Bombay, was there, upon the platform. He had resolved to follow the supposed robber to Calcutta, and farther, if necessary. Passepartout did not observe the detective, who stood in an obscure corner; but Fix heard him relate his adventures in a few words to Mr Fogg.

"I hope that this will not happen again," said Phileas Fogg, coldly, as he got into the train.

Poor Passepartout, quite crestfallen, followed his master without a word. Fix was on the point of entering another carriage, when an idea struck him which induced him to alter his plan.

"No, I'll stay," he muttered. "An offence has been committed on Indian soil. I've got my man."

Just then the locomotive gave a sharp screech, and the train passed out into the darkness of the night.

An Unusual Means of Transport

At half-past twelve the train stopped at Burhampoor, where Passepartout was able to purchase some Indian slippers, ornamented with false pearls, in which, with evident vanity, he proceeded to encase his feet. The travellers made a hasty breakfast and started off for Assurghur, after skirting for a little the banks of the small river Tapty, which empties into the Gulf of Cambray, near Surat.

The train stopped at eight o'clock, in the midst of a glade some fifteen miles beyond Rothal, where there were several bungalows, and workmen's cabins. The conductor, passing along the carriages, shouted, "Passengers will get out here!"

Phileas Fogg looked at Sir Francis Cromarty, his travelling companion from the *Mongolia*, for an explanation; but the general could not tell what meant a halt in the midst of this forest of dates and acacias.

Passepartout, not less surprised, rushed out and speedily returned, crying: "Monsieur, no more railway!"

"What do you mean?" asked Sir Francis.

"I mean to say that the train isn't going on."

The general at once stepped out, while Phileas Fogg calmly followed him, and they proceeded together to the conductor.

"Where are we?" asked Sir Francis.

"At the hamlet of Kholby."

"Do we stop here?"

Certainly. The railway isn't finished."

"What, not finished?"

"No. There's still a matter of fifty miles to be laid from here to Allahabad, where the line begins again."

"Yet you sell tickets from Bombay to Calcutta," retorted Sir Francis, who was growing warm.

"No doubt," replied the conductor; "but the passengers know that they must provide means of transportation for themselves from Kholby to Allahabad."

Sir Francis was furious. Passepartout would willingly have knocked the conductor down, and did not dare to look at his master.

"Sir Francis," said Mr Fogg, quietly, "we will, if you please, look about for some means of conveyance to Allahabad."

"Mr Fogg, this is a delay greatly to your disadvantage."

"No, Sir Francis; it was foreseen."

"What? You knew that the way———?"

"Not at all; but I knew that some obstacle or other would sooner or later arise on my route. Nothing, therefore, is lost. I have two days, which I have

already gained, to sacrifice. A steamer leaves Calcutta for Hong Kong at noon, on the 25th. This is the 22nd, and we shall reach Calcutta in time."

There was nothing to say to so confident a response.

Mr Fogg and Sir Francis Cromarty, after searching the village from end to end, came back without finding any transport.

Happily, Passepartout found a means of conveyance—an elephant. The elephant's name was Kiouni, whose Indian owner told them it could travel rapidly for a long time. Mr Fogg resolved to hire the elephant, but the owner would not agree over the hiring price. Mr Fogg then decided to buy the animal outright, but not until the figure of two thousand pounds was reached would the Indian yield. Mr Fogg paid without hesitation, for it was necessary that he should have the elephant and start travelling without delay.

A young Parsee with an intelligent face who was an accomplished elephant driver offered his services as a guide, which Mr Fogg accepted, promising a generous reward. The elephant was duly equipped with a saddle cloth and some curiously uncomfortable howdahs. Some provisions were purchased at Kholby. Phileas Fogg offered to take Sir Francis with them, and the general gratefully accepted.

When all was ready, Sir Francis and Mr Fogg took the howdahs on either side, Passepartout got astride the saddle-cloth between them. The Parsee perched himself on the elephant's neck, and at nine o'clock they set out from the village, the animal marching off through the dense forest of palms by the shortest cut.

A Procession in the Forest

Phileas Fogg and Sir Francis Cromarty, plunged to the neck in the peculiar howdahs provided for them, were horribly jostled by the swift trotting of the elephant, spurred on as he was by the skilful Parsee; but they endured the discomfort with true British phlegm, talking little, and scarcely able to catch a glimpse of each other. Passepartout, who was mounted on the beast's back, received the direct force of each concussion as he trod along.

After two hours the guide stopped the elephant and gave him an hour for rest, during which Kiouni quenched his thirst at a neighbouring spring.

At noon the Parsee gave the signal for departure. The country soon presented a very savage aspect, vast dry plains dotted with scanty shrubs, and sown with great blocks of syenite.

The principal chain of the Vindhias was crossed by eight in the evening, and another halt was made on the northern slope, in a ruined bungalow. They had gone nearly twenty-five miles that day, and an equal distance still separated them from the station of Allahabad.

As the night was cold, the Parsee lit a fire in the bungalow with a few dry branches, and the warmth was very grateful. The provisions purchased at Kholby sufficed for supper, and the travellers ate ravenously. The conversation, beginning with a few disconnected phrases, soon gave place to loud and steady snores. Nothing occurred during the night to disturb the slumberers.

The journey was resumed at six in the morning, as the guide hoped to reach Allahabad by evening. Towards noon they passed by the village of Kallenger, on the Cani, one of the branches of the Ganges. The guide kept to the open country until Allahabad was now only twelve miles to the north-east. They stopped under a clump of bananas, the fruit of which, as healthy as bread and as succulent as cream, was amply partaken of and appreciated.

At two o'clock the guide entered a thick forest which extended several miles; he preferred now to travel under cover of the woods. They had not as yet had any unpleasant encounters, and the journey seemed on the point of being successfully accomplished, when the elephant, becoming restless, suddenly stopped. It was then four o'clock.

"What's the matter?" asked Sir Francis, putting out his head.

"I don't know officer," replied the Parsee, listening attentively to a confused murmur which came through the thick branches.

The murmur soon became more distinct; it now seemed like a distant concert of human voices accompanied by brass instruments. "A procession of Brahmins is coming this way," said the Parsee. "We must prevent their seeing us."

The guide led the elephant into a thicket, at the same time asking the travellers not to stir. He held himself ready to bestride the animal at a moment's notice, should flight become necessary.

The discordant tones of voices and instruments

drew nearer. The head of the procession soon appeared beneath the trees, a hundred paces away; and the strange figures who performed the religious ceremony were easily distinguished through the branches. First came the priests with mitres on their heads, and clothed in long lace robes. They were surrounded by men, women, and children, who sang a kind of lugubrious psalm, interrupted at regular intervals by tambourines and cymbals; while behind them was drawn a car with large wheels, the spokes of which represented serpents entwined with each other. Upon the car, which was drawn by four richly caparisoned zebus, stood a hideous statue with four arms, the body coloured a dull red, with haggard eyes, dishevelled hair, protruding tongue, and lips tinted with betel. It stood upright upon the figure of a prostrate and headless giant.

Sir Francis, recognizing the statue, whispered, "The Goddess Kali, the goddess of love and death."

The Parsee made a motion to keep silence. Some Brahmins, clad in all the sumptuousness of Oriental apparel, and leading a woman who faltered at every step, followed. This woman was young, and as fair as a European. Her head and neck, shoulders, ears, arms, hands, and toes, were loaded down with jewels and gems—with bracelets, earrings and rings; while a tunic bordered with gold, and covered with a light muslin robe, betrayed the outline of her form.

The guards who followed the young woman presented a violent contrast to her, armed as they were with naked sabres hung at their waists, and long damascened pistols, and bearing a corpse on a palanquin. It was the body of an old man, gorgeously arrayed in the habiliments of a rajah, wearing, as in life, a turban embroidered with pearls, a robe of tissue of silk and gold, a scarf of cashmere sewn with diamonds, and the magnificent weapons of a Hindoo prince. Next came the musicians and the rearguard of capering fakirs, whose cries sometimes drowned the noise of the instruments; these closed the procession.

Sir Francis watched the procession with a sad countenance, and, turning to the guide, said, "A suttee."

The Parsee nodded. The procession slowly wound under the trees, and soon its last ranks disappeared in the depths of the wood. The songs gradually died away; occasionally cries were heard in the distance, until at last all was silence again.

Phileas Fogg had heard what Sir Francis said, and, as soon as the procession had disappeared, asked: "What is a 'suttee'?"

"A suttee," returned the general, "is a human sacrifice, but a voluntary one. The woman you have just seen will be burned tomorrow at the dawn of day, and, if she were not, you couldn't conceive what terrible treatment she would be obliged to submit to from her relatives."

"And the corpse?" asked Mr Fogg.

"Is that of the prince, her husband," said the guide; "an independent rajah of Bundelcund."

"Where are they taking her?" asked Sir Francis.

"To the pagoda of Pillaji, two miles from here; she will pass the night there," the Parsee informed them.

"And the sacrifice will take place—?"

"Tomorrow, at the first light of dawn."

The guide now led the elephant out of the thicket, and leaped upon his neck. Just at the moment that he was about to urge Kiouni forward with a peculiar whistle, Mr Fogg stopped him, and, turning to Sir Francis Cromarty, said, "Suppose we save this woman?"

"Save the woman, Mr Fogg?"

"I have yet twelve hours to spare; I can devote them to that."

"Why, you are a man of heart!"

"Sometimes," replied Phileas Fogg, quietly: "when I have the time."

Passepartout's Daring Feat

They all agreed that the project was a bold one, but they were all willing to risk life or liberty for the sake of the woman.

"I think we must wait till night before acting," suggested Mr Fogg.

"I think so," agreed the guide.

The worthy Indian then gave some account of the victim, who, he said, was a celebrated beauty of the Parsee race, and the daughter of a wealthy Bombay merchant. She has received a thoroughly English education in that city, and, from her manners and intelligence, would be thought European. Her name was Aouda. Left an orphan, she was married against her will to the old rajah of Bundelcund; and, knowing the fate that awaited her, she escaped, was retaken, and devoted by the rajah's relatives, who had an interest in her death, to the sacrifice from which it seemed she could not escape.

The Parsee's narrative only confirmed Mr Fogg and his companions in their generous design. It was decided that the guide should direct the elephant towards the pagoda of Pillaji, which he accordingly approached as quickly as possible. They halted, half an hour afterwards, in a copse, some five hundred feet from the pagoda, where they were well concealed; but they could hear the groans and cries of the gathering.

The Parsee, leading the others, noiselessly crept through the wood, and in ten minutes they found themselves on the banks of a small stream, whence, by the light of the rosin torches, they perceived a pyre of wood, on the top of which lay the embalmed body of the rajah, which was to be burned with his wife. The pagoda, whose minarets loomed above the trees in the deepening dusk, stood a hundred steps away. Much to the guide's disappointment, the guard of the rajah, lighted by torches, were watching at the doors and marching to and fro with naked sabres; probably the priests, too, were watching within.

The Parsee, who was now convinced that it was impossible to force an entrance to the temple, advanced no farther, but led his companions back again.

They waited till midnight; but no change took place among the guards, and it became apparent that their yielding to sleep could not be relied upon.

The hours passed, and the lighter shades now announced the approach of day, though it was not yet light. The guide led them to the rear of the glade, where they were able to observe the sleeping groups.

Meanwhile Passepartout, who had perched himself on the lower branches of a tree, was resolving an idea which had first struck him like a flash, and which was now firmly lodged in his brain.

He had commenced by saying to himself, "What folly!" and then he repeated, "Why not, after all? It's a chance—perhaps the only one!" Thinking thus, he slipped, with the suppleness of a serpent, to the lowest branches, the ends of which bent almost to the ground.

This was the moment. The slumbering multitude became animated, the tambourines sounded, songs and cries arose; the hour of the sacrifice had come. The doors of the pagoda swung open, and a bright light escaped from its interior, in the midst of which Mr Fogg and Sir Francis espied the victim. She seemed, having shaken off a stupor of intoxication, to be striving to escape from her executioner. Sir Francis's heart throbbed; and convulsively seizing Mr Fogg's hand, found in it an open knife. Just at this moment the crowd began to move. The young woman had again fallen into a stupor caused by fumes of hemp, and passed among the fakirs, who escorted her with their wild, religious cries.

Phileas Fogg and his companions, mingling in the rear ranks of the crowd, followed; and in two minutes they reached the banks of the stream, and stopped fifty paces from the pyre, upon which still lay the rajah's corpse. In the semi-obscurity they saw the victim, quite senseless, stretched out beside her husband's body. Then a torch was brought, and the wood, soaked with oil, instantly took fire.

At this moment Sir Francis and the guide seized Phileas Fogg, who, in an instant of mad generosity, was about to rush upon the scene. But he had quickly pushed them aside, when the whole scene suddenly changed. A cry of terror arose. The whole multitude prostrated themselves, terror-stricken, on the ground.

The old rajah was not dead, then, since he rose of a sudden, like a spectre, took up his wife in his arms, and descended from the pyre in the midst of the clouds of smoke, which only heightened his ghostly appearance.

Fakirs and soldiers and priests, seized with instant terror, lay there, with their faces on the ground, not daring to lift their eyes and behold such a prodigy.

The inanimate victim was borne along by the vigorous arms which supported her, and which she did not seem in the least to burden. Mr Fogg and Sir Francis stood erect and the Parsee bowed his head.

The resuscitated rajah approached Sir Francis and Mr Fogg, and, in an abrupt tone, said, "Let us be off!"

It was Passepartout himself, who had slipped upon the pyre in the midst of the smoke, and, profiting by the still overhanging darkness, had delivered the young woman from death! It was Passepartout who, playing his part with a happy audacity, had passed through the crowd amid the general terror.

A moment after, all four of the party had disappeared in the woods, and the elephant was bearing them away at a rapid pace.

Escape Across India

The rash exploit had been accomplished; and for an hour Passepartout laughed gaily at his success. Sir Francis pressed the worthy fellow's hand, and his master said, "Well done!" which, from him, was high commendation; to which Passepartout replied that all the credit of the affair belonged to Mr Fogg.

As for the young Indian woman, she had been unconscious throughout of what was passing, and now, wrapped up in a travelling-blanket, was reposing in one of the howdahs.

The station at Allahabad was reached about ten o'clock, and the interrupted line of railway being resumed, would enable them to reach Calcutta in less than twenty-four hours.

The young woman was placed in one of the waiting-rooms of the station, whilst Passepartout was charged with purchasing for her various articles of toilet, a dress, shawl, and some furs; for which his master gave him unlimited credit.

The train was about to start from Allahabad, and Mr Fogg proceeded to pay the guide the price agreed upon for his service.

"Parsee," said he to the guide, "you have been serviceable and devoted. I have paid for your service, but not for your devotion. Would you like to have this elephant? He is yours."

The guide's eyes glistened.

"Your honour is giving me a fortune!" cried he.

"Take him, guide," returned Mr Fogg, "and I shall still be your debtor."

Soon, Phileas Fogg, Sir Francis Cromarty, and Passepartout, installed in a carriage with Aouda, who had the best seat, were whirling at full speed towards Benares. It was a run of eighty miles, and was accomplished in two hours. During the journey, the young woman fully recovered her senses. What was her astonishment to find herself in this carriage on the railway, dressed in European habiliments, and with travellers who were quite strangers to her! Her companions first set about reviving her with a little liquor, and then Sir Francis narrated to her what had passed, dwelling upon the courage with which Phileas Fogg had not hesitated to risk his life to save her, and recounting the happy sequel of the venture, the result of Passepartout's rash idea.

Aouda pathetically thanked her deliverers, rather with tears than words; her fine eyes interpreted her gratitude better than her lips. Then, as her thoughts strayed back to the scene of the sacrifice, and recalled the dangers which still menaced her, she shuddered with terror.

Phileas Fogg understood what was passing in Aouda's mind, and offered, in ordered to reassure her, to escort her to Hong Kong, where she might remain safely until the affair was hushed up—an offer which she eagerly and gratefully accepted.

At half-past twelve the train stopped at Benares, which was Sir Francis Cromarty's destination, the troops he was rejoining being encamped some miles northward of the city. He bade adieu to Phileas Fogg, wishing him all success, and expressing the hope that he would come that way again in a less original, but more profitable, fashion. Mr Fogg lightly pressed him by the hand. The parting of Aouda, who did not forget what she owed to Sir Francis, betrayed more warmth.

The railway, on leaving Benares, passed for a while along the valley of the Ganges. Through the windows of their carriage the travellers had glimpses of the diversified landscape of Behar, with its mountains clothed in verdure, its fields of barley, wheat, and corn, its jungles peopled with green alligators, its neat villages, and its still thickly-leaved forests.

Night came on; the train passed on at full speed. Calcutta was reached at seven in the morning, and the packet left for Hong Kong at noon; so that Phileas Fogg had five hours before him.

The Arrest

The train entered the station, and Passepartout, jumping out first, was followed by Mr Fogg, who assisted his fair companion to descend. Phileas Fogg intended to proceed at once to the Hong Kong steamer, in order to get Aouda comfortably settled for the voyage. He was unwilling to leave her while they were still on dangerous ground.

Just as he was leaving the station a policeman came up to him, and said, "Mr Phileas Fogg?"

"I am he."

"Is this man your servant?" added the policeman, pointing to Passepartout.

"Yes."

"Be so good, both of you, as to follow me."

Mr Fogg betrayed no surprise whatever. The policeman was a representative of the law, and law is sacred to an Englishman. Passepartout tried to reason about the matter, but the policeman tapped him with his stick, and Mr Fogg made him a signal to obey.

"May this young lady go with us?" asked he.

"She may," replied the policeman.

Mr Fogg, Aouda, and Passepartout were conducted to a palkigari, a sort of four-wheeled carriage, drawn by two horses, in which they took their places and were driven away. No one spoke during the twenty minutes which elapsed before they reached their destination.

The carriage stopped before a modest-looking house, which, however, did not have the appearance of a private mansion. The policeman having asked his prisoners—for so, truly, they might be called—to descend, conducted them into a room with barred windows, and said: "You will appear before Judge Obadiah at half-past eight."

He then retired and closed the door.

"Why, we are prisoners!" exclaimed Passepartout, falling into a chair.

Aouda, with an emotion she tried to conceal, said to Mr Fogg: "Sir, you must leave me to my fate! It is on my account that you receive this treatment; it is for having saved me!"

Phileas Fogg contented himself with saying that it was impossible. It was quite unlikely that he should be arrested for preventing a suttee. The complainants would not dare present themselves with such a charge. There was some mistake. Moreover, he would not in any event abandon Aouda, but would escort her to Hong Kong.

"But the steamer leaves at noon," replied Passepartout, nervously.

"We shall be on board at noon," replied his master placidly.

Appearance in Court

At half-past eight the door opened, the policeman appeared, and, requesting them to follow him, led the way to an adjoining hall. It was evidently a court-room, and a crowd of Europeans and natives already occupied the rear of the apartment.

Mr Fogg and his two companions took their places on a bench opposite the desks of the magistrate and his clerk. Immediately after, Judge Obadiah, a fat, round man, followed by the clerk, entered. He proceeded to take down a wig which was hanging on a nail, and put it hurriedly on his head.

"The first case," he said.

"Phileas Fogg?" demanded Oysterpuff, the clerk.

"I am here," replied Mr Fogg.

"Passepartout?"

"Present!" responded Passepartout.

"Good," said the judge. "You have been looked for, prisoners, for two days on the trains from Bombay."

"But of what are we accused?" asked Passepartout, impatiently.

"You are about to be informed."

"I am an English subject, sir," said Mr Fogg, "and I have a right—"

"Have you been ill-treated?"

"Not at all."

"Very well; let the complainants come in."

A door was swung open by order of the judge and three Indian priests entered.

The priests took their places in front of the judge, and the clerk proceeded to read in a loud voice a complaint of sacrilege against Phileas Fogg and his servant, who were accused of having violated a place held consecrated by the Brahmin religion, the pagoda of Malabar Hill at Bombay.

"You hear the charge?" asked the judge.

"Yes, sir," replied Mr Fogg, consulting his watch, "and I admit it."

"And as proof," added the clerk, "here are the desecrator's very shoes, which he left behind him."

"My shoes!" cried Passepartout.

Fix, the detective, had foreseen the advantage which Passepartout's escapade gave him, and, delaying his departure for twelve hours, had consulted the priests of Malabar Hill. Knowing that the English authorities dealt very severely with this kind of misdemeanour, he promised them a goodly sum in damages, and sent them forward to Calcutta by the next train.

Owing to the delay caused by the rescue of the young widow, Fix and the priests reached the Indian capital before Mr Fogg and his servant.

"Inasmuch," resumed the judge, "as the English law protects equally and sternly the religions of the Indian people, and as the man Passepartout has admitted that he violated the sacred pagoda of Malabar Hill, at Bombay, on the 20th October, I condemn the said Passepartout to imprisonment for fifteen days and a fine of three hundred pounds."

"Three hundred pounds!" cried Passepartout, startled at the largeness of the sum.

"Silence!" shouted the constable.

"And inasmuch," continued the judge, "as it is not proved that the act was not done by the connivance of the master with the servant, and as the master in any case must be held responsible for the acts of his paid servant, I condemn Phileas Fogg to a week's imprisonment and a fine of one hundred and fifty pounds."

Fix rubbed his hands softly with satisfaction; if Phileas Fogg could be detained in Calcutta a week, it would be more than time for the warrant to arrive. Passepartout was stupefied. This sentence ruined his master. A wager of twenty thousand pounds lost, because he, like a precious fool, had gone into that abominable pagoda!

Phileas Fogg, self-composed as if the judgement did not in the least concern him, did not even lift his eyebrows while it was being pronounced. Just as the clerk was calling the next case, he rose, and said, "I offer bail."

"You have that right," returned the judge.

Fix's blood ran cold, but he resumed his composure when he heard the judge announce that the bail required for each prisoner would be one thousand pounds.

"I will pay at once," said Mr Fogg, taking a roll of bank-bills from the carpet-bag, which Passepartout had by him, and placing them on the clerk's desk.

"This sum will be restored to you upon your release from prison," said the judge. "Meanwhile, you are liberated on bail."

"Come!" said Phileas Fogg to his servant.

Mr Fogg offered his arm to Aouda, then departed. Fix still nourished hopes that the robber would not, after all, leave the two thousand pounds behind him, but would decide to serve out his week in jail, and issued forth on Mr Fogg's traces. That gentleman took a carriage, and the party were soon landed on one of the quays.

The *Rangoon* was moored half a mile off in the harbour, its signal of departure at the mast-head. Eleven o'clock was striking; Mr Fogg was an hour in advance of time. Fix saw them leave the carriage and push off in a boat for the steamer, and stamped his feet with disappointment.

The Voyage to Hong Kong

The trip from Calcutta to Hong Kong comprised some three thousand five hundred miles, occupying from ten to twelve days.

During the first days of the journey, Aouda became better acquainted with her protector, and constantly gave evidence of her deep gratitude for what he had done. She also had a relative at Hong Kong whom she hoped to join.

Meanwhile, Fix was in hiding. He had managed to embark on the *Rangoon* at Calcutta without being seen by Passepartout, after leaving orders that, if the warrant should arrive, it should be forwarded to him at Hong Kong.

During the afternoon of Wednesday, October 30th, the *Rangoon* entered the Strait of Malacca, and weighed anchor at Singapore the next day at four a.m. to receive coal, having gained half a day on the prescribed times of her arrival.

At eleven o'clock the *Rangoon* rode out of Singapore harbour, and in a few hours the high mountains of Malacca were lost to view.

Singapore is distant some thirteen hundred miles from the island of Hong Kong. Phileas Fogg hoped to accomplish the journey in six days, so as to be in time for the steamer which would leave on the 6th of November for Yokohama, the principal Japanese port.

The weather, which had hitherto been fine, changed with the last quarter of the moon. The sea rolled heavily, and the wind at intervals rose almost to a storm. During the latter days of the voyage the weather worsened, the wind blew a gale and retarded the steamer. A sort of tempest arose on the 3rd November, the squall knocking the vessel about with fury and the waves running high. The steamer was forced to proceed slowly.

On the 4th November, however, the sea became more calm, and the storm lessened its violence; the wind veered southward, and was once more favourable. Some of the sails were unfurled, and the *Rangoon* resumed its most rapid speed.

The time lost could not, however, be regained. Land was not signalled until five o'clock on the morning of the 6th; Phileas Fogg was twenty-four hours behindhand, and the Yokohama steamer would, of course, be missed.

The pilot went on board at six, and took his place on the bridge, to guide the *Rangoon* through the channels to the port of Hong Kong.

Mr Fogg did not hesitate to approach the pilot and tranquilly ask him if he knew when a steamer would leave Hong Kong for Yokohama.

"At high tide tomorrow morning," answered the pilot.

"What's the steamer's name?" asked Mr Fogg.

"The *Carnatic*."

"Ought she not to have gone yesterday?"

"Yes, sir; but they had to repair one of her boilers, and so her departure was postponed till tomorrow."

"Thank you," returned Mr Fogg, descending mathematically to the saloon.

At one o'clock the *Rangoon* was at the quay, and the passengers were going ashore.

Chance had strangely favoured Phileas Fogg, for, had not the *Carnatic* been forced to lie over for

repairing her boilers, she would have left on the 6th of November, and the passengers for Japan would have been obliged to await for a week the sailing of the next steamer. Mr Fogg was, it is true, twenty-four hours behind his time; but this could not seriously imperil the remainder of his tour.

The *Carnatic* was announced to leave Hong Kong at five the next morning. Mr Fogg had sixteen hours in which to attend to his business there, which was to deposit Aouda safely with her wealthy relative.

But, on enquiry, they learned that he had left China for Europe, probably Holland. It was then decided that Aouda should accompany Mr Fogg and Passepartout to Europe.

Passepartout Is Tricked by Fix

On reaching the quay where they were to embark on the *Carnatic*, Passepartout was astonished to find Fix walking up and down. The detective seemed very much disturbed and disappointed. He had, indeed, good reasons to inveigh against the bad luck which pursued him. The warrant had not come! It was certainly on the way, but as certainly it could not now reach Hong Kong for several days; and this being the last English territory on Mr Fogg's route, the robber would escape unless he could manage to detain him.

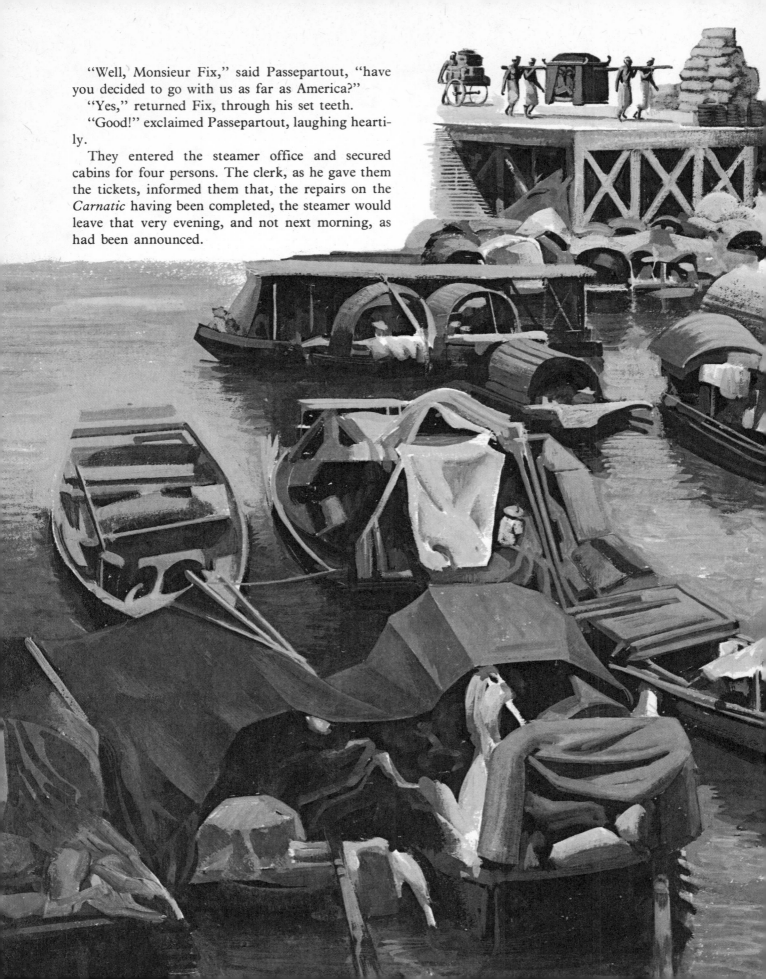

"Well, Monsieur Fix," said Passepartout, "have you decided to go with us as far as America?"

"Yes," returned Fix, through his set teeth.

"Good!" exclaimed Passepartout, laughing heartily.

They entered the steamer office and secured cabins for four persons. The clerk, as he gave them the tickets, informed them that, the repairs on the *Carnatic* having been completed, the steamer would leave that very evening, and not next morning, as had been announced.

"That will suit my master all the better," said Passepartout. "I will go and let him know."

Fix now decided to make a bold move; he resolved to tell Passepartout all. It seemed to be the only possible means of keeping Phileas Fogg several days longer at Hong Kong. He accordingly invited his companion into a tavern which caught his eye on the quay.

They ordered two bottles of port, to which the Frenchman did ample justice, whilst Fix observed him with close attention.

"I want to have a serious talk with you," said Fix.

Passepartout, at this, looked attentively at his companion. Fix's face seemed to have a singular expression.

"What is it that you have to say?"

Fix placed a hand upon Passepartout's arm, and, lowering his voice said, "Listen to me. I am a police detective, sent out here by the London office."

"You, a detective?"

"I will prove it. Here is my commission."

Passepartout was speechless with astonishment when Fix displayed this document, the genuineness of which could not be doubted.

"Listen. On the 28th of last September a robbery of fifty-five thousand pounds was committed at the Bank of England by a person whose description was fortunately secured. Here is the description; it answers exactly to that of Mr Phileas Fogg."

"What nonsense!" cried Passepartout, striking the table with his fist. "My master is the most honourable of men."

"How can you tell? You know scarcely anything about him. You went into his service the day he came away; and he came away on a foolish pretext, without trunks, and carrying a large amount in banknotes. And yet you are bold enough to assert that he is an honest man!"

"Yes, yes," repeated the poor fellow mechanically.

"Would you like to be arrested as his accomplice?"

Passepartout, overcome by what he had heard, held his head between his hands, and did not dare to look at the detective. Phileas Fogg, the saviour of Aouda, that brave and generous man, a robber! And yet how many presumptions there were against him! Passepartout essayed to reject the suspicions which forced themselves upon his mind; he did not wish to believe that his master was guilty.

"Well, what do you want of me?" said he, at last, with an effort.

"See here," replied Fix: "I have tracked Mr Fogg to this place, but as yet I have failed to receive the warrant of arrest for which I sent to London. You must help me to keep him here in Hong Kong—"

"I! But I—"

"I will share with you the two thousand pounds' reward offered by the Bank of England."

"Never!" replied Passepartout, who tried to rise, but fell back, exhausted in mind and body. "Mr Fix," he stammered; "even should what you say be true—if my master is really the robber you are seeking for—which I deny—I have been, am, in his service; I have seen his generosity and goodness; and I will never betray him—not for all the gold in the world. I come from a village where they don't eat that kind of bread!"

"You refuse?"

"I refuse."

"Consider that I've said nothing," said Fix, "and let us drink."

"Yes; let us drink!"

Passepartout felt himself yielding more and more to the effects of the liquor. Fix, seeing that he must at all hazards be separated from his master, wished to overcome him entirely. Some pipes full of opium lay upon the table. Fix slipped one into Passepartout's hand. He took it, put it between his lips, lit it, drew several puffs, and his head, becoming heavy under the influence of the narcotic, fell upon the table.

"At last!" said Fix, seeing Passepartout unconscious. "Mr Fogg will not be informed of the *Carnatic's* departure; and, if he is, he will have to go without this cursed Frenchman!"

And, after paying his bill, Fix left the tavern.

Journey to Yokohama

When Passepartout did not appear the next morning to answer his master's bell, Mr Fogg, not betraying the least vexation, contented himself with taking his carpet-bag, calling Aouda and sending for a palanquin.

It was then eight o'clock; at half-past nine, it being then high tide, the *Carnatic* would leave the harbour. Mr Fogg and Aouda got into the palanquin, their luggage being brought after on a wheelbarrow, and half-an-hour later stepped upon the quay whence they were to embark. Mr Fogg then learned that the *Carnatic* had sailed the evening before. He had expected to find not only the steamer but his domestic, and was forced to give up both; but no sign of disappointment appeared on his face, and he merely remarked to Aouda, "It is an accident, madam; nothing more."

At this moment a man who had been observing him attentively approached. It was Fix, who, bowing, addressed Mr Fogg: "Were you not, like me, sir, a passenger by the *Rangoon*, which arrived yesterday?"

"I was sir," replied Mr Fogg coldly. "But I have not the honour—"

"Pardon me; I thought I should find your servant here."

"Do you know where he is, sir?" asked Aouda anxiously.

"What?" responded Fix, feigning surprise. "Is he not with you?"

"No," said Aouda. "He has not made his appearance since yesterday. Could he have gone on board the *Carnatic* without us?"

"Without you, madam?" answered the detective. "Excuse me, did you intend to sail in the *Carnatic*?"

"Yes sir."

"So did I, madam, and I am excessively disappointed. The *Carnatic*, its repairs being completed, left Hong Kong twelve hours before the stated time, without any notice being given; and we must now wait a week for another steamer."

As he said 'a week' Fix felt his heart leap for joy. Fogg retained at Hong Kong a week! There would be time for the warrant to arrive, and fortune at last favoured the representative of the law. His horror may be imagined when he heard Mr Fogg say, in his placid voice, "But there are other vessels besides the *Carnatic*, it seems to me, in the harbour of Hong Kong."

And, offering his arm to Aouda, he directed his steps towards the docks in search of some craft about to start. Fix, stupefied, followed. For three hours Phileas Fogg had wandered about the docks, when at length he was accosted by a sailor.

"Is your honour looking for a boat?"

"Have you a boat ready to sail?"

"Yes, your honour; a pilot-boat—No. 43—the best in the harbour."

"Does she go fast?"

"Between eight and nine knots an hour. Will you look at her?"

"Yes."

"Your honour will be satisfied with her. Is it for a sea excursion?"

"No; for a voyage."

"A voyage?"

"Yes; will you agree to take me to Yokohama? I have missed the *Carnatic,* and I must get to Yokohama by the 14th at the latest, to make the boat for San Francisco. I offer you a hundred pounds per day, and an additional reward of two hundred pounds if I reach Yokohama in time."

"Well, your honour," replied he, "I could not risk myself, my men, or my little boat of scarcely twenty tons on so long a voyage at this time of year. Besides, we could not reach Yokohama in time, for it is sixteen hundred and sixty miles from Hong Kong. But, it might be arranged another way,—by going to Shanghai, which is only eight hundred miles from here, and picking up the San Francisco steamer there, which is where it starts before putting in at Yokohama and Nagasaki."

"You are sure of that?"

"Perfectly."

"And when does the boat leave Shanghai?"

"On the 11th, at seven in the evening. We have, therefore, four days before us, that is ninety-six hours; and in that time, if we had good luck and a south-west wind, and the sea was calm, we could make those eight hundred miles to Shanghai."

"And could you go—?"

"In an hour; as soon as provisions could be got aboard and the sails put up."

"It is a bargain. Are you the master of the boat?"

"Yes; John Bunsby, master of the *Tankadere.*"

"Here are two hundred pounds on account, sir," added Phileas Fogg, turning to Fix, "if you would like to take the advantage—"

"Thanks, sir; I was about to ask the favour."

"Very well. In half-an-hour we shall go on aboard."

While Fix, in a feverish, nervous state, repaired to the pilot-boat the others directed their course to the police-station at Hong Kong. Phileas Fogg there gave Passepartout's description and left a sum of money to be spent in the search for him.

Mr Fogg and Aouda then stopped at the hotel for the luggage, and returned to the wharf. It was now three o'clock; and pilot-boat No. 43, with its crew on board and its provisions stored away, was ready for departure.

The sails and the English flag were hoisted at ten minutes past three. Mr Fogg and Aouda, who were seated on deck, cast a last glance at the quay.

Knowing the Frenchman's pertinacity, and having had ample evidence of his faithful service, they had not given up all hope of his return. But Passepartout did not appear.

John Bunsby, master, at length gave the order to start, and the *Tankadere,* taking the wind under her brigantine, foresail, and standing-jib bounded briskly forward over the waves.

A Storm off Shanghai

At sunrise the next day, which was November 8th, the boat had made more than one hundred miles, and by evening, the log showed that two hundred and twenty miles had been accomplished from Hong Kong.

At daybreak the wind began to blow hard and the heavens seemed to predict a gale.

The night was really terrible; at times it was a miracle that the craft did not founder. Twice it would have been all over with her if the crew had not been constantly on the watch. Aouda was exhausted, but did not utter a complaint. More than once Mr Fogg rushed to protect her from the violence of the waves.

Day reappeared. The tempest still raged with undiminished fury; but the wind now returned to the south-west and it was a favourable change, and the *Tankadere* again bounded forward on this mountainous sea.

There were some signs of a calm at noon, and these became more distinct as the sun descended toward the horizon. The tempest had been as brief as terrific.

The night was comparatively quiet. Some of the sails were again hoisted, and the speed of the boat was very good. At dawn they espied the coast.

John Bunsby found himself at six o'clock not more than ten miles from the mouth of Shanghai River. Shanghai itself is situated at least twelve miles up the stream. At seven they were still three miles from Shanghai. At this moment, a long, black funnel, crowned with wreaths of smoke, appeared on the edge of the waters. It was the American steamer, leaving for Yokohama at the appointed time.

"Signal her!" said Phileas Fogg quietly. "Hoist your flag!"

The flag was run up at half-mast, and, this being the signal of distress, it was hoped that the American steamer, perceiving it, would change her course a little, so as to succour the pilot-boat.

"Fire!" said Mr Fogg. And the booming of the little cannon resounded in the air.

Passepartout Arrives in Yokohama

Meanwhile, the *Carnatic*, setting sail from Hong Kong at half-past six on the 7th of November, directed her course at full steam towards Japan.

The next day a passenger with a half-stupefied eye, staggering gait, and disordered hair, was seen to

emerge from the second cabin, and to totter to a seat on deck. It was Passepartout and what had happened to him was as follows.

Shortly after Fix had left, the poor fellow awoke, and struggled against the stupefying influence of the narcotic. Staggering and holding himself up by keeping against the walls, falling down and creeping up again, and irresistibly impelled by a kind of instinct, he kept crying out, "The *Carnatic!* The *Carnatic!*

The steamer lay puffing alongside the quay, on the point of starting. Passepartout had but a few steps to go; and, rushing upon the plank, he crossed it, and fell unconscious on the deck, just as the *Carnatic* was moving off. Several sailors, who were evidently accustomed to this sort of scene, carried the poor Frenchman down into the second cabin, and Passepartout did not wake until they were one hundred and fifty miles away from China.

He then realized that his master and Aouda were

not on the steamer and remembered that the time of sailing had been changed, that he should have informed his master of that fact, and that he had not done so. It was his fault, then, that Mr Fogg and Aouda had missed the steamer, but it was still more the fault of the traitor who, in order to separate him from his master and retain the latter at Hong Kong, had inveigled him into getting drunk! He now saw the detective's trick. If Fix ever came within his reach, what a settling of accounts there would be!

After his first depression, Passepartout became calmer and began to study his situation. His passage had fortunately been paid for in advance; and he had five or six days in which to decide upon his future course.

At dawn on the 13th the *Carnatic* entered the port of Yokohama. Passepartout went timidly ashore. He had nothing better to do than, taking chance for his guide, to wander aimlessly through the streets of Yokohama.

Night came, and Passepartout wandered through the streets, lit by vari-coloured lanterns, looking on at the dancers. Then he came to the harbour, which was lit up by the rosin torches of the fishermen, who were fishing from their boats.

Passepartout Is Reunited with His Master

What happened when the pilot-boat came in sight of Shanghai will be easily guessed. The signals made by the *Tankadere* had been seen by the captain of the Yokohama steamer, who, espying the flag at half-mast, had directed his course towards the little craft. Phileas Fogg, after paying the stipulated price of his passage to John Bunsby, and rewarding that worthy with the additional sum of five hundred and fifty pounds, ascended the steamer with Aouda and Fix; and they started at once for Nagasaki and Yokohama.

They reached their destination on the morning of the 14th of November. Phileas Fogg lost no time in going on board the *Carnatic* where he learned, to Aouda's great delight—and perhaps to his own, though he betrayed no emotion—that Passepartout, a Frenchman, had really arrived on her the day before.

The San Francisco steamer was announced to leave that very evening, and it became necessary to find Passepartout, if possible, without delay. And

they did find him. Poor Passepartout was wandering along towards them, looking sad and jaded, until he looked up and saw his master.

"Ah, my master! my master!" he cried.

"Come on, young man!" said Mr Fogg encouragingly, "let us all go to the steamer."

Passepartout thought that the time had not yet arrived to divulge to his master what had taken place between the detective and himself; and in the account he gave of his absence he simply excused himself for having been overtaken by drunkenness in smoking opium at a tavern in Hong Kong.

At half-past six, the very hour of departure, Mr Fogg and Aouda, followed by Passepartout, looking very sorry for himself, stepped upon the American steamer.

Arrival in San Francisco

The steamer making its way to San Francisco belonged to the Pacific Mail Steamship Company, and was named the *General Grant*. She was a large paddle-wheel steamer of two thousand five hundred tons, well equipped and fast.

By making twelve miles an hour, she would cross the ocean in twenty-one days. Phileas Fogg was therefore justified in hoping that he would reach San Francisco by the 2nd of December, New York by the 11th, and London on the 20th—thus gaining several hours on the fatal date of the 21st of December.

A railway train from San Francisco to New York, and a transatlantic steamer from New York to Liverpool would doubtless bringing them to the end of this impossible journey round the world within the period agreed upon.

But where was Fix at this moment?

He was actually on board the *General Grant*. He had found the warrant at Yokohama and had not been able to see Mr Fogg that day, and now the warrant was useless, as Mr Fogg had left English ground. He therefore decided to follow Fogg to England and even to try, if he could, to hasten the journey.

On that very day, however, he met Passepartout face to face on the forward deck. The latter, without a word, made a rush for him, grasped him by the throat, and administered to the detective a perfect volley of blows, which proved the great superiority of French over English pugilistic skill.

When Passepartout had finished, he found himself relieved and comforted. Fix got up in a somewhat rumpled condition, and looking at his adversary, coldly said, "Have you done?"

"For the time—yes."

"Then let me have a word with you, in your master's interest."

Passepartout seemed to be vanquished by Fix's coolness, for he quietly followed him, and they sat down aside from the rest of the passengers.

"You have given me a thrashing," said Fix. "Good; I expected it. Now, Mr Fogg seems to be going back to England. Well, I will follow him there. But hereafter I will do as much to keep obstacles out of his way as I have done up to this time to put them in his path. I've changed my game, you see, and simply because it was for my interest to change it. Your interest is the same as mine; for it is only in England that you will ascertain whether you are in the service of a criminal or an honest man."

Passepartout listened very attentively to Fix, and was convinced that he spoke with entire good faith.

"Are we friends?" asked the detective.

"Friends?—no," replied Passepartout; "but allies, perhaps. At the least sign of treason, however, I'll twist your neck for you."

"Agreed," said the detective quietly.

Eleven days later, on the 3rd of December, the *General Grant* entered the bay of the Golden Gate, and reached San Francisco.

Mr Fogg had neither gained nor lost a single day.

An Encounter with Buffalo

Mr Fogg, on reaching shore, proceeded to find out at what hour the first train left for New York, and learned that this was at six o'clock p.m.; he had, therefore, an entire day to spend in the Californian capital.

He had not proceeded two hundred steps, however, when, by the greatest chance in the world, he met Fix. The detective seemed wholly taken by surprise. What! Had Mr Fogg and himself crossed the Pacific together, and not met on the steamer? At last Fix felt honoured to behold once more the gentleman to whom he owed so much, and as his business recalled him to Europe, he should be

delighted to continue the journey in such pleasant company.

Mr Fogg replied that the honour would be his.

At a quarter before six the travellers reached the station, and found the train ready to depart. They all got into the train, which started off at full speed.

The railroad was to be traversed in seven days, which would enable Phileas Fogg—at least, so he hoped—to take the Atlantic steamer at New York on the 11th for Liverpool.

The travellers were asleep when they passed through Sacramento and later the train entered the range of the Sierra Nevada. San Francisco was reached at seven in the morning; then they entered and passed through the State of Nevada through the Carson Valley and reached Reno at midday, where there was a delay of twenty minutes for breakfast. They then proceeded through prairies, the mountains lining the horizon, and in the distance great herds of buffaloes, massing together, seemed like a moveable dam.

About twelve o'clock a troop of ten or twelve thousand head of buffalo encumbered the track. The locomotive, slackening its speed, tried to clear the way with its cow-catcher; but the mass of animals was too great. The buffaloes marched along with a tranquil gait, uttering now and then deafening bellowings. There was no use in interrupting them, for, having taken a particular direction, nothing can moderate and change their course; it is a torrent of living flesh which no dam could contain.

Passepartout was furious at the delay they occasioned.

The best course was to wait patiently, and regain the lost time by greater speed when the obstacle was removed.

When the track was clear, the train continued its immense journey across this vast country.

The train stopped at the Great Salt Lake, which Mr Fogg and his party were able to spend some time visiting, then sped on through Wyoming territory, over the Rocky Mountains and through limitless plains and prairies, some of which were infested with Indians, who frequently made furious attacks upon the train.

An Indian Attack

There was an occasion when Passepartout showed immense bravery when the train was under a particularly savage assault.

The train had left the important town of North Platte, and had passed Plum Creek, and was pursuing its course when suddenly, savage yells resounded in the air. Cries of terror proceeded from the interior of the cars as the occupants perceived that the train was being attacked by a band of Sioux.

This was not the first attempt of these daring Indians, for more than once they had waylaid trains on the road. A hundred of them had, according to their habit, jumped upon the steps without stopping the train, with the ease of a clown mounting a horse at full gallop.

The Sioux were armed with guns, from which came the reports, to which the passengers, who were almost all armed, responded by revolver-shots.

The Indians had first mounted the engine, and half stunned the engineer and stoker with blows from their muskets. A Sioux chief, wishing to stop the train, but not knowing how to work the regulator, had opened wide instead of closing the steam-valve, and the locomotive was plunging forward with terrific velocity.

The Sioux had at the same time invaded the cars, skipping like enraged monkeys over the roofs, thrusting open the doors, and fighting hand to hand with the passengers. Penetrating the baggage-room, they pillaged it, throwing the trunks out of the train.

The travellers defended themselves bravely; some of the cars were barricaded, and sustained a siege, like moving forts, carried along at a speed of a hundred miles an hour.

Aouda behaved courageously from the first. She defended herself like a true heroine with a revolver, which she shot through the broken windows whenever a savage made his appearance. Twenty Sioux had fallen mortally wounded to the ground, and the wheels crushed those who fell upon the rails as if they had been worms. Several passengers, shot or stunned, lay on the seats.

It was necessary to put an end to the struggle, which had lasted for ten minutes, and which would result in the triumph of the Sioux if the train was not stopped. Fort Kearney station, where there was a garrison, was only two miles distant; but, that once passed, the Sioux would be masters of the train between Fort Kearney and the station beyond.

The conductor was fighting beside Mr Fogg, when he was shot and fell. At the same moment he cried,

"Unless the train is stopped in five minutes, we are lost!"

"It shall be stopped," said Phileas Fogg, preparing to rush from the car.

"Stay, monsieur," cried Passepartout; "I will go."

Mr Fogg had not time to stop the brave fellow, who, opening a door unperceived by the Indians, succeeded in slipping under the car; and while the struggle continued, and the balls whizzed across each other over his head, he worked his way under the cars with amazing agility, holding on to the chains, aiding himself by the brakes and edges of the sashes, creeping from one car to another with marvellous skill, and thus gaining the forward end of the train.

There, suspended by one hand between the baggage-car and the tender, with the other he loosened the safety-chains; but, owing to the traction, he would never have succeeded in unscrewing the yoking-bar, had not a violent concussion jolted this bar out. The train, now detached from the engine, remained a little behind, whilst the locomotive rushed forward with increased speed with Passepartout on board!

Carried on by the force already acquired, the train still moved for several minutes; but the brakes were worked, and at last they stopped, less than a hundred feet from Kearney station.

The soldiers of the fort, attracted by the shots, hurried up; the Sioux had not expected them, and decamped in a body before the train entirely stopped.

Passepartout had at last revived the engineer and together they brought the locomotive to a standstill before returning to join the passenger cars.

There were many wounded, but none mortally. All the passengers got out of the train, the wheels of which were stained with blood. From the tyres and spokes hung ragged pieces of flesh. As far as the eye could reach on the white plains behind, red trails were visible. The last Sioux were disappearing in the south, along the banks of the Republican River.

Everyone was safe—they were all saved through the devotion of the courageous Frenchman.

A Night in New York

The train now passed rapidly across the State of Iowa, by Council Bluffs, Des Moines, and Iowa City. During the night it crossed the Mississippi at Davenport, and by Rock Island entered Illinois. The next day, which was the 10th, at four in the evening, it reached Chicago, already risen from its ruins, and more proudly seated than ever on the borders of its beautiful Lake Michigan.

Nine hundred miles separated Chicago from New York; but trains are not wanting at Chicago. Mr Fogg passed at once from one to the other, and the locomotive of the Pittsburg, Fort Wayne and Chicago Railway left at full speed, as if it fully comprehended that that gentleman had no time to lose. It traversed Indiana, Ohio, Pennsylvania, and New Jersey like a flash, rushing through towns with antique names, some of which had streets and car-tracks, but as yet no houses. At last the Hudson came into view; and at a quarter-past eleven in the evening of the 11th, the train stopped in the station on the right bank of the river, before the very pier of the Cunard line.

The *China*, for Liverpool, had started three-quarters of an hour before!

The *China*, in leaving, seemed to have carried off Phileas Fogg's last hope.

"We will consult about what is best tomorrow. Come," he said coolly.

The party crossed the Hudson in the Jersey City ferryboat, and drove in a carriage to the St. Nicholas Hotel, on Broadway. Rooms were engaged, and the night passed, briefly to Phileas Fogg, who slept profoundly, but very long to Aouda and the others, whose agitation did not permit them to rest.

The next day was the 12th of December. Mr Fogg left the hotel alone, after giving Passepartout instructions to await his return, and inform Aouda to be ready at an instant's notice. He proceeded to the banks of the Hudson, and looked about among the vessels moored or anchored in the river for any that were about to depart.

He seemed about to give up all hope, when he espied, anchored at the Battery, a cable's length off at most, a trading vessel, with a screw, well-shaped, whose funnel, puffing a cloud of smoke, indicated that she was getting ready for departure.

This was the *Henrietta*, bound for Bordeaux.

Mr Fogg was only able to secure his passage for an enormous sum of money, as the Captain was travelling with freight and had no need for passengers. The Captain was offered two thousand dollars apiece for himself and the crew, which totalled eight thousand dollars!

When Passepartout heard what this last voyage was going to cost, he uttered a prolonged "Oh!" which extended throughout his vocal gamut.

As for Fix, he said to himself that the Bank of England would certainly not come out of this affair well indemnified. When they reached England, even if Mr Fogg did not throw some handfuls of bank-bills into the sea, more than seven thousand pounds would have been spent.

Mr Fogg and his party were all on board, when the *Henrietta* made ready to weigh anchor at nine o'clock.

Phileas Fogg Takes Command

At noon the next day a man mounted the bridge to ascertain the vessel's position. It may be thought that this was the captain of the *Henrietta*. Not the least in the world. It was Phileas Fogg, Esquire. As for the captain, Captain Speedy, he was shut up in his cabin under lock and key, and was uttering loud cries, which signified an anger at once pardonable and excessive.

What had happened was very simple. Phileas Fogg wished to go to Liverpool, but the captain would not carry him there. Then Phileas Fogg, during the thirty hours he had been on board, had so shrewdly managed with his banknotes that the sailors and stokers, who were an occasional crew, and were not on the best of terms with the captain, went over to him in a body. This was why Phileas Fogg was in command instead of Captain Speedy. The *Henrietta* was directing her course towards Liverpool. It was very clear, to see Mr Fogg manage the craft, that he had been a sailor. As for Passepartout, he thought Mr Fogg's manoeuvre simply glorious.

On the 13th they passed the edge of the Banks of Newfoundland, a dangerous locality; ever since the evening before, the barometer, suddenly falling, had indicated an approaching change in the atmosphere; and during the night the temperature varied, the cold became sharper, and the wind veered to the south-east. This was a misfortune. Mr Fogg, in order not to deviate from his course, furled his sails and increased the force of the steam; the vessel's speed slackened. But Phileas Fogg was a bold mariner, and knew how to maintain headway against the sea; and

he kept on his course, without even decreasing his steam.

The 16th of December was the seventy-fifth day since Phileas Fogg's departure from London, and the *Henrietta* had not yet been seriously delayed. Half of the voyage was almost accomplished.

But on this day the engineer came on deck, went up to Mr Fogg and began to speak earnestly with him—they were running out of coal! And on the 18th, the engineer, as he had predicted, announced that the coal would give out during the course of the day.

"Do not on any account let the fires go down," said Mr Fogg. "Keep them up to the last. Let the valves be filled."

Towards noon Phileas Fogg, having ascertained their position, called Passepartout, and ordered him to go for Captain Speedy. It was as if the honest fellow had been commanded to unchain a tiger. He went to the poop, saying to himself, "He will be like a madman!"

In a few moments, with cries and oaths, a bomb appeared on the poop-deck. The bomb was Captain Speedy. It was clear that he was on the point of bursting.

"Where are we?" were the first words his anger permitted him to utter.

"Seven hundred and seven miles from Liverpool," replied Mr Fogg, with imperturbable calmness.

"Pirate!" cried Captain Speedy.

"I have sent for you, sir," continued Mr Fogg, "to ask you to sell me your vessel."

"No! By all the devils, no!"

"But I shall be obliged to burn her."

"Burn the *Henrietta!* Burn my vessel!" cried Captain Speedy, "a vessel worth fifty thousand dollars!"

"Here are sixty thousand," replied Phileas Fogg, handing the captain a roll of bank-bills.

This had a prodigious effect on Andrew Speedy. An American can scarcely remain unmoved at the sight of sixty thousand dollars. The captain forgot in an instant his anger, his imprisonment, and all his grudges against his passenger. The *Henrietta* was twenty years old; it was a great bargain. The bomb would not go off, after all.

"Agreed," said Captain Speedy.

During this colloquy, Passepartout was as white as a sheet, and Fix seemed on the point of having an apoplectic fit. Nearly twenty thousand pounds had been expended. It was true, however, that fifty-five thousand pounds had been stolen from the bank.

Then Mr Fogg gave orders to have the interior seats, bunks, and frames pulled down, and burnt. It was necessary to have dry wood to keep the steam up to the adequate pressure, and on that day the poop, cabins, bunks, and the spare deck were sacrificed. On the next day, the 19th of December, the masts, rafts, and spars were burned. The railings, fittings, the greater part of the deck, and top sides, disappeared on the 20th. But on this day they sighted the Irish coast and Fastnet Light, and by ten in the evening they were passing Queenstown; and the steam was about to give out altogether!

Queenstown is the Irish port at which the transatlantic steamers stop to put off the mails. These mails are carried to Dublin by express trains always held in readiness to start; from Dublin they are sent on to Liverpool by the most rapid boats, and thus gain twelve hours on the Atlantic steamers.

Phileas Fogg counted on gaining twelve hours in the same way. The *Henrietta* entered Queenstown Harbour at one o'clock in the morning.

Phileas Fogg at last disembarked on the Liverpool quay, at twenty minutes before twelve, December 21st. He was only six hours distant from London.

But at this moment Fix came up, put his hand upon Mr Fogg's shoulder, and, showing his warrant, said, "You are really Phileas Fogg?"

"I am."

"I arrest you in the Queen's name!"

No Time to Lose

Phileas Fogg was in prison. He had been shut up in the Custom House, and he was to be transferred to London the next day.

If anyone, at this moment, had entered the Custom House, he would have found Mr Fogg seated, motionless, calm, and without apparent anger, upon a wooden bench. He was not, it is true, resigned; but this last blow failed to force him into an outward betrayal of any emotion.

The Custom House clock struck one. Mr Fogg observed that his watch was two hours too fast.

Two hours! Admitting that he was at this moment taking an express train, he could reach London and the Reform Club by a quarter before nine, p.m. His forehead slightly wrinkled.

At thirty-three minutes past two he heard a singular noise outside, then a hasty opening of doors. Passepartout's voice was audible, and immediately after, that of Fix. Phileas Fogg's eyes brightened for an instant.

The door swung open, and he saw Passepartout, Aouda, and Fix, who hurried towards him.

Fix was out of breath, and his hair was in disorder. He could not speak. "Sir," he stammered, "sir—forgive me—a most—unfortunate resemblance—robber arrested three days ago—you—are free!"

Phileas Fogg was free! He walked to the detective, looked him steadily in the face, and with the only rapid motion he had ever made in his life, or which he ever would make, drew back his arm, and with the precision of a machine, knocked Fix down.

Mr Fogg, Aouda, and Passepartout left the Custom House without delay, got into a cab, and in a few moments descended at the station.

Phileas Fogg asked if there was an express train about to leave for London. It was forty minutes past two. The express train had already left. Phileas Fogg then ordered a special train. There were several rapid locomotives on hand; but the railway arrangements did not permit the special train to leave until three o'clock.

At that hour, Phileas Fogg, having stimulated the engineer by the offer of a generous reward, at last set out towards London with Aouda and his faithful servant.

Unfortunately there were forced delays, and when Mr Fogg stepped from the train at the terminus, clocks in London were striking ten minutes before nine.

Having made the tour of the world, he was behindhand five minutes. He had lost the wager!

Defeat

Mr Fogg bore his misfortune with his habitual tranquility. Mr Fogg's course, however, was fully decided upon; he knew what remained for him to do.

A room in the house in Savile Row was set apart for Aouda, who was overwhelmed with grief at her protector's misfortune.

Knowing that Englishmen governed by a fixed idea sometimes resort to the desperate expedient of suicide, Passepartout kept a narrow watch upon his master, though he carefully concealed the appearance of so doing.

The night passed. Mr Fogg went to bed. Aouda did not once close her eyes. Passepartout watched all night, like a faithful dog, at his master's door.

The next day Mr Fogg had no reason for going out, and so he remained at home. He shut himself up in his room, and busied himself putting his affairs in order.

About half-past seven in the evening Mr Fogg sent to know if Aouda would receive him, and in a few moments he found himself alone with her.

Later Passepartout was summoned and appeared immediately. Mr Fogg still held Aouda's hand in his own; Passepartout understood, and his big, round face became as radiant as the tropical sun at its zenith. Phileas Fogg and Aouda had decided to be married!

Mr Fogg asked Passepartout if it was not too late to notify the Reverend Samuel Wilson, of Marylebone parish, that evening.

Passepartout smiled his most genial smile, and said, "Never too late."

It was five minutes past eight.

"Will it be for tomorrow, Monday?"

"For tomorrow, Monday," said Mr Fogg, turning to Aouda.

"Yes; for tomorrow, Monday," she replied.

Passepartout hurried off as fast as his legs could carry him.

The Wager Is Won

On Saturday, the 21st December in the evening, the five antagonists of Phileas Fogg had met in the great saloon of the club. They were in a state of feverish suspense. Would Phileas Fogg reappear before their eyes?

The clock indicated eighteen minutes to nine.

The players took up their cards, but could not keep their eyes off the clock. Certainly, however secure they felt, minutes had never seemed so long to them!

"Seventeen minutes to nine," said Thomas Flanagan, as he cut the cards which Ralph handed to him.

Then there was a moment of silence. The great saloon was perfectly quiet.

"Sixteen minutes to nine!" said John Sullivan, in a voice which betrayed his emotion.

One minute more, and the wager would be won. Andrew Stuart and his partners suspended their game. They left their cards, and counted the seconds.

At the fortieth second, nothing. At the fiftieth, still nothing.

At the fifty-fifth, a loud cry was heard in the street.

The players rose from their seats.

At the fifty-seventh second the door of the saloon opened; and the pendulum had not beat the sixtieth second when Phileas Fogg appeared, followed by an excited crowd who had forced their way through the club doors, and in a calm voice, said, "Here I am, gentlemen!"

Yes; Phileas Fogg in person!

The reader will remember that at five minutes past eight in the evening—about four and twenty hours after the arrival of the travellers in London—Passepartout had been sent by his master to engage the services of the Reverend Samuel Wilson in a certain marriage ceremony, which was to take place the next day.

In thirty minutes Passepartout had returned to Savile Row again, and staggered breathlessly into Mr Fogg's room.

He could not speak.

"What is the matter?" asked Mr Fogg.

"My master," gasped Passepartout, "marriage—impossible, because tomorrow—is Sunday!"

"Monday," replied Mr Fogg.

"No—today—is Saturday."

"Saturday? Impossible!"

"Yes, yes, yes, yes," cried Passepartout. "You have made a mistake of one day! We arrived twenty–four hours ahead of time; but there are only ten minutes left!"

Passepartout had seized his master by the collar, and was dragging him along with irresistible force.

Phileas Fogg, thus kidnapped, without having time to think, left his house, jumped into a cab, promised a hundred pounds to the cabman, and finally reached the Reform Club.

The clock indicated a quarter before nine when he appeared in the great saloon.

Phileas Fogg had accomplished the journey round the world in eighty days.

The cause of the error is very simple.

Phileas Fogg had, without suspecting it, gained one day on his journey, and this merely because he had travelled constantly *eastward*; he would, on the contrary, have lost a day had he gone in the opposite direction, that is, *westward*.

In journeying eastward he had gone towards the sun, and the days therefore diminished for him as many times four minutes as he crossed degrees in this direction. There are three hundred and sixty degrees on the circumference of the earth; and these three hundred and sixty degrees, multiplied by four minutes, give precisely twenty-four hours – that is, the day unconsciously gained. In other words, while Phileas Fogg, going eastward, saw the sun pass the

meridian *eighty* times, his friends in London only saw it pass the meridian *seventy-nine* times. This is why they awaited him at the Reform Club on Saturday, and not Sunday, as Mr Fogg thought.

Phileas Fogg, then, had won the twenty thousand pounds; but as he had spent nearly nineteen thousand on the way, the pecuniary gain was small. His object was, however, to be victorious, and not to win money. He divided the one thousand pounds that remained between Passepartout and the unfortunate Fix, against whom he cherished no grudge.

It need not be said that the marriage took place forty-eight hours after, and that Passepartout, glowing and dazzling, gave the bride away. Had he not saved her, and was he not entitled to this honour?

The next day, as soon as it was light, Passepartout

rapped vigorously at his master's door. Mr Fogg opened it, and asked, "What's the matter, Passepartout?"

"What is it, sir? Why, I've just this instant found out——"

"What?"

"That we might have made the tour of the world in only seventy-eight days."

"No doubt," returned Mr Fogg, "by not crossing India. But if I had not crossed India, I should not have saved Aouda; she would not have been my wife, and——" Mr Fogg quietly shut the door.

Phileas Fogg had won his wager, and had made his journey around the world in eighty days.

TREASURE ISLAND

The Old Sea Dog at the 'Admiral Benbow'

I take up my pen in the year of grace 17–, and go back to the time when my father kept the 'Admiral Benbow' inn, and the brown old seaman, with the sabre cut, first took up his lodging under our roof.

I remember him as if it were yesterday, as he came plodding to the inn door, his sea-chest following behind him in a hand-barrow; a tall, strong, heavy, nut-brown man; his tarry pigtail falling over the shoulders of his soiled blue coat; his hands ragged and scarred, with black, broken nails; and the sabre cut across one cheek, a dirty, livid white. I remember him looking round the cove and whistling to himself as he did so, and then breaking out in that old sea-song that he sang so often afterwards:

"Fifteen men on the dead man's chest—
    Yo-ho-ho, and a bottle of rum!"

Then he rapped on the door with a bit of stick like a handspike that he carried, and when my father appeared, called roughly for a glass of rum. This, when it was brought to him, he drank slowly, like a connoisseur, lingering on the taste, and still looking about him at the cliffs and up at our signboard.

"This is a handy cove," says he, at length; "and a pleasant sittyated grog-shop. Much company, mate?"

My father told him no, very little company, the more was the pity.

"Well, then," said he, "this is the berth for me. Here you, matey," he cried to the man who trundled the barrow: "bring up alongside and help up my chest. I'll stay here a bit," he continued. "I'm a plain man; rum and bacon and eggs is what I want, and that head up there for to watch ships off. What you mought call me? You mought call me captain. Oh, I see what you're at––there;" and he threw down three or four pieces on the threshold. "You can tell me when I've worked through that," says he, looking as fierce as a commander.

He was a very silent man by custom. All day he hung round the cove, or upon the cliffs, with a brass telescope; all evening he sat in a corner of the parlour next the fire, and drank rum and water very strong. He had taken me aside one day, and promised me a silver fourpenny on the first of every month if I would only keep my "weather-eye open for a seafaring man with one leg", and let him know the moment he appeared. Often enough, when the first of the month came round, and I applied to him for my wage, he would only blow through his nose at me, and stare me down; but before the week was out he was sure to think better of it, bring me my fourpenny piece, and repeat his orders to look out for "the seafaring man with one leg".

In one way, he bade fair to ruin us; for he kept on staying week after week, and at last month after month, so that all the money had been long exhausted, and still my father never plucked up the heart to insist on having more. If ever he mentioned it, the captain blew through his nose so loudly, that you might say he roared, and stared my poor father out of the room. I have seen him wringing his hands after such a rebuff, and I am sure the annoyance and the terror he lived in must have greatly hastened his early and unhappy death.

Black Dog Appears and Disappears

It was a bitter cold winter, with long, hard frosts and heavy gales; and it was plain from the first that my poor father was little likely to see the spring. He sank daily, and my mother and I had all the inn upon our hands; and were kept busy enough, without paying much regard to our unpleasant guest.

It was one January morning, very early—mother was upstairs with father; and I was laying the breakfast-table against the captain's return when the parlour door opened, and a man stepped in on whom I had never set my eyes before. He was a pale, tallowy creature, wanting two fingers of the left hand; and, though he wore a cutlass, he did not look much like a fighter. I had always my eye open for seafaring men, with one leg or two, and I remember this one puzzled me. He was not sailorly, and yet he had a smack of the sea about him too.

"Come here, sonny, says he. "Come nearer here."

I took a step nearer.

"Is this here table for my mate Bill?" he asked, with a kind of leer.

I told I did not know his mate Bill and this was for a person who stayed in our house, whom we called the captain.

"Well," said he, "my mate Bill would be called the captain, as like as not. He has a cut on one cheek, and a mighty pleasant way with him, particularly in drink, has my mate Bill. We'll put it, for argument like, that your captain has a cut on one cheek—and we'll put it, if you like, that that cheek's the right one. Ah, well! I told you. Now, is my mate Bill in this here house?"

I told him he was out walking.

"Which way, sonny? Which way is he gone?"

And when I had pointed out the rock and told him how the captain was likely to return, and how soon, and answered a few other questions, "Ah," said he, "this'll be as good as drink to my mate Bill."

The stranger kept hanging about just outside the inn door, peering round the corner like a cat waiting for a mouse. "Ah, here is my mate Bill, with a spy-glass under his arm, bless his old 'art to be sure. You and me'll just go back into the parlour, sonny, and get behind the door and we'll give Bill a little surprise—bless his 'art, I say again."

At last in strode the captain, slammed the door behind him, without looking to the right or left, and marched straight across the room to where his breakfast awaited him.

"Bill," said the stranger, in a voice that I thought he had tried to make bold and big. The captain spun round on his heel and fronted us; all the brown had gone out of his face, and even his nose was blue; he had the look of a man who sees a ghost, or the evil one, or something worse, if anything can be; and, upon my word, I felt sorry to see him, all in a moment, turn so old and sick.

"Come, Bill, you know me; you know an old shipmate, Bill, surely," said the stranger.

The captain made a sort of gasp.

"Black Dog!" said he.

"And who else?" returned the other, getting more at his ease. "Black Dog as ever was, come for to see his old shipmate Billy, at the 'Admiral Benbow' inn. Ah, Bill, Bill, we have seen a sight of time, us two, since I lost them two talons," holding up his mutilated hand.

"Now, look here," said the captain; "you've run me down: here I am; well, speak up: what is it?"

Black Dog bade me go, and leave the door wide open. "None of your keyholes for me, sonny," he said; and I left them together, and retired into the bar.

Then all of a sudden there was a tremendous explosion of oaths and other noises—the chair and table went over in a lump, a clash of steel followed, and then a cry of pain, and the next instant I saw Black Dog in full flight, and the captain hotly pursuing, both with drawn cutlasses, and the former streaming blood from the left shoulder. Just at the door, the captain aimed at the fugitive one last tremendous cut, which would certainly have split him to the chine had it not been intercepted by our big signboard of Admiral Benbow. You may see the notch on the lower side of the frame to this day.

The blow was the last of the battle. Once out upon the road, Black Dog, in spite of his wound, showed a wonderful clean pair of heels, and disappeared over the edge of the hill in half a minute. The captain, for his part, stood staring at the signboard like a bewildered man. Then he passed his hand over his eyes several times, and at last turned back into the house.

"Jim," says he, "rum"; and as he spoke, he reeled a little, and caught himself with one hand against the wall.

"Are you hurt?" cried I.

"Rum," he repeated. "I must get away from here. Rum! Rum!"

I ran to fetch it; but I was quite unsteadied by all that had fallen out, and I broke one glass and fouled the tap, and while I was still getting in my own way, I heard a loud fall in the parlour, and running in, beheld the captain lying full length upon the floor. Dr Livesey came in at this moment on a visit to my father. Between us, with much trouble, we managed to hoist the captain upstairs, and laid him on his bed, where his head fell back on the pillow as if he were almost fainting.

"You have had a stroke," the doctor told him, "I clear my conscience—the name of rum for you is death. He should lie for a week where he is, Jim— that is the best thing for him and you; but another stroke would settle him."

The Black Spot

About noon I stopped at the captain's door with some cooling drinks and medicines. He was lying very much as we had left him, only a little higher, and he seemed both weak and excited.

"Jim," he said, "you're the only one here that's worth anything; and you know I've been always good to you. Never a month but I've given you a silver fourpenny for yourself. And now you see, mate, I'm pretty low, and deserted by all; and, Jim, you'll bring me one noggin of rum, now, won't you, matey?"

"The doctor—" I began.

But he broke in cursing the doctor, in a feeble voice, but heartily. "Doctors is all swabs," he said; "and that doctor there, why, what do he know about seafaring men? Look, Jim, how my fingers fidget," he continued, in a pleading tone. "I can't keep 'em still, not I. I haven't had a drop this blessed day. If I don't have a drain o' rum, Jim, I'll have the horrors; I seen some on 'em already. I seen old Flint in the corner, there, behind you; as plain as print. I'll give you a golden guinea for a noggin, Jim."

"I want none of your money," said I, "but what you owe my father. I'll get you one glass, and no more."

When I brought it to him, he seized it greedily, and drank it out.

"Jim," he said, at length, "you saw that seafaring man today?"

"Black Dog?" I asked.

"Ah, Black Dog," says he. "He's a bad 'un; but there's worse that put him on. Now, if I can't get away nohow, and they tip me the black spot, mind you, it's my old sea-chest they're after; you get on a horse and go to—well, yes,—to that eternal doctor swab, and tell him to pipe all hands—magistrates and sich—and he'll lay 'em aboard at the 'Admiral Benbow'—all old Flint's crew, man and boy, all on 'em that's left. I was first mate, I was, old Flint's first mate, and I'm the on'y one as knows the place. He gave it me in Savannah, when he lay a-dying, like as if I was to now, you see. But you won't peach unless they get the black spot on me, or unless you see a seafaring man with one leg, Jim—him above all."

"But what is the black spot, captain?" I asked.

"That's a summons, mate. I'll tell you if they get that. But keep your weather-eye open, Jim, and I'll share with you equals, upon my honour."

What I should have done had all gone well I do not know. Probably I should have told the whole story to the doctor; for I was in mortal fear lest the captain should repent of his confessions and make an end of me. But as things fell out, my poor father died quite suddenly that evening, which put all other matters on one side. Our natural distress, the visits of the neighbours, the arranging of the funeral, and all the work of the inn to be carried on in the meanwhile, kept me so busy that I had scarcely time to think of the captain, far less to be afraid of him.

So things passed until, the day after the funeral, and about three o'clock of a bitter, foggy, frosty afternoon, I was standing at the door for a moment, full of sad thoughts about my father, when I saw someone drawing slowly near along the road. He was plainly blind, for he tapped before him with a stick, and wore a great green shade over his eyes and nose; and he was hunched, as if with age or weakness, and wore a huge old tattered sea-cloak with a hood, that made him appear positively deformed. I never saw in my life a more dreadful looking figure. He stopped a little from the inn and, raising his voice in an odd sing-song, addressed the air in front of him:

"Will any kind friend inform a poor blind man, who has lost the precious sight of his eyes in the gracious defence of his native country, England, and God bless King George!—where or in what part of this country he may now be?"

"You are at the 'Admiral Benbow', Black Hill Cove, my good man," said I.

"I hear a voice", said he—"a young voice. Will

you give me your hand, my kind young friend, and lead me in?"

I held out my hand, and the horrible, soft-spoken eyeless creature gripped it in a moment like a vice. I was so much startled that I struggled to withdraw; but the blind man pulled me close up to him with a single action of his arm.

"Now, boy," he said, "take me in to the captain."

"Sir," said I, "upon my word I dare not."

"Oh," he sneered, "that's it! Take me in straight, or I'll break your arm."

And he gave it, as he spoke, a wrench.

"Sir," said I, "it is for yourself I mean. The captain is not what he used to be. He sits with a drawn cutlass."

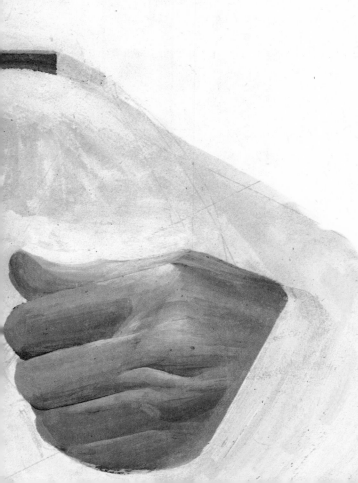

"Come now, march," interrupted he; and I never heard a voice so cruel, and cold, and ugly as that blind man's. It cowed me more than the pain; and I began to obey him at once, walking straight in at the door and towards the parlour, where our sick old buccaneer was sitting, dazed with rum. The blind man clung close to me, holding me in one iron fist, and leaning almost more of his weight on me that I could carry. "Lead me straight up to him, and when I'm in view, cry out, 'Here's a friend for you, Bill.' If you don't, I'll do this!" and with that he gave me a twitch that I thought would have made me faint. Between this and that I was so utterly terrified of the blind beggar that I forgot my terror of the captain, and as I opened the parlour door, cried out the words he had ordered in a trembling voice.

The poor captain raised his eyes, and at one look the rum went out of him, and left him staring sober. The expression of his face was not so much of terror as of mortal sickness. He made a movement to rise, but I do not believe he had enough force left.

"Now, Bill, sit where you are," said the beggar. "If I can't see, I can hear a finger stirring. Business is business. Hold out your left hand. Boy, take his left hand by the wrist, and bring it near to my right."

We both obeyed him to the letter, and I saw him pass something from the hollow of the hand that held his stick into the palm of the captain's, which closed upon it instantly.

"And now that's done," said the blind man; and at the words he suddenly left hold of me, and, with incredible accuracy and nimbleness, skipped out of the parlour and into the road, where, as I still stood motionless, I could hear his stick go tap-tap-tapping into the distance.

It was some time before either I or the captain seemed to gather our senses; but at length, and about at the same moment, I released his wrist, which I was still holding, and he drew in his hand and looked sharply into the palm.

"Ten o'clock!" he cried. "Six hours. We'll do them yet"; and he sprang to his feet.

Even as he did so, he reeled, put his hand to his throat, stood swaying for a moment, and then, with a peculiar sound, fell from his whole height face foremost to the floor.

I ran to him at once, calling my mother. But haste was all in vain. The captain had been struck dead by thundering apoplexy. When I saw that he was dead

I burst into a flood of tears. It was the second death I had known, and the sorrow of the first was still fresh in my heart.

The Sea-Chest

I lost no time, of course, in telling my mother all that I knew, and perhaps should have told her long before, and we saw ourselves at once in a difficult and dangerous position. Something must speedily be resolved upon; and it occurred to us at last to go forth together and seek help in the neighbouring hamlet. No sooner said than done. Bare-headed as we were, we ran out at once in the gathering evening and the frosty fog.

It was already candle-light when we reached the hamlet, and I shall never forget how much I was cheered to see the yellow shine in doors and windows; but that, as it proved, was the best of the help we were likely to get in that quarter. For—you would have thought men would have been ashamed of themselves—no soul would consent to return with us to the 'Admiral Benbow'. The more we told of our troubles, the more—man, woman, and child—they clung to the shelter of their houses. And the short and the long of the matter was, that while we could get several who were willing enough to ride to Dr Livesey's, which lay in another direction, not one would help us to defend the inn.

We returned dejectedly. We slipped along the hedges, noiseless and swift, nor did we see or hear anything to increase our terrors, till, to our huge relief, the door of the 'Admiral Benbow' had closed behind us.

I slipped the bolt at once, and we stood and panted for a moment in the dark, alone in the house with the dead captain's body. Then my mother got a candle in the bar, and, holding each other's hands, we advanced into the parlour. He lay as we had left him, on his back, with his eyes open and one arm stretched out.

"Draw down the blinds, Jim," whispered my mother; "they might come and watch outside. And now," said she, when I had done so, "we have to get the key off *that;* and who's to touch it, I should like to know!" and she gave a kind of sob as she said the words.

I went down on my knees at once. On the floor close to his hand was a little round of paper,

blackened on the one side. I could not doubt that this was the *black spot;* and taking it up, I found written on the other side, in a very good, clear hand, this short message: "You have till ten tonight."

"He had till ten, mother," said I; and just as I said it, our old clock began striking. This sudden noise startled us shockingly; but the news was good, for it was only six.

"Now, Jim," she said, "that key."

I gave her the key and we hurried upstairs and though the lock of the chest was very stiff, she had turned it and thrown back the lid in a twinkling.

A strong smell of tobacco and tar rose from the interior, but nothing was to be seen on the top except a suit of very good clothes, carefully brushed and folded. They had never been worn, my mother said. Under that, the miscellany began—a quadrant, a tin cannikin, several sticks of tobacco, two brace of very handsome pistols, a piece of bar silver, an old Spanish watch and some other trinkets of little value and mostly of foreign make, a pair of compasses mounted with brass, and five or six curious West Indian shells. It has often set me thinking since that he should have carried about these shells with him in his wandering, guilty, and hunted life.

In the meantime, we had found nothing of any value but the silver and the trinkets, and neither of these were in our way. Underneath there was an old boat-cloak whitened with sea-salt on many a harbour-bar. My mother pulled it up with impatience, and there lay before us, the last things in the chest, a bundle tied up in oilcloth, and looking like papers, and a canvas bag, that gave forth, at a touch, the jingle of gold.

"I'll take what is owed," said my mother.

"And I'll take this to square the count," said I, picking up the oilskin packet.

Next moment, we were both groping downstairs, leaving the candle by the empty chest. Then we heard in the silent frosty air the tapping of a stick on the frozen road. "Mother," said I, "we must leave here at once."

The fog was rapidly dispersing; already the moon shone quite clear on the high ground on either side; and it was only in the exact bottom of the dell and round the tavern door that a thin veil still hung unbroken to conceal the first steps of our escape. Far less than halfway to the hamlet, very little beyond the bottom of the hill, we must come forth into the moonlight. Nor was this all; for the sound of several footsteps running came already to our ears, and as we looked back in their direction, a light tossing to and fro and still rapidly advancing, showed that one of the new-comers carried a lantern.

We were just at the little bridge, by good fortune; and I helped my mother, tottering as she was, to the edge of the bank, where suddenly, she gave a sigh and fell on my shoulder. I do not know how I found the strength to do it all, and I am afraid it was roughly done; but I managed to drag her down the bank and a little way under the arch. Farther I could not move her, for the bridge was too low to let me do more than crawl below it. So there we had to stay —my mother almost entirely exposed, and both of us within earshot of the inn.

The Last of the Blind Man

My curiosity, in a sense, was stronger than my fear; for I could not remain where I was, but crept back to the bank again, whence, sheltering my head behind a bush of broom, I might command the road before our door. I was scarcely in position ere my enemies began to arrive, seven or eight of them, running hard, their feet beating out of time along the road, and the man with the lantern some paces in front. Three men ran together, hand in hand; and I made out, even through the mist, that the middle man of this trio was the blind beggar. The next moment his voice showed me that I was right.

"Down with the door!" he cried.

"Ay, ay, sir!" answered two or three; and a rush was made upon the 'Admiral Benbow', the lantern-bearer following; and then I could see them pause, and hear speeches passed in a lower key, as if they were surprised to find the door open. But the pause was brief, for the blind man again issued his commands. His voice sounded louder and higher, as if he was afire with eagerness and rage.

"In, in, in!" he shouted, and cursed them for their delay.

Four or five of them obeyed at once, two remaining on the road with the formidable beggar. There was a pause, then a cry of surprise, and then a voice shouting from the house:

"Bill's dead!"

But the blind man swore at them again for their delay.

"Search him, some of you shirking lubbers, and

the rest of you aloft and get the chest," he cried.

I could hear their feet rattling up our old stairs, so that the house must have shook with it. Promptly afterwards, fresh sounds of astonishment arose; the window of the captain's room was thrown open with a slam and a jingle of broken glass; and a man leaned out into the moonlight, head and shoulders, and addressed the blind beggar on the road below him.

"Pew," he cried, "they've been before us. Someone's turned the chest out alow and aloft."

"Is it there?" roared Pew.

"The money's there."

The blind man cursed the money.

"Flint's map, I mean," he cried.

"We don't see it here, nohow," returned the man.

"Here, you below there, is it on Bill?" cried the blind man again.

At that, another fellow, probably him who had remained below to search the captain's body, came to the door of the inn. "Bill's been overhauled a'ready," said he, "nothin' left."

"It's these people of the inn—it's that boy. I wish I had put his eyes out!" cried the blind man, Pew. "They were here no time ago—they had the door bolted when I tried it. Scatter, lads, and find 'em."

Suddenly another sound came from the top of the hill on the side of the hamlet—the tramp of horses galloping. Almost at the same time a pistol-shot, flash and report, came from the hedge-side. And that was plainly the last signal of danger; for the buccaneers turned at once and ran, separating in every direction, one seaward along the cove, one slant across the hill, and so on, so that in half a minute not a sign of them remained but Pew. Him they had deserted, whether in sheer panic or out of revenge for his ill words and blows, I know not; but there he remained behind, tapping up and down the road in a frenzy, and groping and calling for his comrades. Finally he took the wrong turn, and ran a few steps past me, towards the hamlet, crying:

"Johnny, Black Dog, Dirk," and other names, "you won't leave old Pew, mates—not old Pew!"

Just then the noise of horses topped the rise, and four or five riders came in sight in the moonlight, and swept at full gallop down the slope.

At this Pew saw his error, turned with a scream, and ran straight for the ditch, into which he rolled. But he was on his feet again in a second, and made another dash, now utterly bewildered, right under the nearest of the coming horses.

The rider tried to save him, but in vain. Down went Pew with a cry that rang high into the night; and the four hoofs trampled and spurned him and passed by. He fell on his side, then gently collapsed upon his face, and moved no more.

I leaped to my feet and hailed the riders. They were pulling up, at any rate, horrified at the accident; and I saw what they were. One, tailing out behind the rest, was a lad that had gone from the hamlet to Dr Livesey's; the rest were revenue officers.

"What were they after," enquired the officer in charge, Mr Dance, "money?"

"No, sir; not money, I think," replied I. "In fact, sir, I believe I have the thing in my breast-pocket; and, to tell you the truth, I should like to get it put in safety."

"To be sure, boy; quite right," said he. "I'll take it, if you like."

"I thought, perhaps, Dr Livesey——" I began.

"Perfectly right," he interrupted, very cheerily, "perfectly right—a gentleman and a magistrate. And, now I come to think of it, I might as well ride round there myself and report to him or squire. Master Pew's dead, when all's done; not that I regret it, but he's dead, you see, and people will make it out against an officer of his Majesty's revenue, if make it out they can. Now, I'll tell you, Hawkins: if you like, I'll take you along."

I thanked him heartily for the offer, and we walked back to the hamlet where the horses were. By the time I had told mother of my purpose they were all in the saddle.

"Dogger," said Mr Dance, "you have a good horse; take up this lad behind you."

As soon as I was mounted, holding on to Dogger's belt, the supervisor gave the word, and the party struck out at a bouncing trot on the road to Dr Livesey's house.

The Captain's Papers

We rode hard all the way, till we drew up before Dr Livesey's door. The house was all dark to the front.

Mr Dance told me to jump down and knock, and Dogger gave me a stirrup to descend by. The door was opened almost at once by a maid.

"Is Dr Livesey in?" I asked.

No, she said; he had come home in the afternoon, but had gone up to the Hall to dine and pass the evening with the squire.

"So there we go, boys," said the officer.

This time, as the distance was short, I did not mount, but ran up the long, leafless, moonlit avenue to the white line of the Hall buildings. Here Mr Dance dismounted, and, taking me along with him, was admitted at a word into the house.

I had never seen the squire so near at hand. He was a tall man, over six feet high, and broad in proportion, and he had a bluff, rough-and-ready face, all roughened and reddened and lined in his long travels.

The doctor stood beside him. After introductions and explanations had been made, Dr Livesey spoke.

"And so, Jim," said the doctor, "you have the thing that they were after, have you?"

"Here it is, sir," said I, and gave him the oilskin packet.

"Very well," said the doctor. "Now, then, if Jim is agreeable, we'll open the packet"; and he laid it before him on the table.

The bundle was sewn together, and the doctor had to get out his instrument-case, and cut the stitches with his medical scissors. It contained two things— a book and a sealed paper.

"First of all we'll try the book," observed the doctor.

The squire and I were both peering over his shoulder as he opened it. On the first page there were only some scraps of writing, such as a man with a pen in his hand might make for idleness or practice. "Billy Bones his fancy"; then there was "Mr W. Bones, mate". "No more rum." "Off Palm Key he got itt"; and some other snatches, mostly single words and unintelligible. I could not help wondering who it was that had "got itt", and what "itt" was

that he got. A knife in his back as like as not.

"Not much instruction there," said Dr Livesey, as he passed on.

"And now," said the squire, "for the other."

The paper had been sealed in several places with a thimble by way of a seal; the doctor opened the seals with great care, and there fell out the map of an island, with latitude and longitude, soundings, names of hills, and bays and inlets, and every particular that would be needed to bring a ship to a safe anchorage upon its shores. It was about nine

miles long and five across, and a hill in the centre part marked 'The Spy-glass'. There were several additions of a later date; but, above all, three crosses of red ink—two on the north part of the island, one in the south-west, and beside this last, in the same red ink, and in a small, neat hand, very different from the captain's tottery characters, these words: "Bulk of treasure here."

Over on the back the same hand had written this further information:

Tall tree, Spy-glass shoulder, bearing a point to the N. of N.N.E.

Skeleton Island E.S.E. and by E.

The bar silver is in the north cache; you can find it by the trend of the east hummock, ten fathoms south of the black crag with the face on it.

The arms are easy found, in the sand hill, N. point of north inlet cape, bearing E. and a quarter N.

'J.F.'

"Livesey," said the squire, "you will give up this wretched practice at once. Tomorrow I start for Bristol. In three weeks' time—three weeks!—two weeks—ten days—we'll have the best ship, sir, and the choicest crew in England. Hawkins shall come as cabin-boy. You'll make a famous cabin-boy, Hawkins. You, Livesey, are ship's doctor; I am admiral. We'll take Redruth, Joyce, and Hunter. We'll have favourable winds, a quick passage, and not the least difficulty in finding the spot, and money to eat—to roll in—to play duck and drake with ever after."

I Go to Bristol

It was longer than the squire imagined ere we were ready for the sea, and none of our first plans could be carried out as we intended. The doctor had to go

to London for a physician to take charge of his practice and the squire was hard at work at Bristol.

So the weeks passed on, till one fine day there came a letter addressed to Dr Livesey, with this addition, "To be opened, in the case of his absence, by Tom Redruth, or young Hawkins". Obeying this order, we found, or rather I found—for the game-keeper was a poor hand at reading anything but print—the following important news:

Old Anchor Inn, Bristol, March 1, 17—,

Dear Livesey.—As I do not know whether you are at the Hall or still in London, I send this in double to both places.

The ship is bought and fitted. She lies at anchor, ready for sea. You never imagined a sweeter schooner—a child might sail her—two hundred tons; name, *Hispaniola*.

All I lacked now was a crew. I wished a round score of men and I had the worry of the deuce itself to find so much as half a dozen, till the most remarkable stroke of fortune brought me the very man that I required.

I was standing on the dock, when, by the merest accident, I fell in talk with him. I found he was an old sailor, kept a public house, knew all the seafaring men in Bristol, had lost his health ashore, and wanted a good berth as cook to get to sea again. He had hobbled down there that morning, he said, to get a smell of the salt.

I was monstrously touched—so would you have been—and, out of pure pity, I engaged him on the spot to be ship's cook. Long John Silver, he is called, and has lost a leg; but that I regarded as a recommendation, since he lost it in his country's service under the immortal Hawke. He has no pension, Livesey. Imagine the abominable age we live in!

Well, sire, I thought I had only found a cook, but it was a crew I had discovered. Between Silver and myself we got together in a few days a company of the toughest old salts imaginable—not pretty to look at, but fellows, by their faces, of the most indomitable spirits. I declare we could fight a frigate.

I am in the most magnificent health and spirits, eating like a bull, sleeping like a tree, yet I shall not enjoy a moment till I hear my old tarpaulins tramping round the capstan. Seaward ho! Hang the treasure! It's the glory of the sea that has turned my head. So now, Livesey, come post; do not lose an hour, if you respect me.

Let young Hawkins and Redruth both come full speed to Bristol.

John Trelawney.

The night passed, and the next day, after dinner, Redruth and I were afoot and on the road. I said goodbye to mother and the cove where I had lived since I was born, and the dear old 'Admiral Benbow'. One of my last thoughts was of the captain, who had so often strode along the beach with his cocked hat, his sabre-cut cheek, and his old brass telescope. Next moment we had turned the corner, and my home was out of sight.

The mail picked us up about dusk at the 'Royal George' on the heath. I was wedged in between Redruth and a stout old gentleman, and in spite of the swift motion and the cold night air, I must have dozed a great deal from the very first, and then slept like a log up hill and down dale through stage after stage; for when I was awakened at last, it was by a punch in the ribs, and I opened my eyes, to find that we were standing still before a large building in a city street, and that the day had already broken a long time.

"Where are we?" I asked.

"Bristol," said Tom. "Get down."

Mr Trelawney had taken up his residence at an inn far down the docks, to superintend the work upon the schooner. Thither we had now to walk, and our way, to my great delight, lay along the quays and beside the great multitude of ships of all sizes and rigs and nations. In one, sailors were singing at their work; in another, there were men aloft, high over my head, hanging to threads that seemed no thicker than a spider's. Though I had lived by the shore all my life, I seemed never to have been near the sea till then. The smell of tar and salt was something new. I saw the most wonderful figure-heads, that had all been far over the ocean. I saw, besides, many old sailors, with rings in their ears, and whiskers curled in ringlets, and tarry pigtails, and their swaggering, clumsy sea-walk; and if I had seen as many kings or archbishops I could not have been more delighted.

And I was going to sea myself; to sea in a schooner, with a piping boatswain, and pigtailed singing seamen; to sea, bound for an unknown island, and to seek for buried treasures!

While I was still in this delightful dream, we came suddenly in front of a large inn, and met Squire

Trelawney, all dressed out like a sea-officer, in stout blue cloth, coming out of the door with a smile on his face, and a capital imitation of a sailor's walk.

"Here you are," he said, "and the doctor came last night from London. Bravo! the ship's company complete!"

"Oh, sir," cried I, "when do we sail?"

"Sail!" says he. "We sail tomorrow!"

At the Sign of the 'Spy-Glass'

When I had done breakfasting, the squire gave me a note addressed to John Silver, at the sign of the 'Spy-glass', and told me I should easily find the place by following the line of the docks, and keeping a bright look-out for a little tavern with a large brass telescope for sign. I set off, overjoyed at this opportunity to see some more of the ships and seamen, and picked my way among a great crowd of people and carts and bales, for the dock was now at its busiest, until I found the tavern in question.

The customers were mostly seafaring men; and they talked so loudly that I hung at the door, almost afraid to enter.

As I was waiting, a man came out of a side room, and, at a glance, I was sure he must be Long John. His left leg was cut off close by the hip, and under the left shoulder he carried a crutch, which he managed with wonderful dexterity, hopping about upon it like a bird. He was very tall and strong, with a face as big as a ham—plain and pale, but intelligent and smiling. Indeed, he seemed in the most cheerful spirits, whistling as he moved about among the tables, with a merry word or a slap on the shoulder for the more favoured of his guests.

Now, to tell you the truth, from the very first mention of Long John in Squire Trelawney's letter, I had taken a fear in my mind that he might prove to be the very one-legged sailor whom I had watched for so long at the old 'Benbow'. But one look at the man before me was enough. I had seen the captain, and Black Dog, and the blind man Pew, and I thought I knew what a buccaneer was like—a very different creature, according to me, from this clean and pleasant-tempered landlord.

I plucked up courage at once, crossed the threshold, and walked right up to the man where he stood, propped on his crutch, talking to a customer.

"Mr Silver, sir?" I asked, holding out the note.

"Yes, my lad," said he; "such is my name, to be sure. And who may you be?"

And then as he saw the squire's letter, he seemed to me to give something almost like a start.

"Oh!" said he, quite loud, and offering his hand, "I see. You are our new cabin-boy; pleased to see you."

And he took my hand in his large firm grasp.

"I'll put on my old cocked hat, and step along of you to Cap'n Trelawney," he said.

On our little walk along the quays, he made himself the most interesting companion, telling me about the different ships that we passed by, their rig, tonnage, and nationality, explaining the work that was going forward—how one was discharging, another taking in cargo, and a third making ready for sea; and every now and then telling me some little anecdote of ships or seamen, or repeating a nautical phrase till I had learned it perfectly. I began to see that here was one of the best possible shipmates.

The Voyage

All that night, we were in a great bustle getting things stowed in their places and I was dog-tired when, a little before dawn, the boatswain sounded his pipe, and the crew began to man the capstan-bars.

I am not going to relate the voyage in detail. It was fairly prosperous. The ship proved to be a good ship, the crew were capable seamen, and Smollett, the captain, thoroughly understood his business.

As for Long John Silver, all the crew respected and even obeyed him. He had a way of talking to each, and doing everybody some particular service.

To me he was unweariedly kind; and always glad to see me in the galley, which he kept as clean as a new pin; the dishes hanging up burnished, and his parrot in a cage in one corner.

"Come away, Hawkins," he would say; "come and have a yarn with John. Nobody more welcome than yourself, my son. Sit you down and hear the news. Here's Cap'n Flint—I calls my parrot Cap'n Flint, after the famous buccaneer—here's Cap'n Flint predicting success to our v'yage. Wasn't you, cap'n?"

And the parrot would say, with great rapidity, "Pieces of eight! pieces of eight! pieces of eight!" till you wondered that it was not out of breath, or till John threw his handkerchief over the cage.

It was about the last day of our voyage out, and just after sundown, when all my work was over, and I was on my way to my berth, it occurred to me that I should like an apple. I ran on deck. The watch was all forward looking out for the island. The man at the helm was watching the luff of the sail, and whistling away gently to himself; and that was the only sound excepting the swish of the sea against the bows and around the sides of the ship.

In I got bodily into the apple barrel, which always stood on deck, for anyone to help himself that had a fancy, and found there was scarce an apple left; but, sitting down there in the dark, what with the sound of the waters and the rocking movement of the ship, I had either fallen asleep, or was on the point of doing so, when a heavy man sat down with rather a clash close by. The barrel shook as he leaned his shoulders against it, and I was just about to jump up when the man began to speak. It was Silver's voice, and, before I had heard a dozen words, I understood that the lives of all the honest men aboard depended upon me alone.

What I Heard in the Apple Barrel

"No, not I," said Silver. "Flint was cap'n; I was quartermaster, along of my timber leg. The same broadside I lost my leg, old Pew lost his daylights. There was some that was feared of Pew, and some that was feared of Flint; but Flint his own self was feared of me. Feared he was, and proud. They was the roughest crew afloat, was Flint's; the devil himself would have been feared to go to sea with them. Well, now, I tell you, I'm not a boasting man, and you seen yourself how easy I keep company; but when I was quartermaster, *lambs* wasn't the word for Flint's old buccaneers. Ah, you may be sure of yourself in old John's ship. Israel," continued Silver, for the other man was Israel Hands, our wily old coxswain, "your head ain't much account, nor ever was. But you're able to hear, I reckon; leastways, your ears is big enough. Now, here's what I say: you'll berth forward, and you'll live hard, and you'll speak soft, and you'll keep sober, till I give the word; and you may lay to that, old son."

"Well, I don't say no, do I?" growled the coxswain. "What I say is, when? That's what I say."

"When! by the powers!" cried Silver. "Well, now, if you want to know, I'll tell you when. The last moment I can manage; and that's when. Here's a first-rate seaman, Cap'n Smollett, sails the blessed ship for us. Here's this squire and doctor with a map and such—I don't know where it is, do I? No more do you, says you. Well, then, I mean this squire and doctor shall find the stuff, and help us to get it aboard, by the powers. Then we'll see. If I was sure of you all, sons of double Dutchmen, I'd have Cap'n Smollett navigate us half-way back again before I struck."

"Everybody know'd you was a kind of a chapling, John; but there's others as could hand and steer as well as you," said Israel. "They liked a bit of fun, they did. They wasn't so high and dry, nohow, but took their fling, like jolly companions every one."

"So?" says Silver. "Well, and where are they now? Pew was that sort, and he died a beggar-man. Flint was, and he died of rum at Savannah. Ah, they was a sweet crew, they was! on'y, where are they?"

"But," asked Israel, "when we do lay 'em athwart, what are we to do with 'em, anyhow?"

"There's the man for me!" cried Silver, admiringly. "That's what I call business. Well, what would you think? Put 'em ashore like maroons? That would have been England's way. Or cut 'em down like that much pork? That would have been Flint's or Billy Bones's."

"Billy was the man for that," said Israel. " 'Dead men don't bite,' says he. Well, he's dead now hisself; he knows the long and short of it now; and if ever a rough hand come to port, it was Billy."

You may fancy the terror I was in! I should have leaped out and run for it, if I had found the strength, but my limbs and heart alike misgave me.

Just then a sort of brightness fell upon me in the barrel, and, looking up, I found the moon had risen, and was silvering the mizzen-top and shining white on the luff of the foresail; and almost at the same time the voice of the look-out shouted "Land ho!"

Council of War

There was a great rush of feet across the deck. I could hear people tumbling up from the cabin and the foc's'le; and, slipping in an instant outside my barrel, I dived behind the fore-sail, made a double towards the stern, and came out upon the open deck in time to join Hunter and Dr Livesey in the rush for the weather bow.

There all hands were already congregated. "And now, men," said the captain, when all was sheeted home, "has any one of you ever seen that land ahead?"

"I have, sir," said Silver. 'I've watered there with a trader I was cook in."

"The anchorage is on the south, behind an islet, I fancy?" asked the captain.

"Yes, sir; Skeleton Island they calls it. It were a main place for pirates once, and a hand we had on board knowed all their names for it. That hill to the nor'ard they calls the Fore-mast Hill; there are three hills in a row running south'ard—fore, main, and mizzen, sir. But the main—that's the big 'un with the cloud on it—they usually calls the Spyglass, by reason of a look-out they kept when they was in the anchorage cleaning; for it's there they cleaned their ships, sir, asking your pardon."

"I have a chart here," says Captain Smollett. "See if that's the place."

Long John's eyes burned in his head as he took the chart; but, by the fresh look of the paper, I knew he was doomed to disappointment. This was not the map we found in Billy Bones's chest, but an accurate copy, complete in all things—names and heights and soundings—with the single exception of the red crosses and the written notes.

Sharp as must have been his annoyance, Silver had the strength of mind to hide it.

"Yes, sir," said he, "this is the spot to be sure; and very prettily drawed out."

"Thank you, my man," says Captain Smollett. "I'll ask you, later on, to give us a help. You may go."

Captain Smollett, the squire and Dr Livesey were talking together on the quarter-deck, and, anxious as I was to tell them my story, I durst not interrupt them openly. While I was still casting about in my thoughts to find some probable excuse, Dr Livesey called me to his side. He had left his pipe below, and being a slave to tobacco, had meant that I should fetch it; but as soon as I was near enough to speak and not be overheard, I broke out immediately: "Doctor, let me speak. Get the captain and squire down to the cabin and then make some pretence to send for me. I have terrible news."

The three gentlemen went below, and not long after, word was sent forward that Jim Hawkins was wanted in the cabin.

I found them all three seated around the table, a bottle of Spanish wine and some raisins before them, and the doctor smoking away, with his wig on his lap, and that, I knew, was a sign that he was agitated. The stern window was open, for it was a warm night, and you could see the moon shining behind on the ship's wake.

"Now, Hawkins," said the squire, "you have something to say. Speak up."

I did as I was bid, and, as short as I could make it, told the whole details of Silver's conversation.

Nobody interrupted me till I was done, nor did any one of the three of them make so much as a movement, but they kept their eyes upon my face from first to last.

Talk as we pleased, there were only seven out of the twenty-six on board on whom we knew we could rely; ourselves, Hunter, Joyce and Redruth, and out of these seven one was a boy, so that the grown men on our side were six to their nineteen.

How I Began My Shore Adventure

The appearance of the island when I came on deck next morning was altogether changed. Grey-coloured woods covered a large part of the surface. This even tint was indeed broken up by streaks of yellow sandbreak in the lower lands, and by many tall trees of the pine family, out-topping the others—some singly, some in clumps; but the general colouring was uniform and sad. Buried in among the trees was a block-house and stockade.

We had a dreary morning's work before us, for there was no sign of any wind, and the boats had to be got out and manned, and the ship warped three or four miles round the corner of the island, and up the narrow passage to the haven. I volunteered for one of the boats where I had, of course, no business. The heat was sweltering, and the men grumbled fiercely over their work.

There was not a breath of air moving, nor a sound but that of the surf booming half a mile away along the beaches and against the rocks outside. A peculiar stagnant smell hung over the anchorage—a smell of sodden leaves and rotting tree trunks. I observed the doctor sniffing, like someone tasting a bad egg.

"I don't know about treasure," he said, "but I'll stake my wig there's fever here."

If the conduct of the men had been alarming in the boat, it became truly threatening when they had come aboard. They lay about the deck growling together in talk. The slightest order was received with a black look, and grudgingly and carelessly obeyed. Even the honest hands must have caught the infection, for there was not one man aboard to mend another. Mutiny, it was plain, hung over us like a thunder-cloud.

We held a council in the cabin.

"Sir," said the captain, "if I risk another order, the whole ship'll come about our ears by the run.

You see, sir, here it is. I get a rough answer, do I not? Well, if I speak back, pikes will be going in two shakes; if I don't, Silver will see there's something under that, and the game's up. Now, we've only one man to rely on."

"And who is that?" asked the squire.

"Silver, sir," returned the captain; "he's anxious as you and I to smother things up. This is a tiff; he'd soon talk 'em out of it if he had the chance, and what I propose to do is to give him the chance. Let's allow the men an afternoon ashore. If they all go, why, we'll fight the ship. If they none of them go, well, then, we hold the cabin, and God defend the right. If some go, you mark my words, sir, Silver'll bring 'em aboard again as mild as lambs."

Then it was that there came into my head the first of the mad notions that contributed so much to save our lives. If six men were left by Silver, it was plain our party could not take and fight the ship; and since only six were left, it was equally plain that the cabin party had no present need of my assistance. It occurred to me at once to go ashore. In a jiffy I had slipped over the side, and curled up in the foresheets of the nearest boat, and almost at the same moment she shoved off.

The crews raced for the beach; but the boat I was in having some start, and being at once the lighter and the better manned, shot far ahead of her consort, and the bow had struck among the shore-side trees, and I had caught a branch and swung myself out, and plunged into the nearest thicket, while Silver and the rest were still a hundred yards behind.

"Jim, Jim!" I heard him shouting.

But you may suppose I paid no heed; jumping, ducking and breaking through, I ran straight before my nose. Without taking any notice, I drew near to the foot of a little hill with two peaks, and here a fresh alarm brought me to a standstill with a thumping heart.

The Man of the Island

From the side of the hill, which was here steep and stony, a spout of gravel was dislodged, and fell rattling and bounding through the trees. My eyes turned instinctively in that direction, and I saw a figure leap with great rapidity behind the trunk of a pine. What it was, whether bear or man or monkey,

I could in no wise tell. It seemed dark and shaggy; more I knew not. But the terror of this new apparition brought me to a stand.

Instantly the figure reappeared, and, making a wide circuit, began to head me off. I was tired, at any rate; but had I been as fresh as when I rose, I could see it was in vain for me to contend in speed with such an adversary. From trunk to trunk the creature flitted like a deer, running man-like on two legs, but unlike any man that I had ever seen, stooping almost double as it ran. Yet a man it was, I could no longer be in doubt about that.

He was concealed by this time, behind another tree trunk; but he must have been watching me closely, for as soon as I began to move in his direction he reappeared and took a step to meet me.

Then he hesitated, drew back, came forward again, and at last, to my wonder and confusion, threw himself on his knees and held out his clasped hands in supplication.

At that I once more stopped.

"Who are you?" I asked.

"Ben Gunn," he answered, and his voice sounded hoarse and awkward, like a rusty lock. "I'm poor Ben Gunn, I am; and I haven't spoke with a Christian these three years."

I could now see that he was a white man like myself, and that his features were even pleasing. His skin, wherever it was exposed, was burnt by the sun; even his lips were black; and his fair eyes looked quite startling in so dark a face.

"Three years!" I cried. "Were you shipwrecked?"

79

"Nay, mate," said he—"marooned."

I had heard the word, and I knew it stood for a horrible kind of punishment common enough among the buccaneers, in which the offender is put ashore with a little powder and shot, and left behind on some desolate and distant island.

"Marooned three years agone," he continued, "and lived on goats since then, and berries, and oysters. Wherever a man is, says I, a man can do for himself. But, mate, my heart is sore for Christian diet. You mightn't happen to have a piece of cheese about you, now? No? Well, many's the long night I've dreamed of cheese—toasted, mostly—and woke up again, and here I were."

"If ever I can get aboard again," said I, "you shall have cheese by the stone."

"If ever you can get aboard again, says you?" he repeated. "Why, now, who's to hinder you?"

At this I had a happy inspiration. I began to see that I had found an ally, and I told him my story at once.

"Ah," said he, "that's the hitch, for sure. Well, there's my boat, that I made with my two hands. I keep her under the white rock. If the worst comes to the worst, we might try that after dark. Jim," he continued, "I've lived that rough as you'd be ashamed to hear of. But, Jim"—looking all round him and lowering his voice to a whisper—"I'm rich."

I now felt that the poor fellow had gone crazy in his solitude, and I suppose I must have shown the feeling in my face; for he repeated the statement hotly:

"Rich! rich! I says. And I'll tell you what: I'll make a man of you, Jim. Ah, Jim, you'll bless your stars, you will, you was the first that found me."

And at this there came suddenly a lowering shadow over his face, and he tightened his grasp upon my hand, and raised a forefinger threateningly before my eyes. "Now, Jim, you tell me true; that ain't Flint's ship?" he asked.

"It's not Flint's ship, and Flint is dead; but I'll tell you true, as you ask me—there are some of Flint's hands aboard; worse luck for the rest of us."

"Not a man—with one—leg?" he gasped.

"Silver?" I asked.

"Ah, Silver!" says he; "that were his name."

"Now, I'll tell you what," he went on. "So much I'll tell you and no more. I were in Flint's ship when he buried the treasure; he and six along—six strong

seamen. They was ashore nigh on a week, and us standing off and on in the old *Walrus*. One fine day up went the signal, and here come Flint by himself in a little boat, and his head done up in a blue scarf. The sun was getting up, and mortal white he looked about the cutwater. But, there he was, you mind, and the six all dead—dead and buried. How he done it, not a man aboard us could make out. It was battle, murder, and sudden death, leastways—him against six. Billy Bones was the mate; Long John, he

was quartermaster; and they asked him where the treasure was. 'Ah,' says he, 'you can go ashore, if you like, and stay,' he says; 'but as for the ship she'll beat up for more, by thunder!' That's what he said.

"Well, I was in another ship three years back, and we sighted this island. 'Boys,' said I, 'here's Flint's treasure; let's land and find it.' The cap'n was displeased at that; but my messmates were all of a mind, and landed. Twelve days they looked for it, and every day they had the worse word for me, until

one fine morning all hands went aboard. 'As for you, Benjamin Gunn,' says they, 'here's a musket,' they says, 'and a spade, and pickaxe. You can stay here, and find Flint's money for yourself,' they says. Hi!" he broke out, "what's that?"

For just then, although the sun had still an hour or two to run, all the echoes of the island awoke and bellowed to the thunder of a cannon.

The cannon-shot was followed, after a considerable interval, by a volley of small arms.

Another pause, and then, not a quarter of a mile in front of me, I beheld the Union Jack flutter in the air above a wood.

Narrative Continued by the Doctor: How the Ship Was Abandoned

It was about half past one—three bells in the sea phrase—that the two boats went ashore from the *Hispaniola*. The captain, the squire, and I were talking matters over in the cabin. Had there been a breath of wind we should have fallen on the six mutineers who were left aboard with us, slipped our cable, and away to sea. But the wind was wanting; and, to complete our helplessness, down came Hunter with the news that Jim Hawkins had slipped into a boat and was gone ashore with the rest.

It never occurred to us to doubt Jim Hawkins; but we were alarmed for his safety. The six scoundrels were sitting grumbling under a sail in the forecastle; ashore we could see the gigs made fast, and a man sitting in each, hard by where the river runs in. One of them was whistling *Lillibullero*.

It was decided that Hunter and I should go ashore with the jolly-boat in quest of information. The gigs had leaned to their right; but Hunter and I pulled straight in, in the direction of the stockade.

In the meantime, the squire and the captain stayed on deck, and the latter hailed the coxswain, who was the principal man aboard.

"Mr Hands," he said, "here are two of us with a brace of pistols each. If any one of you six make a signal of any description, that man's dead."

By this time, tumbling things in as they came, we had the jolly-boat loaded as much as we dared. Joyce and I got out through the stern-port and we made for shore again, as fast as oars could take us.

We had soon touched land and set to provision the block-house. All three made the first journey, heavily laden, and tossed our stores over the palisade. Then, leaving Joyce to guard them—one man, to be sure, but with half a dozen muskets—Hunter and I returned to the jolly-boat, and loaded ourselves once more.

The Jolly-Boat's Last Trip

This next trip was quite different from the other. In the first place, the little gallipot of a boat that we were in was gravely overloaded. Five grown men, and three of them—Trelawney, Redruth, and the captain—over six feet high, was already more than she was meant to carry. Add to that the powder, pork, and bread-bags. The gunwale was lipping astern. Several times we shipped a little water, and my breeches and the tails of my coat were all soaking wet before we had gone a hundred yards.

The captain made us trim the boat, and we got her to lie a little more evenly. All the same, we were afraid to breathe.

Suddenly the captain spoke up again, and I thought his voice was a little changed.

"The gun!" said he. "Look astern, doctor."

We had entirely forgotten the big long nine gun on board the ship; and there, to our horror, were the five rogues busy about her, getting off her jacket, as they called the stout tarpaulin cover under which she sailed. But the worst of it was, that with the course I now held, we turned our broadside instead of our stern to the Hispaniola, and offered a target like a barn door.

I could hear, as well as see, that brandy-faced rascal, Israel Hands, plumping down a round-shot on the deck.

"Here come the gigs, sir," said I.

"Give way then," cried the captain. "We mustn't mind if we swamp her now. If we can't get ashore, all's up."

"Only one of the gigs is being manned, sir," I added, "the crew of the other most likely going round by shore to cut us off."

"They'll have a hot run, sir," returned the captain. "It's not them I mind; it's the roundshot."

The gig was no longer to be feared; the little point had already concealed it from our eyes. The ebb-tide, which had so cruelly delayed us, was now making reparation, and delaying our assailants. The one source of danger was the gun.

At that moment, the report sounded. Where the ball passed, not one of us precisely knew; but I fancy it must have been over our heads, and that the wind of it may have contributed to our disaster.

At any rate, the boat sank by the stern, quite gently, in three feet of water, leaving the captain and myself, facing each other, on our feet. The other three took complete headers, and came up again, drenched and bubbling.

We waded ashore as fast as we could, leaving behind us the poor jolly-boat, and a good half of all our powder and provisions.

End of the First Day's Fighting

We made our best speed across the strip of wood that now divided us from the stockade; and at every step we took the voices of the buccaneers rang nearer. Soon we could hear their footfalls as they ran, and the crashing of the branches as they breasted across a bit of thicket.

Forty paces farther we came to the edge of the wood and saw the stockade in front of us. We struck the enclosure about the middle of the south side, and, almost at the same time, seven mutineers, the boatswain at their head—appeared in full cry at the south-western corner.

They paused, as if taken aback; and before they recovered, not only the squire and I, but Hunter and Joyce from the block-house, had time to fire. The four shots came in rather a scattering volley; but they did the business; one of the enemy actually fell, and the rest, without hesitation, turned and plunged into the trees.

In the meantime the captain, whom I had observed to be wonderfully swollen about the chest and pockets, had turned out a great many various stores—the British colours, a Bible, a coil of stoutish rope, pen, ink, the log-book, and pounds of tobacco. He had found a longish fir tree lying felled and cleared in the enclosure, and with the help of Hunter, he had set it up at the corner of the log-house where the trunks crossed and made an angle.

Then, climbing on the roof, he had with his own hand bent and run up the colours.

Just then, with a roar and a whistle, a round-shot passed high above the roof of the log-house and plumped far beyond us in the wood.

At the second trial, the aim was better, and the ball descended inside the stockade, scattering a cloud of sand, but doing no further damage.

"Captain," said the squire, "the house is quite invisible from the ship. It would be the flag they are aiming at. Would it not be wiser to take it in?"

"Strike my colour!" cried the captain. "No, sir, not I"; and, as soon as he had said the words, I think we all agreed with him.

Just as I was wondering over poor Jim Hawkins's fate, there came a hail on the land side.

"Somebody hailing us," said Hunter, who was on guard.

"Doctor! squire! captain! Hullo, Hunter, is that you?" came the cries.

And I ran to the door in time to see Jim Hawkins, safe and sound, come climbing over the stockade. He had soon told his story. I resolved to seek out this Ben Gunn at the first opportunity.

Silver's Embassy
Jim Resumes the Narrative

I was dead tired, and, after I had told my story, I slept like a log of wood. I was awakened by a bustle and the sound of voices.

"Flag of truce!" I heard someone say; and then immediately after, with a cry of surprise, "Silver himself!"

There were two men just outside the stockade, one of them waving a white cloth; the other, no less a person than Long John Silver himself, standing placidly by.

"Keep indoors, men," said the captain. "Ten to one this is a trick."

Then he hailed the buccaneer.

"Who goes? Stand, or we fire."

"Flag of truce," cried Silver.

The captain was in the porch, keeping himself carefully out of the way of a treacherous shot should any be intended. He turned and spoke to us:

"Doctor's watch on the look out. Dr Livesey, take the north side, if you please; Jim, the east; Gray, west. The watch below, all hands to load muskets. Lively, men, and careful."

And then he turned again to the mutineers.

"And what do you want with your flag of truce?" he cried.

This time it was the other man who replied.

"Cap'n Silver, sir, to come on board and make terms," he shouted.

"Cap'n Silver! Don't know him. Who's he?" cried the captain. And we could hear him adding to himself: "Cap'n Silver is it? My heart, and here's promotion!"

Long John answered for himself.

"Me, sir. These poor lads have chosen me cap'n, after your desertion, sir"—laying a particular emphasis upon the word 'desertion'. "We're willing to submit, if we can come to terms, and no bones about it. All I ask is your word, Cap'n Smollett, to let me safe and sound out of this here stockade, and one minute to get out o' shot before a gun is fired."

"My man," said Captain Smollett, "I have not the slightest desire to talk to you. If you wish to talk to me, you can come, that's all."

"You ain't a-going to let me inside, cap'n?" complained Long John. "It's a main cold morning, to be sure, sire, to sit outside upon the sand."

"Why, Silver," said the captain, "if you had pleased to be an honest man, you might have been sitting in your galley. It's your own doing. You're either my ship's cook—and then you were treated handsome—or Cap'n Silver, a common mutineer and pirate, and then you can go hang!"

"Well, here it is," said Silver. "We want that treasure, and we'll have it—that's our point! You would just as soon save your lives, I reckon; and that's yours. You have a chart, haven't you?"

"That's as may be," replied the captain.

"Oh, well, you have, I know that," returned Long John. "You needn't be so husky with a man; there ain't a particle of service in that, and you may lay to it. What I mean is, we want your chart. Now, I never meant you no harm, myself."

"That won't do with me, my man," interrupted the captain. "We know exactly what you mean to do, and we don't care; for now, you see, you can't do it."

And the captain looked at him calmly, and proceeded to fill a pipe.

"Now," resumed Silver, "here it is. You give us the chart to get the treasure by, and drop shooting poor seamen, and stoving of their heads in while

asleep. You do that, and we'll offer you a choice. Either you come aboard along of us, once the treasure's shipped, and then I'll give you my affydavy, upon my word of honour, to clap you somewhere safe ashore. Or, if that ain't to your fancy, some of my hands being rough, and having old scores, on account of hazing, then you can stay here, you can. We'll divide stores with you, man for man; and I'll give my affydavy, as before, to speak the first ship I sight, and send 'em here to pick you up."

"Is that all?" asked Captain Smollett.

"Every last word, by thunder!" answered John. "Refuse that, and you've seen the last of me but musket-balls."

"Very good," said the captain. "Now you'll hear me. You can't find the treasure. You can't sail the ship—there's not a man among you fit to sail the

ship. You can't fight us. Your ship's in irons, Master Silver; you're on a lee shore, and so you'll find. I stand here and tell you so; and they're the last good words you'll get from me; for, in the name of heaven, I'll put a bullet in your back when next I meet you. Tramp, my lad. Bundle out of this, please, hand over hand, and double quick."

Silver's face was a picture; his eyes started in his head with wrath.

"Give me a hand up!" he cried.

"Not I," returned the captain.

"Who'll give me a hand up?" he roared.

Not a man among us moved. With a dreadful oath he stumbled off, ploughed down the sand, was helped across the stockade, after four or five failures, by the man with the flag of truce, and disappeared in an instant afterwards among the trees.

The Attack

The captain looked on for a while in silence. Then he spoke.

"My lads," said he, "I've given Silver a broadside. I pitched it in red-hot on purpose; and before the hour's out we shall be boarded. We're outnumbered, I needn't tell you that, but we fight in shelter; and with discipline. I've no manner of doubt that we can drub them, if you choose."

"Doctor, you will take the door," he resumed. "See, and don't expose yourself; keep within, and fire through the porch. Hunter, take the east side, there. Joyce, you stand by the west, my man. Mr Trelawney, you are the best shot—you and Gray will take this long north side, with the five loopholes; it's there the danger is. If they can get up to it, and fire in upon us through our own ports, things would begin to look dirty. Hawkins, neither you nor I are much account at the shooting; we'll stand by to load and bear a hand."

An hour passed away.

"Hang them!" said the captain. "This is as dull as the doldrums. Gray, whistle for a wind."

And just at that moment came the first news of the attack. Suddenly, with a loud huzza, a little cloud of pirates leaped from the woods on the north side, and ran straight on the stockade. At the same moment, the fire was opened from the woods, and a rifle-ball sang through the doorway, and knocked the doctor's musket into bits.

The boarders swarmed over the fence like monkeys. Squire and Gray fired again and yet again; three men fell, one forwards into the enclosure, two back on the outside. But of these, one was evidently more frightened than hurt, for he was on his feet again in a crack, and instantly disappeared among the trees.

Two had bit the dust, one had fled, four had made good their footing inside our defences; while from the shelter of the woods seven or eight men, each evidently supplied with several muskets, kept up a hot though useless fire on the loghouse.

The four who had boarded made straight before them for the building, shouting as they ran, and the men among the trees shouted back to encourage them. In a moment, the four pirates had swarmed up the mound and were upon us.

"Out lads, out, and fight 'em in the open! Cutlasses!" cried the captain.

I snatched a cutlass from the pile, and someone, at the same time, snatching another, gave me a cut across the knuckles which I hardly felt. I dashed out of the door into the clear sunlight. Someone was close behind, I knew not who. Right in front, the doctor was pursuing his assailant down the hill, and sent him sprawling on his back.

"Round the house, lads! round the house!" cried the captain; and even in the hurly-burly I perceived a change in his voice.

"Fire—fire from the house!" cried the doctor.

But his words were unheeded, no shot was fired, and the last boarder made good his escape, and disappeared with the rest into the wood. In three seconds nothing remained of the attacking party but the five who had fallen, four on the inside, and one on the outside, of the palisade.

How I Began My Sea Adventure

Out of the eight men who had fallen in the action, only three still breathed—that one of the pirates who had been shot at the loophole, Hunter, and Captain Smollett; and of these the first two were as good as dead.

As for the captain, his wounds were grievous indeed, but not dangerous. No organ was fatally injured. The first ball had broken his shoulderblade and touched the lung, not badly; the second had only torn and displaced some muscles in the calf. He was sure to recover, the doctor said, but, in the meantime and for weeks to come, he must not walk nor move his arm, nor so much as speak when he could help it.

The house became stiflingly hot, and with so much blood about me, and so many poor dead bodies lying all around, I took a disgust of the place that was almost as strong as fear. My disgust with my surroundings kept growing stronger and stronger and I began to get another idea in my head, till at last, being near a bread-bag, and no one then observing me, I took the first step towards my escape, and filled both pockets of my coat with biscuit.

I was a fool, if you like, and certainly I was going to do a foolish, over-bold act; but I was determined to do it with all the precautions in my power. These biscuits, should anything befall me, would keep me, at least, from starving till far on in the next day.

The next thing I laid hold of was a brace of pistols, and as I already had a powder-horn and bullets, I felt myself well supplied with arms.

As for the scheme I had in my head, it was not a bad one in itself. I was to go down the sandy spit that divides the anchorage on the east from the open sea, find the white rock, and ascertain whether it was there or not that Ben Gunn had hidden his boat; a thing quite worth doing, as I still believe. But as I was certain I should not be allowed to leave the enclosure, my only plan was to take French leave, and slip out when nobody was watching; and that was so bad a way of doing it as made the thing itself wrong. But I was only a boy, and I had made my mind up.

The squire and Gray were busy helping the captain with his bandages; the coast was clear; I made a bolt for it over the stockade and into the thickest of the trees, and before my absence was observed I was out of cry of my companions.

I took my way straight for the east coast of the island, till thinking I was now got far enough, I took the cover of some thick bushes, and crept warily up to the ridge of the spit.

The white rock, visible enough above the brush, was still some eighth of a mile farther down the spit, and it took me a goodish while to get up with it, crawling, often on all fours, among the scrub. Night had almost come when I laid my hands on its rough sides. Sure enough, there was the boat.

I can give you no fairer idea of Ben Gunn's boat than by saying it was like the first and the worst coracle ever made by man. But the great advantage of the coracle it certainly possessed, for it was exceedingly light and portable.

Well, now that I had found the boat, you would have thought I had had enough of truantry for once; but, in the meantime, I had taken another notion, and become so obstinately fond of it, that I would have carried it out, I believe, in the teeth of Captain Smollett himself. This was to slip out under cover of the night, cut the *Hispaniola* adrift, and let her go ashore where she fancied. I had quite made up my mind that the mutineers, after their repulse of the morning, had nothing nearer their hearts than to up anchor and away to sea; this, I thought, it would be a fine thing to prevent; and now that I had seen how they left their watchmen unprovided with a boat, I thought it might be done with little risk.

The Ebb-Tide Runs

The coracle—as I had ample reason to know before I was done with her—was a very safe boat for a person of my height and weight, both buoyant and clever in a sea-way; but she was the most cross-grained, lop-sided craft to manage. Do as you please, she always made more leeway than anything else, and turning round and round was the manoeuvre she was best at. Even Ben Gunn himself has admitted that she was "queer to handle till you knew her way." By good fortune, the tide carried me till there lay the *Hispaniola,* hardly to be missed.

I at last came to the hawser and laid hold. Just while I was meditating, a puff came, caught the *Hispaniola,* and forced her into the current; and to my great joy, I felt the hawser slacken in my grasp, and the hand by which I held it dip for a second under water.

With that I made my mind up, took out my gully, opened it with my teeth, and cut one strand after another, till the vessel only swung by two. Then I lay quiet, waiting to sever these last when the strain be once more lightened by a breath of wind.

At last the breeze came; the schooner sidled and drew nearer in the dark; I felt the hawser slacken once more, and with a good, tough effort, cut the last fibres through.

The breeze had but little action on the coracle, and I was almost instantly swept against the bows of the *Hispaniola.* At the same time the schooner began to turn upon her heel, spinning slowly, end for end, across the current.

I wrought like a fiend, for I expected every moment to be swamped; and since I found I could not push the coracle directly off, I now shoved straight astern. At length I was clear of my dangerous neighbour; and just as I gave the last impulsion, my hands came across a light cord that was trailing overboard across the stern bulwarks. Instantly I grasped it.

Why I should have done so I can hardly say. It was at first mere instinct; but once I had it in my hands and found it fast, curiosity began to get the upper hand, and I determined I should have one look through the cabin window.

I pulled in hand over hand on the cord, and, when I judged myself near enough, rose at infinite risk to about half my height, and thus commanded the roof and a slice of the interior of the cabin.

By this time the schooner and her little consort were gliding pretty swiftly through the water; indeed, we had already fetched up level with the pirates' camp fire. The ship was talking, as sailors say, loudly, treading the innumerable ripples with an incessant weltering splash; and until I got my eye above the window-sill I could not comprehend why the watchmen had taken no alarm. One glance, however, was sufficient; and it was only one glance that I durst take from that unsteady skiff. It showed me Hands and another man, wearing a red cap, locked together in deadly wrestle, each with a hand upon the other's throat.

I dropped upon the thwart again, none too soon, for I was near overboard. I could see nothing for the moment but these two furious, encrimsoned faces, swaying together under the smoky lamp; and I shut my eyes to let them grow once more familiar with the darkness.

The pirate company about the camp fire had broken into the chorus I had heard so often:

"Fifteen men on the dead man's chest—
    Yo-ho-ho, and a bottle of rum!
Drink and the devil had done for the rest—
    Yo-ho-ho, and a bottle of rum!"

I was just thinking how busy drink and the devil were at that very moment in the cabin of the *Hispaniola,* when I was surprised by a sudden lurch of the coracle. At the same moment she yawed sharply and seemed to change her course. The speed in the meantime had strangely increased.

I opened my eyes at once. All round me were little ripples, combing over with a sharp, bristling sound and slightly phosphorescent. The *Hispaniola* herself, a few yards in whose wake I was still being whirled along, seemed to stagger in her course, and I saw her spars toss a little against the blackness of the night; nay, as I looked longer, I made sure she also was wheeling to the southward.

I glanced over my shoulder, and my heart jumped against my ribs. There, right behind me, was the glow of the camp fire. The current had turned at right angles, sweeping along with it the tall schooner and the little dancing coracle; ever quickening, ever bubbling higher, ever muttering louder, it went spinning through the narrows for the open sea.

Suddenly the schooner in front of me gave a violent yaw, turning, perhaps, through twenty degrees; and almost at the same moment one shout followed another from on board; I could hear feet pounding on the companion ladder; and I knew that the two drunkards had at last been interrupted in their quarrel and awakened to a sense of their disaster.

I lay down flat in the bottom of that wretched skiff, continually beaten to and fro upon the billows,

now and again wetted with flying sprays, and never ceasing to expect death at the next plunge. Gradually weariness grew upon me; a numbness, an occasional stupor, fell upon my mind even in the midst of my terrors; until sleep at last supervened, and in my sea-tossed coracle I lay and dreamed of home and the old 'Admiral Benbow'.

The Cruise of the Coracle

It was broad day when I awoke, and found myself tossing at the south-west end of Treasure Island. The sun was up, but was still hid from me behind the great bulk of the Spy-glass, which on this side descended almost to the sea in formidable cliffs.

There was a great, smooth swell upon the sea. The wind blowing steady and gentle from the south, there was no contrariety between that and the current, and the billows rose and fell unbroken.

I found each wave, instead of the big, smooth glossy mountain it looks from shore, or from a vessel's deck, was for all the world like any range of hills on the dry land, full of peaks and smooth places and valleys. The coracle, left to herself, turning from side to side, threaded, so to speak, her way through these lower parts, and avoided the steep slopes and higher, toppling summits of the wave.

"Well, now," thought I to myself, "it is plain I must lie where I am, and not disturb the balance; but it is plain, also, that I can put the paddle over the side, and from time to time, in smooth places, give her a shove or two towards land." No sooner thought upon than done. There I lay on my elbows, in the most trying attitude, and every now and again gave a weak stroke or two to turn her head to shore.

It was very tiring and slow work, yet I did visibly gain ground; and, as we drew near the Cape of the Woods, though I saw I must infallibly miss the point, I had still made some hundred yards of easting. I was, indeed, close in. I could see the cool green tree-tops swaying together in the breeze, and I felt sure I should make the next promontory without fail.

It was high time, for I now began to be tortured with thirst. The glow of the sun from above, its thousandfold reflection from the waves, the sea-water that fell and dried upon me, caking my very lips with salt. The current had soon carried me past

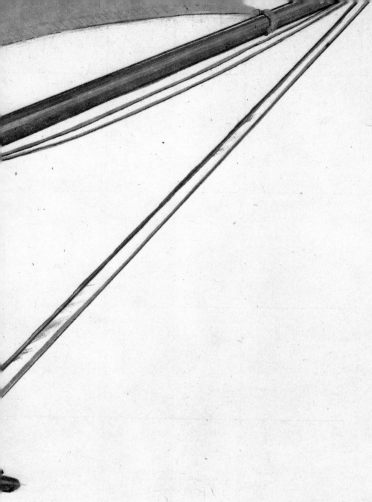

and more to the westward, so that I thought they had sighted me and were going about to chase. At last, however, she fell right into the wind's eye, was taken dead aback, and stood there a while helpless, with her sails shivering.

I was now gaining rapidly on the schooner; I could see the brass glisten on the tiller as it banged about; and still no soul appeared upon her decks. It became plain to me that no one was steering. And, if so, where were the men?

I was not a hundred yards from her when the wind came again in a clap; she filled on the port tack, and was off again, stooping and skimming like a swallow.

My first impulse was one of despair, but my second was towards joy. Round she came, till she was broadside on to me—round still till she had covered a half, and then two-thirds, and then three-quarters of the distance that separated us. I could see the waves boiling white under her forefoot. Immensely tall she looked to me from my coracle.

And then, of a sudden, I began to comprehend. I had scarce time to think—scarce time to act and save myself. I was on the summit of one swell when the schooner came swooping over the next. The bowsprit was over my head. I sprang to my feet, and leaped, stamping the coracle under water. With one hand I caught the jib-boom, while my foot was lodged between the stay and the brace; and as I still clung there panting, a dull blow told me that the schooner had charged down upon and struck the coracle, and that I was left without retreat on the *Hispaniola*.

I Strike the Jolly Roger

I had scarce gained a position on the bowsprit, when the flying jib flapped and filled upon the other tack, with a report like a gun. The schooner trembled to her keel under the reverse; but next moment, the other sails still drawing, the jib flapped back again, and hung idle.

This had nearly tossed me off into the sea; and

the point; and, as the next reach of sea opened out, I beheld a sight that changed the nature of my thoughts.

Right in front of me, not half a mile away, I beheld the *Hispaniola* under sail. I made sure, of course, that I should be taken; but I was so distressed for want of water, that I scarce knew whether to be glad or sorry at the thought; and, long before I had come to a conclusion, surprise had taken entire possession of my mind, and I could do nothing but stare and wonder.

The *Hispaniola* was under her main-sail and two jibs, and the beautiful white canvas shone in the sun like snow or silver. Presently she began to fetch more now I lost no time, crawled back along the bowsprit, and tumbled head foremost on the deck.

There were two watchmen of the night before, sure enough: red-cap on his back, as stiff as a handspike, with his arms stretched out like those of a crucifix, and his teeth showing through his open lips; Israel Hands propped against the bulwarks, his chin on his chest, his lands lying open before him on the deck, his face as white, under its tan, as a tallow candle.

At every jump of the schooner, red-cap slipped to and fro; but—what was ghastly to behold—neither his attitude nor his fixed teeth-disclosing grin was anyway disturbed by this rough usage. At every jump, too, Hands appeared still more to sink into himself and settle down upon the deck, his feet sliding ever the farther out, and the whole body canting towards the stern, so that his face became, little by little, hid from me; and at last I could see nothing beyond his ear and the frayed ringlet of one whisker.

At the same time, I observed, around both of them, splashes of dark blood upon the planks, and began to feel sure that they had killed each other in their drunken wrath.

While I was thus looking and wondering, in a calm moment, when the ship was still, Israel Hands turned partly round, and, with a low moan, writhed himself back to the position in which I had seen him first. The moan, which told of pain and deadly weakness, and the way in which his jaw hung open, went right to my heart. But when I remembered the talk I had overheard from the apple barrel, all pity left me.

I walked aft until I reached the main-mast.

"Come aboard, Mr Hands," I said ironically.

He rolled his eyes round heavily; but he was too far gone to express surprise. All he could do was to utter one word, "Brandy."

Foraging about, I found a bottle with some brandy left, for Hands; and for myself I routed out some biscuit, some pickled fruits, a great bunch of raisins, and a piece of cheese. With these I came on deck, put down my own stock behind the rudder-head, and well out of the coxwain's reach, went forward to the water-breaker, and had a good, deep drink of water, and then, and not till then, gave Hands the brandy.

He must have drunk a gill before he took the bottle from his mouth.

"Aye," said he, "by thunder, but I wanted some o' that!"

I had sat down already in my own corner and begun to eat.

"Much hurt?" I asked him.

He grunted, or rather I might say, he barked.

"By-the-by," I continued, "I can't have these colours, Mr Hands; and, by your leave, I'll strike 'em. Better none than these."

And, again dodging the boom, I ran to the colour lines, handed down their cursed black flag, and chucked it overboard.

"God save the King!" said I, waving my cap; "and there's an end to Captain Silver!"

In three minutes I had the *Hispaniola* sailing easily before the wind along the coast of Treasure Island, with good hopes of turning the northern point ere noon, and beating down again as far as North Inlet before high water, when we might beach her safely, and wait till the subsiding tide permitted us to land.

Then I lashed the tiller and went below to my own chest, where I got a silk handkerchief of my mother's. With this, and with my aid, Hands bound up the great bleeding stab he had received in the thigh, and after he had eaten a little and had a swallow or two more of the brandy, he began to pick up visibly, sat straighter up, spoke louder and clearer, and looked in every way another man.

But there was a shadow of treachery in his expression as he craftily watched, and watched, and watched me at my work.

Israel Hands

All told, we had scarce two miles to run; but the navigation was delicate, the entrance to this northern anchorage was not only narrow and shoal, but lay east and west, so that the schooner must be nicely handled to be got in. I think I was a good, prompt subaltern, and I am very sure that Hands was an excellent pilot; for we went about and about, and dodged in, shaving the banks, with a certainty and a neatness that were a pleasure to behold.

The excitement of these manoeuvres had somewhat interfered with the watch I had kept hitherto, sharply enough, upon the coxswain. Even then I was still so much interested, waiting for the ship to touch, that I had quite forgot the peril that hung over my head, and stood craning over the starboard bulwarks and watching the ripples spreading wide before the bows. I might have fallen without a struggle for my life, had not a sudden disquietude seized upon me, and made me turn my head. Perhaps I had heard a creak, or seen his shadow moving with the tail of my eye; perhaps it was an instinct like a cat's; but, sure enough, when I looked around, there was Hands, already half-way towards me, with a dirk in his right hand.

At the same instant he threw himself forward, and I leapt sideways towards the bows. As I did so, I left hold of the tiller, which sprang sharp to leeward; and I think this saved my life, for it struck hands across the chest, and stopped him, for the moment, dead.

Well, while things stood thus, suddenly the *Hispaniola* struck, staggered, ground for an instant in the sand, and then, swift as a blow, canted over to the port side, till the deck stood at an angle of forty-five degrees, and about a puncheon of water splashed into the scupper-holes, and lay, in a pool, between the deck and bulwark.

We were both of us capsized in a second, and both of us rolled, almost together, into the scuppers; the dead red-cap tumbling stiffly after us.

I was the first afoot again. Quick as thought I sprang into the mizzen shrouds, rattled up hand over hand, and did not draw a breath till I was seated on the cross-trees.

I had been saved by being prompt; the dirk had struck not half a foot below me, as I pursued my upward flight; and there stood Israel Hands with his mouth open and his face upturned to mine, a perfect statue of surprise and disappointment, then, with a pistol in either hand, I addressed him.

"One more step, Mr Hands," said I, "and I'll blow your brains out! Dead men don't bite, you know," I added, with a chuckle.

He stopped instantly. I could see by the working of his face that he was trying to think, and the process was so slow and laborious that, in my new-found security, I laughed aloud. At last, with a swallow or two, he spoke, his face still wearing the same expression of extreme perplexity. In order to speak he had to take the dagger from his mouth, but, in all else, he remained unmoved.

"Jim," says he, "I reckon we're fouled, you and me, and we'll have to sign articles. I'd have had you but for that there lurch; but I don't have no luck, not I; and I reckon I'll have to strike, which comes hard, you see, for a master mariner to a ship's younker like you, Jim."

I was drinking in his words and smiling away, as conceited as a cock upon a wall, when, all in a breath, back went his right hand over his shoulder. Something sang like an arrow through the air; I felt a blow and then a sharp pang, and there I was pinned by the shoulder to the mast. Both my pistols went off and with a choked cry, the coxswain loosed his grasp upon the shrouds, and plunged head first into the water.

"Pieces of Eight"

The hot blood was running over my back and chest. The dirk, where it had pinned my shoulder to the mast, seemed to burn like a hot iron; yet it was not so much these real sufferings that distressed me, for these, it seemed to me, I could bear without a murmur; it was the horror I had upon my mind of falling from the cross-trees into that still green water, beside the body of the coxswain.

I clung with both hands till my nails ached, and I shut my eyes as if to cover up the peril. Gradually my mind came back again, my pulses quieted down to a more natural time, and I was once more in possession of myself.

It was my first thought to pluck forth the dirk; but either it struck too hard or my nerve failed me; and I desisted with a violent shudder. Oddly enough, that very shudder did the business. The knife, in fact, had come the nearest in the world to missing me altogether; it held me by a mere pinch of skin, and this the shudder tore away. The blood ran down the faster, to be sure; but I was my own master again, and only tacked to the mast by the coat and shirt.

These last I broke through with a sudden jerk, and then regained the deck by the starboard shrouds. I went below, and did what I could for my wound.

The red-cap had pitched, as I have said, against the bulwarks, where he lay like some horrible, ungainly sort of puppet; I took him by the waist as if he had been a sack of bran, and, with one good heave, tumbled him overboard.

I was now alone upon the ship; the tide had just turned. The sun was within so few degrees of setting that already the shadow of the pines upon the western shore began to reach right across the anchorage, and fall in patterns on the deck. The

evening breeze had sprung up, and though it was well warded off by the hill with the two peaks upon the east, the cordage had begun to sing a little softly to itself and the idle sails to rattle to and fro.

By this time the whole anchorage had fallen into shadow. It began to be chill; the tide was rapidly fleeting seaward, the schooner settling more and more on her beam-ends.

I scrambled forward and looked over. It seemed shallow enough, and holding the cut hawser in both hands for a last security, I let myself drop softly overboard.

At least, and at last, I was off the sea, nor had I returned thence empty-handed. There lay the schooner, clear at last from buccaneers and ready for our own men to board and get to sea again. I had nothing nearer my fancy than to get home to the stockade and boast of my achievements.

Gradually the night fell blacker; it was all I could do to guide myself even roughly towards my destination; the double hill behind me and the Spy-glass on my right hand loomed faint and fainter; the

stars were few and pale; and in the low ground where I wandered I kept tripping among bushes and rolling into sandy pits.

Suddenly a kind of brightness fell about me. I looked up; a pale glimmer of moonbeams had alighted on the summit of the Spy-glass, and soon after I saw something broad and silvery moving low down behind the trees, and knew the moon had risen.

With this to help me, I passed rapidly over what remained to me of my journey; and, sometimes walking, sometimes running, impatiently drew near to the blockade.

I stole round by the eastern end, keeping close in shadow, and at a convenient place, where the darkness was thickest, crossed the palisade.

To make assurance surer, I got upon my hands and knees, and crawled, without a sound, towards the corner of the house. As I drew nearer, my heart was suddenly and greatly lightened. It is not a pleasant noise in itself, and I have often complained of it at other times; but just then it was like music to hear my friends snoring together so loud and peaceful in their sleep.

By this time I had got to the door and stood up. All was dark within, so that I could distinguish nothing by the eye. As for sounds, there was the steady drone of the snorers, and a small occasional noise, a flickering or pecking that I could in no way account for.

With my arms before me I walked steadily in. And then, all of a sudden, a shrill voice broke forth out of the darkness:

"Pieces of eight! pieces of eight! pieces of eight! pieces of eight! pieces of eight!" and so forth, without pause or change, like the clacking of a tiny mill.

Silver's green parrot, Captain Flint!

I had no time left me to recover. At the sharp, clipping tone of the parrot, the sleepers awoke and sprang up; and with a mighty oath, the voice of Silver cried:

"Who goes?"

In the Enemy's Camp

The pirates were in possession of the house and stores; there was the cask of cognac, there were the pork and bread, as before; and, what tenfold increased my horror, not a sign of any prisoner. I could only judge that all had perished, and my heart smote me sorely that I had not been there to perish with them.

There were six of the buccaneers, all told; not another man was left alive. Five of them were on their feet, flushed and swollen, suddenly called out of the first sleep of drunkenness. The sixth had only risen upon his elbow: he was deadly pale, and the blood-stained bandage round his head told that he had recently been wounded, and still more recently dressed. I remembered the man who had been shot and had run back among the woods in the great attack, and doubted not that this was he.

The parrot sat, preening her plumage, on Long John's shoulder. He himself, I thought, looked somewhat paler and more stern than I was used to. He still wore the fine broadcloth suit in which he had fulfilled his mission, but it was bitterly the worse for wear, daubed with clay and torn with the sharp briers of the wood.

"So," said he, "here's Jim Hawkins, shiver my timbers! Dropped in, like, eh? Well, I take that friendly, and quite a pleasant surprise for poor old John. I see you were smart when first I set my eyes on you; but this here gets away from me clean, it do. Now you see, Jim, so be as you *are* here," says he, "I'll give you a piece of my mind. I've always liked you, I have, for a lad of spirit, and the picter of my own self when I was young and handsome. I always wanted you to jine and take your share, and die a gentleman, and now, my cock, you've got to. You can't go back to your own lot, for they won't have you; and without you start a third ship's company all by yourself, which might be lonely, you'll have to jine with Cap'n Silver."

So far so good. My friend, then, were still alive.

"Yesterday morning, Mr Hawkins," said he, "in the dogwatch, down came Doctor Livesey with a flag of truce. Says he, 'Cap'n Silver, you're sold out. Ship's gone.' Well, maybe we'd been taking a glass, and a song to help it round. I won't say no. Leastways none of us had looked out. 'Well,' says the doctor, 'let's bargain.' We bargained, him and I, and here we are: stores, brandy, block-house, the firewood you was thoughtful enough to cut, and in a manner of speaking, the whole blessed boat, from cross-trees to keelson. As for them, they've tramped; I don't know where's they are. And lest you should take it into that head of yours," he went on, "that

you was included in the treaty, here's the last word that was said: 'How many are you,' says I, 'to leave?' 'Four,' says he—'four, and one of us wounded. As for that boy, I don't know where he is, confound him,' says he, 'nor I don't much care. We're about sick of him.' These was his words."

"Is that all?" I asked.

"Now, look you here, Jim Hawkins," he said, in a steady whisper, that was no more than audible, "you're within half a plank of death, and, what's a long sight worse, of torture. But, you mark, I stand by you through thick and thin. I didn't mean to. I was about desperate to lose that much blunt, and be hanged into the bargain. But I see you was the right sort. I says to myself: You stand by Hawkins, John, and Hawkins'll stand by you. You're his last card, and, by the living thunder, John, he's yours! Back to back, says I. You save your witness, and he'll save your neck!"

I began dimly to understand.

"You mean all's lost?" I asked.

"Ay, by gum, I do!" he answered. "Ship gone, neck gone—that's the size of it. Once I looked into that bay, Jim Hawkins, and seen no schooner—well, I'm tough, but I gave out. As for that lot, mark me, they're outright fools and cowards. I'll save your life —if so be as I can—from them. But, see here, Jim —tit for tat—you save Long John from swinging."

I was bewildered; it seemed a thing so hopeless he was asking—he, the old buccaneer, the ringleader throughout.

"What I can do, that I'll do," I said.

"It's a bargain!" cried Long John. "You speak up plucky, and, by thunder! I've a chance."

He hobbled to the torch, where it stood propped among the firewood, and took a fresh light to his pipe.

"Understand me, Jim," he said, returning. 'I've a head on my shoulders, I have. I'm on squire's side now. I know you've got that ship safe somewheres. How you done it, I don't know, but safe it is. I guess Hands and his mate turned soft. I never much believed in neither of them. Now you mark me. I ask no questions, nor I won't let others. I know when a game's up, I do; and I know a lad that's staunch. Ah, you that's young—you and me might have done a power of good together!"

He drew some cognac from the cask into a tin cannikin.

"Will you taste, messmate?" he asked; and when I had refused: "Well, I'll take a drain myself, Jim," said he. "I need a caulker, for there's trouble on hand. And, talking o' trouble, why did that doctor give me the chart, Jim?"

My face expressed a wonder so unaffected that he saw the needlessness of further questions.

The Treasure Hunt—Flint's Pointer

"And now, Jim," he said, "we're to go in for this here treasure hunting and you and me must stick close, back to back like, and we'll save our necks in spite of fate and fortune."

We made a curious figure, had anyone been there to see us; all in soiled sailor clothes, and all but me armed to the teeth. Silver had two guns slung about him—one before and one behind—besides the great cutlass at his waist, and a pistol in each pocket of his square-tailed coat. To complete his strange appearance, Captain Flint sat perched upon his shoulder and gabbling odds and ends of purposeless sea-talk. I had a line about my waist, and followed obediently after the sea cook, who held the loose end of the rope, now in his free hand, now between his powerful teeth. For all the world, I was led like a dancing bear.

The other men were variously burthened, some carrying picks and shovels—for that had been the very first necessary they brought ashore from the *Hispaniola*—others laden with pork, bread, and brandy for the midday meal.

The party spread itself abroad, in a fan shape, shouting and leaping to and fro. About the centre, and a good way behind the rest, Silver and I followed —I tethered by my rope, he ploughing, with deep pants, among the sliding gravel. From time to time, indeed, I had to lend him a hand, or he must have missed his footing and fallen backward down the hill.

We had thus proceeded for about half a mile, and were approaching the brow of the plateau, when the man upon the farthest left began to cry aloud, as if in terror. Shout after shout came from him, and the others began to run in his direction.

"He can't 'a' found the treasure," said one, hurrying past us from the right, "for that's clean a-top."

Indeed, as we found when we also reached the spot, it was something very different. At the foot of a pretty big pine, and involved in a green creeper, which had even partly lifted some of the smaller bones, a human skeleton lay, with a few shreds of clothing, on the ground. I believe a chill struck for a moment to every heart.

"He was a seaman," said another buccaneer, George Merry, who, bolder than the rest, had gone up close, and was examining the rags of clothing. "Leastways, this is good sea-cloth."

"Ay, ay," said Silver, "like enough; you wouldn't look to find a bishop here, I reckon. But what sort of a way is that for bones to lie? 'Tain't in natur'."

Indeed, on a second glance, it seemed impossible to fancy that the body was in a natural position. But for some disarray (the work, perhaps, of the birds that had fed upon him, or of the slow-growing creeper that had gradually enveloped his remains) the man lay perfectly straight—his feet pointing in one direction, his hands, raised above his head like a diver's, pointing directly in the opposite.

"I've taken a notion into my old numskull," observed Silver. "Here's the compass; there's the tip-top p'int o' Skeleton Island, stickin' out like a tooth. Just take a bearing, will you, along the line of them bones."

It was done. The body pointed straight in the

direction of the island, and the compass read duly E.S.E. and by E.

"I thought so," cried the cook; "this here is a p'inter. Right up there is our line for the Pole Star and the jolly dollars. But, by thunder! if it don't make me cold inside to think of Flint. This is one of his jokes, and no mistake. Him and these six was alone here; he killed 'em, every man; and this one he hauled here and laid down by compass, shiver my timbers!"

We started out again; but in spite of the hot sun and the staring daylight, the pirates no longer ran separate and shouting through the wood, but kept side by side and spoke with bated breath. The terror of the dead buccaneer had fallen on their spirits.

The Voice among the Trees

Partly from the damping influence of this alarm, partly to rest Silver, the whole party sat down as soon as they had gained the brow of the ascent.

The plateau being something tilted towards the west, this spot on which we had paused commanded a wide prospect on either hand. Before us, over the tree-tops, we beheld the Cape of the Woods fringed with surf; behind, we not only looked down upon the anchorage and Skeleton Island, but saw—clear across the spit and the eastern lowlands—a great field of open sea upon the east. Sheer above us rose the Spy-glass, here dotted with single pines, there black with precipices.

There was no sound but that of the distant breakers, mounting from all round, and the chirp of countless insects in the brush. Not a man, not a sail upon the sea; the very largeness of the view increased the sense of solitude.

Silver, as he sat, took certain bearings with his compass.

"There are three 'tall trees'," said he, "about in the right line from Skeleton Island. 'Spy-glass Shoulder', I take it, means that lower p'int there. It's child play to find the stuff now. I've half a mind to dine first."

All of a sudden, out of the middle of the trees in front of us, a thin, high, trembling voice struck up the well-known air and words:

"Fifteen men on the dead man's chest—
    Yo-ho-ho, and a bottle of rum!"

I never have seen men more dreadfully affected.

The colour went from their six faces like enchantment; some leaped to their feet, some clawed hold of others; others grovelled on the ground.

"It's Flint, by—!" cried Merry.

The song had stopped as suddenly as it began—broken off, you would have said, in the middle of a note, as though someone had laid his hand upon the singer's mouth.

Coming so far through the clear, sunny atmosphere among the green tree-tops, I thought it had sounded airily and sweetly; and the effect on my companions was the stranger.

The buccaneers remained rooted to the ground, their eyes starting from their heads. Long after the voice had died away they still stared in silence, dreadfully, before them.

"That fixes it!" gasped one. "Let's go."

"Wait," said Silver, "there's one thing not clear to me. There was an echo. Now, no man ever seen a sperrit with a shadow; well, then, what's he doing with an echo to him, I should like to know? That ain't in natur', surely?"

This argument seemed weak enough to me. But you can never tell what will affect the superstitious, and, to my wonder, George Merry was greatly relieved.

"Well, that's so," he said. 'You've a head upon your shoulders, John, and no mistake. 'Bout ship, mates! This here crew is on a wrong tack, I do believe. And come to think on it, it was like Flint's voice, I grant you, but not just so clearaway like it, after all. It was liker somebody else's voice, now—it was liker—"

"By the powers, Ben Gunn!" roared Silver.

"Why, nobody minds Ben Gunn," cried Merry; and we set forth again.

The first of the tall trees was reached, and by the bearing, proved the wrong one. So with the second. The third rose nearly two hundred feet into the air above a clump of underwood; a giant of a vegetable, with a red column as big as a cottage, and a wide shadow around it in which a company could have manoeuvred. It was conspicuous far to sea both to the east and west, and might have been entered as a sailing mark upon the chart.

But it was not its size that now impressed my companions; it was the knowledge that seven hundred thousand pounds in gold lay somewhere buried below its spreading shadow. The thought of the money, as they drew nearer, swallowed up their

103

previous terrors. Their eyes burned in their heads; their feet grew speedier and lighter; their whole soul was bound up in that fortune, that whole lifetime of extravagance and pleasure, that lay waiting there for each of them.

We were now at the margin of the thicket.

"Huzza, mates, all together!" shouted Merry; and the foremost broke into a run.

And suddenly, not tend yards further, we beheld them stop. A low cry arose. Silver doubled his pace, digging away with the foot of his crutch like one possessed; and next moment he and I had come also to a dead halt.

Before us was a great excavation, not very recent, for the sides had fallen in and grass had sprouted on the bottom. In this were the shaft of a pick broken in two and the boards of several packing-cases strewn around. On one of these boards I saw, branded with a hot iron, the name *Walrus*—the name of Flint's ship.

All was clear to probation. The cache had been found and rifled; the seven hundred thousand pounds were gone!

The Fall of a Chieftain

Each of these six men was as though he had been struck. But with Silver the blow passed almost instantly. Every thought of his soul had been set full-stretch, like a racer, on that money; well, he was brought up in a single second, dead; and he kept his head, found his temper, and changed his plan before the other buccaneers had had time to realise the disappointment.

"Jim," he whispered, "take that, and stand by for trouble."

And he passed me a double-barrelled pistol.

At the same time he began quietly moving northward, and in a few steps had put the hollow between us two and the other five. Then he looked at me and nodded, as much as to say, "Here is a narrow corner," as, indeed, I thought it was.

There was no time left for me to answer in. The buccaneers, with oaths and cries, began to leap, one after another, into the pit, and to dig with their fingers, throwing the boards aside as they did so. One found a piece of gold. He held it up with a perfect spout of oaths. It was a two-guinea piece, and it went from hand to hand among them for a quarter of a minute.

"Two guineas!" roared Merry, shaking it at Silver. "That's your seven hundred thousand pounds, is it? You're the man for bargains, ain't you? You're him that never bungled nothing, you wooden-headed lubber!"

Then they began to scramble out of the pit.

"Mates," said Merry, "there's two of them alone there; one's the old cripple that brought us all here and blundered us down to this; the other's that cub that I mean to have the heart of. Now, mates—"

He was raising his arm and his voice, and plainly meant to lead a charge. But just then—crack! crack! crack!—three musket-shots flashed out of the thicket. Merry tumbled head foremost into the excavation; the man with the bandage spun round like a teetotum, and fell all his length upon his side, where he lay dead, but still twitching; and the other three turned and ran for it with all their might.

And the same moment the doctor and Ben Gunn joined us, with smoking muskets, from among the nutmeg trees.

"Thank ye kindly, doctor," says Silver. "You came in in about the nick, I guess, for me and Hawkins. And so it's you, Ben Gunn!" he added. "Well, you're a nice one to be sure."

"I'm Ben Gunn, I am," replied the maroon,

wriggling like an eel in his embarrassment. "And," he added, after a long pause, "how do, Mr Silver? Pretty well, I thank ye, says you."

"Ben, Ben," murmured Silver, "to think as you've done me!"

The doctor took one of the pickaxes, deserted, in their flight, by the mutineers; and then as we proceeded leisurely downhill to where the boats were lying, related, in a few words, what had taken place. It was a story that profoundly interested Silver; and Ben Gunn, the half-idiot maroon, was the hero from beginning to end.

Ben, in his long, lonely wanderings about the island, had found the skeleton—it was he that had rifled it; he had found the treasure; he had dug it up (it was the shaft of his pickaxe that lay broken in the excavation); he had carried it on his back, in many weary journeys, from the foot of the tall pine to a cave he had on the two-pointed hill at the north-east angle of the island, and there it had lain stored in safety since two months before the arrival of the *Hispaniola*.

When the doctor had wormed this secret from him, on the afternoon of the attack, and when, next morning, he saw the anchorage deserted, he had gone to Silver, given him the chart, which was now useless—given him the stores, for Ben Gunn's cave was well supplied with goat's meat salted by himself —given anything and everything to get a chance of moving in safety from the stockade to the two-pointed hill, there to keep a guard upon the money.

"As for you, Jim," he said, "it went against my heart, but I did what I thought best for those who had stood by their duty; and if you were not one of these, whose fault was it?"

That morning, finding that I was to be involved in the horrid disappointment he had prepared for the mutineers, he had run all the way to the cave, and, leaving squire to guard the captain, had taken the maroon, and started, making the diagonal across the island, to be at hand beside the pine. Soon, however, he saw that our party had the start of him; and Ben Gunn, being fleet of foot, had been despatched in front to do his best alone. Then it had occurred to him to work upon the superstitions of his former shipmates, in which he had been highly successful.

"Ah," said Silver, "it were fortunate for me that I had Hawkins here. You would have let old John be cut to bits, and never given it a thought, doctor."

"Not a thought," replied Doctor Livesey, cheerily.

And by this time we had reached the gigs. The doctor, with the pickaxe, demolished one of them, and then we all got aboard the other and set out to go round by sea for North Inlet.

What a supper I had of it that night, with all my friends around me; and what a meal it was, with Ben Gunn's salted goat, and some delicacies and a bottle of old wine from the *Hispaniola*. Never, I am sure, were people gayer or happier. And there was Silver, sitting back almost out of the firelight, but eating heartily, prompt to spring forward when anything was wanted, even joining quietly in our laughter— the same bland, polite, obsequious seaman of the voyage out.

And Last

All of us had an ample share of the treasure, and used it wisely or foolishly, according to our nature. Captain Smollett is now retired from the sea. As for Ben Gunn, he got a thousand pounds and he still lives, a great favourite, though something of a butt, with the country boys, and a notable singer in church on Sundays and saint's days.

Ben Gunn had connived at Silver's escape in a shore boat and he assured us he had only done so to preserve our lives, which would certainly have been forfeit if "that man with the one leg had stayed aboard." But this was not all. The sea-cook had not gone empty-handed. He had cut through a bulkhead unobserved, and had removed one of the sacks of coin, worth, perhaps, three or four hundred guineas, to help him on his further wanderings.

Of him we have heard no more. That formidable seafaring man with one leg has at last gone clean out of my life forever.

The bar silver and the arms still lie, for all that I know, where Flint buried them; and certainly they shall lie there for me. Oxen and wain-ropes would not bring me back again to that accursed island; and the worst dreams that ever I have are when I hear the surf booming about its coasts, or start upright in bed, with the sharp voice of Captain Flint still ringing in my ears: "Pieces of eight! pieces of eight!"

ROBIN HOOD

Robin Hood

Robin Hood was a gallant outlaw, clad all in Lincoln green, who roamed the forest with his mighty bow, robbing the rich to give to the poor—courteous and dauntless, ever ready for a jest! He was outlawed for breaking laws which the people privately liked to see broken, and all his lawless acts were much juster than the unjust laws. He was the protector of women and of anyone who could not protect himself.

Robin was devout and God-fearing, but he had no use for idle monks and pompous churchmen. He stood out against Prince John, who was oppressing the land while the rightful king was in a foreign prison; but when King Richard himself returned, no subject was more stoutly loyal than Robin Hood.

This brave outlaw was really Robert, Earl of Huntingdon, born at Locksley, near Nottingham, about 1160, in Henry II's reign. His father was one of the last of the Saxon barons, and his mother was a niece of Guy of Warwick and sister to Gamwal of Gamwal Hall. Robin Hood's cousin, William Gamwal, became, later, one of his closest followers (as "Will Scarlet").

After the loss of his parents, home, and lands occurred—sacrificed to the rapacity of Prince John, who usurped the King's place during his absence at the Crusades—Robin saw his castle burnt to the ground by the Normans, who to him were alien robbers. However, he escaped with his life, and fled to Sherwood Forest. There, on the cool grass under a mighty oak, he lay, full of rage, planning vengeance against his enemies. But he loved the forest—the singing birds, the whistling trees, the playful squirrels, the rural scents and sounds, all soothed his troubled spirit. Anger passed and gave place to peaceful calm, and, one with Nature, in the dim evening light of the saddest day in his life, he, an outlaw, fell on his knees and vowed:

"To honour God and the King,

To help the weak and fight the strong,
and to take from the rich and give to the poor."

Robert of Huntingdon thus became "Robin of Sherwood", or, shortly, "Robin Hood."

Those were the days when dense forests covered much of England, when monks ambled along the highways on their ponies and knights rode by on prancing war-steeds, when the poor people told tales at the village merry-making—and when Robin himself and his merry men roamed through the greenwood.

Little John

"No sport have we seen for several days," said Robin Hood one bright spring morning, "so I intend to go abroad to seek adventures forthwith. But listen, my merry men, remember well my call. Three blasts upon my horn I will blow in my hour of need; so come quickly, for I shall want your aid."

With a wave of his hand, he set off, and strode along until he came to a narrow bridge that spanned a little stream. At one end of it there stood a man, a good seven feet tall, who carried a staff that looked like a small tree trunk.

"Now, stand back, my good fellow," said Robin, "and let the better man cross first."

"Nay," answered the stranger; "stand back yourself, for I am the better man here."

"That we shall see," said Robin Hood; "for if you dare to move one step forward I will send a good Nottingham shaft between your ribs."

"You prattle like a coward," said the stranger, "to talk of shooting with your bow, when I have only this plain staff to defend myself."

"Faith, never have I had a coward's name in all my life before," replied Robin, and, so saying, he went to the wood and cut himself a stout oak staff, six feet in length. Then, taking their staffs by the middle with the two hands wide apart, Robin and the stranger stepped upon the narrow bridge and gave blow for blow in one of the stoutest quarterstaff bouts that ever man had witnessed.

Robin smote the stranger upon the ribs until his jacket smoked like a damp straw thatch in the sun, and the stranger gave Robin a crack on the crown that caused the blood to flow, and still both kept their footing. But at last the stranger gave Robin such a blow that he fell head over heels into the water.

"And where are you now, good lad?" cried the stranger, roaring with laughter.

Robin laughed too as soon as he could get his breath, and, scrambling to the bank, said:

"I must own you are a brave soul as well as a stout fellow with the quarterstaff, and have fairly won the fight.

"Yes, a fair fight fairly won!" said Robin Hood. Then he set horn to lip and blew a loud blast. Scarcely had the echo died away than his men appeared, a score or two of stout bowmen, all clad in Lincoln green.

"Good master, how is this?" cried Will Stutely, seeing Robin Hood dripping from head to foot.

"This fellow has tumbled me in the brook," replied Robin.

"Then in he shall go too." And the lads made for the stranger, and would have given him a good ducking and also a drubbing, had not Robin cried out, "Stop! He has beaten me in fair fight, and if he will stay with us and be one of our men he is right welcome." So the stranger was accepted.

"What is your name?" Robin asked, as the stranger gave him his hand.

"John Little," answered the stranger solemnly, at which all the men laughed heartily, and Will Stutely cried out:

"Little you are indeed, and small of bone and sinew, and therefore you shall be christened Little John!"

"Then come, my merry men," laughed Robin Hood, "and we will prepare a christening feast for this fair infant."

So through the forest they went until they came to a great oak tree with broad-spreading branches and 'neath it a seat of green moss, where Robin was wont to sit at feast and merry-making with his good men about him. A brace of fat does from the king's fine herd was brought forth, and a barrel of humming ale was broached.

Then, whilst great fires crackled and the savoury smell of roasting venison filled the glade, some of them held contests with the quarterstaff, and others set up garlands on the branches of trees and shot at them in archery practice. When the feast was ready, all sat down, and Robin Hood placed Little John at his right hand.

And thus, amid jest and song and good cheer, they christened Little John, who was to win renown second only to that of Robin Hood himself.

The Great Shooting Match at Nottingham

Now, all this time, the proud Sheriff of Nottingham was trying in vain to bring Robin Hood to justice. So many times had he tried and failed that the king had spoken harsh and scornful words. Then at last he bethought himself how he might use guile to lay his hands on the daring outlaw.

"It is of no avail," thought the Sheriff, "to seek out that evil knave Robin Hood in his woodland haunts. But if I could only persuade him to come to Nottingham Town, I warrant I would capture him."

So he decided to proclaim a great shooting match to which everyone who could draw a longbow should be bidden. An arrow of gold was to be the prize, and he who won it fairly and squarely should be hailed by all as the greatest archer throughout the length and breadth of the land.

When Robin Hood heard of the Sheriff's proclamation, he called his men about him and said:

"Men, I would have one of us win this fair prize that our sweet friend the Sheriff offers, and therefore will we take our bows and shafts and go to Nottingham Town."

"Have a care, good master," said one of the followers. "I have heard it said that this same shooting match is a trap whereby the knavish Sheriff would draw you into the town and capture you."

"Then," said Robin, "we must meet guile with guile. We shall lay aside our suits of Lincoln green and go in disguise—some as shaven friars, some as rustic peasants, and some as tinkers or as beggars. How like you that plan, my merry men!"

"Good, good!" they cried heartily.

Arrival of the Great Day

The great day arrived, and at the appointed time the Sheriff took his place in the seat of honour near the target. The ten best archers were chosen to shoot again.

"Can you see Robin Hood amongst those ten?" asked the Sheriff of a man-at-arms standing near.

"Nay, I cannot, your worship," answered the man. "Six of them I know right well and of the others none is of Robin Hood's size, except, perhaps, that tattered beggar in scarlet, but he has a beard of brown instead of yellow, and he is blind in one eye."

Each of the ten now shot again, and then from these the three best were chosen for the final contest. One of these was the tattered stranger in scarlet with the patch over one eye; another was Gilbert o' the Red Cap, one of the Sheriff's own archers. Twice they shot, all three, and it was soon seen that the match lay between Gilbert and the tattered stranger. On the third shot Gilbert's shaft lodged close beside the spot that marked the very centre.

"Well done, Gilbert!" cried the Sheriff joyously. "Now, ragged knave, let us see if you can shoot a better shaft than that."

The Ragged Stranger's Shot

All held their breath as the ragged stranger stepped forth. Hitherto he had shot so quickly that one could scarce take breath between the drawing and the shooting, and men marvelled that one blind of one eye could shoot so well. Now he shot with greater care. Straight flew the arrow and so true that it smote a feather from off Gilbert's shaft and lodged in the very centre.

"Here, my good fellow," said the Sheriff. "Take the prize, for well and fairly you have won it. I swear you draw a better bow than that same cowardly Robin Hood, who dared not show his face here today."

That afternoon, in the depths of Sherwood Forest, Robin Hood's men feasted merrily, but the soul of their leader was vexed. "I would like to let the Sheriff know who it was that won the golden arrow from out his hand," said Robin.

Then up spoke Little John: "Let me go to Nottingham Town, and I will send yon Sheriff news of this by a messenger such as he does not expect."

The Sheriff Gets a Surprise

That night, as the Sheriff sat at meat in his great hall, a blunted grey goose shaft with a small scroll attached came through the window and fell upon the table. The Sheriff opened the scroll and grew red with rage, for on it he read:

Now Heaven bless thy grace this day,
Say all in sweet Sherwood,
For thou didst give the prize away
To merry Robin Hood.

How Robin Hood Met Friar Tuck

For a time after the winning of the golden arrow, the merry outlaws kept themselves close in Sherwood Forest. When the larder was well supplied with game the great oak glade was given up to sport. Some would play at bowls, or at dice; others would have wrestling matches, bouts at quarterstaff, or mock duels with sword and buckler. But their favourite and never-ending delight was shooting with the long-bow—that trusty weapon which made them so justly famed and feared.

Little John took a bow-string and hung up a dead squirrel from a bough at five hundred feet away, and after taking careful aim, because the wind swayed the mark, he sped his shaft clean through the squirrel's body amid resounding cheers.

"God's blessing on thy head," said Robin. "Gladly would I walk a hundred miles to see one that could match that."

At this Will Scarlet laughed full heartily.

"That is not so hard to do," said he, "for at Rubygill Abbey there dwells a curtal friar that can beat both him and you."

Then Robin leaped up lightly from the green-sward, where he had been lying.

"Now, by'r Lady," exclaimed he, "neither food nor drink will I touch until I have seen this friar of yours, were he in very truth a hundred miles away.

Make ready to lead us, while I don my cap of steel, broadsword, and buckler, to meet this holy archer."

"It be no hundred miles, good uncle," said Will. "We shall gain Rubygill Abbey ere noon."

So Little John, Will Scarlet and Robin strode through the forest at a quick gait, mile after mile

without a stop, till they came to Needwood Forest, hard by Tutbury, where Friar Tuck had in days past received Will Scarlet to his broad bosom, learned to love him, and taught him all his skill with sword and long-bow and quarterstaff.

When the three outlaws were still some way off they caught sight of the Abbey below them, through a slight opening of the trees.

"There," said Will Scarlet, "you will find the holy man you want."

"Well," said Robin, "you two remain here. I would parley with this man alone."

So saying, he strode forward, leaving Little John and Will behind, till a blast from his bugle should call them. He trudged along till he came to a brook, by the side of which, seated upon the ground among a bunch of tall ferns, he espied a man, with a missal book on his lap and a leather bottle at his lips, in the act of drinking. So long the bottle remained tilted in air that Robin stole close ere the other saw him. Robin stood still, and the bottle was slowly lowered, displaying a perfectly round, fat face as red as a cherry, with small, laughing brown eyes fringed with heavy eyebrows. The cheery friar's shaven crown shone like glass, and it too was fringed with a circlet of curly hair. He had a broad fat neck which was quite bare, and at the back of it was a cowl of rough, brown cloth attached to a loose, flowing robe of the same stuff, covering a powerful and strong-limbed body. Round his middle was buckled a leathern belt that held some keys, a string of beads, and a dagger. Beside him on the ground lay a sword, a buckler, and a steel cap.

As he slowly took the bottle from his lips he beheld the stout yeoman standing there, and straightway such a look of amazement came over his funny red face that Robin burst forth into a loud, hearty laugh. "Holy man," said he, "I thought that bottle was glued to your face, so long and lovingly did it cling to those cherry lips. If there is anything left within it, the draught must be right pleasant. I would like some to sweeten my dry throat."

"Ah! would you now?" was the answer. "Then why not test yon cool, sparkling brook from where the bottle was filled?"

"Nay, nay, good Friar, you wouldn't make such pretty gurgling music with water as I heard from you just now. Precious little water hath passed your lips this many a day."

"Well," said the Friar, "a pious man ought not to

116

deny a stranger who asks a drop to quench his thirst." So saying, he passed the bottle to Robin.

Robin took a long pull and found the liquor so good that he tipped the bottle higher and higher, keeping it so long tilted upright that at last the Friar jumped to his feet with a roar like a bull, saying:

"You greedy guts, by Saint Wilfrid I will part your mouth and my bottle with a cuff over your ribs that will land you on the other side of the brook!"

"Ay," said jolly Robin, smacking his lips, "right good Rhenish water, I trow! Thank you for the loan of the bottle, which I will straight away refill from the brook for your future use."

"Nay," cried the Friar, peering anxiously down the neck of the bottle, "be off while there yet is peace between us."

"Do you know," asked Robin, "of a certain curtal friar in these parts named Tuck?"

"Maybe I do, and maybe I do not. If you mean him of Rubygill Abbey, the place is but a few rods down the glade when you've crossed the brook."

"Ay, truly," said Robin, "but I see no place to cross without wetting my new hose. I pray you, therefore, kind and good Friar, carry me across on those broad shoulders. Come, tuck up your robe and bend your back that I may meet this same curtal friar in seemly fashion."

Then the Friar closed one eye, screwed up his mouth, and placed his finger upon his brow as in deep thought. At last he said: "What—if the good Saint Christopher were so willing, my unworthy self should not refuse." So saying, he laid down his missal and, tucking up his skirts, took Robin Hood on his back. He plunged into the flowing water up to his waist, carefully feeling his way over the pebbles on the bottom, and spake no word, good or bad, until he reached the further bank.

Then Robin leaped lightly from his back and set off briskly for Rubygill Abbey.

"Hold! Not so fast, my fine fellow!" cried the Friar. "For now I think I have left my missal and my steel cap upon the other side."

"Well," said Robin, "There is nothing to stop you going back to get them."

"Nay, but," said the Friar smiling, "one good turn deserves another, and therefore you must carry me back on your shoulders, for with another ducking I may take a chill or fall sick of divers pains and rheums."

"What if I should not?" said Robin.

"Then I will baste your hide with your own sword which I carried safely over and now hold."

Now Robin did not like the thought of playing pack-horse to this burly Friar. But he thought that the fellow spake truly enough concerning the sword, so he bent his back, with no very good grace. Straightway the Friar began to prod his heels into Robin's sides to make him go the faster, though he had to go slowly and carefully over the rough bottom with so weighty a burden. But he spoke no word, and after much floundering and splashing they reached the bank in safety, where the Friar got his steel cap and his buckler.

"Now," said Robin, panting and sweating with his hard work, "it's my turn, and you shall carry me back, or I will put a shaft through your fat body as easily as a maid skewers a capon."

"Why, so I will," said the Friar. "So put up your bow, and come along, for it is ill to shoot a holy man that has done you a service."

So Robin once more mounted the broad back of the lusty Friar, and, becoming jubilant, shouted, "Come up, gee, woa!" rapping with his heels the stout Friar's shins, who quietly plodded along, without a word, toward the middle of the brook. But of a sudden he gave a mighty heave of his shoulders, and Robin flew right over his head into the brook with a loud splash, while the Friar stood holding his broad ribs from bursting with laughter.

"Now my fine fellow," he cried, "choose whether you will sink or swim!"

Robin Hood spoke no word, for his nose and mouth were full of water, and he had no breath to spare. He swam to a bush of broom that overhung the bank and dragged himself ashore. Meanwhile, the Friar leisurely waded out, shaking with mirth. Robin, angry, met him with bow bent and arrow aimed.

"Now, you false Friar, you shall die," he cried, grimly.

But the other never blenched. Raising up his buckler he said:

"Shoot on, you fine fellow. I tell you, if you shoot here all summer's day, I will never flee."

At that Robin lowered his bow. "No," said he, "on second thoughts, I will not shoot you dead where you stand, rascally hedge priest though you are. But with my good broadsword I will let your blood. Therefore, arm yourself and make ready."

"Not so hasty," said the Friar, calmly. "I'm ready

and willing as a maid is to wed." He slowly set his steel cap upon his head, and then, grasping his broadsword firmly in his great fist, he faced Robin with a bold front, bawling out: "Now, my crowing cockerel, I'll clip your comb and spurs, shake your wet feathers!"

Thereupon they rushed together with a loud clash of steel and flying sparks, but before long Robin saw that he must curb his hot blood or soon have it spilled; for the Friar, though angry, was calm and determined, bearing down Robin's guard with his heavy arm. So they fought from right to left, up and down, back and forth in the glade, with a savage fury and noise as if it were a whole company fighting.

Hour after hour the battle went on, with short pauses for rest, both panting and sweating, eyeing each other in silence, for neither had breath to waste in speech. From ten o'clock that morn had they struggled, and now past noon they were still tearing, slashing, and cutting with aching arms and tired backs; yet neither had a scratch.

"Hold!" bellowed the Friar. "Let us give up for a space, take a midday bite and quench our thirst. Then, to it again."

"Not so, you tough mountain of flesh," shouted bold Robin Hood. "Not till my sword has taken toll on some part of your fat body will I give over."

"Now hold your hand for a moment, my doughty fellow," said the Friar. "Will you not let me take off this hot steel cap to cool my brow? For the sweat is blinding me."

"Yes, do so, quickly," said Robin, the better pleased that now the broad shining poll would be a fair mark for his sword. Then the battle began afresh. Do all he could, Robin failed to strike the Friar's crown; and he in turn missed Robin a hundred times—and so the grim fight raged till four in the afternoon.

The ferns and woodland flowers were trodden into a shapeless mass among the soft, black loam. The song-birds had long flown away affrighted at the clashing din. At last bold Robin cried:

"Enough, enough, you curtal Friar! Give me leave to set my horn to my mouth, and to blow three blasts upon it."

"That will I," said the curtal Friar, lowering the point of his sword. "I care not for your blast, though you blow till your eyes fall out."

So Robin set his horn to his lips and blew three loud blasts. Scarce had the Friar heard the echo when he saw two tall archers with shafts ready nocked come running over the grass.

"Whose men are these," cried he, "that come so hastily at your call?"

"These men are mine," said Robin Hood. "And what is that to thee?"

Then the curtal Friar saw that he had been tricked, but he was unabashed.

"A boon, a boon," he cried, mimicking Robin, with a shrewd glint in his eye, "like to that I granted you! Give me but leave to set my fist to my mouth and whistle thrice."

"That will I," said Robin, "for it is but just and fair."

So the Friar put his fist to his mouth and gave three loud whistles. The next moment there came half a dozen great mongrel dogs tearing along, barking loud as they drew nigh.

"Here, you cowardly villain," said the Friar, "are a couple of shaggy hounds for each of your men, and I myself will be enough for you. At 'em, my pets, tear their green jerkins to shreds, my hearties."

Thereupon, two great, ugly mastiffs climbed in front and back of Robin in a trice before he had time to defend himself or flee. At last, torn and ragged, he got him to a tree and sat, with legs astride a stout limb, watching Little John shoot at the fierce brutes. Then he saw what made him doubt his eyes, for the dogs leaped aside from the flying arrows, caught them in their mouths, and broke them in two.

"This is witchcraft," thought Robin, "and the Friar is a wizard, for never might dogs do so of their own nature." His wonder grew when he saw Will Scarlet step forth boldly toward the hounds with no weapon in his hand.

"Down, Beauty; down, Bess," cried Will, cuffing them right and left. Straightway the dogs began to cower down and fawn upon him, and gambolled about him as he stepped toward their master.

"What meaneth this?" said the Friar. "Have my dogs gone daft to love the company of thieves and cutthroats? Have I not, with their aid, kept Rubygill Abbey seven long year and more from baron, knight, and squire, and must I now yield myself to three beggarly yeoman that dare to beard me in my own dale? Tear them, tear their limbs asunder, good dogs!"

Will Scarlet now came forward, petting a great ugly hound.

"Come stout Friar," said he, "cease this brawling and curb your wagging tongue."

"What!" said the Friar. "Do my eyes behold young Will Gamwal in company with such a brace of deer-stealers? Now, I swear by holy Saint Boniface I will——"

"Peace, Friar, and listen," cried Will.

Then, pointing to Robin, he said: "This stout yeoman, who seems ill at ease perched in yonder tree, is none other than Robin Hood. The other tall fellow is Little John, his good righthand man; and they have come to bid you join our merry band of outlaws in Sherwood Forest. Call off your dogs and let us speak together and set matters right."

"Right Will," said the Friar, "I do know Robin Hood by report, but does he think to get me by cracking my bones? In truth I ache and am very sore."

At length, somewhat appeased and soothed by Will's manner and words, he whistled off his hounds. Then Robin climbed down the tree and, Little John with him, approached the Friar.

"For a holy man," said Robin, "truly you are the stoutest fighter that I ever clapped eyes upon."

"Nay, good Robin, you are the better man, for never was I so weary of any man in fight." With that he pushed forth his brawny palm, saying, "Right glad am I to meet the bold outlaws of Sherwood Forest."

"And now," said Robin, "all being well, we will go

together in search of Friar Tuck, whom we came seeking; and you, holy Friar, must guide us."

"By my troth," laughed Will, "you have not far to seek, for that same holy friar now stands before you."

"What?" exclaimed Robin. "Surely you are not Friar Tuck!"

"The same," said the Friar, with a twinkle in his eye, "that gave you a duck in yon stream."

"And the same," laughed Robin, "that drained the bottle of good Rhenish wine. Truly my mouth waters to think on it."

"Then let us share another bottle" beamed the Friar, "before we take the road to Sherwood."

Robin Hood and the Knight

One day Robin, having gone forth with some of his merry men to see what rich men he could surprise and strip of their riches, saw a knight––Sir Richard of the Lees––coming towards him, heavy with grief.

"Good Sir Knight," said Robin, "why are you so sad?"

"Alas," said the knight, "my son had the misfortune to slay a man, and for his defence I had to borrow four hundred pounds from the abbot of St Mary's, York. Unless the money is paid on the morrow, my land will be taken, and I shall be a beggar and my wife with me."

"And what is your land worth, Sir Knight?"

"It is worth four hundred pounds a year."

"I' faith, the abbot wants a good deal for his loan!" cried Robin. Then––for it never took him long to make up his mind––he called Little John and commanded him to give the knight four hundred pounds, with some new clothes and a fine horse, and to go along to York as the knight's servant.

How Sir Richard's Estate Was Saved

"We will give my lord abbot an unpleasant surprise," said Robin. "He wants not your four hundred pounds, but your whole estate––the vile robber!"

So the knight, overwhelmed with joy and gratitude, promised to repay the money at the end of the year, and at once set out for York with Little John, to pay the abbot his debt.

Meanwhile, at the abbey of St Mary, the abbot and his cellarer were rubbing their hands in glee at

the thought that the knight would not be able to pay. How vastly would the unlucky man's estate swell the riches of St Mary's!

Just as the cellarer was adding up to see what sum the land would be worth, the news came that the knight, Sir Richard of the Lees, was at the gate.

Sir Richard came into the abbot's presence humbly enough and pleaded for time to pay; for he wanted to see what would happen. Of course, the abbot and his cellarer refused to hear him, so eager were they to obtain possession of the land.

Then it was that Sir Richard brought out the bag

of gold. The abbot and the cellarer looked at it, scarcely able to believe their eyes. The cellarer was so furious that he tried to set up some legal quibble to keep the knight from paying his debt after all, but there the money was, for all to see—and really the abbot and the cellarer could do nothing but take it.

Sir Richard met his wife, who was waiting at the abbey gate, and together they went home, laughing merrily at the abbot's rage.

Some time afterwards the knight, having lived most carefully that he might save up the money, rode into the depths of Sherwood Forest to pay his debt to Robin Hood. Besides the four hundred pounds, he carried a present of one hundred bows and one hundred sheaves of arrows, each an ell long, with burnished heads, fledged with peacock's feathers, and notched with silver. With Sir Richard rode a hundred men, wearing his livery of white and red.

Now that very day Robin Hood, with two of his men, had gone to the high road to look for plunder. They saw two black-robed monks coming, each on a fine saddle-horse. These monks were on their way to London, carrying treasure packed, as was the custom, in hampers or casks on horses. They were attended by a guard of fifty-two archers.

But the fifty-two archers had no sooner set eyes on Robin and his men than they took to their heels and fled, leaving the treasure to be guarded only by the two monks, a little page boy, and a groom.

Robin laughed to himself—for St Mary's abbot had indeed sent him pay! At a blast of his horn, his companions gathered about him. Then he noticed that one of the monks was the cellarer who, according to Little John's report, had behaved so roughly to the unfortunate knight. But Robin was always polite.

"And pray, sirs, what money do you carry?" he asked the cellarer civilly.

"But twenty poor marks," said he, falsely.

"If you bear but twenty marks," Robin told him, "then I will double the sum; for to the poor, Robin Hood is always bountiful."

But he had no mind to take the monk's word for it. And when he came to look, behold, the treasure was worth some eight hundred pounds! Furthermore, he discovered that the monks were on the way to London to set the law in motion against Sir Richard of the Lees.

That settled the matter for Robin. He took the monks deep into the forest. There he entertained them royally—and sent them off stripped of every penny of their treasure! They turned mournfully back to the abbey, thinking that they could have dined as well— and more cheaply—at Doncaster.

Robin and his merry men were still laughing over this adventure when who should appear but Sir Richard himself, eager to pay his debt, and to present his fine gift of bows and arrows.

"I take not a penny," cried Robin boisterously. "The good cellarer of St Mary's has already paid me! As for the bows and arrows, I accept them gladly, and for them you shall have another four hundred pounds."

Allan-a-Dale and His Bride

One day on the highway Little John overtook a young gentleman and asked him what moneys he had.

"I have but five shillings and a ring," said the youth.

"If that be true," said Little John, "then I want nothing from you."

Just then Robin came up and asked the young man why he looked so sad.

"Ah, you may well ask!" cried young Allan-a-Dale. "This ought to be my wedding morning; but my bride is being given away by her father to an old knight who can offer gold by the bushel for her."

"And where is the church," asked Robin, "in which this wedding is to take place?"

"It is but five miles from here," said Allan, and the tears streamed from his eyes.

Robin Hood would have no tears, but he told young Allan to keep with his merry men and follow him, when summoned, to the church. Then Robin disguised himself cunningly as a harpist, and went off to the home of the bride's father to ask whether he might play music at the wedding feast.

"By all means," said the father. "Here is the bishop; he can tell whether you are a good harpist or no."

"Nay," cried Robin, "there shall be no music from this harp of mine until I have set eyes on the bride and the bridegroom."

The bride came in, pale as snow and drooping with sadness. The bridegroom, who escorted her, was old and wizened as a winter-tossed oak.

"Now, now!" cried Robin, "this is no fit match, sir! Would you wed a snowdrop with an old thistle? By my faith, this bride shall choose her own bridegroom."

At that he blew a lusty blast on his horn, and twenty-four archers answered the call. They were led by Little John, and among them was Allan-a-Dale.

"Now, sweet bride," said Robin, "will you have yonder gnarled trunk for your dear, or will you choose this youth, with five hundred pounds in his pouch and brave young limbs to work for you?"

"Allan! It is Allan!" cried the bride. "He is my love and my dear!"

Allan-a-Dale knelt at her feet and took her hand. The aged bridegroom glanced at the terrified father, then at the sturdy archers, then at Robin Hood— who was merry-eyed enough but resolute in every muscle. Then the bridegroom begged leave to be let off from his bargain.

"But indeed," cried the bride's father, "she cannot marry any but you, sir, for no bishop can wed a pair unless they have been asked three times in church."

"That is soon done!" cried Little John. Then he led the way to the church, and, standing under the desk, he published the banns seven times instead of three, just to make sure.

Then the bishop married the bride and Allan-a-Dale, and every one of the merry men was bidden to the wedding feast.

The Fair Maid Marian

Now Robin Hood loved a certain maiden dearly, and her name was Maid Marian. Maid Marian loved Robin too, but her father would not let her marry him. Bold Robin had given her a ring, and she had sworn to marry no man until King Richard should be freed from his prison and come home again.

One day, as Robin strode on adventure through the wood, disguised as a husbandman, a proud youth appeared in the forest glade, and Robin challenged him. The youth answered him hotly, and drew sword. As the singer of the old ballad tells us:

They drew out their swords, and to cutting they
    went,
    At least an hour or more,
That the blood ran apace from bold Robin's face,
    And the youth was wounded sore.

"Hold!" cried Robin at last—for indeed he was sorry to hurt so brave a lad——"Hold, fair youth! Let us fight no more."

"Why," faltered the brave lad, ready to faint from his labour, "who are you, then?"

"My name is Robin Hood," the outlaw answered with a laugh, "Now you know——"

But the stranger gave a cry and stretched out one white hand; and on a finger of it Robin saw the ring he had given to Maid Marian!

"That ring——"

"You gave me, Robin!"

Then it was that Maid Marian fell forward, and Robin clasped her in his arms.

"Maid Marian—you have come to me—into the wild forest?" he cried in joy and wonder. "And how have I greeted you!"

"Yes, I have come," she said.

Robin blew his horn, and up dashed his merry men.

"Allan-a-Dale," he cried, "I helped you win your wife. Let your wife now look after my bride. She shall wed me——"

"Never!" It was the high-spirited girl herself who interrupted him. "Never—until the King himself shall come to give me away! Would you have me forget my vow?"

"Be it so," said Robin then, and kissed her tenderly. "Yet to-night, when Maid Marian has rested from her brave fight with a quarrelsome husbandman, we shall crown her queen of the forest."

But when she returned home her father, the Baron of Arlingford, was furious. Marian was confined to the castle. He had no intention of letting his daughter marry an outlaw. Her love of the forest and the chase, which he had never before discouraged, was now a matter of serious alarm to him, for he loved his daughter the bewitching Marian very much.

"If you coop me up here, I shall die like a lonely swan on a pool," she cried.

In other words Marian had no intention of giving up her wild sweetheart even though she was prepared to wait to be married.

"I must go to the woods, father," she insisted.

"Must!" said the Baron, "I say you must not!"

"But I am going," said Marian.

"I will have the drawbridge up," said the Baron.

"Then I will swim the moat," said Marian.

"But I will seal the gates," said the Baron.

"Then I shall leap from the battlements," said she.

"So, I will lock you in an upper chamber," said the Baron.

"And I will shred the tapestry, and let myself down."

"Right, I shall lock you in a turret," said the Baron, "where you shall only see light through a loophole."

"Ah, but through the loophole I shall take flight, like a young eagle from its eyrie. Understand, father, let me go freely and I will return willingly, but if you force me to slip through a loophole, you will never see me again."

Marian had her own way. She ranged at liberty, but always kept her promise to return home. This had the effect of giving her father great confidence in her—but it was about to end abruptly.

The Baron was one morning munching his way

through breakfast, when his ears were assailed by a tremendous clamour. A large party of armed men on the other side of the moat were calling in the king's name that the drawbridge be lowered.

The Baron walked along the battlements until he faced his visitors across the moat. As soon as they saw him they yelled again. "Lower the drawbridge and raise the portcullis at once."

"For what and for whom," asked the Baron.

"The Sheriff of Nottingham," said the leader, "lies in bed grievously bruised, many of his men are wounded and some slain. We are here to apprehend William Gamwal, Father Michael and your daughter, Marian Fitzwater, accomplices in this breach of the king's peace."

"Rubbish!" roared the Baron. "What do you mean by coming here with your cock and bull stories —my daughter bruising the Sheriff of Nottingham indeed. You are a set of rascals, be off with you, leave at once!"

"Lord Fitzwater," cried one, "take heed how you resist lawful authority. We shall yet prove ourselves."

By this time the Baron's men had flocked to the battlements, with long-bows, cross-bows, slings and stones, and Marian with her bow and quiver at their head. The assailants, observing the castle so well defended, deemed it expedient to get out. They turned their horses about and galloped away. The Baron turned to his daughter,

"Explain this, Marian, my dear, for I fear there is trouble here."

Marian told him William Gamwal and she had been in the forest, joining in a merry May dance with Friar Michael and a group of foresters, when the Sheriff of Nottingham burst on the scene with a retinue of fifty men and tried to arrest one of the party. All immediately resisted, Marian herself wounding one of the knights.

"I see," said the Baron, "and I can guess who that

forester was—this bold Robin, this courteous Robin, this thief of Sherwood Forest was behind it all. You'll hunt no more in that company, my girl. No more games and feasts, these pranks could mean the loss of my castle and lands, so an end to it I say!"

But Lord Fitzwater was soon to become an outlaw himself. A week later, the heralding of trumpets and waving of banners brought an eminent visitor to the castle gate. Prince John, brother of Richard the Lion Heart, King of England, was announced. Marian's spirits dropped, for on a previous visit to the castle, John had made it very apparent that he wished her to return with him to London. Both she and her father resisted his design, for they were constant to Richard, who was absent on another crusade.

That evening there were bitter words. The Baron insisted that his daughter remain where she was; the Prince, almost shrieking in his frustration, suddenly struck the father down and had him banished to a turret prison and a guard placed over him. The Baron's own men could do nothing to help, since it would put their master's life in jeopardy if they attempted to fight, but young William Gamwal, friend of Marian, heard the voices raised. He knew of John's infatuation for Marian, and, feeling that Robin Hood should be informed about the visit of the Prince, left the castle, ostensibly to return to Gamwal Hall, but in fact to seek out the Outlaw of Sherwood. He located Robin Hood just as darkness closed over the trees.

"Did any of Prince John's men see you leave?" said Robin at length.

"I think not," said William, "in fact no one would have known I was there."

"Then return, go in the open, say you are visiting Marian. Then, with darkness, put some ropes over the battlements. You'll have friends there who'll help. Little John and several of my men will swim the moat and you can draw us up to the top of the wall. Now, sleep, for there is much to be arranged tomorrow."

There was no reason to suspect Will Gamwal of being anything but harmless, so he was admitted into the castle with the excuse of having a message for the Lady Marian, and that night, several ropes were suspended from the battlements, and loyal supporters of the Baron stood by to hand up the brave fellows who would attempt the rescue of Lord Fitzwater and his daughter.

Prince John was not accompanied by many soldiers. His advantage lay in holding the Baron prisoner. So few patrolled the castle walls. Most drank or slept while the Prince attempted to persuade the lovely Marian to follow the direction of his own wishes.

"What do you intend to do with my father?" asked Marian, "you cannot keep him prisoner in his own castle."

"I do not intend to, sweet lady. Tomorrow he goes with me to London, and there he stays until you follow. I will keep him for eternity if necessary."

Marian gave no sign that she had noticed the door latch being raised, and when the heavy door began to inch open, her composure was admirable to behold, and until a dagger was placed at the throat of the Prince, she made barely a movement. Then she was all vigour and activity.

"Robin! William said you would come—I've waited."

"Little John has your father safe. Will is enlisting the aid of the Baron's men. In a moment there will be a battle and we'll pitch this cur and his rabble into the moat," said Robin.

All transpired as Robin had planned, and from the castle walls they watched the soaked and wretched Prince stagger along the road with his defeated followers.

"Prince John will brand me as an outlaw for this night's work," remarked the Baron as Robin and his men were preparing to depart.

"Then join our company whenever you wish, my Lord," laughed the outlaw, "for you will never find a more loyal band of rascals."

The Baron looked glum, but he knew that with Prince John and the Sheriff of Nottingham ranged against him, these staunch rogues might be his only allies. He took the outlaw's hand.

Robin Hood and the Beggar

Now it fell upon a fair afternoon that Robin went alone through a fern-clad forest path. After a while he got upon the high-road, where he met a beggar going sturdily along at a good pace, looking neither to the right nor to the left, noticing no one as he strode on his way. In his hand he held a pike-staff that was both stout and strong, while wound about his body was a clouted cloth folded many times, making an excellent covering from wind and rain.

Tied to a leathern strap there hung from his neck a large mealbag, firmly fastened to a stout, broad buckle, and upon his head were three hats stuck fast together, one above the other, so that wherever he went little did he care either for sun or for rain.

When good Robin spied this oddly attired stranger he stepped boldly right in front of him, for he had a shrewd thought that the beggar was not so poor as he seemed.

"Stay," said Robin, "stay awhile and speak with me."

But the beggar, making as if he had not heard him, went but the faster on his way, without so much as a turn of his head.

"Well," said Robin, "you show me scant courtesy. You must stop, for I have something to say to you."

"By my three hats," cried the beggar, in a harsh voice, "to stay I have no will, for it is getting late, and it is far to my lodging house. Should they have supper before I get there, I shall get no food."

"Now," said good Robin, "I see well that in thinking only of your own supper, you have no care of mine. All this day have I eaten no food, and I have nowhere to lie this night. To the tavern would I go but I have no money. Sir stranger, you must lend me some till we meet again."

The beggar answered peevishly: "I have no money to lend; I think you are as young as I and as strong, I warrant. If you fast till I lend you money, you shall eat naught this year."

"Then," said bold Robin, "since we are together here, if you have but one farthing I'll take it from you ere you go. Come, beggar, cease to stand there staring me in the face; or I will open up all the bags, your tag-rags and bobtails, and rip them to pieces with my hands. Should you make an outcry, I vow by the saints to try how far a broad arrow can pierce a beggar's skin."

The beggar looked at Robin with a wry smile upon his face and made answer:

"Far better let me be; for do not think I care a straw, or be afraid for your nip-crooked tree that you call a bow, nor that I care any whit for your sticks that you call arrows. Here do I defy you to do me harm—for all your loud talk you will get nothing from me but ill."

Such fearless words from a ragged beggar roused Robin's wrath. Straightway he nocked a broad arrow and bent his great bow. But e'er it was drawn a span, the beggar with his stout pike-staff reached forward with so swift a stroke that the bow burst in two. Nothing daunted, Robin with a bound darted to strike down the beggar with his sword, but that proved likewise vain, for the fellow with his pike-staff struck such a fierce blow on Robin's hand that his sword fell to the ground.

Robin could not speak a word, for he was sick at heart and faint from bitter pain. Yet still the beggar with his terrible pike-staff laid lusty blows upon his side and back, till at last Robin fell down on the soft sward, lying helpless and bleeding at the mercy of his terrible foe.

"Stand up, stand up," the beggar man said; "'tis a shame to go to rest. In truth, I think it were best to stay till you get your money. Then go to the tavern and buy both food and wine with the beggar's money. There you can boast of what you did get in the forest."

Robin answered ne'er a word, but lay still as a stone. Closed were both his eyes, and his cheeks were pale as any clay. With a few more blows upon his body the beggar thought him dead, and leaving him to lie stark and still, his face upturned to the sky, he strode on his way.

Now it so happened that by good chance three of Robin's band came walking by the way and found their master lying on the ground, wounded, bleeding, and senseless.

"Who has done this foul deed, comrades?" said one. "Let us take our dear master up, and carry him to yon brook, that we may sprinkle water on his face and so bring him to life." So they took up good Robin, who made a piteous moan, while blood gushed forth from his mouth and nose. Yet though they searched all over his body, they found no cuts, but many cruel bruises. When his brow had been bathed with cold water, Robin at last came to his senses enough to speak a little.

"Tell us, dear master," said his men, "tell us what is the matter, and how you fell into such an evil situation."

Robin sighed deep e'er he began to tell of his disgrace.

"For twenty years and more have I been outlaw and forester in this wood, yet I was never so hard beaten as you have found me here. A beggar with a clouted cloak hath with his pike-staff so mauled my back that I fear 'twill never be well. He went o'er yon hill, and upon his head, he carried three hats. If ever you loved your master, go now to revenge me of

this vile deed and bring him back to me again. Take care that he does not escape."

"One of us shall stay with you, because you are in no state to be left alone, and the other two, I warrant, shall bring the villain beggar back to use as you will."

"Now, by my faith," said good Robin, "enough has been said. Take good heed, for I fear you will both be evil paid if he gets a chance to swing his wicked tree around your noddles."

"Be not afraid, dear master, that we two can be bested by any base beggar that carries naught but a **staff! You shall shortly see that his staff will stand** him in no stead. He shall be brought back again, fast bound, to see if you will have us slay him."

"Be sly then," said Robin, "and by stealth work your way into his path before he is aware."

The two outlaws then left Robin, clinging to a tree like a poor, tottering old man. Now the beggar had mended his pace and was striding along over the hill, giving no thought to the trouble he had caused and only anxious to reach his lodging ere nightfall. The two outlaws ran at full speed by a lower path, careless of the mud and briars along the way, going a distance of over three miles. Then, turning to a little clump of bushes in a glen that the beggar must surely pass, they hid themselves close behind trees on each side of the path, standing ready till the beggar drew nigh. After a little they saw him coming, and just as he got betwixt them both leaped upon him.

Taken off his guard, the beggar was so afraid that he dared not move. He could not run, he could not wield his staff. He was not sure but other outlaws might be near; so in despair, thinking that at last his life's end was near at hand, he began to crave mercy.

"Grant me my life," he pleaded, "and hold away that ugly knife. I never harmed you in all my life, neither by night nor day, and indeed you do a great sin if you slay a poor silly beggar."

"You lie, false and cruel varlet," cried the outlaw who held his staff. "You have near slain the gentlest and kindest man that e'er was born. Back again to him you shall be led, fast bound with thongs, to see if he will have you slain or bid us hang you."

Then the beggar thought that all was done with him, though if he could but escape out of their hands and get hold of his staff he was sure that he would teach them another game. While they made ready to bind him he cudgelled his brains for some wily scheme to free himself. The only way that came into his mind was to tempt them with some money; so he said:

"Brave gentlemen, be good to me, and let me go. It helps you not a flea to take a beggar's blood. 'Twas but to save mine own hide that I did hurt your master, and listen, good friends—I will give you a recompense that shall make you rich if you will but set me free and do me no more harm. I will give you a hundred pounds, and much more odd silver that I have gathered these many years. Under this clouted cloak I have it, far hidden beneath its folds next to my skin and also in the bottom of my meal-bag."

To this neither of the young men answered a word, but each looked at his companion to see whether he would be false to his honour and disgrace the band. One argued, "We will take the money to our captain and tell him that the beggar is slain." The other said: "Our orders were 'Bring him back alive or dead'."

At last they agreed to yield to the beggar's counsel and let him go, then follow after and take him again by stealth when they had his money; for, being swift of foot, they might easily overtake him.

"False knave," said one, "say no more, but get the money and count it out. 'Tis little enough to pay for the ill turn you have done our master; yet come what may, if you give us the money now we will not take you back."

So the beggar thanked them right heartily, and straightway set about loosening his clouted cloak to

spread it on the ground. Then he took from his neck a bag containing over two pecks of meal, which he set down upon the cloak. Opening wide the bag, he bent down and felt in every nook and corner for the money. Both young men drew their faces closer to see the gold appear, when of a sudden the beggar lifted out two great handfuls of meal and flung it in their faces, blinding them so that they could do naught with their hands save strive to wipe the meal from eyes, nose, and mouth. In a trice the beggar grasped his pike-staff and, with a gleeful laugh, cried:

"Now, my pretty pair of blades, if I've done you wrong in mealing your clothes, with my staff I will strike off the meal again."

With that, he began to ply his staff, filling the air with meal from their bodies as his mighty blows fell on their shoulders, necks, and arms. The young outlaws, half blinded and choked, could do nought to help themselves. They turned and ran with all the speed they could muster, leaving the beggar shaking his staff in the air and calling upon them to stay awhile and get well dusted.

"What's all this haste?" he cried. "Stay a while, I'll pay you with a right good will until you have had enough and to spare. The shakings of my meal-bag have by chance blown into your eyes, but what of that? I have a good pike-staff that will soon make them clear."

Thus he went on entreating them in right loving

fashion to tarry, but the young outlaws heard him not, for they were far away. Since the night was creeping on apace, it would be vain to follow and attack him now, so they thought it wise to return, and with sad hearts and downcast looks they got them back to their master.

"Well, my comrades," asked Robin, "how did you speed in your quest?"

They answered him, "Full ill, and we were evil paid."

"That cannot be," said Robin. "A man would think to look at your clothes that you have been working for the miller. Tell me the matter truly— how did you fare, and what have you done with the bold beggar I sent you for."

The young men drooped down, hanging their heads for very shame, and could not speak a word. Then, with true anger in his voice, Robin said:

"Because I fell beneath the cudgel of this beggar fiend I think you feared he would serve you in the same fashion."

At these words, so true and so just, the young men confessed, and told Robin the truth all to the end— how the beggar blinded them with the meal, how he basted their bones so sore to dust it from their clothes, and how they fled to the forest.

Robin cried out: "For shame! We are dishonoured forever. Help me to lift my weary bones, and take me quickly to my bower."

As they carried him along the path he thought he would have revenge, yet even in his pain he smiled to think that two of his merry young men had got a taste of that beggar's pike-staff besides himself.

Robin Sells Pots and Dishes

Robin was angered to the depths of his heart at thought of the beggar's brutishness, for he himself had never in his life struck a fallen foe, to say nothing of beating a man who lay senseless and helpless at his feet. Yet he thought: "I was to blame! I brought it upon my own head, and must perforce bear the pain I got." Such were his thoughts as he painfully dragged his aching bones along, with the help of his two followers, back through the forest to the oak glade. It seemed an age before he got there, and twice he fainted from weakness. Little John met them with a very sad face, and he wept to see his master in such a plight. Then with his strong arms he fairly carried Robin to his bower, there to lie a month or more till his swollen, bruised body grew strong and well once more.

Many a time he bemoaned himself bitterly to Little John because he could not go abroad. Then, with comforting words, mixed with a spice of sound advice, Little John would soothe him, saying:

"In truth, my dear master, you are too prone to fight with quarterstaff against a foe more used to that weapon. With a good long bow, the case is different, for you would always be the victor."

"I cannot in cold blood," said Robin, "send a shaft through a foe's body with but a pace or two between us. Once I slew a man, and never again will I take life save as dire need or in the heat of combat. But, by heaven, I will no longer lie here like a cat tied in a bag."

Again Little John would gently chide his master, bidding him wait at least till he could stand upon his legs without wobbling. "For," said he, "our treasure is ample, our wants are all supplied, and the men content. Be patient, therefore, for in a week or more, once again you will be strong—long before the wintry wind blows through the glade."

At last, toward the end of summer, the three best doctors of the band—Friar Tuck, Arthur-a-Bland, and Little John—agreed that Robin was well enough to go upon short trips to hunt the deer. Shooting contests were held and games resumed, as a change from the more serious work of gathering in the winter stores. It was now the middle of August. The days were warm, the evenings long and light till ten o'clock, so that the band was in a merry mood, as was their wont when all went well.

Thus it was that, on the next day, a bright, fair morn being a Saturday and a market-day, Robin, Little John, and others of the band set forth toward the great highway that ran along the forest edge, to gather tolls from any that were able to pay, and give away, for charity's sake, to those in dire need. Presently they saw a man sitting on the shafts of a rude little cart pulled by a pony. The cart was filled with mugs, basins, and other pottery vessels, which the man bought very cheap at Stoke, where they were made, and carted from town to town to sell at a good profit. He was singing a merry ditty, now and then whipping up his pony that he might reach Nottingham market in good time. It was plain by his looks that he could take good care of his pots as well as himself.

"Here comes a stout potter," said Robin, "he has crossed this forest many a time, yet has never paid one penny of passage money to us. He shall not escape us this time, I warrant."

"Better let him pass, good master," said Little John. "I met the fellow once at Wentbridge, and he gave me three such clouts that I want no more from him, though I gave him clout for clout. I will lay forty shillings there is not a man among us that can make the potter pay toll."

Bold Robin could not let that pass. "Here are forty shillings," he cried, "and more will I lay that I can make that bold potter pay some token for his passage."

"He will give you his staff for a token! I vow that from him you will get no other pay, my master," said John. But Robin, without more words, strode to the middle of the high road, and, standing firm as a rock till the potter drew nigh, laid his hand on the bridle, bidding the man stand.

"Fellow," bawled the potter, "what do you want?"

"All these three years and more, potter," said Robin, "you have passed by this way, yet never paid a penny toll to us."

"What is your name?" said the potter, "and what is your right to ask for passage money on the King's highway?"

"Robin Hood is my name, and king of these woods, to whom it is your duty to pay toll."

"Not a bad farthing shall you get from me," said the potter, "let go my horse, or I vow to strike it off with my staff."

Straightway leaping down from the shaft, he unstrapped from under the cart a stout pike-staff, saying in angry tones:

"Now, bold outlaw, take your hand from my horse."

Robin drew his sword and, with a buckler upon his arm, advanced to meet the potter, who with a powerful balk-stroke smote off the shield. In a trice the haughty pike-staff was brought down with another fierce blow on Robin's neck as he stooped to get his buckler again. So stiff was the stroke that it sent Robin sprawling on the ground.

"Let us go to help our master," cried Little John, "or yon potter will do him harm."

Then, running toward Robin, with shouts of laughter, he said: "Who has won the wager now?

Shall I have the forty shillings, or shall you have mine?"

"Yes, were they a hundred shillings," said Robin, "They are all yours."

"There is little courtesy," said the potter, "as I have heard wise men say, to take from a poor yeoman what little he has while driving along the highway."

"By my faith, you speak the truth," said Robin, "and from this day forth you shall never be hindered; for a friendship would I have with you, and good payment will I give. Make exchange with me of your clothing, for I will sell pots in Nottingham town, and you shall stay here in the forest to feast on good venison. When I come back, if I sell all, you shall be the gainer."

"To that I will agree," said the potter. "You shall find me an honest fellow; and if you can sell my pots well, come back again when you have done so."

Then spoke Little John and his comrades, "Master, take care and beware of the Sheriff, for he would gladly slay you by fair means or foul. Alone, you will be in great jeopardy."

"Nay, my good comrades," said Robin, "let me be, for by the help of our Good Lady, to Nottingham I will go."

So Robin changed clothes with the potter, and, with some touches here and there to make a better disguise, he jumped on the shaft of the cart and drove away in a jolly good mood, singing a merry song. When he reached Nottingham, he drew up his horse close by the Sheriff's gate, and gave it some oats and hay. Then setting forth his pots, both large and small, upon the cart, so as to make the best show, he began to cry out:

"Crocks and pots, jugs and mugs, who wants to buy? I give one extra, no matter how large or small."

This way the bargaining was new to the wives and widows of Nottingham, and soon drew a large crowd round his cart. Not content with throwing in an extra pot, Robin sold pots worth five pence for three pence. This made the women gape, both old and young; and while they bought they said to each other slyly, "This potter will never thrive at this rate."

"You will have none left ere long, if you sell so cheap," said one buxom wife.

"For that cause came I hither," said smiling Robin, "to sell all I have." And he did sell so fast that before noon only five pieces were left.

"Well done, you cunning potter," said Robin to himself.

"These five unsold pots will I give with my compliments to the Sheriff's wife." And so, in fact he did.

"Sir," said the Sheriff's wife, with a tender smile on good Robin. "When you come to this town again I shall buy what pots I want from you, so much do I like your courtesy. Your kindness is truly great, and I would like you to come and dine with the Sheriff and me."

"God's mercy, good lady," said Robin, "your bidding shall be done."

Then a young maid carried in the pots, and Robin followed the Sheriff's wife to the hall, where he met the Sheriff, who spoke to him heartily:

"Look," said the lady, "what this potter has given us for a present—five pots, both large and small."

"He is full welcome," said the Sheriff. "Let us enter and go to dine."

As they sat at the table, with merry talk and laughter, two of the Sheriff's men began to speak of a prize of forty shillings offered for the best shooting with the long-bow among the townspeople that day. "Now, as I am a true Christian man," Robin said to himself, "this shooting-match will I see."

When they had appeased their hunger upon the very best of bread, ale, and wine, to the shooting-butts they all went to see who would win the prize. The Sheriff's men began to shoot, but they were very poor archers, and none of them got nearer the mark than half the length of a long-bow. The potter looked on with great contempt; and when the Sheriff said, "What think you, good potter, of our archery?" he made answer:

"In plain truth, it seems to me to be very poor. If I had a bow, with one shot I would beat them all."

"I warrant you shall have a bow for that one shot," said the Sheriff, "the best you may choose from such as we have. You seem strong and stalwart as any here." He then bade a yeoman that stood by bring some bows for the potter to choose from.

"'Tis the best here," said Robin, as he took up a bow, "though 'tis a poor, weak thing. Nevertheless, with it I will make good my word."

So without more ado he strode up to the line, side by side with the Sheriff's men, who smiled and twitted him upon his impudence in daring to shoot in such company. The potter answered naught, but, pulling the string to his ear, he carelessly shot the arrow within a foot of the mark. Then the Sheriff's men tried once more with little better success. When the potter again took his place to shoot, they had greater respect for his skill and waited anxiously to see what he would do. Taking much more careful aim, he let fly the shaft and cleft the wand apart, much to the wonder of the Sheriff's men, who thought it great shame that a common potter should win the prize from them. But the Sheriff and his wife were both mightily pleased, and said:

"You are a man worthy to bear a bow anywhere."

"In my cart," he made answer, "I have a bow that I had from Robin Hood."

"Knowest you Robin Hood?" asked the surprised Sheriff. "Tell me of him."

"A hundred times," replied the potter, "have I shot with him under his trysting-tree."

"By my faith," said the Sheriff, "I would give a hundred pounds to have that villainous outlaw stand before me here."

"I would win that hundred pounds," said the potter, "and tomorrow after we have taken our breakfast, if you will go with me I will show you Robin Hood."

"I will pay you well," said the Sheriff, joyfully. "By my faith, you shall not repent of serving me in this matter."

Upon the morrow the potter was early ready with horse and cart. Taking leave of the Sheriff's wife, he thanked her heartily for her good cheer.

"Good dame," said he, "for my love to you, be pleased to wear this gold ring."

"Gracious, good sir, I yield to your wish, for I know the Sheriff's heart was never so light to see the fair forest as in the company of so gallant a companion."

So the Sheriff, on his horse, and the potter, seated in his little cart, both set off for Sherwood.

The morning was bright and warm, and the little birds sang merrily among the green leaves. "The

through an opening of the trees they appeared before the potter and addressed him, saying:

"Master, how have you fared in Nottingham? Have you sold all the wares?"

"Yes, Little John. Look you and see. I have brought the Sheriff of Nottingham in exchange for my goods."

"He is welcome," said Little John. "Such tidings make us glad."

It was then that the Sheriff saw the trick that the potter had served him, and he thought he would rather have given a hundred pounds than to have met Robin Hood that day.

"Had I known," said he, "that you were Robin Hood, you would not have seen this fair forest for a thousand years."

"I know that well," said Robin, laughing. "Therefore you shall leave your horse and other gear with us. You came on horseback, and back you shall go afoot to give my greetings to your good wife at home. I shall give her a white palfrey, and you may tell her

greenwood is a merry place," said Robin, "for a man that has nought to spend, and by the sound of my horn we shall soon know if Robin Hood be near at hand." Then he set his horn to his mouth and blew a blast both loud and long, that could be heard far down the forest glade.

"I hear my master's call," said Little John. "Let us haste, and run to see if all be well." Presently that had she used less courtesy you would have fared much more sadly at our hands." Thus the Sheriff parted from Robin, and to Nottingham he took his way.

His wife was there to give him a welcome. "How did you fare in the greenwood?" she said. "Have you brought Robin Hood home?"

The Sheriff swore a great oath and said: "I have been basely scorned, and tricked of all the moneys I took to the greenwood. My large, fine horse, its gold trappings, my pouch with a hundred pounds were all stripped from me amid the jeers and merry quips of that vile band."

Upon that, the good dame laughed loud and long.

"Now," said she, "he has then been well paid for all those pots he gave to us."

So we leave the unhappy Sheriff and return to the greenwood, where Robin called the potter to him, saying, "Good potter, what were the pots worth that I sold in Nottingham market?"

"They were worth two pounds, but I should have traded and made more by my traffic," said the potter.

"You shall have ten pounds," said Robin. "And remember bold potter, when you come to the greenwood you shall ever be welcome."

So they parted as the best of friends, each well satisfied with the other. Then the potter set off blithe and merry on his way back to Stoke, to get his cart refilled with pots and crocks, hoping to make as good a trade again. "But of that," thought he, "I have grave doubts—there is but one Robin Hood."

Robin and Sir Guy of Gisbourne

This latest clever trick of Robin Hood's was the straw that broke the Sheriff's patience. Each man that sat at meat with him or passed him upon the streets of Nottingham town seemed to be Robin Hood in disguise. The disgrace was so much the harder to bear because his wife found delight in constantly talking of the comely, courteous outlaw and his present of the gold ring, which she still wore. So the Sheriff longed for a dire revenge, and searched eagerly for some means whereby he might put an end at once and forever to the troubles he had borne for twenty-odd years.

At last he decided to give a great feast and invite as many as would come of the barons and knights of the shire. For he thought that if they would not help him with money and men they might at least advise him how best to rid the nearby forests of these pests. He had often tried to get the aid of bold yeoman of his town, but they had flatly said him nay, for many of them had received kindness from Robin and his men. So the Sheriff bade his servants prepare the banquet, to which came not a few of the barons and knights.

When they had eaten the good things and drunk well the wine, the Sheriff arose and addressed them, laying bare all his woe. At this one brave knight got upon his feet and said:

"Sir Sheriff, while we grieve with you in this trouble, not one of us can soil his knightly hands to draw sword in so mean a cause—to wit, the catching of a rascally deer-stealer. Such base deeds are meet for your yeoman or the King's foresters."

"Oft have I promised them much gold," said the Sheriff, "but they either will not, or dare not, encounter this band. Yea, they all turn pale at the name of Robin Hood."

"In faith," said the knight, "I know not any other means whereby you can have your will unless some knight down at the heels for want of friends and gold were willing to lead a company of trained men to the forest and drive the outlaws away."

"Do you, Sir Knight, know of such a one?"

"There is one," replied the knight, "who would do your bidding, if the prize were great. This Sir Guy of Gisbourne is bold enough to do any deed you may set for him, nor will he value his knightly honour above five hundred pounds."

After the guests had gone the Sheriff lost no time in seeking out this Sir Guy, and on the morrow he sent a messenger on horseback to the little market-town of Gisbourne in the West Riding of Yorkshire. Now Sir Guy was poor; he had wasted his substance in riotous living; but, instead of repenting, he was ever ready to do any deed, however base, not only because he needed gold, but for the mere love of doing evil.

In his native town he was feared by every man, and abhorred by every wife, widow, or lass. Besides his wickedness he was the ugliest creature in merry England. His naturally savage features were scarred by many wounds and cuts, for he had been to the wars in the Holy Land, in Ireland, in Scotland, and in the South. Everywhere he went, ever fighting; yet

he seemed to bear a charmed life. Utterly cruel, with a black and stony heart, his bold and fierce demeanour affrighted all men. When he was angry, his face and scars turned a livid blue, so awful to look upon that his foes took him for a demon risen from the regions below. It was his wont to go clad from head to foot in the hide of a horse. The ears stood up from a hood, at the back of which hung the mane, and below was the horse's tail. This body covering was tanned soft with the hair outside, so that he who wore it looked more a beast than a man. Such, then, was the evil Sir Guy, whom the Sheriff's messenger went to seek as a leader to fight and destroy the good Robin Hood and his outlaws.

When he reached the little town of Gisbourne, the messenger had little trouble in learning the whereabouts of him he sought.

"What is the price?" roared Sir Guy, when he had heard the tale. "Repeat to me the sum, that I be not mistaken."

"Five hundred pounds in good coin," said the messenger, "for the living body of Robin Hood, or his head if you slay him."

"'Tis a fair sum for so slight a deed," said Sir Guy slowly, "and, to be brief, I will do the Sheriff's will. The outlaw's head is mine; the money is earned. Do you hear that?" Down came his fist with such a crack on the table that the messenger nearly jumped out of his skin.

"Yes, Sir Guy, I hear, and doubt it not."

"What, ho! knavish hind!" he shouted to a servant. "Get my horse, and furnish him for combat. Get me my two Irish daggers and my longest brown Egyptian blade. There is work afoot for us, so choose the toughest yew long-bow and double-pointed shafts, and be ready at once."

All was soon in readiness, and before long the two were riding back toward Nottingham, which they reached late on the following day. Meanwhile, the Sheriff had not been idle. He foresaw that Sir Guy would willingly do a work so much to his taste, especially for a prize so large. He had already gathered together a hundred of his own men and two hundred of the King's foresters. The latter he would place under the command of Sir Guy, and he himself would lead his own servants. He was no coward, though his men were not of the same metal.

When the knight presented himself, the Sheriff's joy was unbounded. "Such a fierce-looking monster did I ne'er behold," he thought. "Surely he will slay bold Robin." Then he said aloud:

"Thrice welcome are you, Sir Knight of Gisbourne. Let us dine and then talk of what we have to do."

So they went into the hall, where Sir Guy seated himself opposite the place where the Sheriff's wife would sit. Unsheathing his two Irish daggers, he laid one shining blade close beside his platter, the other beside his wine-goblet, and prepared to eat. The Sheriff's wife had been told of this man, and what he was about to do, but she was so afraid at the knives and the fellow's evil looks that she fainted dead away in the arms of her husband, who helped the servants to carry her away from the table.

"What is the matter with your good lady, Sir Sheriff?" asked Guy.

"I believe," said he, "she is overcome with joy to know that the outlaw's end is near."

"Ay, by the bones of Saint Withold!" growled Sir Guy, "of truth it is so. But tell me, what manner of man is this Robin Hood, famed as he is to far and wide? Is he big of bone and broad of chest, like King Richard, that all men fear him?"

"No, by the mass," said the Sheriff, "he is as mild as a sucking pig and gentle as a lamb. The cooing turtle-dove could not match him in soft persuasion. But mark you well, Sir Knight, no fox was ever so sly; no adder creeping through the damp sward is so silent as his footfall on the grass."

"And what of his prowess?" asked Sir Guy. "I have heard of his skill in archery, but doubt it."

"Doubt it not, Sir Knight, for no archer lives, nor ever lived, that can match him. With the broadsword and buckler, and also with the quarterstaff, he has men in combat the strongest and best in merry England, and he has drawn them to his band. I know not of any means to take him save to outnumber him. Outwit him—'tis impossible! Outfight him— 'tis doubtful! If you can meet him alone, you may have the better of him. Indeed, rather would I see it done in such a manner than in any other. It were well that you should go before us to tempt the wily fox to single combat. It is well known that he loves such fights; and many, so I hear, have met him, hand to hand, alone in diverse parts of the forest."

"Truly," said the Knight, "the thieving rogue has frightened all the bravery out of Nottinghamshire. Nevertheless, I will do as you bid. A blast from this horn shall tell that he is dead. But come, good Sheriff, we tarry over-long. Rest assured that Robin

Hood shall meet his end before the moon cast her beams through the forest leaves."

So the Sheriff gave command, and soon his three hundred stalwart yeoman and foresters stood ready to follow the two leaders, who, both on horseback, rode in front on their way through the forest to destroy the outlaw's nest.

On that very same morning, just before sunrise, you might have seen all of Robin's merry men wrapped snugly in their night-cloaks, fast asleep on the grassy sward, round about the great oak. On a low-hanging branch above Robin's head sat a throstle, singing so loud that it roused him from his sleep. Half raising himself, he looked at the bird, which kept pouring forth its mellow notes and would not cease to sing. Then Robin said:

"Now, last night I had a dream, and it seemed to me that two strong yeoman fought with me fast and furiously. I thought they did beat me and bind me fast to a tree, taking from me both arrows and bow. If I be Robin, and am awake in this merry wood, I will take revenge on those two."

Little John, who lay by his side, had also been awakened by the song-bird and heard what Robin said.

"Dreams are swift, master," said he, "even as the wind that blows o'er the hill. For if it be never so loud this night, tomorrow it may be still enough."

"That is truth," said Robin, "but I shall go to seek these strong yeomen, if they are in the forest."

So he leaped up, and, throwing off his covering, shouted to his comrades: "My merry men, bestir yourselves, and make ready. Little John, you shall go with me."

So they all cast off their cloaks, took up their bows, and, after partaking of a hearty breakfast, stood ready to march wherever their brave captain should direct. And a fine body of men they were— alert, strong, brave, obedient—so Robin and Little John thought, as they strode past in single file away to the green forest.

By the time the sun had risen high in all his glorious splendour, the birds were singing on every spray and twig; the cool morning air was just crisp enough to make walking in the fair forest a delight and put all in a joyous mood. The band had struck a different path under the leadership of Will Scarlet, though ever within sound of Robin's bugle-call as he strode along by the side of Little John. Soon the two came in sight of a tall figure leaning against a tree.

He had a long sword and two sharp daggers that he wore by his side, and his body was covered with the hide of a horse, ears, mane, and tail complete.

"God-a-mercy," said Robin, "what is this thing? Is it man or beast?"

"Stand still," said Little John, "under this greenwood tree while I go forth to the strange thing to know what it is."

"Ah, John," said Robin, "I see well you set no store by me. When was I ever wont to send my men before and myself behind? Were it not for the breaking of my bow, John, I would break your head."

These words rankled harshly in John's breast. He spoke not a word in answer, but turned aside and then strode swiftly away to join the main band, leaving Robin standing alone.

He had gone but a short distance when he heard sounds. As he hurried forward, the sounds became shouts and cries, and at last, when he came near, he beheld a full pitched battle 'twixt the outlaw band and the Sheriff's men. As he rushed along his heart grew sick with heaviness, for he saw two of the band lying dead in a hollow piece of ground by the side of a glade, and in the distance was Will Scarlet, leaping along over rocks and stones for his very life, with the Sheriff and seven score of his men close at his heels.

"One shot now I will shoot," said John, "with all my might and main to make yon Sheriff that presses on so fast stop in his career."

Then he bent his great long-bow and pulled so hard that it burst in twain and the parts fell down at his feet.

"Woe is me," he cried, "wickedest wood, that ever grew on a tree; for now this day when I need you most, you fail me."

The arrow flew, but with such a bad aim that instead of hitting the Sheriff it struck Will-a-Trent to the ground—one of the Sheriff's men who was very friendly with the band. Little John's heart was crushed, and his hands hung limp by his side. Heedless of all that was going on in the fight, he was caught by a number of the Sheriff's men, who took him and quickly bound him to a tree.

When the Sheriff heard that Little John was taken, he came up to where the outlaw was pinioned, to jeer and mock at him.

"I have you now," snarled he. "You shall be drawn up hill and down dale tied to a horse's tail. Then I will hang you from the topmost tower of

Nottingham Castle."

"Yet," said Little John, unafraid, "you may fail of your purpose if the good saints have their will. Our men are not all in my situation."

"No," roared the Sheriff, "but Robin Hood is now in the toils of the brave Sir Guy of Gisbourne."

Little John knew of this fell knight, and his heart sank lower than ever to think that Robin was left alone with this villain, whom he now knew to be the creature standing by the tree. So he repented sore that he had crossed his dear master and had left him to his fate.

As soon as Little John had gone, Robin Hood marched up to the man in the horse-hide robe.

"Good morrow, good fellow!" said he.

"Good morrow, good fellow, to you," the other made answer.

"I think by that bow you bear in your hand, you should be a fair archer," said Robin.

"I have lost my way," said the stranger, "and know not where to go."

"I'll lead you good fellow, through the forest and be your guide," said Robin.

"I am seeking for an outlaw," the stranger went on, "that men call Robin Hood, and I would give forty pounds if I could meet with him here."

"Then come along with me, bold fellow, and Robin you shall soon see. But first, under this greenwood tree let us test each other's skill with bow and shaft, for we may meet this Robin Hood by some odd chance in the meantime."

"I like the plan, brave archer," said the stranger; and forthwith they cut a thin sapling that grew among the underbush, which they set in the ground, with a little garland on the top, threescore rods away.

"Lead on, good fellow," said Robin, "and shoot."

"Nay, by my faith, good fellow," said the other, "you shall shoot first."

"Well, so be it," said Robin; "I will do as you say."

The first time Robin shot he missed the wand by an inch; and the stranger, though a right good archer, shot a foot or more away. But upon the second trial he placed the arrow inside the garland. Then Robin, as he had done many times before, loosed a shaft that cut the wand in two.

"A blessing upon your heart," said the stranger. "Fellow, that shooting is good; and if your heart be as good as your hand, Robin Hood could do no better. Now tell me your name, brave archer."

"No, by my faith," said bold Robin, "that will I not do till you have told me yours."

"I dwell," said he, "upon the moorlands of Yorkshire, and when I am called by my right name, men call me Sir Guy of Gisbourne."

"My dwelling," slowly said Robin, "is in this very wood, and men know me as Robin Hood."

Then, with his hand upon the hilt of his sword, Sir Guy roared out: "You are he whom I have long sought."

"Well," said Robin, "I am ready. Prepare yourself, for with my good broadsword will I cut short your evil life."

Robin drew his sword, and Sir Guy his, at the same time unsheathing his long, pointed Irish dagger, which he held in his left hand. Facing each other with keen eyes, they watched their chance. Both knew the combat was to be long and fierce; both were equally determined to win. Each found the other a worthy foe, for in skill and hardihood they were well matched. No one was by to see fair play, save the birds, and they were soon scared away by the noise of the clashing swords and the deep, angry oaths of the fell Sir Guy, as he fiercely lunged, parried, and feinted. Robin was well aware of the peril in which he stood. Sir Guy was fighting for a great prize. The victor would live, the vanquished would surely die. It was a grim battle to the death.

Two hours passed. Weary, yet still fighting, the face of Sir Guy changed from a sickly yellow to a livid blue; then, as the fight went on, his blood grew hotter and flowed to his face, darkening the colour to a deep purple. His long black locks were clotted and damp with sweat, and from time to time, at each furious lunge, he swore dreadful oaths because he could not budge his pale-faced, dogged foeman. Never before in all his life did Robin fight so desperately; never before was he so near death—and he knew it. Early in the fight a faintness fell upon him; but he grimly set his teeth, and new strength came. His strokes, though they dealt no wounds, began to tell upon Sir Guy, robed as he was in a hot skin. For all his wickedness, Sir Guy was a bold warrior, as many had found to their cost, and he was too proud to ask for a moment's time to rest. Robin watched him every second, fighting carefully for fear of some false, dishonourable stroke, for he knew that he had to do with a man who would not scruple to kill him by foul means.

All of a sudden Robin slipped on a root, falling on one knee. Sir Guy sprang forward nimbly and struck him in the left side—a base and cowardly deed, for a true knight would have lowered his blade till his foe got upon his feet.

"By our dear Lady," cried Robin, "'tis not a good man's destiny to die before this day. Take that, you villainous cheat!" So saying, he leaped up and straightway, with a sudden stroke, drove his blade right through Sir Guy's body. The knight swayed, his sword dropped from his uplifted arm, and he slowly sank lifeless to the ground.

"There is now an end to one who has been a traitor all his life," said Robin, as he leaned panting upon his sword. "Lie there, Sir Guy! If you had fought as befitted a knight, maybe you would now be alive, and I lying there instead. But your knavishness has undone you and truly the world is well rid of you."

Robin's wound was but a scratch, for he had partly turned the blow. When he had bound it up and rested a little, he doffed his coat of Lincoln green, and clad himself from top to toe in the horse-hide, saying, "Now I will see how my men have fared and what has befallen Little John." Then he put Sir Guy's horn to his lips and blew so loud a blast that the Sheriff heard it as he stood upon a little hill waiting for the welcome sound.

"Hearken," said the Sheriff, "for I hear good tidings. Yonder I hear Sir Guy blowing his horn, as he said he would do when he had slain Robin Hood. Ay, by the mass, yonder comes the good knight, clad in his horse-hide coat. Come hither, come hither to me, good Sir Guy. Ask whatever you will of me!"

"Oh, I will have none of your gold," said Robin, "nor do I crave any reward save only this: now that I have slain the master, let me go and strike down the knavish servant at yonder tree. No other fee will I have."

"You are a madman," said the Sheriff, "and are truly unworthy of a knight's fee." But he pressed him no further, thinking so large a sum were as well in his own pocket. So he granted Robin's request, though in his heart he longed to carry Little John back to Nottingham alive, as his own prisoner.

When Little John heard his master's voice he knew his freedom was close at hand through some good hap, and now he saw Robin coming as fast as he could hie to cut his bonds. The Sheriff and his men followed close upon Robin's heels to witness the end of Little John.

"Stand aback, stand aback," shouted Robin. "Why do you draw so near? It is not the custom in my country for more than one to hear a man's last confession. Put some space between us, while I do this deed."

So then the men backed away; and Robin, pulling forth the Irish knife, quickly loosed the bonds that held Little John's hands and feet. Then, giving him Sir Guy's bow and arrows, he bade him look to himself. Both turned about at the same instant with bows ready bent; and when the Sheriff saw that his prisoner was free, he knew that Robin Hood had again foiled his plans. The shock was so great that he had no heart to stand and brave it out, but turned aside and made all haste to ride toward his home in Nottingham town. He fled fast, and all his company did likewise, for they knew the deadly aim of those two archers who had so just a cause for anger against them. But before the Sheriff could ride out of sight Little John shot an arrow which wounded him in the shoulder. Thus he rode into Nottingham town with the broad arrow sticking from his back.

Then it was that Little John turned to Robin, saying: "My dear good master, I do freely ask your pardon, and should you grant it me I make a vow nevermore to cross your will or leave you again in the lurch."

"No, no, my trusty John, my best of true hearts, 'tis I should ask pardon of you, for I was out of temper and hasty of speech I spoke unkindly."

Thereupon they embraced, then through the forest these two firm friends of over a quarter of a century strode together, in quiet happiness, back home to their trysting-place, where they found most of their comrades safe and happy. So the night was spent in feasting and tales of deeds nobly done on that famous day when Sir Guy of Gisbourne was slain.

The Return of King Richard

For long months, King Richard the Lion-hearted had been held a prisoner in Germany. At home, his evil brother John oppressed the unhappy people, and conspired treacherously with certain of the barons for Richard's ruin. At last the king was ransomed by his loyal subjects, and suddenly he was home again. Then all who had oppressed the people or followed the traitor John had to scurry about and cover up the tracks of their misdoings.

Now the Sheriff of Nottingham and the abbot of St Mary's had evil tracks enough to cover up, and it occurred to them that a fine way to do it would be to bring King Richard report of the lawless deeds of the outlaw Robin Hood and all his band. It would be easy indeed, thought they, to hide from the King the fact that Robin's men, whatever their crimes, had always stood out against the cruel Prince John and had been loyal to the absent king. Very persuasive they were, and many were the stories they told the King of Robin's supposed treachery.

But King Richard, wary and bold, determined to see for himself. Disguised as an abbot, he rode alone into the forest.

He had not gone far when, sure enough, he fell among Robin's men, who of course did not know him and made him prisoner and hurried him off to their camp in the depths of Sherwood Forest. There they intended to banquet him courteously, as was their wont with any unfortunate churchman who fell into their hands, and to set him free again—robbed of all his gold. So:

Robin took the king's horse
   Hastily in that stead,
And said, Sir Abbot, by your leave
   A while you must abide.

We be yeomen of this Forest,
   Under the greenwood tree
We live by our king's deer,
   Other shift have not we.

And you have churches and rents both
   And gold full great plenty.
Give me some of your spending
   For Saint Charity.

But the false abbot pleaded that he had no more than forty pounds; for the king, he said was staying with him, and he found it very expensive. Robin took

the money and distributed half of it among his men. Then he returned the other half to the king.

"Now, indeed," said the seeming abbot, "let me tell you, bold outlaw, that I have a letter for you from the king himself, commanding you to come to him at Nottingham!"

"The king! King Richard! God and the holy saints bless him!" cried Robin Hood eagerly. "The king is come to right the wrongs Prince John has done! Come, my merry men all, a rousing cheer for King Richard!" And they gave it with a will.

"What are you cheering about?" And there came into their midst a lovely maiden, all clothed in brown and gold to match the autumn woodland.

" 'Tis that the king's come home again, sweet Maid Marian!" said Robin. "This worthy abbot brings good news—better news than he supposed. For I love no man in all the world as I love my king!"

"Nor I," said Maid Marian archly, "save only you, Robin Hood, king of the forest!"

The King at the Feast

You may well imagine that King Richard was

amazed at all he heard and saw, and that he eagerly accepted Robin's invitation to feast with them, to see good sport of archery and strong buffeting.

The king played his part as a merry abbot well enough, but he could not help showing unusual strength in buffeting—for Richard was a mighty warrior, as everybody knows, gigantic of stature and great in strength.

"Ha! ha!" cried Maid Marian roguishly, when she saw that the strange abbot had buffeted Robin Hood to his knees. "It gladdens me to see you bow before an abbot!"

Then it was that Richard threw off his abbot's mantle, and stood forth for all to see.

"The king!" exclaimed Robin, falling on one knee —this time without need of buffeting.

"The king!" breathed Maid Marian, and she knelt by Robin's side.

"The king!" shouted all the rest, and bowed themselves.

King Richard was heartily enjoying his jest, and he was thankful enough for the loyalty of bold Robin Hood and his band at a time when his kingdom was rent with quarrels because of Prince John's treach-ery. So he forgave them all and bade them be outlaws no longer. His only condition was that they should leave the forest and the hunting of the king's deer, and serve him faithfully at his court.

"And this maiden, Sir King?" asked Robin Hood, taking Maid Marian's hand. "She has steadily refused to wed me until the king returns."

"The king has come home now!" cried Richard gaily, "and a wedding feast will be to the liking of us all. Afterwards your wife shall grace the court among the best."

Robin Hood Leaves Sherwood Forest

So Sherwood rang no more with the shouts of the merry men, and Robin and Maid Marian were married and lived happily at the court of the king.

But in time bold Robin grew weary of the court. King Richard died, and King John was a bitter enemy. Maid Marian too was dead, and the days weighed heavily on Robin's heart. At last he was

taken so suddenly and violently ill that he knocked at the door of the nunnery of Kirklees, and implored the nuns to bleed him, so that he might recover.

Some say it was the abbess who cut Robin's vein, some say a nun, some say a friar. Whoever it was, instead of binding up the wound, left Robin bleeding, and locked the door on him.

The Last of Bold Robin Hood

Then Robin knew that his last day had come. Weak as he was, he managed to blow a feeble blast on his trusty horn. Little John, lingering near the nunnery where his master lay, just caught the sound, and came rushing to his aid. But it was too late, for Robin Hood was dying.

"I will burn their foul nunnery over their heads!" cried Little John furiously. But Robin shook his head.

"I have never in my whole life hurt a woman," he said, "nor even a man in a woman's company. Should I begin doing such things now?"

Little John's eyes were dim with tears, but Robin smiled at him bravely. Then he told Little John how he must bury him. This, according to the old ballad, is what he said:

Lay me a green sod under my head,
    And another at my feet,
And lay my bent bow at my side,
    Which was my music sweet.

"And where must this grave be made, dear master?" asked Little John.

"Lift me—give me my bow—stretch it for me, and lay the arrow," said Robin, the old smile struggling with his weakness. "Where the arrow falls, there dig my grave."

Then Little John opened the window wide and gently raised his master. The last arrow twanged from Robin's bow.

And exactly where it fell they buried him.

Here underneath this little stone
    Lies Robert Earl of Huntingdon.
Never archer was he so good
    And people called him Robin Hood.
Such outlaws as he and all his men
    Will England never see again.

THE ADVENTURES OF
TOM SAWYER

Aunt Polly

"Tom!"

No answer.

"Tom!"

No answer.

"What's gone with that boy, I wonder? You, Tom!"

The old lady pulled her spectacles down and looked over them, about the room; then she put them up and looked out.

"Well, I lay if I get hold of you, I'll—"

She did not finish, for by this time she was bending down and punching under the bed with the broom—and so she needed breath to punctuate the punches with. She resurrected nothing but the cat.

"I never did see the beat of that boy!"

She went to the open door and stood in it, and looked out among the tomato vines and 'jimpson' weeds that constituted the garden. No Tom. So she lifted up her voice, at an angle calculated for distance, and shouted:

"Y-o-u-u Tom!"

There was a slight noise behind her, and she turned just in time to seize a small boy by the slack of his roundabout and arrest his flight. "There! I migh 'a thought of that closet. What you been doing in there?"

"Nothing."

"Nothing! Look at your hands, and look at your mouth. What is that truck?"

"I don't know, Aunt."

"Well, I know. It's jam, that's what it is. Forty times I've said if you didn't let that jam alone I'd skin you. Hand me that switch."

The switch hovered in the air. The peril was desperate.

"My! Look behind you, Aunt!"

The old lady whirled around and snatched her skirts out of danger, and the lad fled, on the instant, scrambled up the high board fence, and disappeared over it. His Aunt Polly stood surprised a moment, and then broke into a gentle laugh.

"Hang the boy, can't I ever learn anything? Ain't he played me tricks enough, but, he's my own dead sister's boy, poor thing, and I ain't got the heart to lash him somehow. Every time I let him off my conscience does hurt me so; and every time I hit him my old heart 'most breaks. Well-a-well, man that is born of woman is of few days and full of trouble, as the Scripture says, and I reckon it's so. He'll play hookey this evening, and I'll just be obliged to make him work tomorrow, to punish him. It's mighty hard to make him work Saturdays, when all the boys is having a holiday, but he hates work more than he hates anything else, and I've got to do some of my duty by him, or I'll be the ruination of the child."

The Fight

Tom did play hookey, and he had a very good time. He got back home barely in season to help Jim, the small coloured boy, saw next day's wood, and split the kindlings before supper.

The summer evenings were long. It was not dark yet. Presently Tom checked his stride. A stranger was before him; a boy a shade larger than himself. A new-comer of any age or either sex was an impressive curiosity in the poor little village of St. Petersburg. This boy was well dressed, too well dressed on a week-day. The more Tom stared at the splendid marvel, the higher he turned up his nose at his finery, and the shabbier and shabbier his own outfit seemed to him to grow. Neither boy spoke. If one moved the other moved—but only sidewise, in a circle. They kept face to face and eye to eye all the time. Finally, Tom said:

"I can lick you!"

"I'd like to see you try it."

"Well, I can do it."

"No you can't, either."

"Yes I can."

"No you can't."

"I can."

"You can't."

"Can."

"Can't."

Tom drew a line in the dust with his big toe, and said:

"I dare you to step over that, and I'll lick you till you can't stand up. Anybody that'll take a dare will steal a sheep."

The new boy stepped over promptly, and said:

"Now you said you'd do it, now let's see you do it then."

"Don't you crowd me, now; you'd better look out, or else."

"Well, you said you'd do it—why don't you do it? Bet you can't."

"By jingoes, for two cents I will do it."

The new boy took two broad coppers out of his pocket and held them out with derision.

Tom struck them to the ground.

In an instant both boys were rolling and tumbling in the dirt, gripped together like cats; and for the space of a minute they tugged and tore at each other's hair and clothes, punched and scratched each other's noses, and covered themselves with dust and glory. Presently the confusion took form, and through the fog of battle Tom appeared, seated astride the new boy, and pounding him with his fists.

"Hollar 'nuff!" said he.

The boy only struggled to free himself. He was crying, mainly from rage.

"Hollar 'nuff!" and the pounding went on.

At last the stranger got out a smothered "'nuff!" and Tom let him up, and said, "Now that'll learn you. Better look out who you're fooling with next time."

He got home pretty late that night, and when he climbed cautiously in at the window he uncovered an ambuscade in the person of his aunt; and when she saw the state his clothes were in, her resolution to turn his Saturday holiday into captivity at hard labour became adamantine in its firmness.

Tom's Punishment

Saturday morning was come, and all the summer world was bright and fresh, and brimming with life.

Tom appeared on the side-walk with a bucket of white-wash and a long-handled brush. He surveyed the fence, and the gladness went out of nature, and a deep melancholy settled down upon his spirit. Thirty yards of broad fence nine feet high! It seemed to him that life was hollow, and existence but a burden. Sighing, he dipped his brush and passed it along the topmost plank; repeated the operation; did it again; compared the insignificant whitewashed streak with the far-reaching continent of un-whitewashed fence, and sat down on a tree-box discouraged. Jim came skipping out at the gate with a tin pail, and singing Buffalo Gals. Bringing water from the town pump had always been hateful work in Tom's eyes before, but now it did not strike him so.

"Say, Jim; I'll fetch the water if you'll whitewash some."

Jim shook his head, and said:

"Can't, Mar's Tom. Ole missis she tole me I got to go an' git dis water an' not stop foolin' 'roun' wid anybody."

"Oh, never you mind what she said, Jim. That's the way she always talks. Gimme the bucket—I won't be gone only a minute. She won't ever know."

"Oh, I dasn't, Mar's Tom. Ole missis she'd take an' tar de head off'n me. 'Deed she would."

"Jim, I'll give you a marble. I'll give you a white alley!"

Jim began to waver.

"White alley, Jim; and it's a bully tow."

"My; dat's a mighty gay marvel, I tell you. But, Mar's Tom, I's powerful 'fraid ole missis."

But Jim was only human—this attention was too much for him. He put down his pail, took the white alley. In another minute he was flying down the street with his pail and a tingling rear, Tom was whitewashing with vigour, and Aunt Polly was retiring from the field with a slipper in her hand and triumph in her eye.

But Tom's energy did not last. He began to think of the fun he had planned for this day, and his sorrows multiplied. At this dark and hopeless moment an inspiration burst upon him. Nothing less than a great, magnificent inspiration. He took up his brush and went tranquilly to work. Ben Rogers hove in sight presently; the very boy of all boys whose ridicule he had been dreading. Ben's gait was the hop, skip and jump—proof enough that his heart was light and his anticipations high. He was eating an apple, and giving a long melodious whoop at intervals, followed by a deep-toned ding dong dong, ding dong dong, for he was personating a steamboat! As he drew near he slackened speed, took the middle of the street, leaned far over to starboard, and rounded-to ponderously, and with laborious pomp and circumstance, for he was personating the Big Missouri, and considered himself to be drawing deep water. He was boat, and captain, and engine-bells combined, so he had to imagine himself standing on his own hurricane-deck giving the orders and executing them.

"Stop her, sir! Ling-a-ling-ling." The headway ran almost out, and he drew up slowly towards the side-walk. "Ship up to back! Ling-a-ling-ling!" His arms straightened and stiffened down his sides.

"Set her back on the starboard! Ling-a-ling-ling! Chow! ch-chow-wow-chow!" his right hand meantime describing stately circles, for it was representing a forty-foot wheel. "Let her go back on the labboard! Ling-a-ling-ling! Chow-ch-chow-chow!" The left hand began to describe circles.

Tom went on whitewashing—paid no attention to the steamer. Ben stared a moment, and then said:

"Hi-yi! You're up a stump, ain't you!"

No answer. Tom surveyed his last touch with the eye of an artist; then he gave his brush another gentle sweep, and surveyed the result as before. Ben ranged up alongside of him. Tom's mouth watered for the apple, but he stuck to his work. Ben said:

"Hello, old chap; you got to work, hey?"

"Why, it's you, Ben! I warn't noticing."

"Say, I'm going in a swimming, I am. Don't you wish you could? But of course, you'd druther work, wouldn't you? 'Course you would!"

Tom contemplated the boy a bit, and said:

"What do you call work?"

"Why, ain't that work?"

Tom resumed his whitewashing, and answered carelessly:

"Well, maybe it is, and maybe it ain't. All I know is, it suits Tom Sawyer."

"Oh, come now, you don't mean you like it?"

The brush continued to move.

"Like it? Well, I don't see why I oughtn't to like it. Does a boy get a chance to whitewash a fence every day of his life?"

That put the thing in a new light. Ben stopped nibbling his apple. Tom swept his brush daintily back and forth—stepped back to note the effect—added a touch here and there—criticised the effect again, Ben watching every move, and getting more and more interested, more and more absorbed. Presently he said:

"Say, Tom, let me whitewash a little."

Tom considered; was about to consent; but he altered his mind: "No, no; I reckon it wouldn't hardly do, Ben. You see, Aunt Polly's awful particular about this fence—right here on the street, you know—but if it was the back fence I wouldn't mind, and she wouldn't. Yes, she's awful particular about this fence; it's got to be done very careful; I reckon there ain't one boy in a thousand, maybe two thousand, that can do it the way it's got to be done."

"No—is that so? Oh, come now; lemme just try, only just a little. I'd let you, if you was me, Tom."

"Ben, I'd like to, honest injun; but Aunt Polly—well, Jim wanted to do it, but she wouldn't let him. Sid wanted to do it, but she wouldn't let Sid. Now, don't you see how I am fixed? If you was to tackle this fence, and anything was to happen to it—"

"Oh, shucks; I'll be just as careful. Now lemme try. Say—I'll give you the core of my apple."

"Well, here. No, Ben; now don't; I'm afeard—".

"I'll give you all of it!"

Tom gave up the brush with reluctance in his face, but alacrity in his heart. And while the late steamer Big Missouri worked and sweated in the sun, the retired artist sat on a barrel in the shade close by, dangled his legs, munched his apple, and planned the slaughter of more innocents. There was no lack of material; boys happened along every little while; they came to jeer, but remained to whitewash. By the time Ben was fagged out, Tom had traded the next chance to Billy Fisher for a kite in good repair; and when he played out, Johnny Miller bought in for a dead rat and a string to swing it with; and so on, and so on, hour after hour. And when the middle of the afternoon came, from being a poor poverty-stricken boy in the morning, Tom was literally rolling in wealth. He had, besides the things I have mentioned, twelve marbles, part of a jew's harp, a piece of blue bottle-glass to look through, a spool-cannon, a key that wouldn't unlock anything, a fragment of chalk, a glass stopper of a decanter, a tin soldier, a couple of tadpoles, six fire-crackers, a kitten with only one eye, a brass door-knob, a dog collar—but no dog—the handle of a knife, four pieces of orange-peel, and a dilapidated old window-sash. He had had a nice, good, idle time all the while —plenty of company—and the fence had three coats of whitewash on it! If he hadn't run out of whitewash he would have bankrupted every boy in the village.

Tom said to himself that it was not such a hollow world after all. He had discovered a great law of human action, without knowing it, namely, that, in order to make a man or a boy covet a thing, it is only necessary to make the thing difficult to attain.

Tom presented himself before Aunt Polly.

"Mayn't I go and play now, Aunt?"

"What, a'ready? How much have you done?"

"It's all done, Aunt."

"Tom, don't lie to me. I can't bear it."

"I ain't, Aunt; it is all done."

Aunt Polly placed small trust in such evidence. She went out to see for herself; and she would have been content to find twenty per cent of Tom's statement true. When she found the entire fence whitewashed, and not only whitewashed but elaborately coated and recoated, and even a streak added to the ground, her astonishment was almost unspeakable. She said:

"Well, I never! There's no getting around it; you can work when you're a mind to, Tom." And then she diluted the compliment by adding, "But it's powerful seldom you're a mind to, I'm bound to say.

Well, go 'long and play; but mind you get back some time in a week, or I'll tan you."

Tom's New Love

Tom was over the fence and gone. There was a gate, but as a general thing he was too crowded for time to make use of it.

As he was passing by the house where Jeff Thatcher lived, he saw a new girl in the garden—a

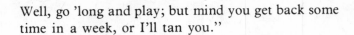

lovely little blue-eyed creature with yellow hair plaited into two long tails, white summer frock, and embroidered pantalettes. The fresh-crowned hero fell without firing a shot. A certain Amy Lawrence vanished out of his heart, and left not even a memory of herself behind. He had thought he loved her to distraction; he had regarded his passion as adoration; and behold it was only a poor little evanescent partiality. He had been months winning her, she had confessed hardly a week ago; he had been the happiest and the proudest boy in the world only seven short days, and here, in one instant of time, she had gone out of his heart like a casual stranger whose visit is done.

He worshipped this new angel with furtive eye, till he saw that she had discovered him; then he pretended he did not know she was present, and began to "show off" in all sorts of absurd boyish ways in order to win her admiration. He kept up this grotesque foolishness for some little time; but by-and-by, while he was in the midst of some dangerous gymnastic performances, he glanced aside, and saw that the little girl was wending to the house. Tom came up to the fence, and leaned on it, grieving, and hoping she would tarry yet a while longer. She halted a moment on the steps, and then moved towards the door. Tom heaved a great sigh as she put her foot on the threshold, but his face lit up, right away, for she tossed a pansy over the fence a moment before she disappeared. The boy ran around and stopped within a short distance of the flower, and then shaded his eyes with his hand, and began to look down the street as if he had discovered something of interest going on in that direction. Presently he picked up a straw and began trying to balance it on his nose, with his head tilted far back; and as he moved from side to side in his efforts he edged nearer and nearer towards the pansy; finally his bare foot rested upon it, his pliant toes closed upon it, and he hopped away with his treasure, and disappeared around the corner. But only for a minute—only while he could button the flower inside his jacket, next his heart, or next his stomach possibly, for he was not much posted in anatomy and not hypercritical anyway.

He wandered far away from the accustomed haunts of boys, and sought desolate places that were in harmony with his spirit. A log raft in the river invited him, and he seated himself on its outer edge, and contemplated the dreary vastness of the stream, wishing the while that he could only be drowned all at once without going through the uncomfortable routine devised by nature. Then he thought of his flower. He got it out rumpled and wilted, and it increased his dismal felicity. He wondered if she would pity him if she knew! Would she cry, and wish that she had a right to put her arms around his neck and comfort him? Or would she turn coldly away like all the hollow world?

This picture brought such an agony of pleasurable suffering that he worked it over and over again in his mind and set it up in varied lights till he wore it threadbare. At last he rose up sighing and departed in the darkness. About half past nine he came along the deserted street to where the adored unknown lived; he paused a moment, no sound fell upon his listening ear; a candle was casting a dull glow upon the curtain of a second-storey window. Was the sacred presence there? He climbed the fence, threaded his stealthy way through the plants, till he stood under that window; he looked up at it long, and with emotion; then he laid him down on the ground under it, disposing himself upon his back, with his hands clasped upon his breast, and holding his poor wilted flower. And thus he would die—out in the cold world with no shelter over his homeless head, no friendly hand to wipe the death-damps from his brow, no loving face to bend pityingly over him when the great agony came. And thus she would see him when she looked out upon the glad morning—and oh, would she drop one tear upon his lifeless form, would she heave one little sigh to see a bright young life so rudely blighted, so untimely cut down?

The window went up; a maid-servant's discordant voice broke the silence, and a deluge of water drenched the prone martyr's remains!

The drowning hero sprang up with a relieving snort; there was a whiz as of a missile in the air, mingled with the murmur of a curse, a sound as of shivering glass followed, and a small vague form went over the fence and shot away in the gloom.

Huckleberry Finn

Monday came and, on his way to school, Tom came upon the juvenile pariah of the village, Huckleberry Finn, son of the town drunkard. Huckleberry was cordially hated and dreaded by all the mothers of the town becausd he was idle, and lawless, and vulgar.

"Hello, Huckleberry!"

"Hello yourself, and see how you like it!"

"What's that you got?"

"Dead cat."

"Lemme see him, Huck. My, he's pretty stiff. Where'd you get him?"

"Bought him off'n a boy."

"What did you give?"

"I give a blue ticket and a bladder that I got at the slaughter house."

"Where'd you get the blue ticket?"

"Bought it off'n Ben Rogers two weeks ago for a hoopstick."

"Say—what is dead cats good for, Huck?"

"Good for? Cure warts with."

"How do you cure 'em with dead cats?"

"Why, you take your cat and go and get in the graveyard, long about midnight, where somebody that was wicked has been buried. When it's midnight a devil will come, or maybe two or three, but you can't see 'em, you can only hear something like the wind, or maybe hear 'em talk; and when they're taking that feller away you heave your cat after 'em and say, 'Devil follow corpse, cat follow devil, warts follow cat. I'm done with ye!' That'll fetch any wart."

"Sounds right. D'you ever try it, Huck?"

"No, but old Mother Hopkins told me."

"Well, I reckon it's so, then, becuz they say she's a witch."

"Say! Why, Tom, I know she is. She witched Pap. Pap says so his own self. He came along one day, and he see she was a witching him, so he took up a rock, and if she hadn't dodged he'd a got her. Well, that very night he rolled off'n a shed wher' he was a layin' drunk, and broke his arm."

"Why that's awful. How did he know she was a witching him?"

"Lord, Pap can tell, easy. Pap says when they keep looking at you right stiddy, they're a witching you, specially if they mumble. Becuz when they mumble they're a saying the Lord's Prayer backwards."

"Say, Hucky, when you going to try the cat?"

"Tonight. I reckon they'll come after old Hoss Williams tonight."

"But they buried him Saturday, Huck. Didn't they get him Saturday night?"

"Why, how you talk! How could their charms work till midnight and then it's Sunday? Devils don't slosh around much of a Sunday, I don't reckon."

"I never thought of that. Lemme go with you?"

"Of course—if you ain't afeard."

"Afeard! 'Tain't likely. Will you meow?"

"Yes, and you meow back if you get a chance. Last time you kep' me a meowing around till old Hays sent to throwing rocks at me, and says, 'Dern that cat!' So I hove a brick through his window—but don't you tell."

"I won't. I couldn't meow that night becuz Auntie was watching me; but I'll meow this time."

School

When Tom reached the little isolated frame school-house, he strode in briskly, with the manner of one who had come with all honest speed. He hung his hat on a peg, and flung himself into his seat with businesslike alacrity. The master, throned on high in his great splint-bottom armchair, was dozing, lulled by the frowsy hum of study. The interruption roused him:

"Thomas Sawyer!"

Tom knew that when his name was pronounced in full, it meant trouble.

"Sir!"

"Come up here. Now, sir, why are you late again, as usual?"

Tom was about to take refuge in a lie, when he saw two long tails of yellow hair hanging down a back that he recognised by the electric sympathy of love; and by that form was the only vacant place on the girl's side of the school-house. He instantly said:

"I STOPPED TO TALK WITH HUCKLEBERRY FINN!"

The master's pulse stood still, and he stared helplessly. The buzz of study ceased; the pupils wondered if this fool-hardy boy had lost his mind. The master said:

"You—you did what?"

"Stopped to talk with Huckleberry Finn."

There was no mistaking the words.

"Thomas Sawyer, this is the most astounding confession I have ever listened to; no mere ferule will answer for this offence. Take off your jacket."

The master's arm performed until it was tired, and the stock of switches notably diminished. Then the order followed:

"Now, sir, go and sit with the girls! And let this be a warning to you."

The titter that rippled around the room appeared to abash the boy, but in reality that result was caused rather more by his worshipful awe of his unknown idol and the dread pleasure that lay in his high good fortune. He sat down upon the end of the pine bench, and the girl hitched herself away from him with a toss of the head. Nudges, winks and whispers traversed the room, but Tom sat still, with his arms upon the long, low desk before him, and seemed to study his book. By and by attention ceased from him, and the accustomed school murmur rose upon the dull air once more.

Becky Thatcher

Presently the boy began to steal furtive glances at the girl. She observed it, 'made a mouth' at him, and gave him the back of her head for the space of a minute. When she cautiously faced around again, a peach lay before her. She thrust it away; Tom gently put it back; she thrust it away again, but with less animosity. Tom scrawled on his slate, 'Please take it —I got more.' The girl glanced at the words, but made no sign. Now the boy began to draw something on the slate, hiding his work with his left hand. For a time the girl refused to notice; but her human curiosity presently began to manifest itself by hardly perceptible signs. The boy worked on, apparently unconscious. The girl made a sort of non-committal attempt to see, but the boy did not betray that he was aware of it. At last she gave in, and hesitatingly whispered:

"Let me see it."

Tom partly uncovered a dismal caricature of a house with two gable ends to it and a cork-screw of

smoke issuing from the chimney. Then the girl's interest began to fasten itself upon the work, and she forgot everything else. When it was finished, she gazed a moment, then she whispered:

"It's nice—make a man."

The artist erected a man in the front yard, that resembled a derrick. He could have stepped over the house; but the girl was not hypercritical; she was satisfied with the monster, and whispered:

"It's a beautiful man—now make me coming along."

Tom drew an hourglass, with a full moon and straw limbs to it, and armed the spreading fingers with a portentous fan. The girl said:

"It's ever so nice—I wish I could draw."

"It's easy," whispered Tom. "I'll learn you."

"Oh, will you? When?"

"At noon. Do you go home to dinner?"

"I'll stay if you will."

"Good—that's a go."

"What's your name?"

"Becky Thatcher."

"What's yours? Oh, I know. It's Thomas Sawyer."

"That's the name they lick me by. I'm Tom when I'm good. You call me Tom, will you?"

"Yes."

Now Tom began to scrawl something on the slate, hiding the words from the girl. But she was not backward this time. She begged to see. Tom said:

"Oh, it ain't anything."

"Yes it is."

"No it ain't; you don't want to see."

"Yes I do, indeed I do. Please let me."

"You'll tell."

"No I won't—deed and deed and double deed I won't."

"You won't tell anybody at all? Ever as long as you live?"

"No, I won't ever tell anybody. Now let me."

"Oh, you don't want to see!"

"Now that you treat me so I will see, Tom"—and she put her small hand on his, and a little scuffle ensued. Tom pretending to resist in earnest, but letting his hand slip by degrees till these words were revealed: 'I love you.'

"Oh you bad thing!" And she hit his hand a smart rap, but reddened and looked pleased nevertheless.

Just at this juncture the boy felt a slow fateful grip closing on his ear, and a steady lifting impulse. In that vice he was borne across the house and

deposited in his own seat, under a peppering fire of giggles from the whole school. Then the master stood over him during a few awful moments, and finally moved away to his throne without saying a word. But although Tom's ear tingled, his heart was jubilant.

As the school quieted down, Tom made an honest effort to study, but the turmoil within him was too great. In turn he took his place in the reading class

and made a botch of it, then in the geography class and turned lakes into mountains, mountains into rivers, and rivers into continents, till chaos was come again; then in the spelling class, and got 'turned down' by a succession of mere baby words till he brought up at the foot and yielded up the pewter medal which he had worn with ostentation for months.

When school broke up at noon, Tom flew to Becky Thatcher, and whispered in her ear.

"Put on your bonnet and let on you're going home; and when you get to the corner, give the rest of 'em the slip, and turn down through the lane and come back. I'll go the other way, and come it over 'em the same way."

Secret Meeting

So the one went off with one group of scholars, and the other with another. In a little while the two met at the bottom of the lane, and when they reached the school they had it all to themselves. Then they sat together, with a slate before them, and Tom gave Becky the pencil and held her hand in his, guiding it, and so created another surprising house. When the interest in art began to wane, the two fell to talking. Tom was swimming in bliss. He said:

"Do you love rats?"

"No, I hate them!"

"Well, I do too—live ones. But I mean dead ones, to swing around your head with a string."

"No, I don't care for rats much, anyway. What I like is chewing gum!"

"Oh, I should say so! I wish I had some now!"

"Do you? I've got some. I'll let you chew it awhile, but you must give it back to me."

That was agreeable, so they chewed it turn about, and dangled their legs against the bench in excess of contentment.

"Was you ever at a circus?" said Tom.

"Yes, and my pa's going to take me again sometime, if I'm good."

"I been to the circus three or four times—lots of times. Church ain't shucks to a circus. There's things going on at a circus all the time. I'm going to be a clown in a circus when I grow up."

"Oh, are you? That will be nice. They're so lovely all spotted up."

"Yes, that's so. And they get slathers of money—most a dollar a day, Ben Rogers says. Say, Becky, was you ever engaged?"

"What's that?"

"Why, engaged to be married."

"No."

"Would you like to?"

"I reckon so. I don't know. What is it like?"

"Like? Why it ain't like anything. You only just tell a boy you won't ever have anybody but him, ever, ever, ever, and then you kiss, and that's all. Anybody can do it."

"Kiss? What do you kiss for?"

"Why that, you know, is to—well, they always do that."

"Everybody?"

"Why, yes, everybody that's in love with each other. Do you remember what I wrote on the slate?"

"Ye—yes."

"What was it?"

"I shan't tell you."

"Shall I tell you?"

"Ye—yes—but some other time."

"No, now."

"No not now—tomorrow."

"Oh, no, now, please, Becky. I'll whisper it, I'll whisper it ever so easy."

Becky hesitating, Tom took silence for consent, and passed his arm about her waist and whispered the tale ever so softly, and with his mouth close to her ear, he added:

"Now you whisper it to me—just the same."

She resisted for a while, and then said:

"You turn your face away, so you can't see, and then I will. But you mustn't ever tell anybody—will you, Tom? Now you won't—will you?"

"No, indeed, indeed I won't. Now, Becky."

He turned his face away. She bent timidly around till her breath stirred his hair, and whispered, "I love you!"

Then she sprang away and ran around and around the desks and benches with Tom after her, and took refuge in a corner at last, with her little white apron to her face. Tom clasped her about her neck and pleaded.

"Now, Becky, it's all over—all over but the kiss. Don't you be afraid of that—it ain't anything at all. Please, Becky."

And he tugged at the apron and the hands.

By-and-by she gave up and let her hands drop; her face, all glowing with the struggle, came up and submitted. Tom kissed the red lips and said:

"Now it's all done, Becky. And always after this, you know, you ain't never to love anybody but me, and you ain't ever to marry anybody but me, never, never and for ever. Will you?"

"No, I'll never love anybody but you, Tom, and I'll never marry anybody but you, and you ain't to ever marry anybody but me, either."

"Certainly. Of course. That's part of it. And always, coming to school, or when we're going home, you're to walk with me, when there ain't anybody looking—and you choose me and I choose you at parties, because that's the way you do when you're engaged."

"It's so nice. I never heard of it before."

"Oh, it's ever so jolly! Why me and Amy Lawrence——"

The big eyes told Tom his blunder, and he stopped, confused.

"Oh, Tom! Then I ain't the first you've ever been engaged to!"

The child began to cry. Tom said:

"Oh, don't cry, Becky. I don't care for her any more."

"Yes you do, Tom—you know you do."

Tom tried to put his arm around her neck, but she pushed him away and turned her face to the wall, and went on crying. Tom tried again, with soothing words in his mouth, and was repulsed again. Then his pride was up, and he strode away and went outside. He stood about, restless and uneasy, for a while, glancing at the door every now and then, hoping she would repent and come to find him. But she did not. Then he began to feel badly, and fear that he was in the wrong. It was a hard struggle with him to make new advances now, but he nerved himself to it and entered. She was still standing back there in the corner, sobbing with her face to the wall. Tom's heart smote him. He went to her and stood for a moment, not knowing exactly what to say. Then he said, hesitatingly:

"Becky, I—I don't care for anybody but you."

No reply—but sobs.

"Becky," pleadingly, "Becky, won't you say something?"

More sobs.

Tom got out his chiefest jewel, a brass knob from the top of an endiron, and passed it around her so that she could see it, and said:

"Please, Becky, won't you take it?"

She struck it to the floor. Then Tom marched out of the house and over the hills and far away, to return to school no more that day. Presently Becky began to suspect. She ran to the door; he was not there. Then she called:

"Tom! Come back, Tom!"

She listened intently, but there was no answer. She had no companions but silence and loneliness. So she sat down to cry again and upbraid herself. By this time the scholars began to gather again, and she had to hide her grief and still her broken heart, and take up the cross of a long dreary aching afternoon with none among the strangers about her to exchange sorrows with.

The Graveyard

At half past nine that night, Tom and Sid, his brother, were sent to bed as usual. They said their prayers, and Sid was soon asleep. Tom lay awake and waited in restless impatience. The raising of a neighbouring window disturbed him. A cry of 'Scat! you devil!' and the crash of an empty bottle against the back of his aunt's wood-shed brought him wide awake, and a single minute later he was dressed and out of the window and creeping along the roof of the 'ell' on all fours. He 'meow'd' with caution once or twice as he went; then jumped to the roof of the wood-shed, and thence to the ground. Huckleberry Finn was there, with his dead cat. The boys moved off and disappeared in the gloom. At the end of half an hour they were wading through the tall grass of the graveyard.

A faint wind moaned through the trees, and Tom feared it might be the spirits of the dead complaining at being disturbed. The boys talked little, and only under their breath, for the time and the place and the pervading solemnity and silence oppressed their spirits. They found the sharp new heap they were seeking, and ensconced themselves within the protection of three great elms that grew in a bunch near to the grave.

Then they waited in silence for what seemed a long time. The hooting of a distant owl was all the sound that troubled the dead stillness. Tom's reflection grew oppressive. He must force some talk. So he said in a whisper:

"Hucky, do you believe the dead people like it for us to be here?"

Huckleberry whispered:

"I wisht I knowed. It's awful solemn like, ain't it?"

"I bet it is."

There was a considerable pause, while the boys canvassed this matter inwardly. Then Tom whispered:

"Say, Hucky—do you reckon Hoss Williams hears us talking?"

"O' course he does. Least his spirit does."

Tom, after a pause:

"I wish I'd said Mister Williams. But I never meant any harm. Everybody calls him Hoss."

"A body can't be too particular how they talk 'bout these yer dead people, Tom."

This was a damper, and conversation died again. Presently Tom seized his comrade's arm and said:

"Sh!"

"What is it, Tom?" And the two clung together with beating hearts.

"Sh! There 'tis again! Didn't you hear it?"

"I—"

"There! Now you hear it!"

"Lord, Tom, they're coming! They're coming, sure. What'll we do?"

"I dono. Think they'll see us?"

"Oh, Tom, they can see in the dark same as cats. I wish I hadn't come!"

"Oh, don't be afeard. I don't believe they'll bother us. We ain't doing any harm. If we keep perfectly still, maybe they won't notice us at all."

"I'll try to, Tom, but Lord, I'm all of a shiver."

"Listen!"

The boys bent their heads together and scarcely breathed. A muffled sound of voices floated up from the far end of the graveyard.

"Look! see there!" whispered Tom. "What is it?"

"It's devil-fire. Oh, Tom, this is awful."

Some vague figures approached through the gloom, swinging an old-fashioned tin lantern that freckled the ground with innumerable little spangles of light. Presently Huckleberry whispered with a shudder:

"It's the devils, sure enough. Three of 'em! Lordy, Tom, we're goners! Can you pray?"

"I'll try, but don't you be afeard. They ain't going to hurt us. 'Now I lay me down to sleep, I—'"

"Sh!"

"What is it, Huck?"

"They're humans! One of 'em is, anyway. One of 'em is old Muff Potter's voice."

"No—'tain't so, is it?"

"I bet I know it. Don't you stir nor budge. He ain't sharp enough to notice us."

"All right, I'll keep still. Now they're stuck. Can't find it. Here they come again. Now they're hot. Cold again. Hot again. Red-hot! They're pinted right, this time. Say, Huck, I know another o' them's voices; it's Injun Joe."

"That's so—that murderin' half-breed! I'd ruther they was devils a dern sight. What kin they be up to Tom?"

The whispers died wholly out now, for the three men had reached the grave, and stood a short distance from the boys' hiding-place.

The Grave Robbers

"Here it is," said the third voice; and the owner of it held the lantern up and revealed the face of young Dr Robinson.

Potter and Injun Joe were carrying a hand-barrow with a rope and a couple of shovels on it. They cast down their load and began to open the grave. The doctor put the lantern at the head of the grave, and came and sat down with his back against one of the elm-trees. He was so close the boys could have touched him.

"Hurry, men!" he said in a low voice. "The moon might come out at any moment!"

For some time there was no noise but the grating sound of the spades discharging their freight of mould and gravel. It was very monotonous. Finally

a spade struck upon the coffin with a dull, woody
accent, and within another minute or two the men
had hoisted it out on the ground. They prised off the
lid with their shovels, got out the body and dumped
it rudely on the ground. The moon drifted from
behind the clouds and exposed the pallid face. The
barrow was got ready and the corpse placed on it,

covered with a blanket, and bound to its place with the rope. Potter took out a large spring-knife and cut off the dangling end of the rope, and then said:

"Now the cussed thing's ready, Sawbones, and you'll just out with another five, or here she stays."

"That's the talk!" said Injun Joe.

"Look here; what does this mean?" said the doctor. "You required your pay in advance and I've paid you."

"Yes, and you done more than that," said Injun Joe, approaching the doctor, who was now standing. "Five years ago you drove me away from your father's kitchen one night when I come to ask for something to eat, and you said I warn't there for any good; and when I swore I'd get even with you if it

took a hundred years, your father had me jailed for a vagrant. Did you think I'd forget? The Injun blood ain't in me for nothing. And now I've got you, and you got to settle you know!"

He was threatening the doctor with his fist in his face by this time. The doctor struck out suddenly, and stretched the ruffian on the ground. Potter dropped his knife, and exclaimed:

"Here, now, don't you strike my pard!" and the next moment he had grappled with the doctor, and the two were struggling with might and main, trampling the grass, and tearing the ground with their heels. Injun Joe sprang to his feet, his eyes flaming with passion, snatched up Potter's knife, and went creeping, catlike, and stooping round and round about the combatants, seeking an opportunity. Just as the doctor knocked Potter unconscious with a heavy blow, Injun Joe drove that knife to the hilt in the young man's breast. He reeled and fell partly upon Potter, flooding him with his blood, and in the same moment the clouds blotted out the dreadful spectacle, and the two frightened boys went speeding away in the dark.

Presently when the moon emerged again Injun Joe

was standing over the two forms, contemplating them. The doctor murmured and gave a long gasp or two, and was still. The half-breed muttered:

"That score is settled, damn you."

Then he robbed the body. After which he put the fatal knife in Potter's open right hand, and sat down on the dismantled coffin. Three—four—five minutes passed, and then Potter began to stir and moan. His hand closed upon the knife, he raised it, glanced at it, and let it fall with a shudder. Then he sat up, pushing the body from him, and gazed at it and then around him confusedly. His eyes met Joe's.

"Lord, how is this, Joe?" he said.

"It's a dirty business," said Joe, without moving. "What did you do it for?"

"I! I never done it!"

"Look here! That kind of talk won't wash."

Potter trembled and grew white. "I thought I'd got sober. I'd no business to drink tonight. But it's in my head yet—worsen' when we started here. I'm all in a muddle; can't recollect anything of it hardly. Tell me, Joe—honest now, old feller—did I do it, Joe? I never meant to; 'pon my soul and honour I never meant to, Joe."

Two or three minutes later the murdered man, the blanketed corpse, the lidless coffin, and the open grave, were under no inspection but the moon's. The stillness was complete again, too.

Witness to Murder

The two boys flew on and on towards the village, speechless with horror. They glanced backward and from time to time as if they feared they might be followed.

"If we can only get to the old tannery before we break down!" whispered Tom, in short catches between breaths. "I can't stand it much longer."

Huckleberry's hard pantings were his only reply, and the boys fixed their eyes on the goal of their hopes, and bent to their work to win it. They gained steadily on it, and at last, breast to breast, they burst in through the open door, and fell, grateful and exhausted, in the sheltering shadows beyond. By and by their pulses slowed down, and Tom whispered:

"Huck, what do you reckon'll come of this?"

"If Dr Robinson dies, I reckon hangin'll come of it."

"Do you, though?"

"Why, I know it, Tom."

Tom thought awhile; then he said:

"Who'll tell? We?"

"What are you talking about? S'pose something happened and Injun Joe didn't hang, why he'd kill us some time or other, just as dead sure as we're a lying here."

"That's just what I was thinking to myself, Huck!"

"If anybody tells, let Muff Potter do it, if he's fool enough. He's generally drunk enough."

Tom said nothing—went on thinking. Presently he whispered:

"Huck, Muff Potter don't know it. How can he tell?"

"What's the reason he don't know it?"

"Because he'd just got that whack when Injun Joe done it. D'you reckon he could see anything? D'you reckon he knowed anything?"

"By hokey, that's so, Tom!"

"And besides, look-a-here—maybe that whack done for him!"

"No, 'tain't likely, Tom. He had liquor in him; I could see that; and besides, he always has. Well, when Pap's full, you might take and belt him over the head with a church and you couldn't phase him. He says so his own self. So it's the same with Muff Potter, of course. But if a man was dead sober, I reckon, maybe that whack might fetch him; I dono."

After another reflective silence, Tom said:

"Hucky, you sure you can keep mum?"

"Tom, we got to keep mum. You know that. That Injun devil wouldn't make any more of drownding us than a couple of cats, if we was to squeak 'bout this and they didn't hang him. Now look-a-here, Tom, less take and swear to one another—that's what we got to do—swear to keep mum."

"Yes, I reckon that's so."

They continued to whisper for some little time. Presently a dog set up a long, low howl just outside—fairly near to them. The boys clasped each other suddenly, in an agony of fright. Then Tom, looking through a crack, exclaimed:

"Oh, Huck, it's a stray dog!"

"Quick, Tom, quick! Who does he mean?"

"Huck, he must mean us both—we're right together."

Tom choked off and whispered:

"Look, Hucky, look! He's got his back to us!"

Hucky looked with joy in his heart.

"Well, he has, by jingoes! Did he before?"

"Yes, he did. But I, like a fool, never thought. Oh, this is bully, you know. Now, who can he mean?"

The howling stopped. Tom pricked up his ears.

"Sh! What's that?" he whispered.

"Sounds like—like hogs grunting. No—it's somebody snoring, Tom."

"That is it? Where'bouts is it, Huck?"

"I b'leeve it's down at t'other end. Sounds so, anyway."

"Hucky, do you das't go if I lead?"

"I don't like to, much, Tom. S'pose it's Injun Joe!"

Tom quailed. But presently the temptation rose up strong and the boys agreed to try, with the understanding that they would take to their heels if the snoring stopped. So they went tip-toeing stealthily down, the one behind the other. When they had got to within five steps of the snorer, Tom stepped on a stick, and it broke with a sharp snap. The man moaned, writhed a little, and his face came into the moonlight. It was Muff Potter. The boys' hearts had stood still, and their bodies too, when the man moved, but their fears passed away now. They tiptoed out, through the broken weather boarding, and stopped at a little distance to exchange a parting word. That long, lugubrious howl rose on the night air again! They turned and saw the strange dog standing close to where Potter was lying, and facing Potter with his nose pointing heaven-ward. Then they separated.

When Tom crept in at his bedroom window, the night was almost spent. He undressed with excessive caution, and fell asleep congratulating himself that nobody knew of his escapade.

Muff Potter Accused

Close upon the hour of noon the whole village was suddenly electrified with the ghastly news. A gory knife had been found close to the murdered man, and it had been recognised by somebody as belonging to Muff Potter—so the story ran. And it was said that a belated citizen had come upon Potter washing himself in the 'branch' about one or two o'clock in the morning, and that Potter had at once sneaked off – suspicious circumstances, especially the washing, which was not a habit with Potter. It was also said

that the town had been ransacked for this 'murderer' (the public are not slow in the matter of sifting evidence and arriving at a verdict), but that he could not be found. Horsemen had departed down all the roads in every direction, and the Sheriff was confident that he would be captured before night.

All the town was drifting towards the graveyard. Tom joined the procession, not because he would not a thousand times rather go anywhere else, but because an awful fascination drew him on. Arrived at the dreadful place, he wormed his small body through the crowd and saw the dismal spectacle. It seemed to him an age since he was there before. Somebody pinched his arm. He turned, and his eyes met Huckleberry's. Then both looked elsewhere at once, and wondered if anybody had noticed anything in their mutual glance. But everybody was talking, and intent upon the grisly spectacle before them.

"Poor fellow!" "Poor young fellow!" "This ought to be a lesson to grave-robbers!" "Muff Potter'll hang for this if they catch him!" This was the drift of remark, and the minister said, "It was a judgement; His hand is here."

Now Tom shivered from head to heel; for his eye fell upon the stolid face of Injun Joe. At this moment the crowd began to sway and struggle, and voices shouted, 'It's him! It's him! He's coming himself!'

"Who? Who?" from twenty voices.

"Muff Potter!"

"Hallo, he's stopped! Look out, he's turning! Don't let him get away!"

People in the branches of the trees over Tom's head said he wasn't trying to get away—he only looked doubtful and perplexed.

"Infernal impudence!" said a bystander; "wanted to come and take a quiet look at his work—didn't expect any company."

The crowd fell apart now, and the Sheriff came through ostentatiously, leading Potter by the arm. The poor fellow's face was haggard, and his eyes showed the fear that was upon him. When he stood before the murdered man, he shook as with a palsy, and he put his face in his hands and burst into tears.

"I didn't do it, friends," he sobbed; "'pon my word and honour I never done it."

"Who's accused you?" shouted a voice.

This shot seemed to carry home. Potter lifted his face and looked around him with a pathetic hopelessness in his eyes. He saw Injun Joe, and exclaimed:

"Oh, Injun Joe, you promised me you'd never——"

"Is that your knife?" and it was thrust before him by the Sheriff.

Potter would have fallen if they had not caught him and eased him to the ground. Then he said:

"Something told me 't if I didn't come back and get——" He shuddered; then waved his nerveless hand with a vanquished gesture and said, "Tell 'em, Joe, tell 'em——it ain't no use any more."

Then Huckleberry and Tom stood dumb and staring, and heard the stony-hearted liar reel off his serene statement. They expecting every moment that the clear sky would deliver God's lightnings upon his head, and wondering to see how long the stroke was delayed. And when he had finished and still stood alive and whole, their wavering impulse to break their oath and save the poor betrayed prisoner's life faded and vanished away, for plainly this miscreant had sold himself to Satan, and it would be fatal to meddle with the property of such a power as that.

"Why didn't you leave? What did you want to come here for?" somebody said.

"I couldn't help it—I couldn't help it," Potter moaned. "I wanted to run away, but I couldn't seem to come anywhere but here." And he fell to sobbing again.

Injun Joe repeated his statement, a few minutes afterwards on the inquest, under oath, and helped to raise the body of the murdered man, and put it in a wagon for removal; and it was whispered through the shuddering crowd that the wound bled a little! The boys thought that this happy circumstance would turn suspicion in the right direction, but they were disappointed, for more than one villager remarked:

"It was very close to Muff Potter when it done it."

Tom's Conscience

Tom's fearful secret and gnawing conscience disturbed his sleep for as much as a week after this; and at breakfast one morning Sid said:

"Tom, you pitch around and talk in your sleep so much that you keep me awake about half the time."

Tom blanched and dropped his eyes.

"It's a bad sign," said Aunt Polly, gravely. "What you got on your mind, Tom?"

"Nothing. Nothing 't I know of." But the boy's hand shook so that he spilled his coffee.

"And you do talk such stuff," Sid said. "Last night you said, 'It's blood, it's blood, that's what it is!' You said that over and over. And you said, 'Don't torment me so—I'll tell.' Tell what?"

Everything was swimming before Tom. There is no telling what might have happened now, but luckily the concern passed out of Aunt Polly's face, and she came to Tom's relief without knowing it. She said:

"Sho! It's that dreadful murder. I dream about it most every night myself. Sometimes I dream it's me that done it."

Tom's sister, Mary, said she had been affected much the same way. Sid seemed satisfied. Tom got out of their presence as quickly as he plausibly could, and after that he complained of toothache for a week, and tied up his jaws every night. He never knew that Sid lay nightly watching, and frequently slipped the bandage free, and then leaned on his elbow listening a good while at a time, and afterwards slipped the bandage back in its place again. Tom's distress of mind wore off gradually, and the toothache grew irksome and was discarded. If Sid really managed to make anything out of Tom's mutterings, he kept it to himself. It seemed to Tom that his schoolmates never would get done holding inquests on dead cats, and thus keeping his trouble present to his mind. Sid noticed that Tom never was coroner at one of these inquiries, though it had been his habit to take the lead in all new enterprises; he noticed, too, that Tom never acted as a witness—and that was strange; and Sid did not overlook the fact that Tom even showed a marked aversion to these inquests, and always avoided them when he could. Sid marvelled, but said nothing. However, even inquests went out of vogue at last, and ceased to torture Tom's conscience.

Every day or two during this time of sorrow, Tom watched his opportunity and went to the little grated jail window and smuggled such small comforts through to the 'murderer' as he could get hold of. The jail was a trifling little brick den that stood in a marsh at the edge of the village, and no guards were afforded for it; indeed, it was seldom occupied. These offerings greatly helped to ease Tom's conscience. The villagers had a strong desire to tar and feather Injun Joe and ride him on a rail for body-snatching, but so formidable was his character that nobody could be found who was willing to take the lead in the matter, so it was dropped. He had been careful to begin both of his inquest statements with the fight, without confessing the grave-robbery that preceded it; therefore it was deemed wisest not to try the case in the courts at present.

Running Away from Home

One morning Tom awoke and wondered where he was. He sat up, rubbed his eyes and looked around; then he comprehended. It was the cool grey dawn, and there was a delicious sense of repose and peace in the deep pervading calm and silence of the woods. For he, Joe Harper and Huck had decided to run away from home and become pirates on Jackson Island.

Tom stirred up the others and they all clattered away with a shout, and in a minute or two were stripped and chasing after and tumbling over each other in the shallow limpid water of the white sandbar. They felt no longing for the little village sleeping in the distance beyond the majestic waste of water. A vagrant current or a slight rise in the river had carried off their raft, but this only gratified them, since its going was something like burning the bridge between them and civilization.

They found plenty of things to be delighted with, but nothing to be astonished at. They discovered that the island was about three miles long and a quarter of a mile wide, and that the shore it lay closest to was only separated from it by a narrow channel. They took a swim about every hour, so it was close upon the middle of the afternoon when they got back to camp. They were too hungry to stop to fish, but they fared sumptuously upon cold ham, brought from home, and then threw themselves down in the shade to talk. But the talk soon began to drag, and then died. The stillness, the solemnity, that brooded in the woods, and the sense of loneliness, began to tell upon the spirits of the boys. They fell to thinking. A sort of undefined longing crept upon them. This took dim shape presently—it was budding homesickness. Even Finn the Red-handed (his new pirate name) was dreaming of his door-steps and empty hogsheads. But they were all ashamed of their weakness, and none was brave enough to speak his thought.

For some time now, the boys had been dully conscious of a peculiar sound in the distance, just as one sometimes is of the ticking of a clock which he takes no distinct note of. But now this mysterious sound became more pronounced, and forced a recognition. The boys started, glanced at each other, and then each assumed a listening attitude. There was a long silence, profound and unbroken; then a deep, sullen boom came floating down out of the distance.

"What is it?" exclaimed Joe, under his breath.

"I wonder," said Tom in a whisper.

"Tain't thunder," said Huckleberry, in an awed tone, "becuz thunder——"

"Hark!" said Tom; "listen—don't talk."

They waited a time that seemed an age, and then the same muffled boom troubled the solemn hush.

"Let's go and see."

They sprang to their feet and hurried to the shore towards the town. They parted the bushes on the bank and peered out over the water. The little steam ferry-boat was about a mile below the village, drifting with the current. Her broad deck seemed crowded with people. There were a great many skiffs rowing about or floating with the stream in the neighbourhood of the ferry-boat, but the boys could not determine what the men in them were doing. Presently a great jet of white smoke burst from the ferry-boat's side, and as it expanded and rose in a lazy cloud, that same dull throb of sound was borne to the listeners again.

"I know now!" exclaimed Tom; "somebody's drownded!"

"That's it," said Huck; "they done that last summer when Bill Turner got drownded; they shoot a cannon over the water, and that makes him come up to the top."

"By jingo, I wish I was over there now," said Joe.

"I do too," said Huck. "I'd give heaps to know who it is."

The boys still listened and watched. Presently a revealing thought flashed through Tom's mind, and he exclaimed:

"Boys, I know who's drownded: it's us!"

They felt like heroes in an instant. Here was a gorgeous triumph; they were missed; they were mourned; hearts were breaking on their account; tears were being shed; accusing memories of unkindness to these poor lost lads were rising up, and unavailing regrets and remorse were being indulged. Best of all, the departed were the talk of the whole town, and the envy of all the boys, as far as this dazzling notoriety was concerned. This was fine. It was worth while to be a pirate, after all.

As twilight drew on, the ferry-boat went back to her accustomed business and the skiffs disappeared. The pirates returned to camp. They caught fish, cooked supper, and ate it, and then fell to guessing at what the village was thinking and saying about them.

As the night deepened, Huck began to nod, and presently to snore; Joe followed next. Tom lay upon his elbow motionless for some time, watching the two intently. At last he got up cautiously on his knees, and went searching among the grass and the flickering reflections flung by the camp-fire. He picked up and inspected several large semi-cylinders of the thin white bark of a sycamore and finally chose two which seemed to suit him. Then he knelt by the fire and painfully wrote something upon each of these with his 'red keel'; one he rolled up and put in his jacket-pocket, and the other he put in Joe's hat and removed it to a little distance from the owner. And he also put into the hat certain schoolboy treasures of almost inestimable value, among them a lump of chalk, an india-rubber ball, three fish hooks, and one of that kind of marbles known as a 'sure 'nough crystal'. Then he tip-toed his way cautiously among the trees till he felt that he was out of hearing, and straightaway broke into a keen run in the direction of the sand-bar.

Tom's Escapade

A few minutes later Tom was in the shoal water of the bar, wading towards the Illinois shore. Before the depth reached his middle he was half-way over: the current would permit no more wading now, so he struck out confidently to swim the remaining distance. He reached the shore finally, and drifted along till he found a low place and drew himself out. He put his hand on his jacket pocket, found his piece of bark safe, and then struck through the woods, following the shore with streaming garments. Shortly before ten o'clock he came out into an open place opposite the village, and saw the ferry-boat lying in the shadow of the trees and the high bank. Everything was quiet under the blinking stars. He crept down the bank, watching with all his eyes, slipped into the water, swam three or four strokes, and climbed into the skiff that did 'yawl' duty at the boat's stern. He laid himself down under the thwarts and waited, panting. Presently the cracked bell tapped, and a voice gave the order to 'cast off'. A minute or two later the skiff's head was standing high up against the boat's swell, and the voyage was begun. Tom felt happy in his success, for he knew it was the boat's last trip for the night. At the end of a long twelve or fifteen minutes the wheels stopped, and Tom slipped overboard and swam ashore in the dusk, landing a short distance down stream, out of danger of possible stragglers. He flew along unfrequented alleys, and shortly found himself at his aunt's back fence. He climbed over, approached the 'ell' and looked in at the sitting room window, for a light was burning there. There sat Aunt Polly, Sid and Mary and Joe Harper's mother, grouped together, talking. They were by the bed, and the bed was between them and the door. Tom went to the door and began to softly lift the latch; then he pressed gently and the door yielded a crack; he continued pushing cautiously, and quaking every time it creaked, till he judged he might squeeze through on his knees; and so he put his head through and began, warily.

"What makes the candle blow so?" said Aunt Polly. Tom hurried up. "Why, that door's open, I

believe. Why, of course it is. No end of strange things now. Go along and shut it, Sid."

Tom disappeared under the bed just in time. He lay and 'breathed' himself for a time, and then crept to where he could almost touch his aunt's foot as she resumed her conversation.

"But as I was saying," said Aunt Polly, "he warn't bad, so to say—only mischeevous. Only just giddy, and harum-scarum, you know. He warn't any more responsible than a colt. He never meant any harm, and he was the best-hearted boy that ever was"—and she began to cry.

"It was just so with my Joe—always full of his devilment, and up to every kind of mischief, but he was just as unselfish and kind as he could be—and, laws bless me, to think I went and whipped him for taking that cream, never once recollecting that I throwed it out myself because it was sour, and I never to see him again in this world, never, never, never, poor abused boy!" Mrs Harper sobbed as if her heart would break.

Tom stayed listening until Mrs Harper gave a sobbing good night and turned to go. Then with a mutual impulse the two bereaved women flung themselves into each other's arms and had a good consoling cry, and then parted. Aunt Polly was tender far beyond her wont in her good night to Sid and Mary. Sid snuffled a bit, and Mary went off crying with all her heart.

Aunt Polly knelt down and prayed for Tom so touchingly, so appealingly, and with such measureless love in her words and her old trembling voice, that he was weltering in tears again long before she was through.

He had to keep still long after she went to bed, for she kept making broken-hearted ejaculations from time to time, tossing unrestfully, and turning over. But at last she was still, only moaning a little in her sleep. Now the boy stole out, rose gradually by the bedside, shaded the candle-light with his hand, and stood regarding her. His heart was full of pity for her. He took out his sycamore scroll and placed it by the candle. But something occurred to him, and he lingered considering. His face lighted with a happy solution of his thought; he put the bark hastily in his pocket, then he bent over and kissed the faded lips, and straightway made his stealthy exit, latching the door behind him.

He threaded his way back to the ferry landing, untied the skiff at the stern, slipped into it, and was soon rowing up-stream. When he had pulled a mile above the village, he started across and bent himself stoutly to his work. He hit the landing on the other side neatly, for this was a familiar bit of work to him. He was moved to capture the skiff, arguing that it might be considered a ship and therefore legit-imate prey for a pirate; but he knew a thorough search would be made for it, and that might end in revelations. So he stepped ashore and entered the wood. He sat down and took a long rest, torturing himself meantime to keep awake, and then started wearily down the home stretch. The night was far

spent. It was broad daylight before he found himself fairly abreast the island bar. He rested again until the sun was well up and gilding the great river with its splendour, and then he plunged into the stream. A little later he paused, dripping, upon the threshold of the camp, and heard Joe say:

"No, Tom's true-blue, Huck, and he'll come back. He won't desert. He knows that would be a disgrace to a pirate, and Tom's too proud for that sort of thing. He's up to something or other. Now, I wonder what?"

"Well, the things is ours anyway, ain't they?"

"Pretty near, but not yet, Huck. The writing says they are if he ain't back to breakfast."

"Which he is!" exclaimed Tom, with fine dramatic effect, stepping grandly into camp.

A sumptuous breakfast of bacon and fish was shortly provided, and as the boys set to work upon it Tom recounted (and adorned) his adventures. They were a vain and boastful company of heroes when the tale was done. Then Tom hid himself away in a shady spot to sleep till noon, and the other pirates got ready to fish and explore.

The Unusual Funeral Sermon

But there was no hilarity in the little town that tranquil afternoon. The Harpers and Aunt Polly's family were being put into mourning with great grief and many tears. An unusual quiet possessed the village, although it was ordinarily quiet enough in all conscience. The villagers conducted their concerns with an abstracted air, and talked little; but they sighed often. The Saturday holiday seemed a burden to the children. They had no heart in their sports, and gradually gave them up.

When the Sunday-school hour was finished the next morning, the bell began to toll, instead of ringing in the usual way. It was a very still Sabbath, and the mournful sound seemed in keeping with the musing hush that lay upon nature. The villagers began to gather, loitering a moment in the vestibule to converse in whispers about the sad event. But there was no whispering in the house; only the funereal rustling of dresses, as the women gathered to their seats, disturbed the silence there. None could remember when the little church had been so full before. There was finally a waiting pause, an expectant dumbness, and then Aunt Polly entered, followed by Sid and Mary, and then by the Harper family, all in deep black. The whole congregation, the old minister as well, rose reverently and stood, until the mourners were seated in the front pew. There was another silence, broken by sobs, then the minister spread his hands abroad and prayed. A moving hymn was sung, and the text followed: "I am the resurrection and the life."

As the service proceeded, the clergyman drew such pictures of the graces, the winning ways, and the rare promise of the lost lads, that every soul there, thinking he recognized these pictures, felt a pang in remembering that he had persistently blinded himself to them always before; and had as persistently seen only faults and flaws in the poor boys. The minister related many a touching incident in the lives of the departed, too, which illustrated their sweet, generous natures, and the people could easily see, now, how noble and beautiful those episodes were, and remembered with grief that at the time they occurred they had seemed rank rascalities, well deserving the cowhide. The congregation became more and more moved as the pathetic tale went on, till at last the whole company broke down and joined the weeping mourners in a chorus of anguished sobs, the preacher himself giving way to his feelings, and crying in the pulpit.

There was a rustle in the gallery which nobody noticed; a moment later the church door creaked; the minister raised his streaming eyes above his handkerchief, and stood transfixed! First one and then another pair of eyes followed the minister's, and then, almost with one impulse, the congregation rose and stared while the three dead boys came marching up the aisle, Tom in the lead, Joe next, and Huck, a ruin of drooping rags, sneaking sheepishly in the rear. They had been hid in the unused gallery, listening to their own funeral sermon!

Aunt Polly, Mary and the Harpers threw themselves upon their restored ones, smothered them with kisses and poured out thanksgivings, while poor Huck stood abashed and uncomfortable, not knowing exactly what to do or where to hide from so many unwelcoming eyes. He wavered, and started to slink away, but Tom seized him and said:

"Aunt Polly, it ain't fair. Somebody's got to be glad to see Huck."

"And so they shall! I'm glad to see him, poor motherless thing!" And the loving attentions Aunt Polly lavished upon him were the one thing capable of making him more uncomfortable than he was before.

Suddenly the minister shouted at the top of his voice:

" 'Praise God from whom all blessings flow'— SING!—and put your hearts in it!"

And they did. The "Old Hundred" hymn swelled up with a triumphant burst, and while it shook the rafters, Tom Sawyer the Pirate looked around upon

the envying juveniles about him, and confessed in his heart that this was the proudest moment in his life.

As the "sold" congregation trooped out, they said they would almost be willing to be made ridiculous again to hear Old Hundred sung like that once more.

Tom got more cuffs and kisses that day—according to Aunt Polly's varying moods—than he had earned before in a year; and he hardly knew which expressed the most gratefulness to God and affection for himself.

The Murder Trial

Time passed and at last the sleepy atmosphere was stirred, and vigorously. The murder trial came on in the court. It became the absorbing topic of village talk immediately. Tom and Huck did as they had often done before—went to the cell grating and gave Potter some tobacco and matches. He was on the ground floor, and there were no guards.

Muff Potter's gratitude for their gifts had always smote their consciences before—it cut deeper than ever, this time. They felt cowardly and treacherous to the last degree when Potter said:

"You've been mighty good to me, boys—better'n anybody else in this town. And I don't forget it, I don't. Often I says to myself, says I, 'I used to mend all the boys' kites and things, and show 'em where the good fishin' places was, and befriend 'em when I could, and now they've all forgot old Muff when he's in trouble, but Tom don't, and Huck don't—they don't forget him,' says I, and I don't forget them!"

All the village flocked to the court-house the next morning, for this was to be the great day. Both sexes were about equally represented in the packed audience. After a long wait the jury filed in and took their places; shortly afterwards, Potter, pale and haggard, timid and hopeless, was brought in with chains upon him, and seated where all the curious eyes could stare at him; no less conspicuous was Injun Joe, stolid as ever. There was another pause, and then the judge arrived, and the Sheriff proclaimed the opening of the court. The usual whisperings among the lawyers and gathering together of papers followed. These details and accompanying delays worked up an atmosphere of preparation that was as impressive as it was fascinating.

Every detail of the damaging circumstances that occurred in the graveyard upon that morning which all present remembered so well was brought out by credible witnesses, but none of them were cross-examined by Potter's lawyer. The perplexity and dissatisfaction of the house expressed itself in murmurs and provoked a reproof from the bench. Counsel for the prosecution now said:

"By the oaths of citizens whose simple word is above suspicion, we have fastened this awful crime beyond all possibility of question upon the unhappy prisoner at the bar. We rest our case here."

A groan escaped from poor Potter, and he put his face in his hands, and rocked his body softly to and fro, while a painful silence reigned in the court-room. Many men were moved, and many women's compassion testified itself in tears. Counsel for the defence rose and said:

"Your Honour, in our remarks at the opening of this trial, we foreshadowed our purpose to prove that our client did this fearful deed while under the influence of a blind and irresponsible delirium produced by drink. We have changed our mind; we shall not offer that plea. (Then to the clerk.) Call Thomas Sawyer."

A puzzled amazement awoke in every face in the house, not even excepting Potter's. Every eye fastened itself with wondering interest upon Tom as he rose and took his place upon the stand. The boy looked wild enough, for he was badly scared. The oath was administered.

"Thomas Sawyer, where were you on the seventeenth of June, about the hour of midnight?"

Tom glanced at Injun Joe's face, and his tongue failed him. The audience listened breathless, but the words refused to come. After a few moments, however, the boy got a little of his strength back, and managed to put enough of it into his voice to make part of the house hear:

"In the graveyard!"

"A little bit louder, please. Don't be afraid. You were——"

"In the graveyard."

A contemptuous smile flitted across Injun Joe's face.

"Were you anywhere near Horse Williams's grave?"

"Yes, sir."

"Speak up just a trifle louder. How near were you?"

"Near as I am to you."

"Were you hidden or not?"

"I was hid."

"Where?"

"Behind the elms that's on the edge of the grave."

Injun Joe gave a barely perceptible start.

"Anyone with you?"

"Yes, sir. I went there with——"

"Wait—wait a moment. Never mind mentioning your companion's name. We will produce him at the proper time. Did you carry anything there with you?"

Tom hesitated and looked confused.

"Speak out, my boy—don't be diffident. The truth is always respectable. What did you take there?"

"Only a–a–dead cat."

There was a ripple of mirth, which the court checked.

"We will produce the skeleton of that cat. Now my boy, tell us everything that occurred—tell it in your own way—don't skip anything, and don't be afraid."

Tom began—hesitatingly at first, but, as he warmed to his subject, his words flowed more and more easily; in a little while every sound ceased but his own voice; every eye fixed itself upon him; with parted lips and bated breath the audience hung upon his words, taking no note of time, rapt in the ghastly fascinations of the tale. The strain upon pent emotion reached its climax when the boy said, "And as the doctor knocked Muff Potter out, Injun Joe jumped with the knife and——"

Crash! Quick as lightning, the half-breed sprang for a window, and was gone!

Tom the Hero

Tom was a glittering hero once more—the pet of the old, the envy of the young. His name even went into immortal print, for the village paper magnified him. There were some that believed he would be President yet, if he escaped hanging.

As usual, the fickle unreasoning world took Muff Potter to its bosom, and fondled him as lavishly as it had abused him before. But that sort of conduct is to the world's credit; therefore it is not well to find fault with it.

Tom's days were days of splendour and exultation to him, but his nights were seasons of horror. Injun Joe infested all his dreams, and always with doom in his eye. Hardly any temptation could persuade the boy to stir abroad after nightfall. Poor Huck was in the same state of wretchedness and terror, for Tom had told the whole story to the lawyer the night before the great day of the trial, and Huck was sore afraid that his share in the business might leak out as yet, notwithstanding Injun Joe's flight had saved him the suffering of testifying in court. The poor fellow had got the attorney to promise secrecy, but what of that? Since Tom's harassed conscience had managed to drive him to the lawyer's house by night and wring a dread tale from lips that had been sealed with the dismalest and most formidable of oaths, Huck's confidence in the human race was well-nigh obliterated.

Daily Muff Potter's gratitude made Tom glad he had spoken; but nightly he wished he had sealed up his tongue. Half the time Tom was afraid Injun Joe would never be captured; the other half he was afraid he would be. He felt sure he never could draw a safe breath again until that man was dead and he had seen the corpse with his own eyes.

Rewards had been offered, the country had been scoured, but no Injun Joe was found. One of those omniscient and awe-inspiring marvels, a detective, came up from St Louis, moused around, shook his head, looked wise, and made that sort of astounding success which members of that craft usually achieve. That is to say, 'he found a clue'. But you can't hang a 'clue' for murder, and so after the detective had got through and gone home, Tom felt just as insecure as he was before.

The slow days drifted on, and each left behind it a slightly lightened weight of apprehension as no news of Injun Joe was heard.

Treasure Hunting

There comes a time in every rightly constructed boy's life when he has a raging desire to go somewhere and dig for hidden treasure. This desire suddenly came upon Tom one day.

Presently he stumbled upon Huck Finn the Red-handed. Huck would answer. Tom took him to a private place, and opened the matter to him

confidentially. Huck was willing. Huck was always
willing to take a hand in any enterprise that offered
entertainment and required no capital, for he had a
troublesome super-abundance of that sort of time
which is not money.

"Where'll we dig?" said Huck.

"Oh, 'most anywhere."

"Why, is it hid all around?"

"No, indeed it ain't. It's hid in mighty particular
places, Huck. They always bury it under a ha'nted
house, or on an island, or under a dead tree that's
got one limb sticking out. Well, we've tried Jackson's
Island a little, and we can try it again sometime; and
there's the old ha'nted house up the Still-House
branch and there's lots of dead-limb trees—dead
loads of 'em."

"Is it under all of them?"

"How you talk! No!"

"Then how you going to know which one to go
for?"

"Go for all of 'em."

"Why Tom, it'll take all summer."

"Well, what of that? Suppose you find a brass pot
with a hundred dollars in it, all rusty and gay, or a
rotten chest full of di'monds. How's that?"

After digging in a dozen places to no avail, Tom
suggested they do some night digging.

"All right. Let's hide the tools in the bushes."

The boys were there that night about the
appointed time. They sat in the shadow waiting. It
was a lonely place, and an hour made solemn by old
traditions. Spirits whispered in the rustling leaves,
ghosts lurked in the murky nooks, the deep baying of
a hound floated up out of the distance, an owl
answered with his sepulchral note. The boys were
subdued by these solemnities, and talked little. By-
and-by they judged that twelve had come; they
marked where the shadow fell and began to dig.
Their hopes commenced to rise. Their interest grew
stronger, and their industry kept pace with it. The
hole deepened and still deepened, but every time
their hearts jumped to hear the pick strike upon
something, they only suffered a new disappointment.
It was only a stone or a chunk. At last Tom said, "It
ain't any use, Huck, we're wrong again."

"Say, Tom, let's give this place up, and try
somewheres else."

"All right, I reckon we better."

"What'll it be?"

Tom considered awhile, and then said, "The ha'nted house. That's it."

"Well, all right. We'll tackle the ha'nted house if you say so; but I reckon it's taking chances."

Noon next day they reached the haunted house. There was something so weird and grisly about the dead silence that reigned there under the baking sun, and something so depressing about the loneliness and desolation of the place, that they were afraid, for a moment, to venture in. Then they crept to the door and took a trembling peep. They saw a weed-grown, floorless room, unplastered, an ancient fireplace, vacant windows, a ruinous staircase; and here, there, and everywhere, hung ragged and abandoned cobwebs. They presently entered softly, with quickened pulses, talking in whispers, ears alert to catch the slightest sound, and muscles tense and ready for instant retreat.

In a little while familiarity modified their fears, and they gave the place a critical and interested examination, rather admiring their own boldness, and wondering at it too. Next they wanted to look upstairs. This was something like cutting off retreat, but they got to daring each other, and of course there could be but one result—they threw their tools into a corner and made the ascent. Up there were the same signs of decay. In one corner they found a closet that promised mystery, but the promise was a fraud—there was nothing in it. Their courage was up now, and well in hand. They were about to go down and begin work when—

"Sh!" said Tom.

"What is it?" whispered Huck, blanching with fright.

"Sh! There! Hear it?"

"Yes! Oh, my! Let's run!"

"Keep still! Don't you budge! They're coming right towards the door."

The boys stretched themselves upon the floor with their eyes to knot-holes in the planking, and lay waiting in a misery of fear.

"They've stopped. No—coming. Here they are. Don't whisper another word, Huck. My goodness, I wish I was out of this!"

Injun Joe Turns Up Again

Two men entered. Each boy said to himself:

"There's the old deaf and dumb Spaniard that's been about town once or twice lately—never saw t'other man before."

'T'other' was a ragged, unkempt creature, with nothing very pleasant in his face. The Spaniard was wrapped in a serape; he had bushy white whiskers, long white hair flowed from under his sombrero, and he wore green goggles. When they came in, 't'other' was talking in a low voice; they sat down on the ground, facing the door, with their backs to the wall, and the speaker continued his remarks. His manner became less guarded and his words more distinct as he proceeded.

"No," said he, "I've thought it all over, and I don't like it. It's dangerous."

"Dangerous!" grunted the 'deaf and dumb' Spaniard, to the vast surprise of the boys. "Milksop!"

This voice made the boys gasp and quake. It was Injun Joe's! There was silence for some time. Then Injun Joe said:

"What's any more dangerous than the job up yonder—but nothing's come of it."

"That's different. Away up the river so, and not another house about. 'Twon't ever be known that we tried, anyway, long as we didn't succeed."

"Well, what's more dangerous than coming here in the daytime?—anybody would suspicion us that saw us."

"I know that. But there wasn't any other place as handy after that fool of a job. I want to quit this shanty. I wanted to yesterday only it wasn't any use trying to stir out of here with those infernal boys playing over there on the hill right in full view."

'Those infernal boys' quaked again under the inspiration of this remark, and thought how lucky it was that they had remembered it was Friday and concluded to wait a day. They wished in their hearts they had waited a year. The two men got out some food and made a luncheon. After a long and thoughtful silence Injun Joe said:

"Look here, lad, you go back up the river where you belong. Wait there till you hear from me. I'll take the chances on dropping into this town just once more, for a look. We'll do that 'dangerous' job after I've spied around a little and think things look well for it. Then for Texas! We'll leg it together!"

"Good idea," said the comrade, who walked across the room, knelt down, raised one of the rearward hearth-stones and took out a bag that jingled pleasantly. He subtracted from it twenty or thirty dollars for himself and as much for Injun Joe, and passed the bag to the latter, who was on his knees in the corner, now, digging with his bowie-knife.

The boys forgot all their fears, all their miseries in an instant. With glaring eyes they watched every moment. Luck!— the splendour of it was beyond all imagination! There was money enough to make half a dozen boys rich! Here was treasure-hunting under the happiest auspices—there would not be any bothersome uncertainty as to where to dig. They nudged each other every moment—eloquent nudges and easily understood, for they simply meant, "Oh, but ain't you glad now we're here!"

Joe's knife struck upon something.

"Hello," said he.

"What is it?" said his comrade.

"Half-rotten plank—no, it's a box, I believe. Here, bear a hand, and we'll see what it's here for. Never mind, I've broke a hole."

He reached his hand in and drew it out.

"Man, it's money."

The two men examined the handful of coins. They were gold. The two boys above were as excited as themselves, and as delighted.

Joe's comrade said:

"We'll make quick work of this. There's an old rusty pick over amongst the weeds in the corner, the other side of the fire-place—I saw it a minute ago."

He ran and brought the boys' pick and shovel. Injun Joe took the pick, looked it over critically, shook his head, muttered something to himself, and then began to use it.

The box was soon unearthed. It was not very large; it was iron-bound and had been very strong before the slow years had injured it. The men contemplated the treasure awhile in blissful silence.

"Pard, there's thousands of dollars here," said Injun Joe.

" 'Twas always said that Murrel's gang used around here one summer," the stranger observed.

"I know it," said Injun Joe; "and this looks like it, I should say."

"Now you won't need to do that job."

The half-breed frowned. Said he:

"You don't know me. Least you don' know all about that thing. 'Tain't robbery altogether—it's revenge!" and a wicked light flamed in his eyes. "I'll need your help in it. When it's finished—then Texas.

Go home to your Nance and your kids, and stand by till you hear from me."

"Well, if you say so. What'll we do with this—bury it again?"

"Yes. (ravishing delight overhead) No! by the great Sachem, no! (profound distress overhead) I'd nearly forgot. That pick had fresh earth on it! (The boys were sick with terror in a moment.) What business has a pick and a shovel here? What business with fresh earth on them? Who brought them here—and where are they gone? Have you heard anybody? Seen anybody? What! bury it again and leave them to come and see the ground disturbed? Not exactly—not exactly. We'll take it to my den."

"Why, of course! Might have thought of that before. You mean number one?"

"No—number two—under the cross. The other place is bad—too common."

"All right. It's nearly dark enough to start."

Injun Joe got up and went about from window to window, cautiously peeping out. Presently he said:

"Who could have brought those tools here? Do you reckon they can be upstairs?"

The boys' breath forsook them. Injun Joe put his hand on his knife, halted a moment, undecided, and then turned towards the stairway. The boys thought of the closet, but their strength was gone. The steps came creaking up the stairs—the intolerable distress of the situation woke the stricken resolution of the lads—they were about to spring for the closet, when there was a crash of rotten timbers, and Injun Joe landed on the ground amid the debris of the ruined stairway. He gathered himself up cursing, and his comrade said:

"Now what's the use of all that? If it's anybody, and they're up there, let them stay there—who cares? If they want to jump down, now, and get into trouble, who objects? It will be dark in fifteen minutes—and then let them follow us if they want to; I'm willing. In my opinion, whoever hove those things in here caught a sight of us, and took us for ghosts or devils. I'll bet they're running yet."

Joe grumbled awhile; then he agreed with his friend that what daylight was left ought to be economised in getting things ready for leaving. Shortly afterwards they slipped out of the house in the deepening twilight, and moved towards the river with their precious box.

Tracking Down Injun Joe

The adventure of the day mightily tormented Tom's dreams that night. But the incidents of his adventure grew sensibly sharper and clearer under the attrition of thinking them over, and so he presently found himself leaning to the impression that the thing might not have been a dream after all. This uncertainty must be swept away. He would snatch a hurried breakfast, and go and find Huck.

Huck was sitting on the gunwale of a flat boat, listlessly dangling his feet in the water, and looking very melancholy. Tom concluded to let Huck lead up to the subject. If he did not do it, then the adventure would be proved to have been only a dream.

"Hello, Huck!"

"Hello, yourself."

Silence for a minute.

"Tom, if we'd a left the blame tools at the dead tree we'd a got the money. Oh, ain't it awful!"

" 'Tain't a dream, then, 'tain't a dream! Somehow I 'most wish it was. Dog'd if I don't."

"What ain't a dream?"

"Oh, that thing yesterday. I ben half thinking it was."

"Dream! If them stairs hadn't broke down you'd a seen how much a dream it was! I've had dreams enough all night, with that patch-eyed Spanish devil going for me all through 'em, rot him!"

"No, not rot him. Find him! Track the money!"

"Tom, we'll never find him. A feller don't only have one chance for such a pile, and that one's lost. I'd feel mighty shaky if I was to see him, anyway."

"Well, so'd I; but I'd like to see him anyway, and

track him out—to his number two."

"Number two; yes, that's it. I ben thinking 'bout that. But I can't make nothing out of it. What do you reckon it is?"

"I dono. It's too deep. Say, Huck—maybe it's the number of a house!"

"Goody! No, Tom, that ain't it. If it is, it ain't in this one-horse town. They ain't no numbers here."

"Well, that's so. Lemme think a minute. Here—it's the number of a room—in a tavern, you know!"

"Oh, that's the trick! They ain't only two taverns. We can find out quick."

"You stay here, Huck, till I come."

Tom was off at once. He did not care to have Huck's company in public places. He was gone half an hour. He found that in the best tavern, number two had long been occupied by a young lawyer, and was still so occupied. In the less ostentatious house number two was a mystery. The tavern-keeper's young son said it was kept locked all the time, and he never saw anybody go into it or come out of it except at night. He did not know any particular reason for this state of things, had had some little curiosity, but it was rather feeble; had made the most of the mystery by entertaining himself with the idea that the room was 'ha'nted'; had noticed that there was a light in there the night before.

"That's what I've found out, Huck. I reckon that's the very number two we're after."

"I reckon it is, Tom. Now what are you doing to do?"

"Lemme think."

Tom thought a long time. Then he said:

"I'll tell you. The back door of that number two is the door that comes out into that little close alley between the tavern and the old rattle-trap of a brick-store. Now you get hold of all the door keys you can find and I'll nip all of Auntie's, and the first dark night we'll go there and try 'em. And mind you keep a look out for Injun Joe, because he said he was going to drop into town and spy around once more for a chance to get his revenge. If you see him, you just follow him; and if he don't go to that number two, that ain't the place."

"Lordy, I don't want to foller him by myself!"

"Why, it'll be night, sure. He mightn't ever see you—and if he did, maybe he'd never think anything."

"Well, if it's pretty dark I reckon I'll track him. I dono—I dono. I'll try."

"You bet I'll follow him if it's dark, Huck! Why, he might a found out he couldn't get his revenge, and be going right after that money."

"It's so, Tom, it's so. I'll foller him; I will, by jingoes."

"Now you're talking! Don't you ever weaken, Huck, and I won't."

Finding Injun Joe

That night Tom and Huck were ready for their adventure. They hung about the neighbourhood of the tavern until after nine, one watching the alley at a distance and the other the tavern door. Nobody entered the alley or left it; nobody resembling the Spaniard entered or left the tavern door. The night promised to be a fair one; so Tom went home with the understanding that if a considerable degree of darkness came on, Huck was to come and 'meow', whereupon he would slip out and try the keys. But the night remained clear, and Huck closed his watch and retired to bed in an empty sugar hogshead about twelve.

Tuesday the boys had the same ill-luck. Also Wednesday. But Thursday night promised better. Tom slipped out in good season with his aunt's old tin lantern, and a large towel to blindfold it with. He hid the lantern in Huck's sugar hogshead and the watch began. An hour before midnight the tavern closed up, and its lights (the only ones thereabouts) were put out. No Spaniard had been seen. Nobody had entered or left the alley.

Tom got his lantern, lit it in the hogshead, wrapped it closely in the towel, and the two adventurers crept in the gloom towards the tavern. Huck stood sentry and Tom felt his way into the alley. Then there was a season of waiting anxiety that weighed upon Huck's spirits like a mountain. He began to wish he could see a flash from the lantern—it would frighten him, but it would at least tell him that Tom was alive yet.

It seemed hours since Tom had disappeared. Surely he must have fainted; maybe he was dead; maybe his heart had burst under terror and excitement. In his uneasiness Huck found himself drawing closer and closer to the alley, fearing all sorts of dreadful things, and momentarily expecting some catastrophe to happen that would take away his breath. There was not much to take away, for he seemed only able to inhale it by thimblefuls, and his heart would soon wear itself out, the way it was beating. Suddenly there was a flash of light, and Tom came tearing by him:

"Run!" said he. "Run for your life!"

He needn't have repeated it; once was enough; Huck was making thirty or forty miles an hour before the repetition was uttered. The boys never stopped till they reached the shed of a deserted slaughter-house at the lower end of the village. Just as they got within its shelter a storm burst and the rain poured down. As soon as Tom got his breath he said:

"Huck, it was awful! I tried two of the keys just as soft as I could; but they seemed to make such a power of racket that I couldn't hardly get my breath, I was so scared. They wouldn't turn in the lock either. Well, without noticing what I was doing, I took hold of the knob, and open comes the door! It wasn't locked! I hopped in and shook off the towel and, great Caesar's ghost!"

"What!—what'd you see, Tom?"

"Huck, I most stepped on to Injun Joe's hand!"

"No!"

"Yes. He was laying there, sound asleep on the floor, with his old patch on his eye and his arms spread out."

"Lordy, what did you do? Did he wake up?"

"No, never budged. Drunk, I reckon. I just grabbed that towel and started!"

"I'd never a thought of the towel, I bet!"

"Well, I would. My aunt would make me mighty sick if I lost it."

"Say, Tom, did you see that box?"

"Huck, I didn't wait to look around. I didn't see the box, I didn't see the cross. I didn't see anything but a bottle and a tin cup on the floor by Injun Joe! Yes, and I saw two barrels and lots more bottles in the room. Don't you see, now, what's the matter with that ha'nted room?"

"How?"

"Why, it's ha'nted with whisky! Maybe all the Temperance Taverns have got a ha'nted room?"

"Well, I reckon maybe that's so. Who'd a thought such a thing? But say, Tom, now's a mighty good time to get that box, if Injun Joe's drunk."

"It is that! You try it!"

"Well, no—I reckon not."

"And I reckon not, Huck. Only one bottle alongside of Injun Joe ain't enough. If there'd been three he'd be drunk enough and I'd do it." There was a long pause for reflection, and then Tom said:

"Looky here, Huck, let's not try that thing any more till we know Injun Joe's not there. It's too scary. Now if we watch every night, we'll be dead sure to see him go out some time or other, then we'll snatch that box quicker 'n lightning."

"Well, I'm agreed. I'll watch the whole night long, and I'll do it every night, too, if you'll do the other part of the job."

"All right, I will. All you got to do is to trot up Hooper Street a block and meow—and if I'm asleep, you throw some gravel at the window and that'll fetch me."

"Agreed, and good as wheat!"

"Now, Huck, the storm's over, and I'll go home. It'll begin to be daylight in a couple of hours. You go back and watch that long, will you?"

"I said I would, Tom, and I will. I'll ha'nt that tavern every night for a year. I'll sleep all day and I'll stand watch all night."

"That's all right. Now where are you going to sleep?"

"In Ben Roger's hayloft."

Becky's Picnic

The first thing Tom heard on Friday morning was a glad piece of news—Judge Thatcher's family had come back to town the night before, after spending the summer vacation in their Constantinople home. Both Injun Joe and the treasure sank into secondary importance for a moment, and Becky took the chief place in the boy's interest. He saw her, and they had an exhausting good time playing 'hi-spy' and 'gully-keeper' with a crowd of their schoolmates. The day was completed and crowned in a peculiarly satisfactory way: Becky teased her mother to appoint the next day for a picnic, and she consented. The child's delight was boundless, and Tom's not more moderate. The invitations were sent out before sunset, and straightway the young folks of the village were thrown into a fever of preparation and pleasureable anticipation. Tom's excitement enabled him to keep awake until a pretty late hour, and he had good hopes of hearing Huck's 'meow' and of having his treasure to astonish Becky and the picnickers with, next day; but he was disappointed. No signal came that night.

Morning came eventually, and by ten or eleven o'clock a giddy and rollicking company were gathered at Judge Thatcher's, and everything was ready for a start. It was not the custom for elderly people to mar picnics with their presence. The children were considered safe enough under the wings of a few young ladies of eighteen and a few young gentlemen of twenty-three or thereabouts. The old steam ferry-boat was chartered for the occasion: presently the gay throng filed up the main street laden with provision baskets. Sid was sick and had to miss the fun; Mary remained at home to entertain him. The last thing Mrs Thatcher said to Becky was:

"You'll not get back till late. Perhaps you'd better stay all night with some of the girls that live near the ferry landing, child!"

"Then I'll stay with Susy Harper, mamma."

"Very well. And mind and behave yourself, and don't be any trouble."

Presently, as they tripped along, Tom said to Becky:

"Say—I'll tell you what we'll do. 'Stead of going to Joe Harper's, we'll climb right up the hill and stop at Widow Douglas's. She'll have ice-cream! She has it 'most every day—dead loads of it. And she'll be awful glad to have us."

"Oh, that will be fun!"

Then Becky reflected a moment, and said:

"But what will mamma say?"

"How'll she ever know?"

The girl turned the idea over in her mind, and said reluctantly:

"I reckon it's wrong—but——"

"But—shucks! Your mother won't know, and so what's the harm? All she wants is that you'll be safe; and I bet you she'd a said go there if she'd a thought of it. I know she would."

The Widow Douglas's splendid hospitality was a tempting bait. It and Tom's persuasions presently carried the day. So it was decided to say nothing to anybody about the night's programme.

Presently it occurred to Tom that maybe Huck might come this very night and give the signal. The thought took a deal of the spirit out of his anticipations. Still he could not bear to give up the fun at Widow Douglas's. And why should he give it up, he reasoned—the signal did not come the night

before, so why should it be any more likely to come tonight? The sure fun of the evening outweighed the uncertain treasure; and, boy-like, he determined to yield to the stronger inclination and not allow himself to think of the box of money another time that day.

Three miles below town, the ferry-boat stopped at the mouth of a woody hollow and tied up. The crowd swarmed ashore, and soon the forest distances and craggy heights echoed far and near with shouting

and laughter. All the different ways of getting hot and tired were gone through with, and by-and-by the rovers straggled back to camp fortified with responsible appetites, and then the destruction of the good things began. After the feast there was a refreshing season of rest and chat in the shade of spreading oaks. By-and-by somebody shouted:

"Who's for the cave?"

Everybody was. Bundles of candles were produced, and straightway there was a general scamper up the hill. The mouth of the cave was high up the hill-side, an opening shaped like the letter A. Its massive oaken door stood unbarred. Within was a small chamber, chilly as an ice-house, and walled by Nature with solid lime-stone that was dewy with a cold sweat. It was romantic and mysterious to stand

here in the deep gloom and look out upon the green valley shining in the sun.

The procession moved along the main avenue some three quarters of a mile, and then groups and couples began to slip aside into branch avenues, fly along the dismal corridors, and take each other by surprise at points where the corridors joined again. Parties were able to elude each other for the space of half an hour without going beyond the 'known' ground.

By-and-by one group after another came straggling back to the mouth of the cave, panting, hilarious, smeared from head to foot with tallow drippings, daubed with clay, and entirely delighted with the success of the day. Then they were astonished to find that they had been taking no note of time, and that night was about at hand. The clanging bell had been calling for half an hour. However, this sort of close to the day's adventures was romantic and therefore satisfactory. When the ferry-boat with her wild freight pushed into the stream, nobody cared sixpence for the wasted time but the captain.

Huckleberry Finn to the Rescue

Huck was already upon his watch when the ferry-boat's lights went glinting past the wharf. Huck waited what seemed a weary long time when a noise fell upon his ear. He was all attention in an instant. The alley door closed softly. He sprang to the corner of the brick-store. The next moment two men brushed by him, and one seemed to have something under his arm. It must be that box! So they were going to remove the treasure. Why call Tom now? It would be absurd—the men would get away with the box and never be found again. No, he would stick to their wake and follow them; he would trust to the darkness for security from discovery. So Huck stepped out and glided along behind the men, like a cat, with bare feet, allowing them to keep just far enough ahead not to be visible.

He followed them a long way, through streets, past the quarry until they came to Widow Douglas's grounds. 'Very well', he thought, 'let them bury it there; it won't be hard to find.'

Now there was a low voice—Injun Joe's:

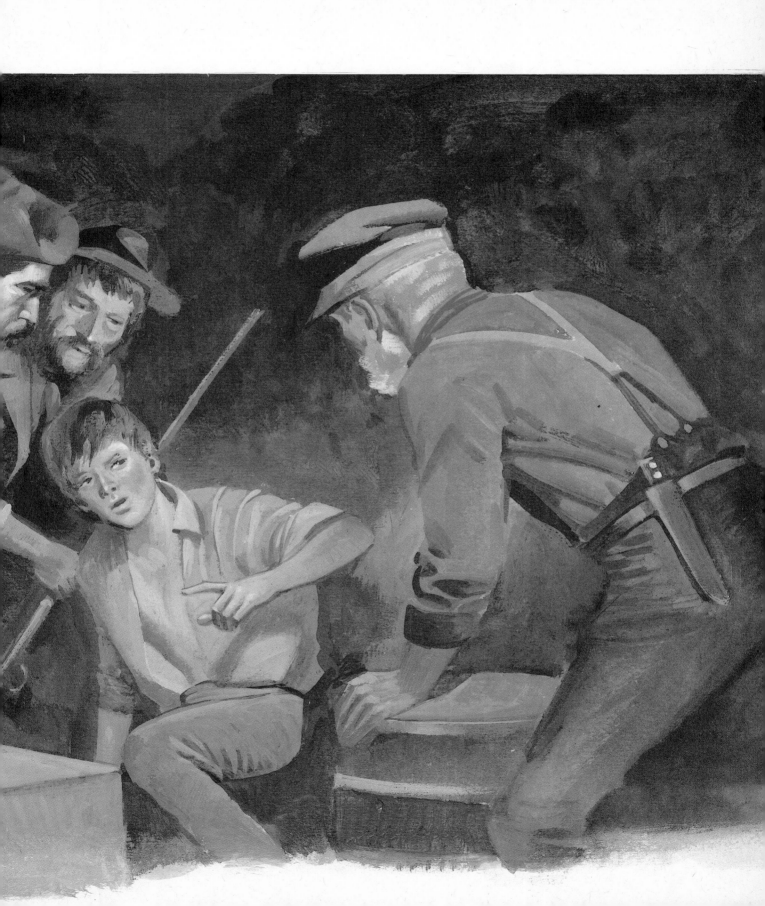

"Damn her, maybe she's got company—there's lights, late as it is."

"I can't see any."

This was that stranger's voice—the stranger of the haunted house. A deadly chill went to Huck's heart—this, then, was the 'revenge' job! His thought was to fly. Then he remembered that the Widow Douglas had been kind to him more than once, and maybe these men were going to murder her. He wished he dared venture to warn her; but he knew he didn't dare—they might come and catch him. He thought all this and more in the moment that elapsed between the stranger's remark and Injun Joe's next —which was:

"Because the bush is in your way. Now—this way —now you see, don't you?"

"Yes. Well, there is company there, I reckon. Better give it up."

"Give it up, and I just leaving this country for ever! Give it up, and maybe never have another chance. I tell you again, as I've told you before, I don't care for her swag—you may have it. But her husband was rough on me—many times he was rough on me—and mainly he was the justice of the peace that jugged me for a vagrant. And that ain't all! He had me horse-whipped! Like a nigger with all the town looking on! Do you understand? He took advantage of me and died. But I'll take it out of her!"

"Oh, don't kill her! Don't do that!"

"Kill? Who said anything about killing? I would kill him if he was here; but not her. When you want to get revenge on a woman you don't kill her—bosh! You go for her looks. You slit her nostrils—you notch her ears like a sow's!"

"By God, that's——"

"Keep your opinion to yourself! It will be safest for you. I'll tie her to the bed, and you'll help me —that's why you're here. If you flinch, I'll kill you! And if I have to kill you, I'll kill her—and then I reckon nobody'll ever know much about who done this business. We'll wait till the lights are out, and we'll do it!"

Huck stepped gingerly back a few paces, then ran down past the quarry until he reached the old Welshman's cottage. He banged at the door, and presently the heads of the old man and his two stalwart sons were thrust from windows.

"What's the row there? Who's banging? What do you want?"

"Let me in—quick! I'll tell everything."

"Why, who are you?"

"Huckleberry Finn—quick, let me in!"

"Let him in, lads, and let's see what's the trouble."

"Please don't ever tell I told you," were Huck's first words when he got in. "Please don't——I'd be killed sure—but the Widow's been good friend to me sometimes, and I want to tell—I will tell if you'll promise you won't ever say it was me."

"By George, he has got something to tell, or he wouldn't act so!" exclaimed the old man. "Out with it, and nobody here'll ever tell, lad."

Three minutes later the old man and his sons, well armed, were up the hill, and just entering the path on tip-toe, their weapons in their hands. Huck accompanied them no farther. He hid behind a great boulder and fell to listening. There was a lagging, anxious silence, and then all of a sudden there was an explosion of firearms and a cry. Huck waited for no particulars. He sprang away and sped down the hill as fast as his legs could carry him.

Huckleberry Finn the Hero

As the earliest suspicion of dawn appeared on Sunday morning, Huck came groping up the hill and rapped gently at the old Welshman's door. The inmates were asleep, but it was a sleep that was set on a hair-trigger, on account of the exciting episode of the night. A call came from a window:

"Who's there?"

Huck's scared voice answered in a low tone:

"Do please let me in! It's only Huck Finn!"

"It's a name that can open this door night or day, lad! Welcome!"

These were strange words to the vagabond boy's ears, and the pleasantest he had ever heard. He could not recollect that the closing word had ever been applied in his case before.

The door was quickly unlocked and he entered. Huck was given a seat, and the old man and his brace of tall sons speedily dressed themselves.

"Now, my boy, I hope you're good and hungry, because breakfast will be ready as soon as the sun's up, and we'll have a piping hot one, too—make yourself easy about that. I and the boys hoped you'd turn up and stop here last night."

"I was awful scared," said Huck, "and I run. I took out when the pistols went off, and I didn't stop for three mile. I've come now becuz I wanted to know about it, you know; and I come before daylight becuz I didn't want to run into them devils, even if they was dead."

"Well, poor chap, you do look as if you'd had a hard time of it—but there's a bed here for you when you've had your breakfast," said the Welshman.

Just as breakfast was completed there was a knock at the door. Huck jumped for a hiding-place, for he had no mind to be connected even remotely with the late event. The Welshman admitted several ladies and gentlemen, among them the Widow Douglas, and noticed that groups of citizens were climbing the hill to stare at the stile. So the news had spread.

The Welshman had to tell the story of the night to the visitors. The Widow's gratitude for her preservation was outspoken.

"Don't say a word about it, madam. There's another that you're more beholden to than you are to me and my boys maybe, but he don't allow me to tell his name. We wouldn't ever have been there but for him."

Of course this excited a curiosity so vast that it almost belittled the main matter.

Tom and Becky Missing

Mrs Thatcher addressed Mrs Harper:

"Is my Becky going to sleep all day?"

"Your Becky?"

"Yes," with a startled look. "Didn't she stay with you last night?"

"Why, no."

Mrs Thatcher turned pale, and sank into a chair just as Aunt Polly, talking briskly with a friend, approached, and said:

"Good morning Mrs Thatcher, good morning, Mrs Harper, my Tom seems to be missing, did he stay with either of you last night?"

"He didn't stay with us," said Mrs Harper, beginning to look uneasy. A marked anxiety came into Aunt Polly's face.

Early in the forenoon of the next day parties of jaded men began to straggle into the village after a long search, but the strongest of the citizens continued searching for the pair. All the news that could be gained was that remotenesses of the cavern were being ransacked that had never been visited before; that every corner and crevice was going to be thoroughly searched; that wherever one wandered through the maze of passages, lights were to be seen flitting hither and thither in the distance, and shoutings and pistol-shots sent their hollow reverberations to the ear down the sombre aisles. In one place, far from the section usually traversed by tourists, the names 'Becky' and 'Tom' had been found traced upon the rocky wall with candle smoke, and near at hand a grease-soiled bit of ribbon.

Lost in the Cave

Now to return to Tom and Becky's share in the picnic. Tom had found a subterranean lake which stretched its dim length away until its shape was lost in the shadows. He wanted to explore its borders, but concluded that it would be best to sit down and rest a while first. Now for the first time the deep stillness of the place laid a clammy hand upon the spirits of the children. Becky said:

"Why, I didn't notice, but it seems ever so long since I heard any of the others."

"Come to think, Becky, we are away down below them, and we couldn't hear them here."

Becky grew apprehensive.

"I wonder how long we've been down here, Tom? We better start back."

"Yes, I reckon we better."

"Can you find the way, Tom? It's all a mixed-up crookedness to me."

"I reckon I could find it, but then the bats. If they put both our candles out, it will be an awful fix. Let's try some other way, so as not to go through there."

"Well, but I hope we won't get lost. It would be so awful!" and the child shuddered at the thought of the dreadful possibilities.

They started through a corridor, and traversed it in silence a long way, glancing at each new opening, to see if there was anything familiar about the look of it; but they were all strange. Every time Tom made an examination, Becky would watch his face for an encouraging sign, and he would say cheerily:

"Oh, it's all right. This ain't the one, but we'll

come to it right away!" But he felt less and less hopeful with each failure, and presently began to turn off into diverging avenues at sheer random, in the desperate hope of finding the one that was wanted. He still said it was 'All right' but there was such a leaden dread at his heart, that the words had lost their ring, and sounded as if he had said, 'All is lost!' Becky clung to his side in an anguish of fear, and tried hard to keep back the tears, but they would come. At last she said:

"Oh, Tom, let's go back that way! We seem to get worse off all the time."

Tom stopped.

"Listen!" said he.

Profound silence; silence so deep that even their breathings were conspicuous in the hush. Tom shouted. The call went echoing down the empty aisles, and died out in the distance in a faint sound that resembled a ripple of mocking laughter.

"Oh, don't do it again, Tom, it is too horrid," said Becky.

"It is horrid, but I better, Becky; they might hear us, you know," and he shouted again.

They moved on and by-and-by Tom took Becky's candle and blew it out. This economy meant so much. Words were not needed. Becky understood, and her hope died again. She knew that Tom had a whole candle and three or four pieces in his pocket——yet he must economise.

The children wandered about more passages uselessly then groped their way to a spring to rest and eat some remains of cake they had left from the picnic. The weary time dragged on; they slept and awoke famished and woe-stricken. They had lost all sense of time.

Now an idea struck Tom. There were some side-passages near at hand. It would be better to explore some of these than bear the weight of the heavy time in idleness. He took a kite-line from his pocket, tied it to a projection, and he and Becky started, Tom in the lead, unwinding the line as he groped along. At the end of twenty steps the corridor ended in a 'jumping-off' place. Tom got down on his knees and felt below, and then as far around the corner as he could reach with his hands conveniently; he made an effort to stretch yet a little further to the right, and at the moment, a short distance away, a human hand, holding a candle, appeared from behind a rock! Tom lifted up a glorious shout, and instantly that hand was followed by the body it belonged to—

Injun Joe's! Tom was paralysed; he could not move. He was vastly gratified the next moment to see the Spaniard take to his heels and get himself out of sight. Tom wondered that Joe had not recognised his voice, and come over and killed him for testifying in court. But the echoes must have disguised the voice. Without that was it, he reasoned. Tom's fright weakened every muscle in his body. He said to himself that if he had strength enough to get back to the spring he would stay there, and nothing should tempt him to run the risk of meeting Injun Joe again. He was careful to keep from Becky what it was that he had seen. He told her he had only shouted 'for luck'.

But hunger and wretchedness rise superior to fears in the long run. Another tedious wait at the spring, and another long sleep brought changes. The children awoke, tortured with a raging hunger. Tom believed it must be Wednesday or Thursday or even Friday or Saturday now, and if there was a search for them, it had been given over. He proposed to explore another passage. He felt willing to risk Injun Joe and all other terrors. But Becky was very weak. She had sunk into a dreary apathy, and would not be roused. She told Tom to go with the kite-line and explore if he chose; but she implored him to come back every little while and speak to her.

Tom kissed her, with a choking sensation in his throat, and made a show of being confident of finding the searchers or an escape from the cave; then he took the kite-line in his hand and went groping down one of the passages on his hands and knees, distressed with hunger and sick with bodings of coming doom. . . .

Home Again

Tom lay upon a sofa with an eager auditory about him, and told the history of the wonderful adventure, putting in many striking additions to adorn it withal; and closed with a description of how he left Becky and went on an exploring expedition; how he followed two avenues as far as his kite-line would reach; how he followed a third to the fullest stretch of the kite-line, and was about to turn back when he glimpsed a far-off speck that looked like daylight; dropped the line and groped towards it, pushed his head and shoulders through a small hole and saw the

broad Mississippi rolling by! And if it had only happened to be night he would not have seen that speck of daylight, and would not have explored that passage any more! He told how he went back for Becky and broke the good news, and she told him not to fret her with such stuff, for she was tired, and knew she was going to die, and wanted to. He described how he laboured with her and convinced her, and how she almost died for joy when she had groped to where she actually saw the blue speck of daylight; how he pushed his way out of the hole and then helped her out; how they sat there and cried for gladness; how some men came along in a skiff, and Tom hailed them and told them their situation and their famished condition; how the men didn't believe the wild tale at first, "because," said they, "you are five miles down the river below the valley the cave is in"; then took them aboard, rowed to a house, gave them supper, made them rest till two or three hours after dark, and then brought them home.

After a couple of weeks passed and Tom had recovered, he decided to stop by and see Becky, who was growing stronger now. The Judge was there and said:

"Well, at least nobody will get lost in that cave any more."

"Why?"

"Because I had its big door sheathed with boiler iron two weeks ago, and triple locked; and I've got the keys."

Tom turned as white as a sheet.

"What's the matter, boy? Here, run, somebody! Fetch a glass of water!"

The water was brought and thrown into Tom's face.

"Ah, now you're all right. What was the matter with you, Tom?"

"Oh, Judge, Injun Joe's in the cave!"

Final Search for Injun Joe

Within a few minutes the news had spread, and a dozen skiff-loads of men were on their way to McDougal's cave, and the ferry-boat, well filled with passengers, soon followed. Tom Sawyer was in the skiff that bore Judge Thatcher. When the cave door was unlocked, a sorrowful sight presented itself in the dim twilight of the place. Injun Joe lay stretched upon the ground, dead, with his face close to the crack of the door, as if his longing eyes had been fixed to the latest moment upon the light and the cheer of the free world outside.

Injun Joe was buried near the mouth of the cave; and people flocked there in boats and wagons from the town and from all the farms and hamlets for seven miles around. They brought their children and all sorts of provisions, and confessed that they had had almost as satisfactory a time at the funeral as they could have had at the hanging.

The morning after the funeral, Tom took Huck to a private place to have an important talk. Huck had just found out that the Temperance Tavern had been closed down for selling whisky. He knew all about Tom's adventure from the Welshman and the Widow Douglas by this time, but Tom said he reckoned there was one thing they had not told him. Huck's face saddened. He said:

"I know what it is. You got into number two, and never found anything but whisky. Nobody told me it was you, but I just knowed it must a ben you, soon as I heard 'bout that whisky business; and I knowed you hadn't got the money becuz you'd a got at me some way or other, and told me, even if you was mum to everybody else. Tom, something's always told me we'd never get hold of that swag.

"Why, Huck, I never told on that tavern-keeper. You know his tavern was all right the Saturday I went to the picnic. Don't you remember you was to watch there that night?"

"Oh, yes! Why it seems 'bout a year ago. It was that very night that I follered Injun Joe."

"You followed him?"

"Yes—but you keep mum. I reckon Injun Joe's left friends behind him. I don't want 'em souring on me, and doing me mean tricks. If it hadn't been for me he'd be down in Texas now, all right."

Then Huck told his entire adventure in confidence to Tom, who had only heard of the Welshman's part of it before.

"Well," said Huck presently, coming back to the main question, "whoever nipped the whisky in number two nipped the money too, I reckon—anyways it's a goner for us, Tom."

"Huck, that money wasn't ever in number two!"

"What!" Huck searched his comrade's face keenly. "Tom, have you got on the track of that money again?"

"Huck, it's in the cave!"

Huck's eyes blazed.

"Say it again, Tom!"

"The money's in the cave!"

"Tom—honest injun, now—is it fun or earnest?"

"Earnest, Huck—just as earnest as ever I was in my life. Will you go with me and help get it out?"

"I bet I will! I will if it's where we can blaze our way to it and not get lost."

"Huck, we can do that without the least little bit of trouble in the world. I'll take you right to it in a skiff, the way that nobody but me knows of!"

"Let's start right off, Tom!"

Finding the Treasure

They got to the hole where Tom had discovered the speck of daylight and climbed inside, Tom in the lead. The boys began to quiet down to whispers, now, for the stillness and gloom of the place oppressed their spirits. They went on with their kite-lines and presently entered and followed a corridor until they reached the 'jumping-off place'. Their candles revealed the fact that it was not really a precipice, but only a steep clay hill. Tom whispered:

"Now I'll show you something, Huck."

He held his candle aloft and said:

"Look as far around the corner as you can. Do you see that? There—on the big rock over yonder —done with candle smoke."

"Tom, it's a cross!"

"Now where's your number two? 'Under the cross', hey? Right yonder's where I saw Injun Joe poke up his candle, Huck. We'll climb down there and have a hunt for that box."

Tom went first, cutting rude steps in the clay hill as he descended. Huck followed. Four avenues opened out of the small cavern which the great rock stood in. The boys examined three of them with no result. They found a small recess in the one nearest the base of the rock, with a pallet of blankets spread down in it; but there was no money-box. The lads searched and re-searched this place but in vain.

Then, Tom said:

"Looky here, Huck, there's foot-prints and some candle-grease on the clay about one side of this rock, but not on the other sides. Now, what's that for? I bet you the money is under the rock. I'm going to dig in the clay."

Then Huck began to dig and scratch also. Some boards were soon uncovered and removed. They had concealed a natural chasm which led under the rock. Tom got into this and held his candle as far under the rock as he could, but said he could not see the end of the rift. He proposed to explore. He stooped and passed under; the narrow way descended gradually. He followed its winding course, first to the right, then to the left, Huck at his heels. Tom turned a short curve by-and-by, and exclaimed:

"My goodness, Huck, looky here!"

It was the treasure-box sure enough, occupying a snug little cavern.

"Got it at last!" said Huck, ploughing among the tarnished coins with his hands. "My, but we're rich, Tom!"

"Huck, I always reckoned we'd get it. It's just too good to believe, but we have got it, sure! Say, let's not fool around here, let's snake it out. Lemme see if I can lift the box."

It weighed about fifty pounds. Tom could lift it after an awkward fashion, but could not carry it conveniently.

"I thought so," he said: "they carried it like it was heavy that day at the ha'nted house—I noticed that. I reckon I was right to think of fetching the money bags along."

The money was soon in the bags, and the boys took it up to the cross rock.

They presently emerged into a clump of bushes, looked warily out, found the coast clear, and were soon lunching in the skiff. As the sun dipped towards the horizon they pushed out and got under way. Tom skimmed up the shore through the long twilight, chattering cheerily to Huck, and landed shortly after dark.

"Now, Huck," said Tom, "we'll hide the money in the loft of the Widow's wood shed, and I'll come up in the morning and we'll count and divide, and then we'll hunt up a place out in the woods for it where it will be safe. Just you lay quiet here and watch the stuff till I run and hook Benny Taylor's little wagon. I won't be a minute."

He disappeared, and presently returned with the wagon, put the bags into it, threw some old rags on top of them, and started off, dragging his cargo behind him. When the boys reached the Welshman's house they stopped to rest. Just as they were about to move on, the Welshman stepped out and said:

"Hallo, who's that?"

"Huck and Tom Sawyer."

"Good! Come along with me, boys, you are keeping everybody waiting. Here, hurry up, trot ahead; I'll haul the wagon for you. Why, it's not as light as it might be. Got bricks in it, or old metal?"

"Old metal," said Tom.

"I judged so; the boys in this town will take more trouble and fool away more time hunting up six bits' worth of old iron to sell to the foundry, than they would to make twice the money at regular work. But that's human nature. Hurry along, hurry along!"

The boys wanted to know what the hurry was about.

"Never mind; you'll see when we get to the Widow Douglas's."

Huck said with some apprehension, for he was long used to being falsely accused:

"We haven't been doing nothing."

"Well, I don't know, Huck, my boy. I don't know about that. Ain't you and the Widow good friends?"

"Yes. Well, she's ben a good friend to me, anyways."

"All right, then. What do you want to be afraid for?"

This question was not entirely answered in Huck's slow mind before he found himself pushed, along with Tom, into Mrs Douglas's drawing-room. The Welshman left the wagon near the door and followed.

The Final Reward

The place was grandly lighted, and everybody that was of any consequence in the village was there. The Thatchers were there, the Harpers, the Rogerses, Aunt Polly, Sid, Mary, the minister, the editor, and a great many more, and all dressed in their best. The Widow received the boys as heartily as anyone could well receive two such looking beings. They were covered with clay and candle-grease. Aunt Polly blushed crimson with humiliation, and frowned and shook her head at Tom. Nobody suffered half as much as the two boys did, however. The Welshman said:

"Tom wasn't at home, yet, so I gave him up; but I stumbled on him and Huck right at my door, and so I just brought them along in a hurry."

"And you did just right," said the Widow. "Come with me, boys."

She took them to a bedchamber and said:

"Now wash and dress yourselves. Here are two new suits of clothes—shirts, socks, everything complete. They're Huck's—no, no thanks, Huck—the Welshman, Mr Jones, bought one and I the other. But they'll fit both of you. Get into them. We'll wait—come down when you are slicked up enough."

Then she left.

After they had put on their new togs, which made Huck so disgusted, Tom knew he'd be back in his old rags as soon as he could, they went downstairs.

The Widow was so grateful for Huck's part in saving her from Injun Joe, she promised him a home with her and money for a business.

"But Huck don't need it," Tom said. "He's rich. Huck's got money. Maybe you don't believe it, but he's got lots of it. Oh, you needn't smile, I reckon I can show you. You just wait a minute." And they both ran out to the wagon and brought in the money bags. Everyone gasped when they counted out twelve thousand dollars, which was more than anyone present had ever seen at one time before, and after explanations it was agreed that the money should be invested for them.

The weeks passed but Huck was none too happy under the Widow's discipline and being rich didn't impress him either, so one day he ran off. Tom found him three days later, and after promising him that he could join his 'robber gang', got him to go back to the Widow's home, and that's where he's been ever since that day.

HEIDI

On the Mountain

Heidi had never felt so happy in her life before as she felt when, as a five year old orphan, she was brought by her Aunt Dete to live with her grandfather up on Alm Mountain.

Dete had received an offer of a good working position and no longer wanted the responsibility of looking after Heidi. She was dubious as to whether she should take Heidi to her grandfather, who was not very well thought of by the villagers. Apparently, when young he had gambled away all his properties and had lived a reckless life. Some said he had become a soldier in Naples and had killed a man in a brawl and when he returned home with Tobias, his son, and without his wife, who had died, he could find no one willing to look after the boy.

He was so disappointed in the villagers he would have no more to do with them and became a hermit whom the villagers named "Alm Uncle", and his son was apprenticed elsewhere.

When Tobias had grown up, he married Dete's sister Adelaide, and Heidi was their daughter. When Adelaide died, and Tobias had been killed in an accident, Dete found herself responsible for Heidi.

So Dete saw that there was no alternative but to take Heidi up the mountain to the simple hut where Heidi's true grandfather lived, despite protestations from the villagers.

So they took the winding path from the old and pleasantly situated village of Mayenfeld, through green and shady meadows to the foot of the mountains, which on this side look down from their stern and lofty heights upon the valley below. The view grows gradually wider as the path ascends.

Half way up the mountain they found an old dilapidated hut, which seemed to tremble in the wind. This was the home of Peter, the goat-herd, who was eleven years old, and lived there with his mother and blind grandmother. Every morning Peter went down to Dorfli to fetch the goats and drive them up onto the mountain, where they were to browse till evening on the mountain plants.

Immediately behind the goat-herd's hut, the path continued, rising in a steep ascent up the mountain side. After a climb of more than three quarters of an hour, they reached Alm Uncle's hut. It stood on a projection of the rock, exposed to the winds, but where every ray of sun could rest upon it, and a full view could be had of the valley beneath.

Behind the hut stood three old fir trees with long, thick, unlopped branches. Beyond these rose a further wall of mountain, the lower heights still overgrown with beautiful grass and plants, above which were stonier slopes, covered only with scrub that led gradually up to the steep, bare, rocky summits.

Against the hut, on the side looking towards the valley, Alm Uncle had put up a seat, and here he was sitting when they arrived, with his thickset grey, bushy eyebrows and immense beard, his pipe in his mouth and his hands on his knees, quietly looking out.

It was a surprise to him, and not an unhappy one, when he found he was to care for little Heidi.

He took to Heidi quite readily and made her a comfortable bed in the hay loft, which she loved, and he also made her a three legged stool, like his own, especially for her to sit on.

He found that Heidi was a very intelligent little girl, and she found her grandfather to be warm and generous and kind-hearted; and so Heidi came to settle in very well.

A Day with the Goats

Heidi would never forget the first time her grandfather allowed her to go with Peter and the goats, up to the mountain summits where the animals could graze.

Peter was already outside the grandfather's hut in the early morning. Heidi ran forward to wish good morning to him and the goats.

"Do you want to go with them on to the mountain?" asked her grandfather. Nothing could have pleased Heidi better, and she jumped for joy in answer. As she was getting ready, her grandfather gave her lunch to Peter to look after and told him to milk one of the goats so that Heidi should have a drink with her lunch.

Heidi started joyfully for the mountain. During the night the wind had blown away all the clouds; the dark blue sky was spreading overhead, and in its midst was the bright sun shining down on the green slopes of the mountain, where the flowers opened their little blue and yellow cups, and looked up to him smiling. Heidi went running hither and thither and shouting with delight, for here were whole patches of delicate red primroses, and there the blue gleam of the lovely gentian, while above them all laughed and nodded the tender-leaved golden cistus.

Enchanted with all this waving field of brightly-coloured flowers, Heidi forgot even Peter and the goats. She ran on in front and then off to the side, tempted first one way and then the other, as she caught sight of some bright spot of glowing red or yellow. And all the while she plucking whole handfuls of the flowers which she put into her little apron, for she wanted to take them all home and stick them in the hay, so that she might make her bedroom look just like the meadows outside. Peter had therefore to be on the alert, and his round eyes had more work than they could manage, for the goats were as lively as Heidi; they ran in all directions, and Peter had to follow whistling and calling and swinging his stick to get all the runaways together again.

"Come along here," called Peter. "You are not to fall over the rocks, your grandfather gave orders that you were not to do so."

When they reached the top, Heidi unfastened her apron and, rolling it carefully round the flowers, laid it beside Peter's wallet containing the lunch, in a hollow; she then sat down beside his outstretched figure and looked about her. The valley lay far below, bathed in the morning sun. In front of her rose a broad snow-field, high against the dark blue sky, while to the left was a huge pile of rocks, on either side of which a bare lofty peak that seemed to pierce the blue, looked frowningly down upon her. The child sat without moving, her eyes taking in the whole scene, and all around was a great stillness, only broken by soft, light puffs of wind that swayed the light bells of the blue flowers, and the shining gold heads of the cistus, and set them nodding merrily on their slender stems.

Peter had fallen asleep after his exertion, and the goats were climbing about among the bushes overhead. Heidi drank in the golden sunlight, the fresh air, the sweet smell of the flowers, and wished for nothing better than to remain there for ever. So the time went on, while to Heidi, who had so often looked up from the valley at the mountains above, these seemed now to have faces, and to be looking down at her like old friends.

Peter woke up later and called to the goats, and they all came springing down the rocks until they were assembled on the green plateau. Heidi played with them for a while and then they ate their lunch and drank the goat's milk. Heidi offered Peter some of her food, and he was unable to speak for astonishment, for never in his life had he had any food to give away. She really pressed him until he finally took some. Then Peter taught her the names of all the goats, including Greenfinch, Snowflake and Great Turk, the prettiest being Little Swan and Little Bear, which belonged to her grandfather.

And thus, imperceptibly, the day had crept on to its close, and now the sun was on the point of sinking out of sight behind the high mountains. Heidi was again sitting on the ground, silently gazing at the blue bell-shaped flowers, as they glistened in the evening sun, for a golden light lay on the grass and flowers, and the rocks above were beginning to shine and glow. All at once she sprang to her feet, "Peter! Peter! everything is on fire! All the rocks are burning, and the great snow mountain and the sky! O look, look! the high rock up there is red with flame! O the beautiful, fiery snow! Stand up, Peter! Everything is on fire!"

"It is always like that," said Peter composedly, "but it is not really fire."

"What is it then?" cried Heidi, as she ran backwards and forwards to look first one side and

then the other, for she felt she could not have enough of such a beautiful sight.

"It gets like that of itself with the sun," explained Peter.

"Look, look!" cried Heidi in fresh excitement, "now they have turned all rose coloured! Look at that one covered with snow, and that with the high, pointed rocks! O how beautiful, look at the crimson snow! And up there on the rocks there are ever so many roses! Oh! now they are turning grey! Oh! oh! now all the colour has died away! It's all gone, Peter." And Heidi sat down on the ground, looking as full of distress as if everything had really come to an end.

Peter explained that it would come again tomorrow and, feeling happier, she and Peter returned home again, to find the grandfather sitting waiting for them under the fir trees.

Heidi had loved that day and was delighted when Peter asked her to go again in the morning and all night she slept soundly on her bed of hay in the loft, dreaming of nothing but shining mountains with red roses all over them, among which happy little goats went leaping in and out.

After that Peter always liked Heidi to accompany him, as she was full of fun and showed him kindness he'd never known before; and so it went on day after day till Heidi, passing her life among the grass and flowers, was burnt brown with the sun and grew so strong and healthy that nothing ever ailed her.

A Visit to Grandmother

The autumn came and the wind blew louder and stronger and the grandfather would say sometimes, "Today you must stay at home, Heidi; a sudden gust of wind would blow a little thing like you over the rocks into the valley below in a moment."

Whenever Peter heard that he must go alone, he looked very unhappy, for he did not know how he should bear the long, dull day without Heidi.

When it grew very cold, Peter would come up early in the morning, blowing on his fingers to keep them warm, and soon he stopped coming, for one night there was a heavy fall of snow and not a single green leaf was to be seen anywhere upon the mountain. Heidi looked through the window watching with wonderment as the snowflakes fell, until the snow was up to the window. Heidi's grandfather went out the next day, when the snowing ceased, to clear it away from the doors and windows.

One afternoon, when Heidi and her grandfather were sitting on their three legged stools before the fire, there came a great thump at the door. It was Peter, white all over with snow from fighting his way through snow drifts. He had been determined not to be beaten, for it was a week now since he had seen Heidi.

Peter stayed for some refreshment and passed a pleasant afternoon there. Then he explained that now he couldn't take the goats about, he had to attend school for the winter months, but he said, "I shall come again next Sunday, and grandmother sent word that she would like you to come and see her one day."

It was quite a new idea to Heidi that she should go and pay anybody a visit, and she could not get it out of her head; so the first thing she said to her grandfather the next day was, "I must go down to see the grandmother today, she will expect me."

"The snow is too deep," answered the grandfather, trying to put her off. But Heidi had made up her mind to go.

On the fourth day, when with every step one took the ground crackled with frost and the whole vast field of snow was hard as ice, Heidi was sitting on her high stool at dinner with the bright sun shining in upon her through the window, and again repeated her little speech, "I must certainly go down to see the grandmother today or else I shall keep her waiting too long."

The grandfather rose from the table, climbed up to the hay loft and brought down the thick sack that was Heidi's coverlet, and said, "Come along then!" The child skipped gleefully after him into the glittering world of snow.

The grandfather had gone into the shed and he now came out dragging a large hand-sleigh along with him. He got into the sleigh and lifted the child on to his lap; then he wrapped her up in the sack, that she might keep nice and warm, and put his left arm closely round her, for it was necessary to hold her tight during the coming journey. The sleigh shot down the mountainside with such rapidity that Heidi thought they were flying through the air, and she shouted with delight.

Suddenly they came to a standstill, and there they were at Peter's hut. Her grandfather lifted her out and unwrapped her.

"There you are, now go in, and when it begins to grow dark, I shall come to meet you."

Heidi went in and walked through the kitchen, where she found a small room. In the corner was the grandmother, bent at the spinning wheel, and Peter's mother, Brigitta.

Heidi soon made friends with the grandmother and Peter's mother, who was surprised to learn that "Alm Uncle" was taking such good care of Heidi.

Heidi was very distressed to learn that the grandmother was blind and would always be so, but the grandmother assured her that Heidi herself would be the light of her life, as she was so cheerful and happy and good to listen to, and it would be such a pleasure if Heidi could come and talk to her often.

So every fine winter's day the child was brought down in her sleigh. She also persuaded her grandfather to patch up the hut, as the rattling of the loose boards and shutters used to frighten the old lady so much she thought her home would one day collapse about her.

So the winter went by. After many years of joyless life, the blind grandmother had at last found something to make her happy. Her days were no longer passed in weariness and darkness, and she would listen every day for the sound of Heidi's footsteps coming, and when she heard the door open and knew the child was really there, she would call out, "God be thanked, she has come again!"

Two Unexpected Visitors

So the winter passed quickly, and still more quickly the bright glad summer, and now another winter was drawing to its close. Heidi was still as light-hearted and happy as the birds, and looked forward with more delight each day to the coming spring, when the warm south wind would roar through the fir trees and blow away the snow, and the warm sun would entice the blue and yellow flowers to show their heads, and the long days out on the mountain would come again, which seemed to Heidi the greatest joy that the earth could give. Heidi was now in her eighth year; she had learnt all kinds of useful things from her grandfather; she knew how to look after the goats as well as anyone, and Little Swan and Little Bear would follow her like two faithful dogs.

One day in March, when the snow had melted, the

pastor came to try and persuade Alm Uncle to send Heidi to school, but the grandfather was adamant that she should not go, and when he explained that the winter journeys to and from school would be treacherous, the pastor agreed. But then he tried with great warmth to persuade Alm Uncle to come down the mountain to Dorfli and live again amongst the people, but it was to no avail.

The next day another visitor arrived; it was Dete, dressed finely in a long trailing skirt and wearing a fine feathered hat.

Dete wanted to take Heidi away. She knew of an immensely wealthy family near Frankfurt, who needed a companion for their only daughter, who was young and an invalid, obliged to go about in a wheelchair. Dete saw it as a good opening for Heidi, and she had come at once for the child.

When Alm Uncle refused to let the child go, Dete leaped up from her seat like a rocket and cried, "If that is all you have to say about it, why then I will give you a piece of my mind. The child is now eight years old and knows nothing, and you will not let her learn. You will not send her to church or school, as I was told down in Dorfli, and she is my own sister's child. I am responsible for what happens to her, and when there is such an opportunity for the child as this which offers for Heidi, only a person who cares for nobody and never wishes good to anyone would think of not jumping at it. But I am not going to give in, and that I tell you; I have everybody in Dorfli on my side; there is not one person there who will not take my part against you; and I advise you to think well before bringing it into court, if that is your intention; there are certain things which might be brought up against you which you would not care to hear, for when one has to do with law-courts there is a great deal raked up that had been forgotten."

"Be silent!" thundered the Alm Uncle, and his eyes flashed with anger. "Go and be done with you! But don't ever bring her back to me. Never let me see her with a hat and feather, and such words on her tongue as you come with today!" And with that he strode out of the hut.

"You have made grandfather angry," said Heidi, and her dark eyes had anything but a friendly expression in them as she looked at Dete.

223

"He will soon be all right again; come now," said Dete hurriedly, "and show me where your clothes are."

"I am not coming," said Heidi.

"Nonsense," continued Dete; then, altering her tone to one half-coaxing, half-cross, "Come, come, you do not understand any better than your grandfather; you will have all sorts of good things that you never dreamed of." Then she went to the cupboard and, taking out Heidi's things, rolled them up in a bundle. "Come along now, there's your hat; it is very shabby but will do for the present; put it on and let us make haste off."

"I am not coming," repeated Heidi.

"Listen to me; you saw your grandfather was angry and heard what he said, that he did not wish to see us ever again; he wants you now to go away with me and you must not make him angrier still. You can't think how nice it is at Frankfurt, and what a lot of things you will see, and if you do not like it you can come back again, your grandfather will be in a good temper again by that time."

"Can I return at once and be back home again here this evening?" asked Heidi.

"What are you talking about, come along now! I tell you that you can come back here when you like. Today we shall go as far as Mayenfeld, and early tomorrow we shall start in the train, and that will bring you home again in no time when you wish it, for it goes as fast as the wind."

Dete had now got the bundle under her arm and the child by the hand, and so they went down the mountain together.

Peter saw them approaching and he exclaimed, "Where are you going, Heidi?"

"I am only just going over to Frankfurt for a little visit with Dete," she replied; "but I must first run to grandmother, she will be expecting me."

"No, no, you must not stop to talk; it is already too late," said Dete, holding Heidi, who was struggling to get away, fast by the hand. "You can go in when you come back, you must come along now," and she pulled the child on with her, fearing that if she let her go in Heidi might take it into her head again that she did not wish to come, and that the grandmother might stand by her.

Peter ran in to tell the grandmother, who was shocked and heart-broken to hear that Heidi was being dragged away.

From that day forward Alm Uncle looked fiercer and more forbidding than ever when he came down and passed through Dorfli. He spoke to no one, and looked such an ogre as he came along with his pack of cheeses to sell on his back, his immense stick in his hand, and his thick, frowning eyebrows, that the women would call to their little ones, "Take care! get out of Alm Uncle's way or he may hurt you."

The days were sad again now for the old blind woman, and not one passed but what she would murmur complainingly, "Alas! all our happiness and pleasure has gone with the child, and now the days are so long and dreary! Pray God I see Heidi again once more before I die!"

A New Life

Clara, the little daughter of Herr Sesemann, was lying pale and thin on the invalid couch in the study of their house in Frankfurt, impatiently awaiting the arrival of her companion. Her two soft blue eyes were fixed on the clock in the corner of the cosy room. This was where she was accustomed to take her lessons from a tutor and in here also was a handsome bookcase with glass doors.

Meanwhile, Dete and Heidi had arrived late in the evening and Fräulein Rottenmeier was interviewing them in her office. Fräulein Rottenmeier was not at all pleased with Heidi. She was disappointed in her

appearance, and thought she was too young and was shocked when she found Heidi could not read or write. But Dete was determined to leave Heidi there and left before Fräulein Rottenmeier could do much about it.

Fräulein Rottenmeier was the housekeeper and, as the mistress of the house had died, she was often left in charge when Herr Sesemann was away. She always wore a mysterious-looking loose garment with a large collar or shoulder-cape that gave a certain solemnity to her appearance, which was enhanced by a very lofty dome-shaped headdress. Whilst Herr Sesemann was absent though, his daughter was to have a full voice in all matters and nothing was to be done against her wish, and after meeting Heidi it was Clara's wish that Heidi should stay.

It came about that Heidi and Clara got along together very well. Heidi made Clara laugh, especially in her lessons, as Heidi found difficulty in learning the letters and would say unexpected things. Fräulein Rottenmeier was not happy about this at all.

Then, one day, when Heidi had been frightened by carriages passing the house, for she had never heard them before, she had inadvertently upset a lot of things on the table and had made Fräulein Rottenmeier very cross.

But the one thing which really did upset Fräulein Rottenmeier was when Heidi had tried to climb a church tower, looking for the view of the valley, and had found some kittens and brought them home. Fräulein Rottenmeier had been terrified of the 'beastly' things. But Clara and Heidi had been so taken with the kittens that they had entrusted Sebastian, a kindly servant, with them and he had agreed to hide them so that they could play with them from time to time. Later, Fräulein Rottenmeier had been looking in Clara's wardrobe for some more 'fitting' clothes for Heidi, when she accidentally came across the kittens and had gone almost hysterical in the outcome.

So accordingly, when Herr Sesemann returned home, Fräulein Rottenmeier informed him that Heidi had been absolutely impossible and that the child was almost out of her mind because of the strange things she would do. Herr Sesemann was very concerned about this, but on observing the girl for himself and finding that Clara and she were the best of friends and that Clara seemed much improved in herself, it was decided that Heidi must definitely stay on, especially as he was to be going away again shortly.

But Heidi missed her grandfather so, and the mountains and Peter and the grandmother so much that at times she was very distressed, especially at having to endure the frowning Fräulein Rottenmeier, who seemed overpoweringly unfair to her.

Clara's Grandmother Arrives

There was much expectation and preparation about the house on a day of the following week, and it was easy to see that the lady who was coming, the grandmother of Clara, was one whose opinion was highly thought of, and for whom everybody had a great respect.

Tinette, the maid, had a new white cap on her head, and Sebastian collected all the footstools he could find and placed them in convenient spots, so that the lady might find one ready to her feet whenever she chose to sit. Fräulein Rottenmeier went about surveying everything, very upright and dignified, as if to show that, though a rival power was expected, her own authority was not going to be extinguished.

And now the carriage came driving up to the door, and Tinette and Sebastian ran down the steps, followed with a slower and more stately step by the lady, who advanced to greet the guest. Heidi had been sent up to her room and ordered to remain there until called down, as the grandmother would certainly like to see Clara alone first.

When she was called down, Heidi walked up to her and said very distinctly in her clear voice, "Good evening," and then wishing to follow her instructions from Fräulein Rottenmeier, called her what would be in English "Mrs Madam," by mistake. Fräulein Rottenmeier glared at her.

"Well!" said the grandmother laughing, "is that how they address people in your home on the mountain?"

"No," replied Heidi gravely, "I never knew anyone with that name before."

"Nor I neither," laughed the grandmother again as she patted Heidi's cheek. "Never mind! When I am with the children I am always grandmamma; you won't forget that name, will you?"

"No, no," Heidi assured her, "I often used to say it at home."

"I understand," said the grandmother, with a cheerful little nod of the head. Then she looked more closely at Heidi, giving another nod from time to time, and the child looked back at her with steady, serious eyes, for there was something kind and warm-hearted about this newcomer that pleased Heidi, and indeed everything to do with the grandmother attracted her, so that she could not turn her eyes away. She had such beautiful white hair, and two long lace ends hung down from the cap on her head and waved gently about her face every time she moved, as if a soft breeze were blowing round her, which gave Heidi a peculiar feeling of pleasure.

"And what is your name, child?" the grandmother now asked.

"I am always called Heidi; but as I am now to be called Adelaide, as Fräulein Rottenmeier wishes, I will try and take care—" Heidi stopped short, for she felt a little guilty; she had not yet grown accustomed to this name; she continued not to respond when Fräulein Rottenmeier suddenly addressed her by it, and the lady was at this moment entering the room.

"Frau Sesemann will no doubt agree with me," she interrupted, "that it was necessary to choose a name that could be pronounced easily, if only for the sake of the servants."

"My worthy Rottenmeier," replied Frau Sesemann, "if a person is called 'Heidi' and has grown accustomed to that name, I call her by the same, and so let it be."

Grandmother's Book

When, on the following day, Clara lay down as usual on her couch after dinner, the grandmother sat down beside her for a few minutes and closed her eyes, then she got up again as lively as ever, and trotted off into the dining-room. No one was there. "She is asleep, I suppose," she said to herself, and then going up to Fräulein Rottenmeier's room she gave a loud knock at the door. She waited a few minutes and then Fräulein Rottenmeier opened the door and drew back in surprise at this unexpected visit.

"Where is the child, and what is she doing all this

time? That is what I came to ask," said Frau Sesemann.

"She is sitting in her room, where she could well employ herself if she had the least idea of making herself useful; but you have no idea, Frau Sesemann, of the out-of-the-way things this child imagines and does, things which I could hardly repeat in good society."

"I should do the same if I had to sit in there like that child, I can tell you; I doubt if you would then like to repeat what I did in good society! Go and fetch the child and bring her to my room; I have some pretty books with me that I should like to give her."

"That is just the misfortune," said Fräulein Rottenmeier with a despairing gesture, "what use are books to her? She has not been able to learn her A B C even, all the time she has been here."

"That is very strange," said Frau Sesemann, "she does not look to me like a child who would be unable to learn her alphabet. However, bring her now to me, she can at least amuse herself with the pictures in the books."

Heidi now appeared and gazed with open-eyed delight and wonder at the beautiful coloured pictures in the books which the grandmother gave her to look at. All of a sudden, as the latter turned over one of the pages to a fresh picture, the child gave a cry. For a moment or two she looked at it with brightening eyes, then the tears began to fall, and at last she burst into sobs. The grandmother looked at the picture – it represented a green pasture, full of young animals, some grazing and others nibbling at the shrubs. In the middle was a shepherd leaning upon his staff and looking on at his happy flock. The whole scene was bathed in golden sunlight, for the sun was just sinking below the horizon.

The grandmother laid her hand kindly on Heidi's. "Don't cry, dear child, don't cry," she said, "the picture has reminded you perhaps of something. But see, there is a beautiful tale to the picture which I will tell you this evening. And there are other nice tales of all kinds to read and to tell again. But now we must have a little talk together, so dry your tears and come and stand in front of me, so that I may see you well – there, now we are happy again."

When at last she saw that Heidi was growing calmer, she said, "Now I want you to tell me something. How are you getting on with your reading lessons?"

"It's of no use," said Heidi in the tone of one who was ready to endure what could not be cured.

"Of course it isn't. Listen to what I have to say," continued the grandmother. "As soon as you are able to read, you shall have that book for your own, and then you will know all about the sheep and the goats, and what the shepherd did, and the wonderful things that happened to him, just as if someone were telling you the whole tale. You will like to hear about all that, won't you?"

Heidi had listened with eager attention to the grandmother's words and now with a sigh exclaimed, "Oh, if only I could read now!"

"It won't take you long now to learn, that I can see; and now we must go down to Clara; bring the books with you." And hand in hand the two returned to the study.

Heidi understood that Herr Sesemann would think it ungrateful of her if she wished to leave, and she believed that the grandmother and Clara would think the same. So there was nobody to whom she dared confide her longing to go home, for she would not for the world have given the grandmother, who was so kind to her, any reason for being as angry with her as Fräulein Rottenmeier had been.

But the weight of trouble on the little heart grew heavier and heavier; she could no longer eat her food, and every day she grew a little paler. She lay awake for long hours at night, for as soon as she was alone and everything was still around her, the picture of the mountain with its sunshine and flowers rose vividly before her eyes; and when at last she fell asleep it was to dream of the rocks and the snow-field turning crimson in the evening light, and waking in the morning she would think herself back at the hut and prepare to run joyfully out into the sun – and then – there was her large bed, and here she was in Frankfurt far, far away from home. And Heidi would often lay her face down on the pillow and weep long and quietly so that no one might hear her.

Heidi's unhappiness did not escape the grandmother's notice. She took her again into her room one day, and drawing the child to her said, "Now tell me, Heidi, what is the matter; are you in trouble?"

But Heidi, afraid if she told the truth the grandmother would think her ungrateful, and would then leave off being so kind to her, answered, "I can't tell you."

"Well, could you tell Clara about it?"

"Oh no, I cannot tell anyone," said Heidi in so positive a tone, and with a look of such trouble on her face, that the grandmother felt full of pity for the child.

Heidi, despite her unhappiness, did now learn to read and would indeed read to Clara often, and the grandmother gave Heidi the book she had so longed for.

When Heidi went to her room at night she looked at her book before going to bed, and from that day forth her chief pleasure was to read the tales which belonged to the beautiful pictures over and over again, especially the tale with the shepherd leaning on his staff with his flock around him in the midst of the green pasture, because it reminded her of Peter.

That was Heidi's favourite tale, which she read over and over again, aloud and to herself, and she was never tired of hearing it. As there were other tales in the book besides, with reading and looking at the pictures the days passed quickly away, and the time drew near for the grandmother to return home.

Herr Sesemann had left before the arrival of the grandmother and after the grandmother had left, the house seemed so silent and empty that Heidi's longing for the old familiar and beautiful things grew daily stronger, so that now only to read a word

that recalled them to her remembrance brought her to the verge of tears, which with difficulty she suppressed.

So the autumn and winter passed, and again the sun came shining down on the white walls of the opposite houses, and Heidi would think to herself that now the time had come for Peter to go out again with the goats, to where the golden flowers of the cistus were glowing in the sunlight, and all the rocks around turned to fire at sunset. Heidi would go and sit in a corner of her lonely room and put her hands up to her eyes that she might not see the sun shining on the opposite wall; and then she would remain

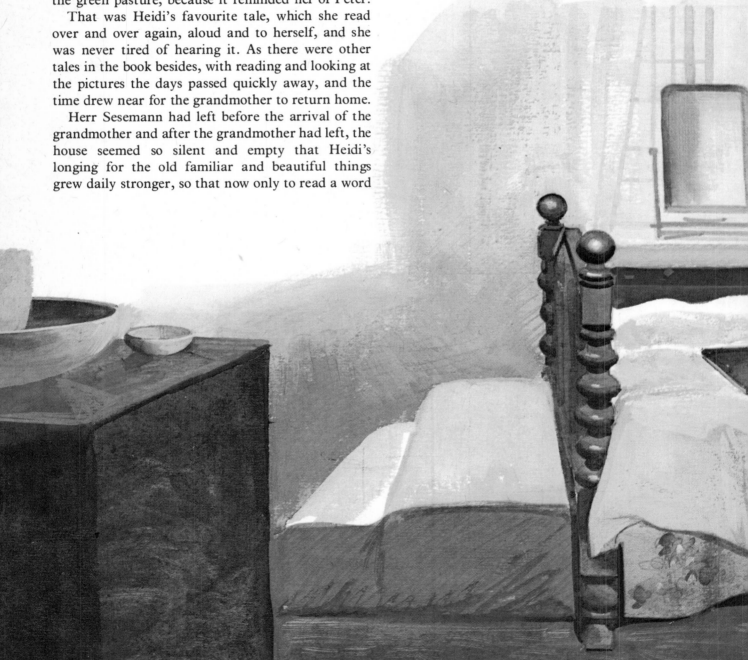

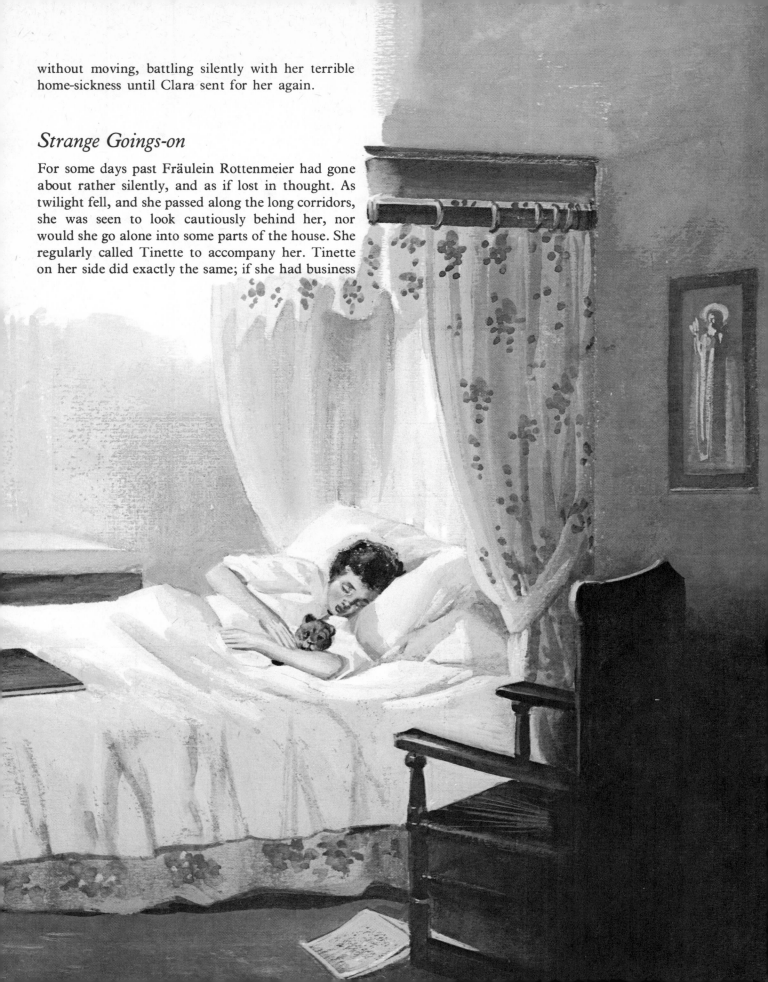

without moving, battling silently with her terrible home-sickness until Clara sent for her again.

Strange Goings-on

For some days past Fräulein Rottenmeier had gone about rather silently, and as if lost in thought. As twilight fell, and she passed along the long corridors, she was seen to look cautiously behind her, nor would she go alone into some parts of the house. She regularly called Tinette to accompany her. Tinette on her side did exactly the same; if she had business

upstairs or down, she called Sebastian to accompany her. For something very strange and mysterious was going on in Herr Sesemann's house. Every morning, when the servants went downstairs, they found the front door wide open, although nobody could be seen far or near to account for it.

During the first few days that this happened, every room and corner was searched in great alarm, to see if anything had been stolen, for the general idea was that a thief had been hiding in the house and had gone off in the night with the stolen goods; but not a thing in the house had been touched; everything was safe in its place. The door was doubly locked at night, and for further security the wooden bar was fastened across it; but it was no good—next morning the door again stood open.

At last, after a great deal of persuasion from Fräulein Rottenmeier, Sebastian and John, another servant, plucked up courage and agreed to sit up one night in the room next the large council-chamber and to watch and see what would happen.

On the appointed night the two sat down and began to take some strengthening cordial, which at first made them very talkative and then very sleepy, so that they leant back in their seats and slept.

At last, as one o'clock struck, John got up with a great show of courage and said, "Come, Sebastian, we must go outside and see what is going on; you need not be afraid, just follow me." Whereupon he opened the door wide and stepped into the hall. Just as he did so a sudden gust of air blew through the open front door and put out the light which John held in his hand. He started back, almost overturning Sebastian, whom he clutched and pulled back

into the room, and then shutting the door quickly he turned the key as far as he could make it go. Then he pulled out his matches and lighted his candle again.

In the light Sebastian gave a cry of alarm, for John was trembling all over and as white as a ghost.

"What's the matter? What did you see outside?" asked Sebastian, horror-struck.

"The door partly open," gasped John, "and a white figure standing at the top of the steps—there it stood, and then all in a minute it disappeared."

Sebastian felt his blood run cold. The two sat down close to one another and did not dare move again till the morning broke and the streets began to be alive again. Then they went upstairs to tell Fräulein Rottenmeier of their experience.

Fräulein Rottenmeier, however, was determined not to pass any more days in a state of fear, and she knew the right course to pursue. She had as yet said nothing to the children of the ghostly apparitions, for she knew if she did that the children would not remain alone for a single moment, and that might entail discomfort for herself. But now she walked straight off into the study, and there in a low mysterious voice told the two children everything that had taken place. Clara immediately screamed out that she could not remain another minute alone, her father must come home, and Fräulein Rottenmeier must sleep in her room at night, and Heidi too must not be left by herself, for the ghost might do something to her. She insisted that they should all sleep together in one room and keep a light burning all night, and Tinette had better be in the next room, and Sebastian and John come upstairs and spend the night in the hall, so they might call out and frighten the ghost the instant they saw it appear on the steps. Clara, in short, grew very excited, and Fräulein Rottenmeier had great difficulty in quieting her.

She promised to write at once to her father, and to have her bed put in her room and not to be left alone for a moment. They could not all sleep in the same room, but if Heidi was frightened, why, Tinette must go into her room. But Heidi was far more frightened of Tinette than of ghosts, of which the child had never before heard, so she assured the others she did not mind the ghost, and would rather be alone at night.

Herr Sesemann Returns

The letter was successful, and two days later Herr Sesemann stood at his front door and rang the bell. Herr Sesemann greeted Sebastian abruptly and went up without a moment's delay into his daughter's room. Clara greeted him with a cry of joy, and seeing her so lively and apparently as well as ever, his face cleared, and the frown of anxiety passed gradually away from it as he heard from his own daughter's lips that she had nothing the matter with her, and moreover was so delighted to see him that she was quite glad about the ghost, as it was the cause of bringing him home again.

"And how is the ghost getting on?" he asked, turning to Fräulein Rottenmeier, with a twinkle of amusement in his eye.

"It is no joke, I assure you," replied the lady. "You will not laugh yourself tomorrow morning, Herr Sesemann; what is going on in the house points to some terrible thing that has taken place in the past and been concealed."

"Well, I know nothing about that," said the master of the house, "but I must beg you not to bring suspicion on my worthy ancestors. And now will you kindly call Sebastian into the dining-room, as I wish to speak to him alone."

As Sebastian appeared Herr Sesemann said: "Go, and take a message to my old friend the doctor, give him my kind regards, and ask if he will come to me tonight at nine o'clock without fail; I have come by express from Paris to consult him. I shall want him to spend the night here, so bad a case is it; so will he arrange accordingly. You understand?"

"Yes, sir," replied Sebastian, "I will see to the matter as you wish." Then Herr Sesemann returned to Clara, and begged her to have no more fear, as he would soon find out all about the ghost and put an end to it.

Punctually at nine o'clock, after the children had gone to bed and Fräulein Rottenmeier had retired, the doctor arrived. He was a grey-haired man with a fresh face, and two bright, kindly eyes.

Herr Sesemann recounted to him how the front door was nightly opened by somebody, according to the testimony of the combined household, and he had therefore provided two loaded revolvers, so as to be prepared for anything that happened; for either the whole thing was a joke got up by some friend of the servants, just to alarm the household while he was away—and in that case a pistol fired into the air would procure him a wholesome fright—or else it was a thief, who, by leading everybody at first to think there was a ghost, made it safe for himself when he came later to steal, as no one would venture to run out if they heard him, and in that case too a good weapon would not be amiss.

The two men took up their quarters for the night in the same room in which Sebastian and John had kept their watch. A bottle of wine was placed on the table, for a little refreshment would be welcome from time to time if the night was to be passed sitting up. Beside it lay the two revolvers, and two good-sized lamps had also been lighted, for Herr Sesemann was determined not to wait for ghosts in any half light.

The door was shut close to prevent the light being seen in the hall outside, which might frighten away the ghost. And now the two gentlemen sat comfortably back in the arm chairs and began talking of all sorts of things, now and then pausing to take a good draught of wine, and so one o'clock struck before they were aware.

The 'Ghost' is Caught

There was not a sound about the house, nor in the street outside. Suddenly the doctor lifted his finger.

"Hush! Sesemann, don't you hear something?"

They both listened, and they distinctly heard the bar softly pushed aside and then the key turned in the lock and the door opened. Herr Sesemann put out his hand for his revolver.

"You are not afraid, are you?" said the doctor as he stood up.

"It is better to take precautions," whispered Herr Sesemann, and seizing one of the lights in his other hand, he followed the doctor who, armed in like manner with a light and a revolver, went softly on in front. They stepped into the hall. The moonlight was shining in through the open door and fell on a white figure standing motionless in the doorway.

"Who is there?" thundered the doctor in a voice that echoed through the hall, as the two men advanced towards the figure.

It turned and gave a cry. There in her little white nightgown stood Heidi, with bare feet, staring with wild eyes at the lights and the revolvers, and trembling from head to foot like a leaf in the wind. The two men looked at one another in surprise.

"Why, I believe it is your little Heidi," said the doctor.

"Child, what does this mean?" said Herr Sesemann. "What did you want? why did you come down here?"

White with terror, and hardly able to make her voice heard, Heidi answered, "I don't know."

But now the doctor stepped forward. "This is a matter for me to see to, Sesemann; go back to your chair. I must take the child upstairs to her bed."

And with that he put down his revolver and gently taking the child by the hand led her upstairs. "Don't be frightened," he said as they went up side by side, "it's nothing to be frightened about; it's all right, only just go quietly."

On reaching Heidi's room the doctor put the candle down on the table, and taking Heidi up in his arms laid her on the bed and carefully covered her over. Then he sat down beside her and waited until Heidi had grown quieter and no longer trembled so violently. He then took her hand and said in a kind, soothing voice, "There, now you feel better, and now tell me where you were wanting to go to?"

"I did not want to go anywhere," said Heidi. "I did not know I went downstairs, but all at once—"

"I see, and had you been dreaming, so that you seemed to see and hear something very distinctly?"

"Yes, I dream every night, and always about the same things. I think I am back with grandfather, and I hear the sound in the fir trees outside, and I see the stars shining so brightly, and then I open the door quickly and run out, and it is all so beautiful! But when I wake I am still in Frankfurt." And Heidi struggled as she spoke to keep back the sobs which seemed to choke her.

"And have you no pain anywhere? No pain in your head or back?"

"No, only a feeling as if there were a great stone weighing on me here."

"As if you had eaten something that would not go down."

"No, not like that; something heavy as if I wanted to cry very much."

"I see, and then do you have a good cry?"

"Oh, no, I mustn't; Fräulein Rottenmeier forbade me to cry."

"So you swallow it all down, I suppose? Are you happy here in Frankfurt?"

"Yes," was the low answer; but it sounded more like "No."

"And where did you live with your grandfather?"

"Up on the mountain."

"That wasn't very amusing; rather dull at times, eh?"

"No, no, it was beautiful, beautiful!" Heidi could go no further; the remembrance of the past, the excitement she had just gone through, the long suppressed weeping, were too much for the girl's strength; the tears began to fall fast, and she broke into violent weeping.

The doctor stood up and laid her head kindly down on the pillow. "There, there, go on crying, it will do you good, and then go to sleep: it will be all right tomorrow."

Then he left the room and went downstairs to Herr Sesemann. "Sesemann," he said, "let me first tell you that your little charge is a sleep-walker; she is the ghost who has nightly opened the front door and put your household into this fever of alarm. Secondly, the child is consumed with home-sickness, to such an extent that she is nearly a skeleton already, and soon will be quite one; something must be done at once. For the first trouble, due to her over-excited nerves, there is but one remedy, to send her back to her native mountain air; and for the second trouble there is also but one cure, and that the same. So tomorrow the child must start for home; there you have my prescription."

Herr Sesemann stood still; the doctor's words were a shock to him. "If you put it so, doctor, there is assuredly only one way—and the thing must be seen to at once." And then he and the doctor walked up and down for a while arranging what to do, after

which the doctor said goodbye, for some time had passed since they first sat down together, and as the master himself opened the hall door this time the morning light shone down through it into the house.

Home Again

Heidi climbed up the steep path from Dorfli as quickly as she could; she was obliged, however, to pause now and again to take breath, for the basket she carried was rather heavy, and the way got steeper as she drew nearer the top. One thought alone filled Heidi's mind; would she find the grandmother sitting in her usual corner by the spinning-wheel, was she still alive? At last Heidi caught sight of the grandmother's house in the hollow of the mountain and her heart began to beat louder and louder—and now she had reached the house, but she trembled so she could hardly open the door—and then she was standing inside, unable in her breathlessness to utter a sound.

"Ah, my God!" cried a voice from the corner, "that was how Heidi used to run in; if only I could

have her with me once again! Who is there?"

"It's I, I, grandmother," cried Heidi as she ran and flung herself on her knees beside the old woman, and seizing her hands, clung to her, unable to speak for joy. And the grandmother herself could not say a word for some time, so unexpected was this happiness. At last she put out her hand and stroked Heidi's curly hair, and said, "Yes, yes, that is her hair, and her voice, thank God He has granted my prayer!" And tears of joy fell from the blind eyes on to Heidi's hand. "Is it really you, Heidi, have you really come back to me?"

"Yes, grandmother, I am really here," answered Heidi in a reassuring voice. "Do not cry, for I have really come back and I am never going away again, and I shall come every day to see you, and you won't have any more hard bread to eat for some days, for look, look!" And Heidi took some white rolls that Clara had given her from the basket, and piled the whole twelve on grandmother's lap.

"Ah, child! child! what a blessing you bring with you!" the old woman exclaimed, as she felt and seemed never to come to the end of the rolls. "But you yourself are the greatest blessing, Heidi," and again she touched the child's hair and passed her hand over her hot cheeks and said, "Say something, child, that I may hear your voice."

Then Heidi told her how unhappy she had been, thinking that the grandmother might die while she was away and that then she would never, never see her again.

Peter's mother now came in and stood for a moment overcome with astonishment. "Why, it's Heidi," she exclaimed, "and yet how can it be?"

And now Heidi clasped the old woman's hand. "I must go home to grandfather," she said. "But tomorrow I shall come again. Goodnight, grandmother."

"Yes, come again, be sure you come again tomorrow," begged the grandmother, as she pressed Heidi's hands in hers, unwilling to let her go.

Down in Dorfli, where Heidi had left her trunk to

be picked up later, the miller was telling the astounded villagers how a young gentleman called Sebastian had brought her to Mayenfeld and seen her off, and had given him her fare without any bargaining, and extra money for himself to take Heidi from the station at Mayenfeld to Dorfli in his miller's cart. What was more, the child had assured him that she had had everything she wanted where she had been, and that it was her own wish to return to her grandfather. This information caused great surprise and was soon repeated all over Dorfli, and that evening there was not a house in the place in which the astounding news was not discussed, of how Heidi had of her own accord given up a luxurious home to return to her grandfather.

Heidi continued her way up the mountain, her basket on her arm. All around her the steep green slopes shone bright in the evening sun, and soon the great gleaming snow-field up above came in sight. Heidi was obliged to keep on pausing to look behind her, for the higher peaks were behind her as she climbed. Suddenly a warm red glow fell on the grass at her feet; she looked back again—she had not remembered how splendid it was, nor seen anything to compare to it in her dreams—for there the two high mountain peaks rose into the air like two great flames, the whole snow-field had turned crimson, and rosy-coloured clouds floated in the sky above.

The grass upon the mountainsides had turned to gold, the rocks were all aglow, and the whole valley was bathed in golden mist. As Heidi stood gazing around her at all this splendour, the tears ran down her cheeks for very delight and happiness.

Not until the glory began to fade could she tear herself away. Then she ran on so quickly that in a very little while she caught sight of the tops of the fir trees above the hut roof, then the roof itself, and at last the whole hut, and there was grandfather sitting as in the old days, smoking his pipe, and she could

see the fir trees waving in the wind. Quicker and quicker went her little feet, and before Alm Uncle had time to see who was coming, Heidi had rushed up to him, thrown down her basket and flung her arms round his neck, unable in the excitement of seeing him again to say more than "Grandfather! Grandfather! Grandfather!" over and over again.

The old man himself said nothing. For the first time for many years his eyes were wet, and he had to pass his hand across them. Then he unloosed Heidi's arms, put her on his knee, and, after looking at her for a moment, "So you have come back to me, Heidi," he said, "how is that? You don't look much of a grand lady. Did they send you away?"

"Oh, no, grandfather," said Heidi eagerly; "you must not think that; they were all so kind—Clara, and grandmamma, and Herr Sesemann. But you see, grandfather, I did not know how to bear myself till I got home again to you. I used to think I should die, for I felt as if I could not breathe; but I never said anything because it would have been ungrateful. And then suddenly one morning quite early Herr Sesemann said to me—but I think it was partly the doctor's doing—but perhaps it's all in the letter," and Heidi jumped down and fetched the roll of money and the letter that Sebastian had given to her when they parted, and handed them both to her grandfather.

"That belongs to you," said the latter, laying the roll down on the bench beside him. Then he opened the letter, read it through, and without a word put it in his pocket.

"Do you think you can still drink milk with me, Heidi?" he asked, taking the child by the hand to go into the hut. "But bring your money with you; you can buy a bed and bedclothes and dresses for a couple of years with it."

"I am sure I do not want it," replied Heidi. "I have got a bed, and Clara has put so many clothes in my box that I shan't want any more."

"Take it and put it in the cupboard; you will want it some day I have no doubt."

Heidi obeyed and skipped happily after her grandfather into the house; she ran into all the corners, delighted to see everything again, and then went up the ladder—but there she came to a pause, and called down in a tone of surprise and distress, "Oh, grandfather, my bed's gone."

"We can soon make it up again," he answered her from below. "I did not know that you were coming back; come along now and have your milk."

Heidi came down, sat herself on her high stool in the old place, and then, taking up her bowl, drank her milk eagerly, as if she had never come across anything so delicious, and as she put down her bowl, she exclaimed, "Our milk tastes nicer than anything else in the world, grandfather."

Back with Peter and the Goats

A shrill whistle was heard outside. Heidi darted out like a flash of lightning. There were the goats leaping and springing down the rocks, with Peter in their midst. When he caught sight of Heidi he stood still with astonishment and gazed speechlessly at her. Heidi called out, "Good evening, Peter," and then ran in among the goats. "Little Swan! Little Bear! do you know me again?" And the animals evidently recognised her voice at once, for they began rubbing their heads against her and bleating loudly as if for joy, and as she called the other goats by name one after the other, they all came scampering towards her helter-skelter and crowding round her. The impatient Greenfinch sprang into the air and over two of her companions to get nearer, and even the shy little Snowflake butted the Great Turk out of her way in quite a determined manner, which left him standing taken aback by her boldness, and lifting his beard in the air as much as to say, "You see who I am."

Heidi was out of her mind with delight at being among all her old friends again; she flung her arms round the pretty little Snowflake, stroked Greenfinch, while she herself was thrust at from all sides by the affectionate and confiding goats; and so at last she got near to where Peter was standing, not having yet got over his surprise.

"Come down, Peter," cried Heidi, "and say good evening to me."

"So you are back again?" he found words to say at last, and now ran down and took Heidi's hand, which she was holding out in greeting, and immediately put the same question to her which he had been in the habit of doing in the old days when they returned home in the evening, "Will you come out with me again tomorrow?"

"Not tomorrow, but the day after perhaps, for tomorrow I must go down to grandmother."

"I am glad you are back," said Peter, while his whole face beamed with pleasure, and then he prepared to go on with his goats; but he never had had so much trouble with them before, for when at last, by coaxing and threats, he had got them all together, and Heidi had gone off with an arm over either head of her grandfather's two goats, the whole flock suddenly turned and ran after her. Heidi had to go inside the stall with her two and shut the door, or Peter would never have got home that night. When Heidi went indoors after this she found her bed already made up for her; the hay had been piled high for it and smelt deliciously, and the grandfather had carefully spread and tucked in the clean sheets. It was with a happy heart that Heidi lay down in it that night, and her sleep was sounder than it had been for a whole year past. The grandfather got up at least ten times during the night and mounted the ladder to see if Heidi was all right and showing no signs of restlessness, and to feel that the hay he had stuffed into the round window was keeping the moon from shining too brightly upon her. But Heidi did not stir; she had no need now to wander about, for the great burning longing of her heart was satisfied; she had seen the high mountains and rocks alight in the evening glow, she had heard the wind in the fir trees, she was at home again on the mountains.

Preparation for a Visitor

It was the month of May. Another long winter had passed, during which the doctor had come from Frankfurt to visit Heidi and her grandfather, and had spent a very happy few days with them. From every height the full fresh streams of spring were flowing down into the valley. The clear warm sunshine lay upon the mountain, which had turned green again. The last snows had disappeared and the sun had already coaxed many of the flowers to show their bright heads above the grass. Up above the gay young wind of spring was singing through the fir trees, and shaking down the old dark needles to make room for the new bright green ones that were soon to deck out the trees in their spring finery. The golden sunshine lit up the grandfather's hut, and all the ground about it was warm and dry again so that one might sit out where one liked. Heidi was running backwards and forwards in her accustomed way on the mountain, not knowing which spot was most delightful.

Now she stood still to listen to the deep, mysterious voice of the wind, as it blew down to her from the mountain summits, coming nearer and nearer and gathering strength as it came, till it broke with force against the fir trees, bending and shaking them, and seeming to shout for joy, so that she too, though blown about like a feather, felt she must join in the chorus of exulting sounds. Then she would run round again to the sunny space in front of the hut, and, seating herself on the ground, would peer closely into the short grass to see how many little flower cups were open or thinking of opening. She rejoiced with all the myriad little beetles and winged insects that jumped and crawled and danced in the sun, and drew in deep draughts of the spring scents that rose from the newly-awakened earth, and thought the mountain was more beautiful than ever. All the tiny living creatures must be as happy as she, for it seemed to her there were little voices all round

her singing and humming in joyful tones, "On the mountain! On the mountain!"

Heidi was especially happy, as a party from Frankfurt were coming to visit. The doctor had thought it would be good for Clara to sample the mountain air and see her friend Heidi again.

From the shed at the back came the sound of sawing and chopping, and Heidi listened to it with pleasure, for it was the old familiar sound she had known from the beginning of her life up here. Suddenly she jumped up and ran round, for she must know what her grandfather was doing. In front of the shed door already stood a finished new chair, and a second was in the course of construction under the grandfather's skilful hand.

"Oh, I know what these are for," exclaimed Heidi in great glee. "We shall want them when they all come from Frankfurt. This one is for grandmamma, and the one you are now making is for Clara, and then—then there will, I suppose, have to be another," continued Heidi with more hesitation in her voice, "or do you think, grandfather, that perhaps Fräulein Rottenmeier will not come with them?"

"Well, I cannot say just yet," replied her grandfather, "but it will be safer to make one so that we can offer her a seat if she does."

A Letter from Frankfurt

While Heidi was watching her grandfather, there approached a whistling, calling, and other sounds which Heidi immediately recognised. She ran out and found herself surrounded by her four-footed friends. They were apparently as pleased as she was to be among the heights again, for they leaped about and bleated for joy, pushing Heidi this way and that, each anxious to express his delight with some sign of affection. But Peter sent them flying to right and left, for he had something to give to Heidi. When he at last got up to her he handed her a letter. "There!" he exclaimed, leaving the further explanation of the matter to Heidi herself.

The letter to Heidi had been given him the evening before by the postman at Dorfli. Heidi read the address carefully; then she ran back to the shed holding out her letter to her grandfather in high glee. "From Frankfurt! from Clara! Would you like to hear it?"

The grandfather was ready and pleased to do so, as also was Peter, who had followed Heidi into the shed. He leant his back against the doorpost, as he felt he could follow Heidi's reading better if firmly supported from behind, and so stood prepared to listen.

"DEAREST HEIDI—Everything is packed and we shall start in two or three days, as soon as papa himself is ready to leave; he is not coming with us as he has first to go to Paris. The doctor comes every day, and as soon as he is inside the door, he cries, 'Off now as quickly as you can, off to the mountain.' He is most impatient about our going. You cannot think how much he enjoyed himself when he was with you back in the winter when he came to visit to see if the area would be beneficial to me. He has called nearly every day since, and each time he has come into my room and said he must tell me about everything again. And then he sits down and describes all he did with you and the grandfather, and talks of the mountains and the flowers and of the great silence up there far above all towns and villages, and of the fresh delicious air, and often adds, 'No one can help getting well up there.' He himself is quite a different man since his visit, and looks quite young again and happy, which he had not been for a long time before. Oh, how I am looking forward to seeing everything and to being with you on the mountain, and to making the acquaintance of Peter and the goats.

"I shall have first to go through a six week's cure at Ragatz; this the doctor has ordered, and then we shall move up to Dorfli, and every fine day I shall be carried up the mountain in my chair and spend the day with you. Grandmamma is travelling with me and will remain with me; she also is delighted at the thought of paying you a visit. But just imagine, Fräulein Rottenmeier refuses to come with us. Almost every day grandmamma says to her, 'Well, how about this Swiss journey, my worthy Rottenmeier? Pray say if you really would like to come with us.' But she always thanks grandmamma very politely and says she has quite made up her mind. I

think I know what has done it: Sebastian gave such a frightful description of the mountain, of how the rocks were so overhanging and dangerous that at any minute you might fall into a crevasse, and how it was such steep climbing that you feared at every step to go slipping to the bottom, and that goats

alone could make their way up without fear of being killed. She shuddered when she heard him tell of all this, and since then she has not been so enthusiastic about Switzerland as she was before. Fear has also taken possession of Tinette, and she also refuses to come. So grandmamma and I will be alone; Sebastian will go with us as far as Ragatz and then return here.

"I can hardly bear waiting till I see you again. Goodbye dearest Heidi; grandmamma sends you her best love and all good wishes—your affectionate friend,

CLARA."

Peter, as soon as the conclusion of the letter had been reached, left his reclining position and rushed out, twirling his stick in the air in such a reckless fashion that the frightened goats fled down the mountain before him with higher and wider leaps than usual. Peter followed at full speed, his stick still raised in the air in a menacing manner as if he was longing to vent his fury on some invisible foe. This foe was indeed the prospect of the arrival of the Frankfurt visitors, the thought of whom filled him with exasperation.

A Talk with Grandmother

Heidi seized the first possible moment next day to go down and tell the grandmother who was coming, and also particularly who was not coming. These details would be of great interest to her, for grandmother knew well all the persons named from Heidi's description, and had entered with deep sympathy into all that the child had told her of her life and surroundings in Frankfurt. Heidi paid her visit in the early afternoon, for she could now go alone again; the sun was bright in the heavens and the days were growing longer, and it was delightful to go racing down the mountain.

The grandmother was in her corner at her spinning-wheel, but there was an expression on her face of mournful anxiety. Peter had come in the evening before brimful of anger and had told her about the large party who were coming up from Frankfurt, and he did not know what other things might happen after that; and the old woman had not slept all night, pursued by the thought of Heidi being taken from her. Heidi ran in, and taking her little stool immediately sat down by grandmother, and began eagerly pouring out all her news, growing more excited with her pleasure as she went on. But all of a sudden she stopped short and said anxiously, "What's the matter, grandmother, aren't you a bit pleased with what I am telling you?"

"Yes, yes, of course, child, since it gives you so much pleasure," she answered, trying to look more cheerful.

"But I can see all the same that something troubles you. Is it because you think after all that Fräulein Rottenmeier may come?" asked Heidi, beginning to feel anxious herself.

"No, no! it is nothing, child," said the grandmother, wishing to reassure her. "Just give me your hand, that I may feel sure you are there. No doubt it would be the best thing for you, although I feel I could scarcely survive it."

"I do not want anything of the best if you could scarcely survive it," said Heidi in such a determined tone of voice that the grandmother's fears increased, as she felt sure the people from Frankfurt were coming to take Heidi with them, since now she was well again they naturally wished to have her with them once more. But she was anxious to hide her trouble from Heidi if possible, as the latter was so sympathetic that she might refuse perhaps to go away, and that would not be right.

When the evening came, Heidi returned home up the mountain. The stars came out overhead one by one, so bright and sparkling that each seemed to send a fresh ray of joy into her heart; she was obliged to pause continually to look up, and the whole sky at last grew spangled with them. The stars with their glistening eyes continued to nod to her till she reached home, where she found her grandfather also standing and looking up at them, for they had seldom been more glorious than they were this night.

A Visitor for Heidi

One day at the end of June, Heidi, having finished her domestic duties, ran out with the intention of paying first a visit to the fir trees, and then going up higher to see if the bush of rock roses was yet in bloom, for its flowers were so lovely when standing open in the sun. But just as she was turning the corner of the hut, she gave such a loud cry that her grandfather came running out of the shed to see what had happened.

"Grandfather, grandfather!" she cried, beside herself with excitement. "Come here! look! look!"

The old man was by her side by this time and looked in the direction of her outstretched hand.

A strange-looking procession was making its way up the mountain; in front were two men carrying a sedan chair, in which sat a girl well wrapped up in shawls; then followed a horse, mounted by a stately-looking lady who was looking about her with great interest and talking to the guide who walked beside her; then a reclining chair, which was being pushed up by another man, it having evidently been thought safer to send the invalid to whom it belonged up the steep path in a sedan chair. The procession wound up with a porter with such a bundle of cloaks, shawls, and furs on his back that it rose well above his head.

"Here they come! here they come!" shouted Heidi, jumping with joy. And sure enough it was the party from Frankfurt; the figures came nearer and nearer, and at last they had actually arrived. The men in front put down their burden, Heidi rushed forward and the two children embraced each other with mutual delight. Grandmamma, having also reached the top, dismounted, and gave Heidi an affectionate greeting, before turning to the grandfather, who had meanwhile come up to welcome his guests. There was no constraint about the meeting, for they both knew each other perfectly well from hearsay and felt like old acquaintances.

After the first words of greeting had been exchanged grandmamma broke out into lively expressions of admiration. "What a magnificent residence you have, Uncle! I could hardly have believed it was so beautiful! A king might envy you! And how well my little Heidi looks—like a wild rose!" she continued, drawing the child towards her and stroking her fresh pink cheeks. "I don't know which way to look first, it is all so lovely! What do you say to it, Clara, what do you say?"

Clara was gazing round entranced; she had never imagined, much less seen, anything so beautiful. She gave vent to her delight in cries of joy. "Oh grandmamma," she said, "I should like to remain here for ever."

The grandfather had meanwhile drawn up the invalid chair and spread some of the wraps over it; he now went up to Clara.

"Supposing we carry the little daughter now to her accustomed chair; I think she will be more comfortable, the travelling sedan is rather hard," he said, and without waiting for anyone to help him, he lifted the child in his strong arms and laid her gently down on her own couch. He then covered her over carefully and arranged her feet on the soft cushion, as if he had never done anything all his life but attend to invalids. The grandmamma looked on with surprise.

The sky spread blue and cloudless over the hut and the fir trees and far above over the high rocks, the grey summits of which glistened in the sun. Clara could not feast her eyes enough on all the beauty around her.

"Oh Heidi, if only I could walk about with you," she said longingly, "if I could but go and look at the fir trees and at everything I know so well from your description, although I have never been here before. Look at the bushes of red flowers, and all the nodding blue-bells! Oh, if I could but get out and pick some!"

Heidi ran off at once and picked her a large nosegay of them.

"But these are nothing, Clara," she said, laying the flowers on her lap. "If you could come up higher to where the goats are feeding, then you would indeed see something! Bushes on bushes of the red centaury, and ever so many more of the blue-bell flowers; and then the bright yellow rock roses, that gleam like pure gold, and all crowding together in the one spot. And then there are others with large leaves that grandfather calls Bright Eyes, and the brown ones with little round heads that smell so delicious. Oh, it is beautiful up there, and if you sit down among them you never want to get up again, everything looks and smells so lovely!"

Heidi's eyes sparkled with the remembrance of what she was describing; she was longing herself to see it all again, and Clara caught her enthusiasm and looked back at her with equal longing in her soft blue eyes.

"Grandmamma, do you think I could get up there? Is it possible for me to go?" she asked eagerly. "If only I could walk, climb about everywhere with you, Heidi!"

"I am sure I could push you up, the chair goes so easily," said Heidi.

The grandfather, in the meantime, had not been idle. He had by this time put the table and extra chairs in front of the seat, so that they might all sit out here and eat the dinner that was preparing inside. The milk and the cheese were soon ready, and then the company sat down in high spirits.

Grandmamma was enchanted, as the doctor had been, with their dining-room, whence one could see far along the valley, and far over the mountains to the farthest stretch of blue sky. A light wind blew refreshingly over them as they sat at table, and the rustling of the fir trees made a festive accompaniment to the repast.

"I never enjoyed anything as much as this. It is really superb!" cried grandmamma two or three times over; and then suddenly in a tone of surprise,

"Do I really see you taking a second piece of toasted cheese, Clara!"

There, sure enough, was a second golden-coloured slice of cheese on Clara's plate.

"Oh, it does taste so nice, grandmamma—better than all the dishes we have at Ragatz," replied Clara, as she continued eating with appetite.

"That's right, eat what you can!" exclaimed Uncle. "It's the mountain air, which makes up for the deficiencies of the kitchen."

Clara Stays with Heidi

So the meal went on. Grandmamma and Alm Uncle got on very well together. The time passed merrily, and then grandmamma looked towards the west and said,—

"We must soon get ready to go, Clara, the sun is a good way down; the men will be here directly with the horse and sedan."

Clara's face fell, and she said beseechingly, "Oh, just another hour, grandmamma, or two hours. We haven't seen inside the hut yet, or Heidi's bed, or any of the other things. If only the day was ten hours long!"

"Well, that is not possible," said grandmamma, but she herself was anxious to see inside the hut, so they all rose from the table and Uncle wheeled Clara's chair to the door. But there they came to a standstill, for the chair was much too broad to pass through the door. Uncle, however, soon settled the difficulty by lifting Clara in his strong arms.

Grandmamma went all round and examined the household arrangements, and was very much amused and pleased at their orderliness and the cosy appearance of everything. "And this is your bedroom up here, Heidi, is it not?" asked the grandmamma, as without trepidation she mounted the ladder to the hay loft. "Oh, it does smell sweet; what a healthy place to sleep in." She went up to the round window and looked out, and grandfather followed up with Clara in his arms, Heidi springing up after them. Then they all stood and examined Heidi's wonderful hay-bed, and grandmamma looked thoughtfully at it and drew from time to time fragrant draughts of the hay-perfumed air, while Clara was charmed beyond words with Heidi's sleeping apartment.

"It is delightful for you up here, Heidi! You can look from your bed straight into the sky, and then

such a delicious smell all round you! and outside the
fir trees waving and rustling! I have never seen such
a pleasant, cheerful bedroom before."

Uncle looked across at the grandmamma. "I have
been thinking," he said to her, "that if you were
willing to agree to it, your little granddaughter
might remain up here, and I am sure she would grow
stronger. You have brought up all kinds of shawls
and covers with you, and we could make up a soft
bed out of them, and as to the general looking after
the child, you need have no fear, for I will see to
that."

Clara and Heidi were as overjoyed at these words
as if they were two birds let out of their cages.

"You are indeed kind, my dear Uncle," said grandmamma. "I thank you sincerely, I thank you from my whole heart, Uncle." And she took his hand and gave it a long and grateful shake.

Grandmamma did not care to stay alone in Dorfli, and therefore decided to return to Ragatz, and thence to make excursions up the mountain from time to time.

The climax to all the beautiful things that Clara had already seen upon the mountain came at the close of the day.

As she lay on the large soft bed in the hay loft, with Heidi near her, she looked out through the round open window right into the middle of the shining clusters of stars, and she exclaimed in delight, "Heidi, it's just as if we were in a high carriage and were going to drive straight into Heaven."

The two children now sat up and said their prayers, and then Heidi put her head down on her little round arm and fell off to sleep at once, but Clara lay awake some time, for she could not get over the wonder of this new experience of being in bed up here among the stars. She had indeed seldom seen a star, for she never went outside the house at night, and the curtains at home were always drawn before the stars came out. Each time she closed her eyes she felt she must open them again to see if the two very large stars were still looking in, and nodding to her as Heidi said they did. There they were, always in the same place, and Clara felt she could not look long enough into their bright sparkling faces, until at last her eyes closed of their own accord, and it was only in her dreams that she still saw the two large friendly stars shining down upon her.

Life on the Mountain

The sun had just risen above the mountains and was shedding its first golden rays over the hut and the valley below. Alm Uncle, as was his custom, had been standing in a quiet and devout attitude for some little while, watching the light mists gradually lifting, and the heights and valley emerging from their twilight shadows and awakening to another day.

The light morning clouds overhead grew brighter and brighter, till at last the sun shone out in its full glory, and rock and wood and hill lay bathed in golden light.

Uncle now stepped back into the hut and went softly up the ladder. Clara had just opened her eyes and was looking with wonder at the bright sunlight that shone through the round window and danced and sparkled about her bed. She could not at first think what she was looking at or where she was. Then she caught sight of Heidi sleeping beside her, and now she heard the grandfather's cheery voice asking her if she had slept well.

She assured him she was not tired, and that when she had once fallen asleep she had not opened her eyes again all night. The grandfather was satisfied at this and immediately began to attend upon her with so much gentleness and understanding that it seemed as if his chief calling had been to look after sick children.

Heidi now awoke and was surprised to see Clara dressed, and already in the grandfather's arms ready to be carried down. She must be up too, and she went through her toilette with lightning-like speed. She ran down the ladder and out of the hut, and there further astonishment awaited her, for grandfather had been busy the night before after they were in bed. Seeing that it was impossible to get Clara's chair through the hut door, he had taken down two of the boards at the side of the shed and made an opening large enough to admit the chair; these he left loose so that they could be taken away and put up at pleasure. He was at this moment wheeling Clara out into the sun; he left her in front of the hut while he went to look after the goats, and Heidi ran up to her friend.

The fresh morning breeze blew round the children's faces, and every fresh puff brought a waft of fragrance from the fir trees. Clara drew it in with delight and lay back in her chair with an unaccustomed feeling of health and comfort.

"Oh, Heidi, if only I could stay up here for ever with you," she exclaimed happily, turning in her chair from side to side that she might drink in the air and sun from all quarters.

"Now you see that it is just what I told you," replied Heidi delighted. "That it is the most beautiful thing in the world to be up here with grandfather."

The latter at that moment appeared from the goat shed bringing two small foaming bowls of snow-white milk – one for Clara and one for Heidi.

"That will do the little daughter good," he said, nodding to Clara; "it is from Little Swan and will make her strong. To your health, child! drink it up."

Clara had never tasted goat's milk before; she hesitated and smelt it before putting it to her lips, but seeing how Heidi drank hers up without hesitating, and how much she seemed to like it, Clara did the same, and drank till there was not a drop left, for she too found it delicious, tasting just as if sugar and cinnamon had been mixed with it.

"Tomorrow we will drink two," said the grandfather, who had looked on with satisfaction at seeing her follow Heidi's example.

Peter now arrived with the goats. They carried Heidi along with them a little way, which was what Peter wanted. "You will have to come with them," he called to her.

"I cannot," Heidi called back from the midst of her friends, "and I shall not be able to come for a long, long time—not as long as Clara is with me. Grandfather, however, has promised to go up the mountain with both of us one day."

Heidi had now extricated herself from the goats and she ran back to Clara. Peter doubled his fists and made threatening gestures towards the invalid on her couch, and then climbed up some distance without pause until he was out of sight, for he was afraid Uncle might have seen him, and he did not care to know what Uncle might have thought.

Letters to Grandmother

Clara and Heidi had made so many plans for themselves that they hardly knew where to begin. Heidi suggested that they should first write to grandmamma, to whom they had promised to send word every day, for grandmamma had not felt sure whether it would in the long run suit Clara's health to remain up the mountain, or if she would continue to enjoy herself there. With daily news of her granddaughter she could stay on without anxiety at Ragatz, and be ready to go to Clara at a moment's notice.

Heidi was prepared to arrange everything for the letter writing, and then they both began writing to grandmamma. But Clara paused after every sentence to look about her; it was too beautiful for much letter writing.

The morning passed, the children hardly knew how, and now grandfather came with the midday bowls of steaming milk, for the little daughter, he said, was to remain out as long as there was a gleam of sun in the sky. Then Heidi pushed Clara's chair under the fir trees, for they had agreed to spend the afternoon under their shade and there tell each other all that had happened since Heidi left Frankfurt. So they sat and chatted under the trees and the hours flew by and all at once, it seemed, the evening had come with the returning Peter, who still scowled and looked angry.

As Clara saw the grandfather leading away Little Swan to milk her, she was suddenly taken with a longing for another bowlful of the fragrant milk, and waited impatiently for it. When grandfather at last brought her the evening milk, she drank it up so quickly that she had emptied her bowl before Heidi and then she asked for a little more. The grandfather went inside with both the children's bowls, and when he brought them out again full he had something else to add to their supper. He had walked over that afternoon to a herdsman's house where the sweetly-tasting butter was made, and had brought home a large pat, some of which he had now spread thickly on two good slices of bread. He stood and watched with pleasure while Clara and Heidi ate their appetising meal with childish hunger and enjoyment.

That night, when Clara lay down in her bed and prepared to watch the stars, her eyes would not keep open, and she fell asleep as soon as Heidi and slept soundly all night—a thing she never remembered having done before. The following day and the day after passed in the same pleasant fashion.

Meanwhile grandmamma down at Ragatz was rejoicing at the excellent news of the invalid which reached her daily from the mountain. Clara found the life more charming each day and could not say enough of the kindness and care which the grandfather lavished upon her, nor of Heidi's lively and amusing companionship, for the latter was more entertaining even than when in Frankfurt with her, and Clara's first thought when she woke each morning was, "Oh, how glad I am to be here still."

Having such fresh assurances each day that all was going well with Clara, grandmamma thought she might put off her visit to the children a little longer, for the steep ride up and down was somewhat of a fatigue to her.

Clara had now been on the mountain for three weeks. For some days past the grandfather, each morning after carrying her down, had said, "Won't the little daughter try if she can stand for a minute or two?" And Clara had made the effort in order to please him, but had clung to him as soon as her feet touched the ground, exclaiming that it hurt her so. He let her try a little longer, however, each day.

Heidi never tired of telling Clara that only higher up on the mountain could the full glory of the flower colours be rightly seen. She had just been expatiating on the flowers as she sat with Clara under the fir trees one evening, and had been telling her again of the wonderful light from the evening sun, when such an irrepressible longing came over her to see it all once more that she jumped up and ran to her grandfather, who was in the shed, calling out almost before she was inside,—

"Grandfather, will you take us out with the goats tomorrow? Oh, it is so lovely up there now!"

"Very well," he answered, "but if I do, the little daughter must do something to please me: she must try her best again this evening to stand on her feet."

Heidi ran back with the good news to Clara, and the latter promised to try her very best as the grandfather wished, for she looked forward immensely to the next day's excursion.

Clara and Heidi got into their beds that night full of delightful anticipation of the morrow; they were so full of their plans that they agreed to keep awake all night and talk over them until they might venture to get up. But their heads had no sooner touched their soft pillows than the conversation suddenly ceased, and Clara fell into a dream of an immense field, which looked the colour of the sky, so thickly inlaid was it with blue bell-shaped flowers; and Heidi heard the great bird of prey calling to her from the heights above, "Come! Come! Come!"

Peter's Bad Deed

Uncle went out early the next morning to see what kind of a day it was going to be. There was a reddish gold light over the higher peaks; a light breeze was springing up and the branches of the fir trees moved gently to and fro—the sun was on its way.

The old man stood and watched the green slopes

under the higher peaks gradually growing brighter with the coming day and the dark shadows lifting from the valley, until at first a rosy light filled its hollows, and then the morning gold flooded every height and depth—the sun had risen.

Uncle wheeled the chair out of the shed ready for the coming journey, and then went in to call the children and tell them what a lovely sunrise it was.

Peter came up at this moment. The goats did not gather round him so trustfully as usual, but seemed to avoid him timidly, for Peter had reached a high pitch of anger and bitterness, and was laying about him with his stick very unnecessarily, and where it fell the blow was no light one. For weeks now he had not had Heidi all to himself as formerly. When he came up in the morning the invalid child was always already in her chair and Heidi fully occupied with her. And it was the same thing over again when he came down in the evening. She had not come out with the goats once this summer, and now today she was only coming in company with her friend and the chair, and would stick by the latter's side the whole time. It was the thought of this which was making him particularly cross this morning. There stood the chair on its high wheels; Peter seemed to see something proud and disdainful about it, and he glared at it as at an enemy that had done him harm and was likely to do him more still today. He glanced round—there was no sound anywhere, no one to see him. He sprang forward like a wild creature, caught hold of it, and gave it a violent and angry push in the direction of the slope. The chair rolled swiftly forward and in another minute had disappeared.

Peter now sped up the mountain as if on wings, not pausing till he was well in shelter of a large blackberry-bush, for he had no wish to be seen by Uncle. But he was anxious to see what had become of the chair, and his bush was well placed for that. Himself hidden, he could watch what happened below and see what Uncle did without being discovered himself. So he looked, and there he saw his enemy running faster and faster downhill, then it turned head over heels several times, and finally, after one great bound, rolled over and over to its complete destruction. The pieces flew in every direction—feet, arms, and torn fragments of the padded seat and bolster—and Peter experienced a feeling of such unbounded delight at the sight that he leapt in the air, laughing aloud and stamping for joy; then he took a run round, jumping over bushes

on the way, only to return to the same spot and fall into fresh fits of laughter. He was beside himself with satisfaction, for he could see only good results for himself in this disaster to his enemy. Now Heidi's friend would be obliged to go away, for she would have no means of going about, and when Heidi was alone again she would come out with him as in the old days, and everything would go on in the proper way again. But Peter did not consider that when we do a wrong thing trouble is sure to follow.

Heidi now came running out of the hut and round to the shed. Grandfather was behind with Clara in his arms. The shed stood wide open, the two loose planks having been taken down, and it was quite light inside. Heidi looked into every corner and ran from one end to the other, and then stood still wondering what could have happened to the chair. Grandfather now came up.

"How is this, have you wheeled the chair away, Heidi?"

"I have been looking everywhere for it, grandfather; you said it was standing ready outside," and she again searched each corner of the shed with her eyes.

At that moment the wind, which had risen suddenly, blew open the shed door and sent it banging back against the wall.

"It must have been the wind, grandfather," exclaimed Heidi, and her eyes grew anxious at this sudden discovery. "Oh! if it has blown the chair all the way down to Dorfli we shall not get it back in time, and shall not be able to go."

"If it has rolled as far as that it will never come back, for it is in a hundred pieces by now," said the grandfather, going round the corner and looking down. "But it's a curious thing to have happened!" he added as he thought over the matter, for the chair would have had to turn a corner before starting downhill.

"Oh, I am sorry," lamented Clara, "for we shall not be able to go today, or perhaps any other day. I shall have to go home, I suppose, if I have no chair. Oh, I am so sorry, I am so sorry!"

"Grandfather, you will be able to do something, won't you, so that it need not be as Clara says, and so that she is not obliged to go home."

"Well, for the present we will go up the mountain as we had arranged, and then later on we will see what can be done," he answered, much to the children's delight.

Clara Goes Up the Mountain

He went indoors, fetched out a pile of shawls, and laying them on the sunniest spot he could find set Clara down upon them. Then he fetched the children's morning milk and had out his two goats.

"Why is Peter not here yet?" thought Uncle to himself, for Peter's whistle had not been sounded that morning. The grandfather now took Clara up on one arm, and the shawls on the other.

"Now then we will start," he said, "the goats can come with us."

Heidi was pleased at this and walked on after her grandfather with an arm over either of the goats' necks, and the animals were so overjoyed to have her again that they nearly squeezed her flat between them out of sheer affection. When they reached the spot where the goats usually pastured they were surprised to find them already feeding there, climbing about the rocks, and Peter with them, lying his full length on the ground.

"I'll teach you another time to go by like that, you lazy rascal! What do you mean by it?" Uncle called to him.

Peter, recognising the voice, jumped up like a shot. "No one was up," he answered.

"Have you seen anything of the chair?" asked the grandfather.

"Of what chair?" Peter called back in answer in a morose tone of voice.

Uncle said no more. He spread the shawls on the sunny slope, and setting Clara upon them asked if she was comfortable.

"As comfortable as in my chair," she said, thanking him, "and this seems the most beautiful

spot. Oh Heidi, it is lovely, it is lovely!" she cried, looking round her with delight.

The grandfather prepared to leave them. They would now be safe and happy together, he said, and when it was time for dinner Heidi was to go and fetch the bag from the shady hollow where he had put it; Peter was to bring them as much milk as they wanted, but Heidi was to see that it was Little Swan's milk. He would come and fetch them towards evening; he must now be off to see after the chair and ascertain what had become of it.

Some hours went by, and Heidi began to think that she might just go over to the spot where all the flowers grew to see if they were fully blown and looking as lovely as the year before. Clara could not go until grandfather came back that evening, when the flowers probably would be already closed. The longing to go became stronger and stronger, till she felt she could not resist it.

"Would you think me unkind, Clara," she said rather hesitatingly, "if I left you for a few minutes? I should run there and back very quickly. I want so to see how the flowers are looking—but wait—" for an idea had come into Heidi's head. She ran and picked a bunch or two of green leaves, and then took hold of Snowflake and led her up to Clara.

"There, now you will not be alone," said Heidi, giving the goat a little push to show her she was to lie down near Clara, which the animal quite understood. Heidi threw the leaves into Clara's lap, and the latter told her friend to go at once to look at the flowers as she was quite happy to be left with the goat; she liked this new experience. Heidi ran off, and Clara began to hold out the leaves one by one to Snowflake, who snuggled up to her new friend in a confiding manner and slowly ate the leaves from her hand.

Heidi had meanwhile reached her field of flowers, and as she caught sight of it she uttered a cry of joy. The whole ground in front of her was a mass of shimmering gold, where the cistus flowers spread their yellow blossoms. Above them waved whole bushes of the deep blue bell-flower; while the fragrance that arose from the whole sunlit expanse was as if the rarest balsam had been flung over it. The scent, however, came from the small brown flowers, the little round heads of which rose modestly here and there among the yellow blossoms. Heidi stood and gazed and drew in the delicious air. Suddenly she turned round and reached Clara's side out of breath with running and excitement. "Oh, you must come," she called out as soon as she came in sight, "it is more beautiful than you can imagine, and perhaps this evening it may not be so lovely. I believe I could carry you, don't you think I could?"

Clara looked at her and shook her head. "Why, Heidi, what can you be thinking of; you are smaller than I am. Oh, if only I could walk!"

The Field of Flowers

Heidi looked round as if in search of something, some new idea had evidently come into her head. Peter was sitting up above looking down on the two children. He had been sitting and staring before him in the same way for hours, as if he could not make out what he saw. He had destroyed the chair so that the friend might not be able to move anywhere and that her visit might come to an end, and then a little while after she had appeared right up here under his

very nose with Heidi beside her. He thought his eyes must deceive him, and yet there she was and no mistake about it.

Heidi now looked up to where he was sitting and called out in a peremptory voice, "Peter, come down here!"

"I don't wish to come," he called in reply.

"But you are to, you must; I cannot do it alone, and you must come here and help me; make haste and come down," she called again.

"I am coming," he said reluctantly, and came down the slope.

As soon as he reached them, Heidi gave her orders: Peter was to take hold of Clara under the arms on one side and she on the other, and together they were to lift her up. This first movement was successfully carried through, but then came the difficulty. As Clara could not even stand, how were they to support her and get her along? Heidi was too small for her arm to serve Clara to lean upon.

"You must put one arm well round my neck—so, and put the other through Peter's and lean firmly upon it, then we shall be able to carry you."

Peter, however, had never given his arm to anyone in his life. Clara put hers in his, but he kept his own hanging down straight beside him like a stick.

"That's not the way, Peter," said Heidi in an authoritative voice. "You must put your arm out in the shape of a ring, and Clara must put hers through it and lean her weight upon you, and whatever you do, don't let your arm give way; like that I am sure we shall be able to manage."

Peter did as he was told, but still they did not get on very well. Clara was not such a light weight, and the team did not match very well in size; it was up one side and down the other, so that the supports were rather wobbly.

Clara tried to use her own feet a little, but each time drew them quickly back.

"Put your foot down firmly once," suggested Heidi. "I am sure it will hurt you less after that."

"Do you think so?" said Clara hesitatingly, but she followed Heidi's advice and ventured one firm step on the ground and then another; she called out a little as she did it; then she lifted her foot again and went on, "Oh, that was less painful already," she exclaimed joyfully.

"Try again," said Heidi encouragingly.

Clara went on putting one foot out after another until all at once she called out, "I can do it, Heidi!

Look! Look! I can make proper steps!"

Heidi cried out with even greater delight, "Can you really make steps, can you really walk? Really walk by yourself? Oh, if only grandfather were here!" and she continued gleefully to exclaim, "You can walk now, Clara, you can walk!"

Clara still held on firmly to her supports, but with every step she felt safer on her feet, as all three became aware, and Heidi was beside herself with joy.

"Now we shall be able to come up here together every day, and just go where we like; and you will be able all your life to walk about as I do, and not have to be pushed in a chair, and will get quite strong and well. It is the greatest happiness we could have had!"

And Clara heartily agreed, for she could think of no greater joy in the world than to be strong and able to go about like other people, and no longer to have to lie from day to day in her invalid chair.

They had not far to go to reach the field of flowers, and could already catch sight of the cistus flowers glowing gold in the sun. As they came to the bushes of the blue bell-flowers, with sunny, inviting patches of warm ground between them, Clara said, "Mightn't we sit down here for a while?"

This was just what Heidi enjoyed, and so the children sat down in the midst of the flowers, Clara for the first time on the dry, warm mountain grass, and she found it indescribably delightful. Clara sat silent, overcome with the enchantment of all that her eye rested upon, and with the anticipation of all the happiness that was now before her. There seemed hardly room in her heart for all her joyful emotions, and these and the ecstasy aroused by the sunlight and the scent of the flowers held her dumb.

Peter also lay among the flowers without moving or speaking, for he was asleep. The breeze came blowing softly and caressingly from behind the sheltering rocks, and passed whisperingly through the bushes overhead. Heidi got up now and then to run about, for the flowers waving in the warm wind seemed to smell sweeter and to grow more thickly whichever way she went, and she felt she must sit down at each fresh spot to enjoy the sight and scent. So the hours went by.

When all three had got back to their old quarters for lunch, Heidi ran and brought forward the bag. She had seen her grandfather putting in all sorts of good things. Heidi took the food out of the bag and divided it into three portions, and each was of a goodly size. She gave the other two their dinners and

sat down with her own beside Clara, and they all three ate with a good appetite after their great exertions.

Peter's Guilt

Peter ate up every bit of food to the last crumb, but there was something wanting to his usual enjoyment of a good dinner, for every mouthful he swallowed seemed to choke him, and he felt something gnawing inside him.

They were so late at their dinner that they had not long to wait after they had finished before grandfather came up to fetch them.

Heidi rushed forward to meet him as soon as he appeared, as she wanted to be the first to tell him the good news. She was so excited that she could hardly get her words out when she did get up to him, but he soon understood, and a look of extreme pleasure came into his face. He hastened up to where Clara was sitting and said with a cheerful smile, "So we've made the effort, have we, and won the day!"

Then he lifted her up, and putting his left arm behind her and giving her his right to lean upon, made her walk a little way, which she did with less trembling and hesitation than before now that she had such a strong arm round her.

Heidi skipped along beside her in triumphant glee, and the grandfather looked too as if some happiness had befallen him. But now he took Clara up in his arms. "We must not overdo it," he said, "and it is high time we went home," and he started off down the mountain path, for he was anxious to get her indoors that she might rest after her unusual fatigue.

When Peter got to Dorfli that evening he found a large group of people collected round a certain spot, pushing one another and looking over each other's shoulders in their eagerness to catch sight of something lying on the ground. Peter thought he should like to see too, and poked and elbowed till he made his way through.

There it lay, the thing he had wanted to see. Scattered about the grass were the remains of Clara's chair; part of the back and the middle bit, and enough of the red padding and the bright nails to show how magnificent the chair had been.

"I was here when the men passed carrying it up," said the baker, who was standing near Peter. "I'll

bet anyone that it was worth twenty-five pounds at least. I cannot think how such an accident could have happened."

"Uncle said the wind might perhaps have done it," remarked one of the women, who could not sufficiently admire the red upholstery.

"It's a good job that no one but the wind did it," said the baker again, "or he might smart for it! No doubt the gentleman in Frankfurt, when he hears what has happened, will make all inquiries about it. I am glad for myself that I have not been seen up the mountain for a good two years, as suspicion is likely to fall on anyone who was about up there at the time."

After hearing this, Peter crept quietly away and then took to his heels and ran off home as fast as he could, as if he thought someone was after him. The baker's words had filled him with fear and trembling. He was sure now that any day a constable might come over from Frankfurt and inquire about the destruction of the chair, and then everything would come out, and he would be seized and carried off to Frankfurt and there put in prison. The whole picture of what was coming was clear before him, and his hair stood on end with terror.

He reached home in this disturbed state of mind. He would not open his mouth in reply to anything that was said to him; he would not eat his potatoes; all he did was to creep off to bed as quickly as possible and hide under the bedclothes and groan.

Grandmamma's Visit

Grandmamma wrote the day before her arrival to let the children know that they might expect her without fail. Peter brought up the letter early the following morning, when bringing up the goats.

Heidi now set about tidying the hut, as grandmamma must find everything clean and in good order when she arrived.

Clara looked on amused and interested to watch the busy Heidi at her work. So the morning went by, and grandmamma might now be expected at any minute. The children dressed themselves and went and sat together outside on the seat.

Grandfather joined them, that they might see the splendid bunch of blue gentians which he had been up the mountain to gather, and the children exclaimed with delight at the beauty of the flowers as they shone in the morning sun. The grandfather then carried them indoors. Heidi jumped up from time to time to see if there was any sign of grandmamma's approach.

At last she saw the procession winding up the mountain just in the order she had expected. First there was the guide, then the white horse with

grandmamma mounted upon it, and last of all the porter with a heavy bundle on his back, for grandmamma would not think of going up the mountain without a full supply of wraps and rugs.

Nearer and nearer wound the procession; at last it reached the top and grandmamma was there looking down on the children from her horse. She no sooner saw them, however, sitting side by side, than she began quickly dismounting, as she cried out in a shocked tone of voice, "Why is this? Why are you not lying in your chair, Clara? What are you all thinking about?" But even before she had got close to them she threw up her hands in astonishment, exclaiming further, "Is it really you, dear child? Why, your cheeks have grown quite round and rosy! I should hardly have known you again!" And she was hastening forward to embrace her when Heidi slipped down from the seat, and, Clara leaning on her shoulder, the two children began walking along quite coolly and naturally. Then indeed grandmamma was surprised, or rather alarmed, for she thought at first that it must be some unheard of proceeding

walk about with her, she went up to the old man, and then letting go Clara's arm she seized his hands.

"My dear Uncle! My dear Uncle! How much we have to thank you for! It is all your doing! It is your care and nursing—"

"And God's good sun and mountain air," he interrupted her, smiling.

"Yes, and don't forget the beautiful milk I have," put in Clara. "Grandmamma, you can't think what a quantity of goat's milk I drink, and how nice it is!"

"I can see that by your cheeks, child," answered grandmamma. "I really should not have known you; you have grown quite strong and plump, and taller too; I never hoped or expected to see you look like that. I cannot take my eyes off you, for I can hardly yet believe it. But now I must telegraph without delay to your father in Paris, and tell him he must come here at once. I shall not say why; it will be the greatest happiness he has ever known. My dear Uncle, how can I send a telegram; have you dismissed the men yet?"

"They have gone," he answered, "but if you are in a hurry I will fetch Peter, and he can take it for you later."

Grandmamma thanked him, for she was anxious that the good news should not be kept from her son a day longer than was possible.

So now they could all sit down in peace to their dinner round the table in front of the hut, and grandmamma was given a detailed account of all that had taken place. Clara and Heidi could not get over their delight at the success of the surprise they had so carefully arranged for grandmamma, and at the latter's continued astonishment.

Another Surprise

Meanwhile Herr Sesemann, who had finished his business in Paris, had also been preparing a surprise. Without saying a word he got into the train one sunny morning and travelled that day to Basle; the next morning he continued his journey, for a great longing had seized him to see his little daughter from whom he had been separated the whole summer.

So while they had been dining, Herr Sesemann had made his way up the mountain and was delighted to have come to the last steep bit of his journey. In another minute or two he would be with

of Heidi's devising.

But no—Clara was actually walking steadily and uprightly beside Heidi—and now the two children turned and came towards her with beaming faces and rosy cheeks. Laughing and crying she ran to them and embraced first Clara and then Heidi, and then Clara again, unable to speak for joy. All at once she caught sight of Uncle standing by the seat and looking on smiling at the meeting. She took Clara's arm in hers, and with continual expressions of delight at the fact that the child could now really his little daughter, and he pleased himself with the thought of her surprise. But the company above had seen his approaching figure and recognised who it was, and they were preparing something he little expected as a surprise on their part.

As he stepped on to the space in front of the hut two figures came towards him. One a tall girl with fair hair and pink cheeks, leaning on Heidi, whose dark eyes were dancing with joy. Herr Sesemann suddenly stopped, staring at the two children, and all at once the tears started to his eyes. What memories arose in his heart! Just so had Clara's mother looked, the fair-haired girl with the delicate pink-and-white complexion. Herr Sesemann did not know if he was awake or dreaming.

"Don't you know me, papa?" called Clara to him, her face beaming with happiness. "Am I so altered since you saw me?"

Then Herr Sesemann ran to his child and clasped her in his arms. "Yes, you are indeed altered! How is it possible? Is it true what I see?" And the delighted father stepped back to look full at her again, and to make sure that the picture would not vanish before his eyes.

And now grandmamma came up, anxious for a sight of her son's happy face. "Well, what do you say now, dear son?" she exclaimed. "You have given us a pleasant surprise, but it is nothing in comparison to what we have prepared for you, you must confess," and she gave her son an affectionate kiss as she spoke. "But now," she went on, "you must come and pay your respects to Uncle, who is our chief benefactor."

"Yes, indeed, and with the little inmate of our own house, our little Heidi, too," said Herr Sesemann, shaking Heidi by the hand. "Well? are you still well and happy in your mountain home? But I need not ask, no Alpine rose could look more blooming. I am glad, child, it is a pleasure to me to see you so."

Heidi looked up with equal pleasure into Herr Sesemann's kind face. How good he had always been to her! That he should find such happiness awaiting him up here on the mountain made her heart beat with gladness.

Grandmamma now led her son to introduce him to Uncle, and while the two men were shaking hands and Herr Sesemann was expressing his heartfelt thanks and boundless astonishment to the old man, grandmamma wandered round to the back to see the old fir trees again.

Here another unexpected sight met her gaze, for there, under the trees where the long branches had left a clear space on the ground, stood a great bush of the most wonderful dark blue gentians, as fresh and shining as if they were growing on the spot. She clasped her hands, enraptured with their beauty.

"How exquisite! what a lovely sight!" she exclaimed. "Heidi, dearest child, come here! Is it you who have prepared this pleasure for me? It is perfectly wonderful!"

The children ran up.

"No, no, I did not put them there," said Heidi, "but I know who did."

"They grow just like that on the mountain, grandmamma, only if anything they look more beautiful still," Clara put in; "but guess who brought those down today," and as she spoke she gave such a pleased smile that the grandmother thought for a moment the child herself must have gathered them. But that was hardly possible.

Peter

At this moment a slight rustling was heard behind the fir trees. It was Peter, who had just arrived. He had made a long round, having seen from a distance who it was standing beside Uncle in front of the hut, and he was trying to slip by unobserved. But grandmamma had seen and recognised him, and suddenly the thought struck her that it might be Peter who had brought the flowers and that he was now trying to get away unseen, feeling shy about it; but she could not let him go off like that, he must have some little reward.

"Come along, boy; come here, do not be afraid," she called to him.

Peter stood still, petrified with fear. After all he had gone through that day he felt he had no longer any power of resistance left. All he could think was, "It's all up with me now." Every hair of his head stood on end, and he stepped forth from behind the fir trees, his face pale and distorted with terror.

"Courage, boy," said grandmamma in her effort to dispel his shyness, "tell me now straight out without hesitation, was it you who did it?"

Peter did not lift his eyes and therefore did not see at what grandmamma was pointing. But he knew that Uncle was standing at the corner of the hut, fixing him with his grey eyes, while beside him stood the most terrible person that Peter could conceive—the police constable from Frankfurt. Quaking in every limb, and with trembling lips he muttered a low, "Yes."

"Well, and what is there dreadful about that?" said grandmamma.

"Because—because—it is all broken to pieces and no one can put it together again." Peter brought out his words with difficulty and his knees knocked together so that he could hardly stand.

Grandmamma went up to Uncle. "Is that poor boy a little out of his mind?" she asked sympathetically.

"Not in the least," Uncle assured her, "it is only that he was the wind that sent the chair rolling down the slope, and he is expecting his well-deserved punishment."

Grandmamma found this hard to believe, for in her opinion Peter did not look an entirely bad boy, nor could he have had any reason for destroying such a necessary thing as the chair. But Uncle had only given expression to the suspicion that he had had from the moment the accident happened. The angry looks which Peter had from the beginning cast at Clara, and the other signs of his dislike to what had been taking place on the mountain had not escaped Uncle's eye. Putting two and two together he had come to the right conclusion as to the cause of the disaster, and he therefore spoke without hesitation when he accused Peter. The lady broke out into lively expostulations on hearing this.

"No, no, dear Uncle, we will not punish the poor boy any further. One must be fair to him. Here are all these strangers from Frankfurt who come and carry away Heidi, his one sole possession, and he is left to sit alone day after day for weeks, with nothing to do but brood over his wrongs. No, no, let us be fair to him; his anger got the upper hand and drove him to an act of revenge—a foolish one, I own, but then we all behave foolishly when we are angry." And saying this she went back to Peter, who still stood frightened and trembling. She sat down on the seat under the fir trees and called him to her kindly, and then she forgave him. He suddenly felt as if the weight of a mountain had fallen off him, and he went off running and leaping with even more than his usual agility. All trouble and trembling had disappeared.

All Ends Happily

Later, after dinner, Herr Sesemann went over to where Uncle and grandmamma were engaged in lively conversation. Uncle stood up as he approached, and Herr Sesemann, taking him by the hand, said,

"Dear friend, let us exchange a few words with one another. You will believe me when I tell you that I have known no real happiness for years past. What worth to me were money and property when they were unable to make my poor child well and happy? With the help of God you have made her whole and strong, and you have given new life not only to her but to me. Tell me now, in what way can I show my gratitude to you? I can never repay all you have done, but whatever is in my power to do is at your service. Speak, friend, and tell me what I can do?"

Uncle had listened to him quietly, with a smile of pleasure on his face as he looked at the happy father.

"Herr Sesemann," he replied in his dignified way, "believe me that I too have my share in the joy of your daughter's recovery, and my trouble is well repaid by it. I thank you heartily for all you have said, but I have need of nothing; I have enough for myself and the child as long as I live. One wish alone I have, and if that could be satisfied I should have no further care in life."

"Speak, dear friend, and tell me what it is."

"I am growing old," Uncle went on, "and shall not be here much longer. I have nothing to leave the child when I die, and she has no relations, except one person who will always like to make what profit out of her she can. If you could promise me that Heidi shall never have to go and earn her living among strangers, then you would richly reward me for all I have done for your child."

"There could never be any question of such a thing as that, my dear friend," said Herr Sesemann quickly. "I look upon the child as our own. You may be sure that we will never allow the child to be left in anyone else's care! I give you here my hand upon it. I promise you Heidi shall never have to go and earn her living among strangers."

Herr Sesemann had been arranging that he and his mother should make a little tour in Switzerland, first ascertaining if Clara was in a fit state to go some part of the way with them. But now he would have the full enjoyment of his daughter's company, and that being so, he did not want to miss any of these beautiful days of late summer, but to start at once on the journey that he now looked forward to with such additional pleasure. And so he proposed that they should spend the night in Dorfli and that next day he should come and fetch Clara, then they would all three go down to Ragatz and make that their starting point.

Clara was rather upset at first at the thought of saying goodbye like this to the mountain; she could not help being pleased, however, at the prospect of the journey.

Heidi was adamant that they should all come down and meet the grandmother before they departed. Heidi kept jumping for joy as she and grandmamma walked along side by side, and grandmamma asked all about grandmother, how she lived, and what she did, especially in the winter when it was so cold. And Heidi gave her a minute account of everything, and told her how grandmother sat crouching in her corner and trembling with cold. Grandmamma listened with interest and sympathy until they came to grandmother's.

Heidi sprang through the door and across to the corner and threw her arms round grandmother.

The latter smiled, but said a little sadly,—"I ought to be glad to think they are taking you with them but I shall not outlive it long."

"What is this I hear? Who has been telling my good grandmother such tales?" exclaimed a kindly voice, and grandmother felt her hand taken and warmly pressed, for grandmamma had followed Heidi in and heard all that was said. "No, no, there is no thought of such a thing! Heidi is going to stay with you and make you happy. We want to see her again, but we shall come to her; and when we do we shall bring you some extra blankets for the winter, as Heidi has told us how you feel the cold so."

And now grandmother's face was lighted up with genuine happiness, and she pressed Frau Sesemann's hand over and over again, unable to speak her thanks, while two large tears of joy rolled down her aged cheeks.

The next day there were many goodbyes and many tears before Heidi and Peter and the grandmother and grandfather were alone again. It was difficult to say which of them looked the happiest at being together again, and at the recollection of all the wonderful things that had happened.

ROBINSON CRUSOE

My Early Life

I was born in the year 1632, in the city of York, of a good family, though not of that country, my father being a foreigner of Bremen, who settled first at Hull: he got a good estate by merchandise, and, leaving off his trade, lived afterwards at York, from whence he had married my mother, whose relations were named Robinson, a very good family in that country, and from whom I was called Robinson Kreutznaer; but, by the usual corruption of words in England, we are now called, nay, we call ourselves, and write our name, Crusoe, and so my companions always called me.

I had two elder brothers, one of which was lieutenant-colonel to an English regiment of foot in Flanders, and was killed at the battle near Dunkirk against the Spaniards: what became of my second brother I never knew, any more than my father or mother did know what was become of me.

Being the third son of the family, and not bred to any trade, my head began to be filled very early with rambling thoughts. My father had given me a competent share of learning, and designed me for the law; but I would be satisfied with nothing but going to sea, and my inclination to this led me so strongly against the will, nay, the commands of my father, and against all the entreaties and persuasions of my mother and friends, that there seemed to be something fatal in that propension of nature tending directly to the life of misery which was to befall me.

My father, a wise and grave man, gave me serious and excellent counsel against what he foresaw was my design. I was sincerely affected with this discourse, but, alas! a few days wore it all off; and, in short, to prevent any of my father's further importunities, in a few weeks after I resolved to run quite away from him.

My First Voyage

Being one day at Hull, where I went casually, and without any purpose of making an elopement, and one of my friends being going to sea to London in his father's ship, and prompting me to go with them, I consulted neither father nor mother any more, and in an ill hour, on the 1st of September, 1651, I went on board a ship bound for London. Never any young adventurer's misfortunes, I believe, began sooner, or continued longer than mine. The ship was no sooner gotten out of the Humber but the wind began to blow, and the waves to rise in a most frightful manner. After a violent storm, our ship was wrecked off Yarmouth. I had not the sense to go back to Hull, but continued on to London, where I went on a vessel bound for the coast of Africa.

My next voyage was on a Guinea trader, and I fell into terrible misfortunes on this voyage––namely, our ship, making her course towards the Canary Islands, was surprised in the grey of the morning by a Turkish rover of Sallee, and we were all carried prisoners into Sallee, a port belonging to the Moors. I was held as a slave for several years, until I eventually made my escape on board a ship bound for the Brazils.

In Brazil I prospered, and became a successful planter and merchant for many years; however I was not content, but must go to sea again, and boarded a ship bound for Guinea. The same day I went on board we set sail, standing away to the northward upon our own coast, with design to stretch over for

the African coast. We had very good weather all the way upon our own coast, till we came to the height of Cape St. Augustino; from whence, keeping farther off at sea, we lost sight of land. Then a violent tornado or hurricane took us quite out of our knowledge. It began from the south-east, came about to the north-west, and then settled in the north-east; from whence it blew in such a terrible manner that for twelve days together we could do nothing but drive, and, scudding away before it, let it carry us whither ever fate and the fury of the winds directed.

Shipwrecked

A second storm then came upon us, and carried us away with the same impetuosity westward, and drove us so out of the way of all human commerce, that, had our lives been saved as to the sea, we were rather in danger of being devoured by savages than ever returning to our own country.

In this distress, the wind still blowing very hard, one of our men early in the morning called out "Land!" and we had no sooner run out of the cabin to look out in hopes of seeing whereabouts in the world we were, but the ship struck upon a sand, and in a moment, her motion being so stopped, the sea broke over her in such a manner, that we expected we should all have perished immediately, and we were driven into our close quarters to shelter us from the very foam and spray of the sea.

It is not easy for anyone who has not been in the like condition to describe or conceive the consternation of men in such circumstances; we were in a dreadful condition indeed, and had nothing to do but to think of saving our lives as best we could. We had a boat on board, but how to get her off into the sea was a doubtful thing. However, there was no room for debate, for we fancied the ship would break in pieces every minute. The mate of the vessel lays hold of the boat, and with the help of the rest of the men, they got her slung over the ship's side, and, getting all into her, we let go, and committed ourselves to God's mercy and the wild sea.

And now our case was very dismal indeed, for we all saw plainly that the sea went so high, that the boat could not live, and that we should be inevitably drowned. After we had rowed, or rather driven, about a league and a half, a raging wave, mountain-like, came rolling astern of us, and plainly bade us expect the *coup-de-grâce*. In a word, it took us with such a fury, that it overset the boat at once, and we were all swallowed up in a moment.

Nothing can describe the confusion of thought which I felt when I sunk into the water; for though I swam very well, yet I could not deliver myself from the waves so as to draw breath, till that a wave, having driven me, or rather carried me, a vast way on towards the shore, and having spent itself, went back, and left me upon the land almost dry, but half-dead with the water I took in. I had so much presence of mind as well as breath left that, seeing myself nearer the mainland than I expected, I got upon my feet, and endeavoured to make on towards the land as fast as I could, before another wave should return and take me up again. But I soon found it was impossible to avoid it; for I saw the sea come after me as high as a great hill and as furious as an enemy which I had no means or strength to contend with. My business was to hold my breath and rise myself upon the water if I could, and so by swimming pilot myself towards the shore.

The wave that came upon me again buried me at once twenty or thirty feet deep in its own body; and I could feel myself carried with a mighty force and swiftness towards the shore a very great way. I was covered again with water for a good while, but I held out until it had spent itself and begun to subside. Then I struck forward against the return of the waves, and felt ground again with my feet. I stood still a few moments to recover breath, till the water went from me, and then took to my heels and ran with what strength I had farther towards the shore.

The final surge, though it broke over me, did not swallow me up, and the next run I took got me to the mainland, where I sat down upon the grass, quite out of reach of the wild sea.

I Am Saved

I was now landed, and safe on shore, but as for my comrades, I never saw them afterwards, or any sign of them, except three of their hats, one cap, and two shoes that were not fellows.

After a while I began to look round me to see what kind of place I was in, and what was next to be done. I soon found my comforts abate, and that in a word I had a dreadful deliverance: for I was wet, had no clothes to shift me, nor anything either to eat or drink to comfort me, neither did I see any prospect before me, but that of perishing with hunger, or being devoured by wild beasts; and that which was particularly afflicting to me was that I had no weapon either to hunt and kill any creature for my sustenance, or to defend myself against any other creature that might desire to kill me for theirs. In a word, I had nothing about me but a knife, a tobacco-pipe, and a little tobacco in a box; this was all my provision, and this threw me into terrible agonies of mind, that for a while I ran about like a madman. Night coming upon me, I began with a heavy heart to consider what would be my lot if there were any ravenous beasts in that country, seeing at night they always come abroad for their prey.

All the remedy that offered to my thoughts at the time was to get up into a thick bushy tree like a fir, but thorny, which grew near me, and where I resolved to sit all night, and consider the next day what death I should die, for as yet I saw no prospect of life. I walked about a furlong from the shore, to see if I could find any fresh water to drink, which I did, to my great joy; and having drunk and put a little tobacco in my mouth to prevent hunger, I went to the tree, and getting up into it, endeavoured to place myself so as that if I should sleep I might not fall; and having cut me a short stick, like a truncheon, for my defence, I took up my lodging, and having been excessively fatigued, I fell fast asleep and slept as comfortably as, I believe, few could have done in my condition, and found myself the most refreshed with it that I think I ever was on such an occasion.

I Visit the Wreck

When I waked it was broad day, the weather clear, and the storm abated, so that the sea did not rage and swell as before; but that which surprised me most was that the ship was lifted off in the night from the sand where she lay, by the swelling of the tide, and was driven up almost as far as the rocks; this being within about a mile from where I was, and the ship seeming to stand upright still, I wished myself on board, that, at least, I might save some necessary things for my use.

When I came down from my apartment in the tree, I looked about me again, and the first thing I found was the boat, which lay as the wind and the sea had tossed her up upon the land, about two miles on my right hand. I walked as far as I could upon the shore to have got to her, but found a neck or inlet of water between me and the boat, which was about half a mile broad, so I came back for the present, being more intent upon getting at the ship, where I hoped to find something for my present subsistence.

A little after noon I found the sea very calm, and the tide ebbed so far out that I could come within a quarter of a mile of the ship; and here I found a fresh renewing of my grief, for I saw evidently that if we had kept on board, we had been all safe, that is to say, we had all got safe on shore, and I had not been so miserable as to be left entirely destitute of all comfort and company, as I now was; this forced tears from my eyes again, but as there was little relief, I resolved, if possible, to get to the ship, so I pulled off my shirt, for the weather was hot to extremity, and took the water, but when I came to the ship, my difficulty was still greater to know how to get on board, for as she lay aground, and high out of the water, there was nothing within my reach to lay hold of. I swam round her twice, and the second time I spied a small piece of a rope, which I wondered I did not see at first, hang down by the forechains so low as that with great difficulty I got hold of it, and by the help of that rope, got up into the forecastle of the ship. My first work was to search and to see what was spoiled and what was free; and first I found that all the ship's provisions were dry and untouched by the water, and being very well disposed to eat, I went to the bread-room and filled my pockets with biscuit, and ate it as I went about other things, for I had no time to lose. I also found some rum in the great cabin, of which I took a large dram, and which I had indeed need enough of to spirit me for what was before me. Now I wanted nothing but a boat to furnish myself with many things which I foresaw would be very necessary to me.

I Build a Raft

It was in vain to sit still and wish for what was not to be had, and this extremity roused my application. We had several spare yards, and two or three large spars of wood, and a spare top-mast or two in the ship; I resolved to fall to work with these, and I flung as many of them over board as I could manage for their weight, tying every one with a rope that they might not drive away; when this was done I went down the ship's side, and pulling them to me, I tied four of them fast together at both ends as well as I could, in the form of a raft, and laying two or three short pieces of plank upon them crossways, I found I could walk upon it very well, but that it was not able to bear any great weight, the pieces being too light; so I went to work, and with the carpenter's saw I cut a spare top-mast into three lengths, and added them to my raft, with a great deal of labour and pains; but hope of furnishing myself with necessaries encouraged me to go beyond what I

should have been able to have done upon another occasion.

My raft was now strong enough to bear any reasonable weight. I first laid all the planks or boards upon it that I could get. I then got three of the seamen's chests, which I had broken open and emptied, and lowered them down upon my raft; the first of these I filled with provision, viz. bread, rice, three Dutch cheeses, five pieces of dried goat's flesh, which we lived much upon, and a little remainder of European corn which had been laid by for some fowls which we brought to sea with us, but the fowls were killed; there had been some barley and wheat together, but, to my great disappointment, I found afterwards that the rats had eaten or spoiled it all; as for liquors, I found several cases of bottles belonging to our skipper, in which were some cordial waters, and in all about five or six gallons of rack; these I stored by themselves, there being no need to put them into the chest, nor room for them.

Next, tools to work with on shore, and it was after long searching that I found out the carpenter's chest, which was indeed a very useful prize to me; I got it down to my raft, even whole as it was, without losing time to look into it, for I knew in general what it contained.

My next care was for some ammunition and arms; there were two very good fowling-pieces in the great cabin, and two pistols; these I secured first, with some powder-horns, and a small bag of shot, and two old rusty swords; I knew there were three barrels of powder in the ship, but knew not where our gunner had stowed them, but with much search I found them, two of them dry and good, the third had taken water; those two I got to my raft, with the arms; and now I thought myself pretty well freighted, and began to think how I should get to shore with them, having neither sail, oar, nor rudder, and the least cap full of wind would have overset all my navigation.

I had three encouragements: first, a smooth calm sea; second, the tide rising, and setting in to the shore; third, what little wind there was blew me towards the land; and thus, having found two or three broken oars belonging to the boat, and besides the tools which were in the chest, I found two saws, an axe, and a hammer, and with this cargo I put to sea.

At length I spied a little cove on the right shore of the creek, to which with great pain and difficulty I guided my raft, and at last got so near, that, reaching ground with my oar, I could thrust her directly in; but here I had like to have dipped all my cargo in the sea again; for that shore lying pretty steep, that is to say sloping, there was no place to land but where one end of my float, if it ran on shore, would lie so high, and the other sink lower as before, that it would endanger my cargo again. All that I could do was to wait till the tide was at the highest, keeping the raft with my oar like an anchor to hold this side of it fast to the shore; near a flat piece of ground, which I expected the water would flow over; and so it did. As soon as I found water enough, for my raft drew about a foot of water, I thrust her on upon that flat piece of ground, and there fastened or moored her by sticking my two broken oars into the ground, one on one side near one end, and one on the other side near the other end; and thus I lay till the water ebbed away and left my raft and all my cargo safe on shore.

My next work was to view the country, and seek a proper place for my habitation. There was a hill not above a mile from me, which rose up very steep and high, and which seemed to over-top some other hills, which lay as in a ridge from it northward. I took out one of the fowling-pieces, and one of the pistols, and a horn of powder, and thus armed I travelled for discovery up to the top of that hill, where, after I had with great labour and difficulty got to the top, I saw that I was in an island environed every way with the sea, no land to be seen, except some rocks which lay a great way off, and two small islands less than this, which lay about three leagues to the west.

My Second Voyage to the Wreck

Contented with this discovery, I came back to my raft, and fell to work to bring my cargo on shore, which took me up the rest of that day. At night, I barricaded myself round with the chests and boards I had brought on shore, and made a kind of hut for my lodging.

I now began to consider that I might yet get a great many things out of the ship, which would be useful to me, and particularly some of the rigging, and sails, and such other things as might come to land, and I resolved to make another voyage on board the vessel.

Having got my second cargo on shore, I went to work to make me a little tent with the sail and some poles which I cut for that purpose, and into this tent I brought everything that I knew would spoil, either with rain or sun, and I piled all the empty chests and casks up in a circle round the tent, to fortify it from any sudden attempt, either from man or beast.

When I had this done I blocked up the door of the tent with some boards within, and an empty chest set up on end without, and spreading one of the beds upon the ground, laying my two pistols just at my head, and my gun at length by me, I went to bed for the first time, and slept very quietly all night, for I was very weary and heavy; for the night before I had slept little, and had laboured very hard all day, as well to fetch all those things from the ship, as to get them on shore.

After this I went every day on board, and brought away what I could get.

I had now been thirteen days on shore, and had been eleven times on board the ship. But preparing the twelfth time to go on board, I found the wind begin to rise; however, at low water I went on board, and though I thought I had rummaged the cabin so effectually as that nothing more could be found, yet I discovered a chest with drawers in it, in one of which I found two or three razors, and one pair of scissors, with some ten or a dozen of good knives and forks; in another I found about thirty-six pounds' value in money, some European coin, some Brazilian, some pieces of eight, some gold, some silver. I smiled to myself at the sight of this money. "O drug!" said I aloud, "what art thou good for? Thou art not worth to me, no, not the taking off of the ground; one of those knives is worth all this heap; I have no manner of use for thee, even remain where thou art, and go to the bottom as a creature whose life is not worth saving."

However, upon second thoughts, I took it away, and wrapping all this in a piece of canvas, I began to think of making another raft, but while I was preparing this, I found the sky overcast, and the wind began to rise, and in a quarter of an hour it blew a fresh gale from the shore; it presently occurred to me that it was in vain to pretend to make a raft with the wind off shore, and that it was my business to be gone before the tide of flood began, otherwise I might not be able to reach the shore at all. Accordingly I let myself down into the water, and swam across the channel which lay between the ship and the sand, and was at last gotten home to my little tent, where I lay with all my wealth about me very secure.

My New Home

In search of a place to settle permanently, I found a little plain on the side of a rising hill, whose front towards this little plain was steep as a house-side, so that nothing could come down upon me from the top; on the side of this rock there was a hollow place worn a little way in like the entrance or door of a cave, but there was not really any cave or way into the rock at all.

On the flat of the green, just before this hollow place, I resolved to pitch my tent. This plain was not above an hundred yards broad, and about twice as long, and lay like a green before my door, and at the end of it descended irregularly every way down into the low grounds by the sea side. It was on the N.N.W. side of the hill, so that I was sheltered from the heat every day, till it came to a west and by south sun, or thereabouts, which in those countries is near the setting.

Before I set up my tent, I drew a half circle before the cave entrance which took in about ten yards in its semi-diameter from the rock, and twenty yards in its diameter, from its beginning and ending.

In this half circle I pitched two rows of strong stakes, driving them into the ground till they stood very firm like piles, the biggest end being out of the ground about five foot and a half, and sharpened on the top. The two rows did not stand above six inches from one another.

Then I took some pieces of cable which I had brought from the ship, and I laid them in rows one upon another, within the circle, between these two rows of stakes, up to the top, placing other stakes in the inside, leaning against them, about two foot and a half high, like a spur to a post, and this fence was so strong that neither man or beast could scale it.

The entrance into this place I made by a short ladder to go over the top. Into this fence or fortress, with infinite labour, I carried all my riches, all my provisions, ammunition, and stores.

After I had been there about ten or twelve days, it came into my thoughts that I should lose my reckoning of time for want of books and pen and ink, and should even forget the sabbath days from the working days; but to prevent this I cut it with my knife upon a large post, in capital letters, and making it into a great cross I set it up on the shore where I first landed, viz. "I came on shore here on the 30th of Sept. 1659." Upon the sides of this square post I cut every day a notch with my knife, and every seventh notch was as long again as the rest, and every first day of the month as long again as that long one, and thus I kept my calendar, or weekly, monthly, and yearly reckoning of time. And I must not forget that we had in the ship a dog and two cats, of whose eminent history I may have occasion to say something in its place; for I carried both the cats with me, and as for the dog, he jumped out of the ship of himself, and swam on shore to me the day after I went on shore with my first cargo, and was a trusty servant to me many years; I wanted nothing that he could fetch me, nor any company that he could make up to me, I only wanted to have him talk to me, but that would not do. As I observed before, I found pen, ink, and paper, and I husbanded them to the utmost, and I shall show, that while my ink lasted, I kept things very exact, but after that was gone I could not, for I could not make any ink by any means that I could devise.

And now I began to apply myself to make such necessary things as I found I most wanted, as particularly a chair and a table; for without these I was not able to enjoy the few comforts I had in the world; I could not write, or eat, or do several things with so much pleasure without a table. So I went to work; I made abundance of things, even without tools, and some with no more tools than an adze and a hatchet. But having gotten over these things in some measure, and having settled my household stuff and habitation, made me a table and a chair, and all as handsome about me as I could, I began to keep my journal, of which I shall here give you the copy (though in it will be told all these particulars over again) as long as it lasted, for having no more ink I was forced to leave it off.

My Journal

September 30, 1659

I, poor, miserable Robinson Crusoe, being ship-wrecked during a dreadful storm in the offing, came on shore on this dismal unfortunate island, which I called the Island of Despair, all the rest of the ship's company being drowned, and myself almost dead.

All the rest of that day I spent in afflicting myself at the dismal circumstances I was brought to, viz. I had neither food, house, clothes, weapon, nor place to fly to, and in despair of any relief, saw nothing but death before me, either that I should be devoured by wild beasts, murdered by savages, or starved to death for want of food. At the approach of night, I slept in a tree for fear of wild creatures, but slept soundly though it rained all night.

October 1

In the morning I saw to my great surprise the ship had floated with the high tide, and was driven on shore again much nearer the island. I went upon the sand as near as I could, and then swam on board; this day also it continued raining, though with no wind at all.

From the 1st October to the 24th

All these days entirely spent in many several voyages to get all I could out of the ship.

Oct. 20

I overset my raft and all the goods I had got upon it, but being in shoal water, and the things being chiefly heavy, I recovered many of them when the tide was out.

Oct. 25

It rained all night and all day, with some gusts of wind, during which time the ship broke in pieces.

Oct. 26

I walked about the shore almost all day to find out a place to fix my habitation, greatly concerned to secure myself from an attack in the night, either from wild beasts or men. Towards night, I fixed upon a proper place under a rock, and marked out my encampment, which I resolved to strengthen with a wall.

From the 26th to the 30th

I worked very hard in carrying all my goods to my new habitation, though some part of the time it rained exceeding hard.

The 31st

In the morning I went out into the island with my gun to see for some food, and discover the country, when I killed a she-goat, and her kid followed me home, which I afterwards killed also because it would not feed.

November 1

I set up my tent under a rock, and lay there for the first night, making it as large as I could with stakes driven in to swing my hammock upon.

Nov. 2

I set up all my chests and boards, and the pieces of timber which made my rafts, and with them formed a fence round me, a little within the place I had marked out for my fortification.

Nov. 3

I went out with my gun and killed two fowls like ducks, which were very good food. In the afternoon went to work to make me a table.

Nov. 4

This morning I began to order my times of work, of going out with my gun, time of sleep, and time of diversion.

Nov. 5

This day went abroad with my gun and my dog, and killed a wild cat.

Nov. 6

After my morning walk I went to work with my table again, and finished it, though not to my liking; nor was it long before I learned to mend it.

Nov. 7

Now it began to be settled fair weather. The 7th, 8th, 9th, 10th, and part of the 12th (for the 11th was Sunday) I took wholly up to make me a chair.

Nov. 13

This day it rained, which refreshed me exceedingly, and cooled the earth, but it was accompanied with terrible thunder and lightning, which frighted me dreadfully for fear of my powder.

Nov. 14, 15, 16

These three days I spent in making little square chests or boxes, which might hold a pound or two pound, at most, of powder, and so putting the powder in, I stowed it in places as secure and remote from one another as possible. On one of these three days I killed a large bird that was good to eat, but I know not what to call it.

Nov. 17

This day I began to dig behind my tent into the rock to make room for my farther conveniency. Note: Three things I wanted exceedingly for this work, viz. a pick-axe, a shovel, and a wheel-barrow or basket; so I desisted from my work, and began to consider how to supply that want and make me some tools; as for a pick-axe, I made use of the iron crows, which were proper enough, though heavy; but the next thing was a shovel or spade; this was so absolutely necessary, that indeed I could do nothing effectually without it, but what kind of one to make I knew not.

Nov. 18

The next day in searching the woods I found a tree of that wood, or like it, which in the Brazils they call the iron tree, for its exceeding hardness; of this, with great labour and almost spoiling my axe, I cut a piece, and brought it home too with difficulty enough, for it was exceedingly heavy.

The excessive hardness of the wood, and having no other way, made me a long while upon this machine, for I worked it effectually by little and little into the form of a shovel or spade, the handle exactly shaped like ours in England, only that the broad part having no iron shod upon it at bottom, it would not last me so long; however, it served well enough for the uses which I had occasion to put it to; but never was a shovel, I believe, made after that fashion, or so long a making.

I was still deficient, for I wanted a basket or a wheel-barrow; a basket I could not make by any means, having no such things as twigs that would bend to make wicker ware, at least none yet found out; and as to a wheel-barrow, I fancied I could make all but the wheel, but that I had no notion of, neither did I know how to go about it; besides, I had no possible way to make the iron gudgeons for the spindle or axis of the wheel to run in, so I gave it over, and so for carrying away the earth which I dug out of the cave, I made me a thing like a hod, which the labourers carry mortar in when they serve the bricklayers.

This was not so difficult to me as the making the shovel; and yet this, and the shovel, and the attempt which I made in vain to make a wheel-barrow, took me up no less than four days; I mean, always excepting my morning walk with my gun, which I seldom failed, and very seldom failed also bringing home something fit to eat.

Nov. 23

My other work having now stood still, because of my making these tools, when they were finished I went on, and working every day, as my strength and time allowed, I spent eighteen days entirely in widening and deepening my cave, that it might hold my goods commodiously.

Note:

During all this time, I worked to make this room or cave spacious enough to accommodate me as a warehouse or magazine, a kitchen, a dining-room, and a cellar; as for my lodging, I kept to the tent, except that sometimes in the wet season of the year, it rained so hard that I could not keep myself dry, which caused me afterwards to cover all my place within my pale with long poles in the form of rafters leaning against the rock, and load them with flags and large leaves of trees like a thatch.

A Lucky Escape

December 10

I began now to think my cave or vault finished,

when on a sudden (it seems I had made it too large) a great quantity of earth fell down from the top and one side, so much that in short it frightened me, and not without reason too; for I had had a lucky escape. Upon this disaster I had great deal of work to do over again; for I had the loose earth to carry out, and which was of more importance, I had the ceiling to prop up, so that I might be sure no more would come down.

Dec. 11

This day I went to work with it accordingly, and got two shores or posts pitched upright to the top, with two pieces of boards across over each post; this I finished the next day; and setting more posts up with boards, in about a week more I had the roof secured, and the posts, standing in rows, served me for partitions to part of my house.

Dec. 17

From this day to the twentieth I placed shelves, and knocked up nails on the posts to hang everything

up that could be hung up, and now I began to be in some order within doors.

Dec. 20

Now I carried everything into the cave, and began to furnish my house, and set up some pieces of boards, like a dresser, to order my victuals upon, but boards began to be very scarce with me; also I made me another table.

Dec. 24

Much rain all night and all day; no stirring out.

Dec. 25

Rain all day.

Dec. 26

No rain, and the earth much cooler than before, and pleasanter.

Dec. 27

Killed a young goat, and lamed another so that I caught it, and led it home in a string; when I had it home, I bound and splintered up its leg, which was broken. N.B. I took such care of it that it lived, and the leg grew well, and as strong as ever; but by my nursing it so long it grew tame, and fed upon the little green at my door, and would not go away. This was the first time that I entertained a thought of breeding up some tame creatures, that I might have food when my powder and shot was all spent.

Dec. 28, 29, 30

Great heats and no breeze; so that there was no stirring abroad, except in the evening for food; this time I spent in putting all my things in order within doors.

January 1

Very hot still, but I went abroad early and late with my gun, and lay still in the middle of the day. This evening, going farther into the valleys which lay towards the centre of the island, I found there was plenty of goats, though exceeding shy and hard to come at; however I resolved to try if I could not bring my dog to hunt them down.

Jan. 2

Accordingly, the next day I went out with my dog, and set him upon the goats; but I was mistaken, for they all faced about upon the dog, and he knew his danger too well, for he would not come near them.

Jan. 3

I began my fence or wall; which, being still jealous of my being attacked by somebody, I resolved to make very thick and strong.

All this time I worked very hard on my wall, and made my rounds in the woods every day.

Exploring the Island

It was the 15th of July that I began to take a more particular survey of the island itself. I went up the creek first, where, as I hinted, I brought my rafts on shore. I found, after I came about two miles up, that the tide did not flow any higher, and that it was no more than a little brook of running water, and very fresh and good; but this being the dry season, there was hardly any water in some parts of it, at least not enough to run in any stream.

I spent all that evening there, and went not back to my habitation, which, by the way, was the first night, as I might say, I had lain from home. In the night I took my first contrivance, and got up into a tree, where I slept well, and the next morning proceeded upon my discovery, travelling nearly four miles, as I might judge by the length of the valley, keeping still due north, with a ridge of hills on the south and northside of me.

At the end of this march I came to an opening, where the country seemed to descend to the west, and a little spring of fresh water, which issued out of the side of the hill by me, ran the other way, that is, due east; and the country appeared so fresh, so green, so flourishing, everything being in a constant verdure or flourish of spring, that it looked like a planted garden.

I descended a little on the side of that delicious vale, surveying it with a secret kind of pleasure (though mixed with my other afflicting thoughts)—to think that this was all my own, that I was king and lord of all this country indefeasibly, and had a right of possession; and if I could convey it, I might have it in inheritance as completely as any lord of a manor in England. I saw here abundance of cocoa trees, orange, and lemon, and citron trees; but all wild, and very few bearing any fruit, at least not then. However, the green limes that I gathered were not only pleasant to eat, but very wholesome; and I mixed their juice afterwards with water, which made it very wholesome, and very cool and refreshing. I found melons on the ground in great abundance, and grapes upon the trees.

I found now I had business enough to gather and carry home; and I resolved to lay up a store, as well of grapes as limes and lemons, to furnish myself for the wet season, which I knew was approaching. Having spent three days on this journey, I then returned home; for so I must now call my cave.

My First Boat

Two more seasons passed, then, one day, travelling about my island, I came within view of the sea to the west, and it being a very clear day I fairly descried land; whether an island or continent I could not tell.

This at length put me upon thinking whether it was not possible to make myself a canoe, or periagua, such as the natives of those climates make, even without tools, or, as I might say, without hands, viz. of the trunk of a great tree. I was so intent upon my voyage over the sea in it, that I never once considered how I should get it off the land; and it was really in its own nature more easy for me to guide it over forty five miles of sea, than about forty fathoms of land, where it lay, to set it afloat in the water.

I went to work upon this boat the most like a fool that ever man did, who had any of his senses awake. I pleased myself with the design, without determining whether I was ever able to undertake it; not but that the difficulty of launching my boat came often into my head; but I put a stop to my own enquiries into it, by this foolish answer which I gave myself, "Let's first make it, I'll warrant I'll find some way or other to get it along when 'tis done."

This was a most preposterous method; but the eagerness of my fancy prevailed, and to work I went. I felled a cedar tree: I question much whether Solomon ever had such a one for the building of the temple of Jerusalem. It was five foot ten inches diameter at the end of twenty two foot, after which it lessened for a while, and then parted into branches. It was not without infinite labour that I felled this tree; I was twenty days hacking and hewing at it at the bottom; I was fourteen more getting the branches and limbs and the vast spreading head of it cut off, which I hacked and hewed through with axe and hatchet, and inexpressible labour; after this, it cost me a month to shape it, and dub it to a proportion, and to something like the bottom of a boat, that it might swim upright as it ought to do. It cost me near three months more to clear the inside, and work it out so as to make an exact boat of it. This I did indeed without fire, by mere mallet and chisel, and by the dint of hard labour, till I had brought it to be a very handsome periagua, and big enough to have carried me and all my cargo.

When I had gone through this work, I was

extremely delighted with it. The boat was really much bigger than I ever saw a canoe that was made of one tree, in my life. Many a weary stroke it had cost, you may be sure; and there remained nothing but to get it into the water; and had I gotten it into the water, I make no question but I should have begun the maddest voyage, and the most unlikely to be performed, that ever was undertaken.

But all my devices to get it into the water failed me; though they cost me infinite labour too. This grieved me heartily, and now I saw, though too late, the folly of beginning a work before we count the cost, and before we judge rightly of our own strength to go through with it.

Making an Umbrella

I saved the skins of all the creatures that I killed, I mean four-footed ones, and I had hung them up stretched out with sticks in the sun, by which means some of them were so dry and hard that they were fit for little, but others, it seems, were very useful. The first thing I made of these was a great cap for my head, with the hair on the outside to shoot off the rain; and this I performed so well, that after this I made me a suit of clothes wholly of these skins, that is to say, a waistcoat, and breeches open at knees, and both loose, for they were rather wanting to keep me cool than to keep me warm. I must not omit to acknowledge that they were wretchedly made; for if I was a bad carpenter, I was a worse tailor. However, they were such as I made good shift with; and when I was abroad, if it happened to rain, the hair of my waistcoat and cap being outermost, I was kept very dry.

After this I spent a great deal of time and pains to make me an umbrella; I was indeed in great want of one, and had a great mind to make one; I had seen them made in Brazil, where they are very useful in the great heats which are there; and I felt the heats every jot as great here, and greater too, being nearer the equinox; besides, as I was obliged to be much abroad, it was a most useful thing to me, as well for the rains as the heats. I took a world of pains at it, and was a great while before I could make anything likely to hold; nay, after I thought I had hit the way, I spoiled two or three before I made one to my mind; but at last I made one that answered indifferently well. The main difficulty I found was to make it to let down. I could make it to spread, but if it did not let down too, and draw in, it was not portable for me any way but just over my head, which would not do. However, at last, as I said, I made one to answer, and covered it with skins, the hair upwards, so that it cast off the rains like a penthouse, and kept off the sun so effectually, that I could walk out in the hottest of the weather with greater advantage than I could before in the coolest, and when I had no need of it, could close it and carry it under my arm.

My "Family"

Being now in the eleventh year of my residence, I set myself to study some art to trap and snare the wild goats that roamed the island, to see whether I could not catch some of them alive. To this purpose, I made snares to hamper them, and at length resolved to try a pit-fall, in which I trapped three kids. In about a year and a half I had a flock of about twelve goats, and in two years more I had three and forty. Now I not only had goats flesh to feed on when I pleased, but milk too, sometimes a gallon or two in a day.

It would have made a Stoic smile to have seen me and my little family sit down to dinner, and to see how like a king I dined, too, all alone, attended by my servants. Poll, the young parrot I had caught and tamed, was the only person permitted to talk to me, like a favourite. My dog—who was now grown very old and crazy—sat always at my right hand; and two cats, the descendants of those I had brought on shore, one on one side the table and one on the other, expecting now and then a bit from my hand, as a mark of special favour.

Had anyone in England been to meet such a man as I was, it must either have frighted them, or raised a great deal of laughter. Be pleased to take a sketch of my figure as follows.

I had my great, high shapeless cap, made of a goat's skin, with a flap hanging down behind, as well to keep the sun from me as to shoot the rain off from running into my neck. I had a short jacket of goatskin, the skirts coming down to about the middle of my thighs; and a pair of open-kneed breeches of the same—the breeches were made of the skin of an old he-goat, whose hair hung down such a length on either side, that like pantaloons it reached to the middle of my legs; stockings and shoes I had none,

but had made me a pair of somethings, I scarce know what to call them, but they were of a most barbarous shape— as indeed were the rest of my clothes.

I had on a broad belt of goatskin dried, and in a kind of a frog on either side of this, instead of a sword and dagger hung a little saw and hatchet. I had another belt not so broad, which hung over my shoulder; and at the end of it hung two pouches, both made of goat's skin too—in one of which hung my powder, in the other my shot. I carried my gun on my shoulder; and over my head a great clumsy, ugly, goatskin umbrella—but which, after all, was the most necessary thing I had about me, next to my gun.

As for my face, the colour of it was not really so Mulatto-like as one might expect. My beard I had once suffered to grow until it hung about a quarter of a yard long, but as I had both scissors and razors sufficient, I had cut it pretty short, except what grew on my upper lip, which I had trimmed into a large pair of whiskers, of a length and shape monstrous enough, and such as in England would have passed for frightful.

During this time I built another canoe, which I fitted with mast and sail, and used for short voyages on the sea, but I never ventured far from my little creek.

A Mysterious Footprint

It happened one day about noon going towards my boat, I was exceedingly surprised with the print of a man's naked foot on the shore, which was very plain to be seen in the sand. I stood like one thunder-struck, or as if I had seen an apparition; I listened, I looked round me, I could hear nothing, nor see anything; I went up to a rising ground to look farther; I went up the shore and down the shore, but it was all one, I could see no other impression but that one.

I slept none that night; the farther I was from the occasion of my fright, the greater my apprehensions were, which is something contrary to the nature of such things, and especially to the usual practice of all creatures in fear: but I was so embarrassed with my own frightful ideas of the thing, that I formed nothing but dismal imaginations to myself, even

though I was now a great way off it. Some times I
fancied it must be the devil; and reason joined in
with me upon this supposition; for how should any
other thing in human shape come into the place?
Where was the vessel that brought them? What
marks were there of any other footsteps? And how
was it possible a man should come there?

Now I began to take courage, and to peep abroad
again, for I had not stirred out of my castle for three
days and nights, so that I began to starve for
provision; for I had little or nothing within doors but
some barley cakes and water. Then I knew that my
goats wanted to be milked too, which usually was my
evening diversion; and the poor creatures were in
great pain and inconvenience for want of it; and
indeed, it almost spoiled some of them, and almost
dried up their milk.

For several years, I went about the whole island,
then, one day, when wandering more to the west
point of the island than I had ever gone yet, and
looking out to sea, I thought I saw a boat upon the
sea, at a great distance; I had found a perspective
glass or two in one of the seamen's chests, which I
saved out of our ship; but I had it not about me, and
this was so remote that I could not tell what to make
of it, though I looked at it till my eyes were not able
to hold to look any longer. Whether it was a boat or
not, I do not know; but as I descended from the hill,
I could see no more of it, so I gave it over; only I
resolved to go no more out without a perspective
glass in my pocket.

When I was come down the hill to the end of the
island, where indeed I had never been before, I was
presently convinced that the seeing the print of a
man's foot was not such a strange thing in the
islands as I imagined; and but that it was a special
providence that I was cast upon the side of the island
where the savages never came, I should easily have
known that nothing was more frequent than for the
canoes from the main, when they happened to be a
little too far out at sea, to shoot over to that side of
the island for harbour; likewise as they often met
and fought in their canoes, the victors, having taken
any prisoners, would bring them over to this shore,
where according to their dreadful customs, being all
cannibals, they would kill and eat them; of which
hereafter.

When I was come down the hill to the shore, as I
said above, being the S.W. point of the island, I was
perfectly confounded and amazed; nor is it possible

for me to express the horror of my mind, at seeing the shore spread with skulls, hands, feet, and other bones of human bodies; and particularly I observed a place where there had been a fire made, and a circle dug in the earth, like a cockpit, where it is supposed the savage wretches had sat down to their inhuman feastings upon the bodies of their fellow creatures.

I was so astonished with the sight of these things, that I entertained no notions of any danger to myself from it for a long while; all my apprehensions were buried in the thoughts of such a pitch of inhuman, hellish brutality, and the horror of the degeneracy of human nature. I could not bear to stay in the place a moment longer so I got me up the hill again with all the speed I could, and walked on towards my own habitation.

Thus the years passed, and I began to be very well contented with the life I led, if it might but have been secured from the dread of the savages.

But it was otherwise directed; and it may not be amiss for all people who shall meet with my story, to make this just observation from it, namely, how frequently, in the course of our lives, the evil which in itself we seek most to shun and which when we are fallen into it is the most dreadful to us, is often times the very means or door of our deliverance, by which alone we can be raised again from the affliction we are fallen into.

A Cannibal Feast

It was now the month of December, in my twenty-third year; and this being the southern solstice, for winter I cannot call it, was the particular time of my harvest, and required my being pretty much abroad in the fields; when going out pretty early in the morning, even before it was thorough day-light, I was surprised with seeing a light of some fire upon the shore, at a distance from me of about two miles towards the end of the island, where I had observed some savages had been as before; but not on the other side; but to my great affliction, it was on my side of the island.

I was indeed terribly surprised at the sight, and stopped short within my grove, not daring to go out, lest I might be surprised; and yet I had no more peace within, from the apprehensions I had that if these savages, in rambling over the island, should find my corn standing or cut, or any of my works and improvements, they would immediately conclude that there were people in the place, and would then never give over till they had found me out. In this extremity I went back directly to my castle, pulled up the ladder after me, and made all things without look as wild and natural as I could.

Then I prepared myself within, putting myself in a posture of defence; I loaded all my cannon, as I called them, that is to say, my muskets which were mounted upon my new fortification, and all my pistols, and resolved to defend myself to the last gasp, not forgetting seriously to commend myself to the divine protection, and earnestly to pray to God to deliver me out of the hands of the barbarians; and in this posture I continued about two hours; but began to be mighty impatient for intelligence abroad, for I had no spies to send out.

After sitting a while, and musing what I should do, I was not able to bear sitting in ignorance any longer; so setting up my ladder to the side of the hill, I mounted to the top. Pulling out my perspective glass, which I had taken on purpose, I laid me down flat on my belly on the ground, and began to look for the place; I presently found there was no less than nine naked savages, sitting round a small fire they had made, not to warm them, for they had no need of that, the weather being extremely hot; but, as I supposed, to dress some of their barbarous diet of human flesh, which they had brought with them, whether alive or dead I could not know.

They had two canoes with them, which they had hauled up upon the shore; and as it was then tide of ebb, they seemed to me to wait for the return of the flood, to go away again; it is not easy to imagine what confusion this sight put me into, especially seeing them come on my side the island, and so near me too; but when I observed their coming must always be with the current of the ebb, I began afterwards to be more sedate in my mind, being satisfied that I might go abroad with safety all the time of the tide of flood, if they were not on shore before: and having made this observation, I went abroad about my harvest work with the more composure.

As I expected, as soon as the tide made to the westward, I saw them all take the boat, and row (or paddle as we call it) all away. I should have observed, that for an hour and more before they went off, they went to dancing, and I could easily

discern their postures and gestures by my glasses: I could not perceive, by my nicest observation, but that they were stark naked, and had not the least covering upon them; but whether they were men or women, that I could not distinguish.

As soon as I saw them shipped and gone, I took two guns upon my shoulders, and two pistols at my girdle, and my great sword by my side, without a scabbard, and with all the speed I was able to make, I went away to the hill, where I had discovered the first appearance of all; and as soon as I got thither, which was not less than two hours (for I could not go apace, being so loaded with arms as I was), I perceived there had been three canoes more of savages on that place; and looking out farther, I saw they were all at sea together, making over for the main.

This was a dreadful sight to me, especially when going down to the shore, I could see the marks of horror which the dismal work they had been about had left behind it, viz. the blood, the bones, and part of the flesh of human bodies, eaten and devoured by those wretches, with merriment and sport. I was so filled with indignation at the sight, that I began now to premeditate the destruction of the next that I saw there, let them be who or how many soever.

I Rescue a Savage

Two more years passed, then I was surprised one morning early, with seeing no less than five canoes all on shore together on my side the island; and the people who belonged to them all landed and out of my sight. The number of them broke all my measures, for seeing so many, and knowing that they always came four or six, or sometimes more in a boat, I could not tell what to think of it, or how to take my measures to attack twenty or thirty men single handed; so I lay still in my castle, perplexed and discomforted; however, I put myself into all the same postures for an attack that I had formerly provided, and was just ready for action, if anything had presented. Having waited a good while, listening to hear if they made any noise, at length, being very impatient, I set my guns at the foot of my ladder, and clambered up to the top of the hill; standing so, however, that my head did not appear above the hill,

so that they could not perceive me by any means; here I observed, by the help of my perspective glass, that they were no less than thirty in number, they had a fire kindled, and they had meat dressed. How they had cooked it, that I knew not, or what it was; but they were all dancing in I know not how many barbarous gestures and figures, their own way round the fire.

While I was thus looking on them, I perceived by my perspective two miserable wretches dragged from the boats, where it seems they were laid by, and were now brought out for the slaughter: I perceived one of them immediately fell, being knocked down, I suppose with a club or wooden sword, for that was their way, and two or three others were at work immediately cutting him open for their cookery, while the other victim was left standing by himself, till they should be ready for him. In that very moment this poor wretch seeing himself a little at liberty, nature inspired him with hopes of life, and he started away from them, and ran with incredible swiftness along the sands directly towards me, I mean that part of the coast where my habitation was.

I was dreadfully frightened when I perceived him to run my way, and especially when, as I thought, I saw him pursued by the whole body. However, I kept my station, and my spirits began to recover when I found that there were not above three men that followed him, and still more was I encouraged when I found that he outstripped them exceedingly in running, and gained ground on them, so that if he could but hold it for half an hour, I saw easily he would fairly get away from them all.

There was between them and my castle the creek; and this, I saw plainly, he must necessarily swim over, or the poor wretch would be taken there. But when the savage escaping came thither, he made nothing of it, though the tide was then up, but plunging in, swam through in about thirty strokes or thereabouts, landed, and ran on with exceeding strength and swiftness; when the three persons came to the creek, I found that two of them could swim, but the third could not, and that standing on the other side, he looked at the others, but went no further, and soon after went softly back again, which, as it happened, was very well for him in the main.

I observed that the two who swam were yet more than twice as long swimming over the creek as the fellow was that fled from them. It came now very warmly upon my thoughts, and indeed irresistibly, that now was my time to get me a servant, and perhaps a companion or assistant; and that I was called plainly by providence to save the poor creature's life, I fetched my two guns, and getting up again with the same haste to the top of the hill, I crossed towards the sea; and making a short cut, nearly all downhill, placed myself between pursuers and pursued. I shouted to him that fled, and beckoned for him to come back. I then turned to the two who followed. The first I knocked down with the stock of my piece, the second, while he was raising his bow and arrow, I killed with my first shot.

The poor savage who fled had now stopped and though he saw his enemies lying dead, was so fearful that he stood stock still, and made no effort to come forward. I smiled and made signs to him to advance. At length he did so, then kneeling down placed his face upon the ground. He then took my foot and placed it upon his head, thus displaying that he was my slave forever.

My Man Friday

I took him up and made much of him, and encouraged him all I could. I gave him bread and raisins to eat, and a draught of water. And, having refreshed him, I made signs for him to lie down and sleep, which he did straight away.

He was a comely, handsome fellow, perfectly well made, with straight strong limbs, not too large, tall and well shaped, and about twenty-six years of age. He had a very good countenance, especially when he smiled. His hair was long and black, his forehead very high and large, and a great vivacity and sparkling sharpness in his eyes. The colour of his skin was not quite black, but very tawny.

After he had slumbered, I made him know his name should be Friday, which was the day I saved his life. I likewise taught him that my name was to be Master and taught him to say it, and Yes and No, and to know the meaning of them.

The night came and we slept. In the morning I beckoned him to come with me. I gave him the sword, bows and arrows, and one of the guns to carry, and we marched away to the place these creatures had been.

When we arrived there, my blood chilled in my veins, for all variety of human remnants littered the ground; skulls, bones, flesh and blood covered half eaten morsels. In short, evidence of a wild cannibal feast. Friday conveyed to me that they had brought over four prisoners to feast upon. Three had been eaten, and he was to be the fourth.

I told Friday to gather all the remains and burn them. When this had been done we returned to my castle. There I kitted out my savage. I gave him a pair of linen drawers which I had out of the poor gunner's chest I mentioned, and which I found in the wreck; and which with a little alteration fitted him very well.

Never man had a more faithful, loving, sincere servant, than Friday was to me; without passions, sullenness, or designs, perfectly obliged and engaged; his very affections were tied to me, like those of a child to a father; and I dare say he would have sacrificed his life for the saving mine upon any occasion whatsoever. The many testimonies he gave me of this put it out of doubt, and soon convinced me that I needed to use no precautions as to my safety on his account.

I was greatly delighted with him, and made it my business to teach him everything that was proper to make him useful, handy, and helpful; but especially to make him speak, and understand me when I spake; and he was the aptest scholar that ever was, and particularly was so merry, so constantly diligent, and so pleased, when he could but understand me, or make me understand him, that it was very pleasant to talk to him.

This was the pleasantest year of all the life that I led in this place. Friday began to talk pretty well, and understand the names of almost everything I had occasion to call for, and of every place I had to send him to, and to talk a great deal to me. Besides the pleasure of talking to him, I had a singular satisfaction in the fellow himself. His simple, unfeigned honesty appeared to me more and more every day.

He told me that up a great way beyond the moon, that was, beyond the setting of the moon, which must be W. from their country, there dwelt white men, like me; and that they had killed "much mans", that was his word. By all which I understood, he meant the Spaniards, whose cruelties in America had been spread over the whole country, and was remembered by all the nations from father to son.

I enquired if he could tell me how I might come from this island, and get among those white men; he told me, "yes, yes", I might go "in two canoe"; I could not understand what he meant, or make him describe to me what he meant by "two canoe", till at last, with great difficulty, I found he meant it must be in a large great boat, as big as two canoes.

This part of Friday's discourse began to relish with me very well, and from this time I entertained some hopes, that one time or other, I might find an opportunity to make my escape from this place; and that this poor savage might be a means to help me to do it.

After Friday and I became more intimately acquainted, and that he could understand almost all I said to him and speak fluently, though in broken English, to me, I acquainted him with my own story, or at least so much of it is as related to my coming into the place, how I had lived there, and how long. I let him into the mystery, for such it was to him, of gunpowder and bullet, and taught him how to shoot; I gave him a knife, which he was wonderfully delighted with, and I made him a belt, with a frog hanging to it, such as in England we wear hangers in; and in the frog, instead of a hanger, I gave him a hatchet, which was not only as good a weapon in some cases, but much more useful upon other occasions.

Preparing for a Voyage

I showed him the ruins of our boat, which we lost when we were wrecked, and which I could not stir with my whole strength then, but was now fallen almost to pieces. Upon seeing this boat, Friday stood musing a great while, and said nothing. I asked him what it was he studied upon; at last said he, "Me see such boat like come to place at my nation."

I did not understand him a good while; but at last, when I had examined farther into it, I understood by him that a boat, such as that had been, came on shore upon the country where he lived; that is, as he explained it, was driven thither by stress of weather. I presently imagined that some European ship must have been cast away upon their coast, and the boat might get loose, and drive ashore; but was so dull, that I never once thought of men making escape from a wreck thither, much less whence they might come; so I only inquired after a description of the boat.

Friday described the boat to me well enough; but brought me better to understand him, when he added with some warmth, "We save the white mans from drown." Then I presently asked him if there was any white mans, as he called them, in the boat. 'Yes,' he said, "the boat full white mans." I asked him how many; he told upon his fingers seventeen. I asked him then what became of them; he told me, "They live, they dwell at my nation."

From this time I confess I had a mind to venture over, and see if I could possibly join with these men, who I had no doubt were Spaniards or Portuguese; not doubting but if I could, we might find some method to escape from thence, being upon the continent, and a good company together; better than I could from an island forty miles off the shore, and alone without help. So after some days I took Friday to work again, by way of discourse, and told him I would give him a boat to go back to his own nation; and accordingly I carried him to my frigate which lay on the other side of the island, and having cleared it of water, for I always kept it sunk in the water, I brought it out, showed it him, and we both went into it.

I found he was a most dexterous fellow at managing it, he would make it go almost as swift and fast again as I could; so when he was in, I said to him, "Well now, Friday, shall we go to your nation?" He looked very dull at my saying so, which it seems was because he thought the boat too small to go so far.

Upon the whole, I was by this time so fixed upon my design of going over with him to the continent, that I told him we would go and make one as big as required and he should go home in it. There were trees enough in the island to have built a little fleet, not of periaguas and canoes, but even of good large vessels. But the main thing I looked at, was to get

one so near the water that we might launch it when it was made, to avoid the mistake I committed at first.

At last, Friday pitched upon a tree, for I found he knew much better than I what kind of wood was fittest for it, nor can I tell to this day what wood to call the tree we cut down, except that it was very like the tree we call fustic, or between that and the Nicaragua wood, for it was much the same colour and smell. Friday was for burning the hollow or cavity of the tree out to make it for a boat. But I showed him how rather to cut it out with tools, which, after I had showed him how to use, he did very handily, and in about a month's hard labour we finished it, and made it very handsome, especially when with our axes, which I showed him how to handle, we cut and hewed the outside into the true shape of a boat; after this, however, it cost us near a fortnight's time to get her along as it were inch by inch upon great rollers into the water. But when she was in, she would have carried twenty men with great ease.

I had a farther design, and that was to make a mast and sail and to fit her with an anchor and cable. As to a mast, that was easy enough to get; so

I pitched upon a straight young cedar–tree, which I found near the place, and which there was great plenty of in the island, and I set Friday to work to cut it down, and gave him directions how to shape and order it. I was preparing daily for the voyage; and the first thing I did was to lay by a certain quantity of provisions, being the stores for our voyage; and intended, in a week or a fortnight's time, to open the dock and launch our boat.

More Cannibals

I was busy one morning upon some thing of this kind, when I called to Friday, and bade him go to the sea shore, and see if he could find a turtle or tortoise, a thing which we generally got once a week, for the sake of the eggs as well as the flesh. Friday had not been long gone, when he came running back, and flew over my outer wall, or fence, like one that felt not the ground, or the steps he set his feet on; and before I had time to speak to him, he cried out to me, "O master; O master! O sorrow! O bad!" "What's the matter, Friday?" said I. "O yonder, there," said he, "one, two, three canoe! One, two, three!" By his way of speaking, I concluded there were six; but on inquiry, I found it was but three. "Well, Friday," said I, "do not be frightened"; so I heartened him up

as well as I could. However, I saw the poor fellow was most terribly scared.

I entered the wood, with all possible wariness and silence, Friday following close at my heels. I marched till I came to the skirt of the wood, on the side which was next to them; only that one corner of the wood lay between me and them; here I called softly to Friday, and showing him a great tree, which was just at the corner of the wood, I bade him go to the tree, and bring me word if he could see there plainly what they were doing. He did so, and came immediately back to me, and told me they might be plainly viewed there; that they were all about their fire, eating the flesh of one of their prisoners; and that another lay bound upon the sand, a little from them, which he said they would kill next, and which fired all the very soul within me; he told me it was not one of their nation, but one of the bearded men, who he had told me of, that came to their country in the boat. I was filled with horror at the very naming of the white bearded man, and going to the tree, I saw plainly by my glass a white man who lay upon the beach of the sea, with his hands and his feet tied, with flags, or things like rushes; and that he was a European, and had clothes on.

We Rescue a Spaniard

There was another tree, and a little thicket beyond it, about fifty yards nearer to them than the place where I was, which by going a little way about, I saw I might come at undiscovered, and that then I should be within half shot of them; so I withheld my passion, though I was indeed enraged to the highest degree, and going back about twenty paces, I got behind some bushes, which held all the way till I came to the other tree; and then I came to a little rising ground, which gave me a full view of them, at the distance of about eighty yards.

I had not a moment to lose; for nineteen of the dreadful wretches sat upon the ground, all close huddled together, and had just sent the other two to butcher the poor Christian, and bring him, perhaps limb by limb to their fire, and they were stooped down to untie the bands at his feet; I turned to Friday. "Now, Friday," said I, "do as I bid thee;" Friday said he would. "Then, Friday," said I, "do exactly as you see me do, fail in nothing." So I set down one of the muskets and the fowling-piece upon

the ground, and Friday did the like by his; and with the other musket I took my aim at the savages, bidding him do the like. Then asking him if he was ready, he said "Yes." "Then fire at them," said I; and the same moment I fired also.

Friday took his aim so much better than I, that on the side that he shot, he killed two of them and wounded three more; and on my side, I killed one, and wounded two. They were, you may be sure, in a dreadful consternation; and all of them who were not hurt, jumped up upon their feet, but did not immediately know which way to run, or which way to look; for they knew not from whence their destruction came. Friday kept his eyes close upon me, that, as I had bid him, he might observe what I did. So as soon as the first shot was made, I threw down the piece and took up the fowling-piece, and Friday did the like; he saw me cock and present; he did the same again. "Are you ready, Friday?" said I. "Yes," said he. "Let fly then," said I, "in the name of God," and with that I fired again among the amazed wretches, and so did Friday; and as our pieces were now loaded with what I called swan-shot, or small pistol bullets, we found only two drop; but so many were wounded, that they ran about yelling and screaming like mad creatures, all bloody and miserably wounded, most of them; whereof three more fell quickly after, though not quite dead.

"Now, Friday," said I, laying down the discharged pieces, and taking up the musket which was yet loaded, "follow me," which he did, with a great deal of courage. Upon which I rushed out of the wood, and showed myself, and Friday close at my foot. As soon as I perceived they saw me, I shouted as loud as I could, and bade Friday do so too; and running as fast as I could, which by the way, was not very fast, being loaded with arms as I was, I made directly towards the poor victim, who was, as I said, lying upon the beach or shore, between the place where they sat and the sea. The two butchers who were just going to work with him had left him at the surprise of our first fire, and fled in a terrible fright to the seaside and had jumped into a canoe, and three more of the rest made the same way. I turned to Friday, and bade him step forwards and fire at them. He understood me immediately, and running about forty yards to be near them, he shot at them, and I thought he had killed them all; for I saw them fall of a heap into the boat; though I saw two of them up again quickly. However, he killed two of them and wounded the third; so that he lay down in the bottom of the boat, as if he had been dead.

While my man Friday fired at them, I pulled out my knife and cut the flags that bound the poor victim, and loosing his hands and feet, I lifted him up, and asked him in the Portuguese tongue what he was. He answered in Latin, "Christianus"; but was so weak and faint that he could scarce stand or speak. I took my bottle out of my pocket and gave it him, making signs that he should drink, which he did; and I gave him a piece of bread, which he ate. Then I asked him what countryman he was, and he said, "Espagniole"; and being a little recovered, let me know by all the signs he could possibly make, how much he was in my debt for his deliverance. "Seignior," said I, with as much Spanish as I could make up, "we will talk afterwards, but we must fight now. If you have any strength left, take this pistol and sword, and lay about you." He took them very thankfully, and no sooner had he the arms in his hands, but, as if they had put new vigour into him, he flew upon his murderers like a fury, and had cut two of them in pieces in an instant. For the truth is, as the whole was a surprise to them, so the poor creatures were so much frighted with the noise of our pieces, that they fell down for mere amazement and fear; and had no more power to attempt their own escape, than their flesh had to resist our shot. And that was the case of those five that Friday shot at in the boat; for as three of them fell with the hurt they received, so the other two fell with the fright.

I kept my piece in my hand still, without firing, being willing to keep my charge ready, because I had given the Spaniard my pistol and sword; so I called to Friday, and bade him run up to the tree from whence we first fired, and fetch the arms which lay there, which he did with great swiftness; and then giving him my musket, I sat down myself to load all the rest again, and bade them come to me when they wanted. While I was loading these pieces, there happened a fierce engagement between the Spaniard and one of the savages, who made at him with one of their great wooden swords, the same weapon that was to have killed him before, if I had not prevented it. The Spaniard, who was as bold and as brave as could be imagined, though weak, had fought this Indian a good while, and had cut him two great wounds on his head; but the savage being a stout lusty fellow, closing in with him, had thrown him down (being faint) and was wringing my sword out

of his hand, when the Spaniard, though undermost, wisely quitting the sword, drew the pistol from his girdle, shot the savage through the body, and killed him upon the spot, before I, who was running to help him, could come near him.

Friday, being now left to his liberty, pursued the flying wretches with no weapon in his hand but his hatchet; and with that he dispatched those three who, as I said before, were wounded at first and fallen, and all the rest he could come up with; and the Spaniard coming to me for a gun, I gave him one of the fowling-pieces, with which he pursued two of the savages, and wounded them both; but as he was not able to run, they both got from him into the wood, where Friday pursued them and killed one of them; but the other was too nimble for him, and though he was wounded, yet had plunged himself into the sea, and swam with all his might off to those two who were left in the canoe, which three in the canoe, with one wounded, who we know not whether he died or no, were all that escaped our hands of one and twenty.

My thoughts were a little suspended when I had a serious discourse with the Spaniard, and when I understood that there were sixteen more of his countrymen and Portuguese, who having been cast away, and made their escape to that side, lived there at peace indeed with the savages, but were very sore put to it for necessaries and indeed for life.

He told me they were all of them very civil, honest men, and they were under the greatest distress imaginable, having neither weapons nor clothes, nor any food, but at the mercy and discretion of the savages; out of all hopes of ever returning to their own country; and that he was sure, if I would undertake their relief, they would live and die by me.

Having prepared a larger stock of food for all the guests I expected, I gave the Spaniard leave to go over to the main, to see what he could do with those he had left behind him there. I gave him a strict charge in writing not to bring any man with him who would not first swear that he would in no way injure, fight with, or attack the person he should find in the island.

A Ship Approaches

It was no less than eight days I had waited for them,

when a strange and unforeseen accident intervened. I was fast asleep in my hutch one morning, when my man Friday came running in to me, and called aloud, "Master, master, they are come, they are come!"

I jumped up, and regardless of danger, I went out, as soon as I could get my clothes on, through my little grove, which by the way was by this time grown to be a very thick wood. I say, regardless of danger, I went without my arms, which was not my custom to do; but I was surprised, when turning my eyes to the sea, I presently saw a boat at about a league and a half's distance, standing in for the shore, with a shoulder of mutton sail, as they call it; and the wind blowing pretty fair to bring them in; also I observed presently that they did not come from that side which the shore lay on, but from the southernmost end of the island. Upon this I called Friday in, and bade him lie close, for these were not the people we looked for, and that we might not know yet whether they were friends or enemies.

Having fetched my perspective glass, and climbed the ladder, I had scarce set my foot on the hill when my eye plainly discovered a ship lying at anchor, at about two leagues and a half's distance from me south-south-east, but not above a league and a half from the shore. By my observation it appeared plainly to be an English ship, and the boat appeared to be an English long-boat.

I cannot express the confusion I was in, though the joy of seeing a ship, and one who I had reason to believe was manned by my own countrymen, and consequently friends, was such as I cannot describe; but yet I had some secret doubts hung about me, I cannot tell from whence they came, bidding me keep upon my guard.

In the first place, it occurred to me to consider what business an English ship could have in that part of the world, since it was not the way to or from any part of the world where the English had any traffic; and I knew there had been no storms to drive them in there. It was most probable that they were here upon no good design.

I saw the boat draw near the shore, as if they looked for a creek to thrust in at for the convenience of landing; however, as they did not come quite far enough, they did not see the little inlet where I formerly landed my rafts; but ran their boat on shore upon the beach, at about half a mile from me, which was very happy for me; for otherwise they would have landed just, as I may say, at my door, and would soon have beaten me out of my castle, and perhaps have plundered me of all I had. When they were on shore, I was fully satisfied that they were Englishmen; at least most of them. One or two I thought were Dutch, but it did not prove so.

Mutiny

There were in all eleven men, whereof three of them I found were unarmed, and, as I thought, bound; and when the first four or five of them were jumped on shore, they took those three out of the boat as prisoners. One of the three I could perceive using passionate gestures of entreaty, affliction, and despair, even to a kind of extravagance; the other two I could perceive lifted up their hands sometimes, and appeared concerned indeed, but not to such a degree as the first.

I was perfectly confounded at the sight, and knew not what the meaning of it should be. Friday called out to me in English, as well as he could. "O master! you see English mans eat prisoner as well as savage mans." "Why," said I, "Friday, do you think they are a-going to eat them then?" "Yes," said Friday, "they will eat them." "No, no, Friday, I am afraid they will murder them indeed, but you may be sure they will not eat them."

All this while I had no thought of what the matter really was, but stood trembling with the horror of the sight, expecting every moment when the three prisoners should be killed; nay, once I saw one of the villains lift up his arm with a great cutlass, to strike one of the poor men; and I expected to see him fall every moment, at which all the blood in my body seemed to run chill in my veins.

After I had observed the outrageous usage of the three men by the insolent seamen, I observed the fellows run scattering about the land, as if they wanted to see the country. I observed that the three other men had liberty to go also where they pleased; but they sat down all three upon the ground, very pensive, and looked like men in despair.

This put me in mind of the first time when I came on shore, and began to look about me; how I gave myself over for lost; how wildly I looked round me; what dreadful apprehensions I had; and how I lodged in the tree all night for fear of being devoured by wild beasts.

As I knew nothing that night of the supply I was to receive by the providential driving of the ship nearer the land, by the storms and tide, by which I have since been so long nourished and supported; so these three poor desolate men knew nothing how certain of deliverance and supply they were, how near it was to them, and how effectually and really they were in a condition of safety, at the same time that they thought themselves lost, and their case desperate.

It was just at the top of high-water when these people came on shore, and while partly they stood parleying with the prisoners they brought, and partly while they rambled about to see what kind of a place they were in, they had carelessly stayed till the tide was spent and the water was ebbed considerably away, leaving their boat aground.

They had left two men in the boat, who, as I found afterwards, having drank a little too much brandy, fell asleep; however, one of them waking sooner than the other, and finding the boat too fast aground for him to stir it, hallooed for the rest who were straggling about, upon which they all soon came to the boat; but it was past all their strength to launch her, the boat being very heavy, and the shore on that side being a soft oozy sand, almost like a quick-sand.

In this condition, like true seamen who are perhaps the least of all mankind given to forethought, they gave it over, and away they strolled about the country again; and I heard one of them say aloud to another, calling them off from the boat, "Why, let her alone, Jack, can't ye, she will float next tide," by which I was fully confirmed in the main enquiry, of what countrymen they were.

I knew it was no less than ten hours before the boat could be afloat again, and by that time it would be dark, and I might be at more liberty to see their motions, and to hear their discourse, if they had any. In the meantime, I fitted myself up for a battle, as before, though with more caution, knowing I had to do with another kind of enemy than I had at first. I ordered Friday also, who I had made an excellent marksman with his gun, to load himself with arms. I took myself two fowling-pieces, and I gave him three muskets. My figure indeed was very fierce; I had my formidable goat-skin coat on, with the great cap I have mentioned, a naked sword by my side, two pistols in my belt, and a gun upon each shoulder.

The English Captain

It was my design, as I said above, not to have made any attempt till it was dark; but about two o'clock, being the heat of the day, I found that in short they were all gone straggling into the woods, and, as I thought, were laid down to sleep. The three poor distressed men, too anxious for their condition to get any sleep, were however sat down under the shelter of a great tree, at about a quarter of a mile from me, and, as I thought, out of sight of any of the rest.

Upon this I resolved to discover myself to them, and learn something of their condition. Immediately I marched in the figure as above, my man Friday at a good distance behind me, as formidable for his arms, as I, but not making quite so staring a spectre-like figure as I did.

I came as near them undiscovered as I could and then, before any of them saw me, I called aloud to them in Spanish, "What are ye, gentlemen?"

They started up at the noise, but were ten times more confounded when they saw me, and the uncouth figure that I made. They made no answer at all, but I thought I perceived them just going to fly from me, when I spoke to them in English.

"Gentlemen," said I, "do not be surprised at me; perhaps you may have a friend near you when you did not expect it." "He must be sent directly from heaven then," said one of them gravely to me, and pulling off his hat at the same time to me, "for our condition is past the help of man." "All help is from heaven, sir," said I. "But can you put a stranger in the way how to help you, for you seem to me to be in some great distress? I saw you when you landed, and when you seemed to make applications to the brutes that came with you, I saw one of them lift up his sword to kill you."

The poor man, with tears running down his face, and trembling, looked like one astonished, returned, "Am I talking to God or man?" "I am an Englishman and disposed to assist you," I said. "I have one servant only; we have arms and ammunition; tell us freely, can we serve you? What is your case?"

"Our case," said he, 'sir, is too long to tell you, while our murderers are so near; but in short, sir, I was commander of that ship; my men have mutinied against me; they have been hardly prevailed upon not to murder me, and at last have set me on shore in this desolate place, with these two men with me, one my mate, the other a passenger, where we expected to perish, believing the place to be uninhabited, and know not yet what to think of it."

"Have they any fire-arms?" said I. He answered they had only two pieces, and one which they left in the boat. "Well then," said I, "leave the rest to me; I see they are all asleep, it is an easy thing to kill them all; but shall we rather take them prisoners?" He told me there were two desperate villains among them, that it was scarce safe to show any mercy to; but if they were secured, he believed all the rest would return to their duty. I asked him which they were. He told me he could not at that distance describe them; but he would obey my orders in anything I would direct. "Well," said I, "let us retreat out of their view or hearing, lest they awake, and we will resolve further"; so they willingly went back with me, till the woods covered us from them.

"Now," said I, "here are three muskets for you, with powder and ball; tell me next what you think is proper to be done." He showed me all the testimony of his gratitude that he was able; but offered to be wholly guided by me. I told him I thought it was hard venturing anything; but the best method I could think of was to fire upon them at once, as they lay; and if any was not killed at the first volley, and offered to submit, we might save them, and so put it wholly upon God's providence to direct the shot.

He said very modestly, that he was loth to kill them, if he could help it, but that those two were incorrigible villains, and had been the authors of all the mutiny in the ship, and if they escaped, we should be undone still; for they would go on board and bring the whole ship's company, and destroy us all. "Well then," says I, "necessity legitimates my advice, for it is the only way to save our lives." However, seeing him still cautious of shedding blood, I told him they should go themselves, and manage as they found convenient.

We Make Our Plans

In the middle of this discourse, we heard some of them awake, and soon after we saw two of them on their feet. I asked him if either of them were of the men who he had said were the heads of the mutiny. He said, "No." "Well then," said I, "you may let them escape, and Providence seems to have wakened them on purpose to save themselves. Now," says I, "if the rest escape you, it is your fault."

Animated with this, he took the musket I had given him in his hand and a pistol in his belt, and his two comrades with him, with each man a piece in his hand. The two men who were with him, going first, made some noise, at which one of the seamen who

was awake turned about, and seeing them coming, cried out to the rest; but it was too late then; for the moment he cried out, they fired—I mean the two men, the captain wisely reserving his own piece. They had so well aimed their shot at the men they knew, that one of them was killed on the spot, and the other very much wounded; but not being dead, he started up upon his feet, and called eagerly for help to the other; but the captain, stepping to him, told him, 'twas too late to cry for help, he should call upon God to forgive his villainy, and with that word knocked him down with the stock of his musket, so that he never spoke more. There were three more in the company, and one of them was also slightly wounded. By this time I was come, and when they saw their danger, and that it was in vain to resist, they begged for mercy. The captain told them he would spare their lives, if they would give him an assurance of their abhorrence of the treachery they had been guilty of, and would swear to be faithful to him in recovering the ship, and afterwards in carrying her back to Jamaica, from whence they

came. They gave him all the protestations of their sincerity that could be desired, and he was willing to believe them, and spare their lives, which I was not against; only I obliged him to keep them bound hand and foot while they were upon the island.

While this was doing, I sent Friday with the captain's mate to the boat, with orders to secure her and bring away the oars and sail, which they did; and by and by, three straggling men that were (happily for them) parted from the rest, came back upon hearing the guns fired, and seeing their captain, who before was their prisoner, now their conqueror, they submitted to be bound also; and so our victory was complete. Our business now was to consider how to recover the ship.

He agreed with me as to that, but told me he was perfectly at a loss what measures to take; for that there were still six and twenty hands on board, who having entered into a cursed conspiracy, by which they had all forfeited their lives to the law, would be hardened in it now by desperation; and would carry it on, knowing that if they were reduced, they should be brought to the gallows as soon as they came to England, or to any of the English colonies; and that therefore there would be no attacking them with so small a number as we were.

I mused for some time upon what he had said, and found it was a very rational conclusion; and that therefore some thing was to be resolved on very speedily, as well to draw the men on board into some snare for their surprise, as to prevent their landing upon us, and destroying us. Upon this it presently occurred to me that in a little while the ship's crew, wondering what was become of their comrades and of the boat, would certainly come on shore in their other boat to seek for them, and that then perhaps they might come armed, and be too strong for us. This he allowed was rational.

Upon this, I told him the first thing we had to do was to stave the boat which lay upon the beach, so that they might not carry her off; and taking everything out of her, leave her so far useless as not to be fit to swim. Accordingly we went on board, took the arms which were left on board out of her, and whatever else we found there, which was a bottle of brandy and another of rum, a few biscuit cakes, a horn of powder, and a great lump of sugar in a piece of canvas; the sugar was five or six pounds; all which was very welcome to me, especially the brandy and sugar, of which I had had none left for many years.

We knocked a great hole in her bottom, so that if they had come strong enough to master us, yet they could not carry off the boat. Indeed, it was not much in my thoughts that we could be able to recover the ship; but my view was that if they went away without the boat, I did not much question to make her fit again, to carry us away to the Leeward Islands, and call upon our friends, the Spaniards, in my way, for I had them still in my thoughts.

While we were thus preparing our designs, and had first by main strength heaved the boat upon the beach, so high that the tide would not float her off at high-water-mark, we heard the ship fire a gun, and saw her make a waft with her antient, as a signal for the boat to come on board; but no boat stirred; and they fired several times, making other signals for the boat. At last, when all their signals and firing proved fruitless, and they found the boat did not stir, we saw them, by the help of my glasses, hoist another boat out, and row towards the shore; and we found as they approached that there were no less than ten men in her, and that they had fire-arms

with them.

As the ship lay almost two leagues from the shore, we had a full view of them as they came, and a plain sight of the men, even of their faces, because the tide having set them a little to the east of the other boat, they rowed up under shore, to come to the same place where the other had landed, and where the boat lay.

The captain knew the persons and characters of all the men in the boat, of whom he said that there were three very honest fellows, but that as for the boatswain, who it seems was the chief officer among them and all the rest, they were as outrageous as any of the ship's crew.

We had, upon the first appearance of the boat's coming from the ship, considered of separating our prisoners, and had indeed secured them effectually.

Two of them, of whom the captain was less assured than ordinary, I sent with Friday and one of the three (delivered men) to my cave, and he stood sentinel over them at the entrance. The other prisoners had better usage; two of them were kept pinioned indeed, because the captain was not free to trust them; but the other two were taken into my service upon their captain's recommendation, and upon their solemnly engaging to live and die with us; so with them and the three honest men, we were seven men, well armed; and I made no doubt we should be able to deal well enough with the ten that were coming, considering that the captain had said there were three or four honest men among them also. As soon as they got to the place where their other boat lay, they run their boat in to the beach and came all on shore, hauling the boat up after them, which I was glad to see; for I was afraid they would rather have left the boat at anchor, some distance from the shore, with some hands in her to guard her; and so we should not be able to seize the boat.

Being on shore, the first thing they did, they ran all to their other boat, and it was easy to see that they were under a great surprise, to find her stripped as above, of all that was in her, and a great hole in her bottom.

After they had mused a while upon this, they set up two or three great shouts, hallooing with all their might, to try if they could make their companions hear; but all was to no purpose. Then they came all close in a ring, and fired a volley of their small arms, which indeed we heard, and the echoes made the woods ring, but it was all one; those in the cave we were sure could not hear, and those in our keeping, though they heard it well enough, yet dared give no answer to them.

They were so astonished at the surprise of this, that as they told us afterwards, they resolved to go all on board again to their ship, and let them know that the men were all murdered, and the long-boat staved; accordingly they immediately launched their boat again, and got all of them on board.

The captain was terribly amazed and even confounded at this, believing they would go on board the ship again, and set sail, giving their comrades for lost, and so he should still lose the ship, which he was in hopes we should have recovered; but he was quickly as much frighted the other way.

They had not been long put off with the boat, but we perceived them all coming on shore again; but with this new measure in their conduct, which it seems they consulted together upon, namely to leave three men in the boat, and the rest to go on shore, and go up into the country to look for their fellows.

This was a great disappointment to us; for now we were at a loss what to do; for our seizing those seven men on shore would be of no advantage to us if we let the boat escape; because they would then row away to the ship, and then the rest of them would be sure to weigh and set sail, and so our recovering the ship would be lost.

However, we had no remedy but to wait and see what the issue of things might present. The seven men came on shore, and the three who remained in the boat put her off to a good distance from the shore, and came to anchor to wait for them; so that it was impossible for us to come at them in the boat.

Those that came on shore kept close together, marching towards the top of the little hill under which my habitation lay; and we could see them plainly, though they could not perceive us. We could have been very glad they would have come nearer to us, so that we might have fired at them, or that they would have gone farther off, that we might have come abroad.

We waited a great while though very impatient for their removing; and were very uneasy, when after long consultations, we saw them start all up and march down towards the sea.

It seems they had such dreadful apprehensions upon them of the danger of the place, that they resolved to go on board the ship again, give their companions over for lost, and so go on with their intended voyage with the ship.

Battle with the Mutineers

As soon as I perceived them go towards the shore, I imagined it to be as it really was, that they had given over their search, and were for going back again; and the captain, as soon as I told him my thoughts, was ready to sink at the apprehensions of it; but I presently thought of a stratagem to fetch them back again, and which answered my end to a tittle.

I ordered Friday and the captain's mate to go over the little creek westward, and bade them halloo as loud as they could, and wait till the seamen heard them; that as soon as they heard the seamen answer them, they could return it again, and then keeping out of sight, take a round, always answering when the other hallooed, to draw them as far into the island, and among the woods, as possible, and then wheel about again to me, by such ways as I directed them.

They were just going into the boat, when Friday and the mate hallooed, and they presently heard them, and answering, ran along the shore westward, towards the voice they heard, where they were presently stopped by the creek, where the water being up, they could not get over, and called for the boat to come up and set them over, as indeed I expected.

When they had set themselves over, I observed that the boat being gone up a good way into the creek, and as it were, in a harbour within the land, they took one of the three men out of her to go along with them, and left only two in the boat, having fastened her to the stump of a little tree on the shore.

This is what I wished for, and immediately leaving Friday and the captain's mate to their business, I took the rest with me, and crossing the creek out of their sight, we surprised the two men before they were aware; one of them lying on shore, and the other being in the boat. The fellow on shore was between sleeping and waking, and going to start up; the captain, who was foremost, ran in upon him and knocked him down, and then called out to him in the boat to yield, or he was a dead man.

There needed very few arguments to persuade a single man to yield, when he saw five men upon him, and his comrade knocked down; besides, this was, it seems, one of the three who were not so hearty in the mutiny as the rest of the crew, and therefore was easily persuaded, not only to yield, but afterwards to join sincerely with us.

In the meantime, Friday and the captain's mate so well managed their business with the rest, that they drew them by hallooing and answering, from one hill to another, and from one wood to another, till they not only heartily tired them, but left them where they were very sure they could not reach back to the boat before it was dark; and indeed they were heartily tired themselves also by the time they came back to us.

We had nothing now to do but to watch for them in the dark, and to fall upon them, so as to make sure work with them.

It was several hours after Friday came back to me, before they came back to their boat; and we could hear the foremost of them long before they came quite up, calling to those behind to come along, and could also hear them answer and complain how lame and tired they were, and not able to come any faster, which was very welcome news to us.

At length they came up to the boat; but 'tis impossible to express their confusion when they found the boat fast aground in the creek, the tide ebbed out, and their two men gone. We could hear them call to one another in a most lamentable manner, telling one another they were gotten into an enchanted island; that either there were inhabitants in it, and they should all be murdered, or else there were devils and spirits in it, and they should be all carried away and devoured.

They hallooed again, and called their two comrades by their names a great many times, but no answer. After some time, we could see them, by the little light there was, run about wringing their hands like men in despair; and that sometimes they would go and sit down in the boat to rest themselves, then come ashore again, and walk about again, and so over the same thing again.

My men would fain have me give them leave to fall upon them at once in the dark; but I was willing to take them at some advantage, so to spare them, and kill as few of them as I could; and especially I was unwilling to hazard the killing any of our own men, knowing the others were very well armed. I resolved to wait to see if they did not separate; and therefore to make sure of them, I drew my ambuscade nearer, and ordered Friday and the captain to creep upon their hands and feet as close to the ground as they could, that they might not be discovered, and get as near them as they could possibly, before they offered to fire.

They had not been long in that posture, but that the boatswain, who was the principal ringleader of the mutiny, and had now shown himself the most dejected and dispirited of all the rest, came walking towards them with two more of their crew; when they came nearer, the captain and Friday, starting up on their feet, let fly at them.

The boatswain was killed upon the spot, the next man was shot in the body and fell just by him, though he did not die till an hour or two after; and the third ran for it.

At the noise of the fire, I immediately advanced with my whole army, which was now eight men, namely myself generalissimo, Friday my lieutenant-general, the captain and his two men, and the three prisoners-of-war, who we had trusted with arms.

We came upon them indeed in the dark, so that they could not see our number; we bade them surrender, as the captain was standing by with fifty men ready to attack. This, of course, was a fiction as our active force numbered only eight in all. But it worked.

My army came up and seized them all, upon their boat, only I kept myself and one more out of sight, for reasons of state.

Our next work was to repair the boat, and think of seizing the ship.

Upon the captain's coming to me, I told him my project for doing this, which he liked wonderfully well, and resolved to put it in execution the next morning, but first it would be necessary to divide the prisoners.

I told him that he should go and take three of the worst of them, and send them pinioned to the cave where the others lay. This was committed to Friday and the two men who came on shore with the captain.

Retaking the Ship

With the coming of morning the captain had no difficulty before him, but to furnish his two boats,

stop the breach of one, and man them. He made his passenger captain of one, with four other men; and himself, and his mate, and five more, went in the other; and they contrived their business very well, for they came up to the ship about midnight. As soon as they came within call of the ship, he hailed them and told them they had brought off the men and the boat, but that it was a long time before they had found them, and the like; holding them in a chat till they came to the ship's side; when the captain and the mate, entering first with their arms, immediately knocked down the second mate and carpenter with

the butt-end of their muskets. Being very faithfully seconded by their men, they secured all the rest that were upon the main and quarter decks, and began to fasten the hatches to keep them down who were below, when the other boat and their men, entering at the fore chains, secured the fore-castle of the ship, and the scuttle which went down into the cook-room, making three men they found there prisoners.

When this was done, and all safe upon deck, the captain ordered the mate with three men to break into the round-house where the new rebel captain lay, and having taken the alarm, was gotten up, and with two men and a boy had gotten fire-arms in their hands; and when the mate with a crow split open the door, the new captain and his men fired boldly among them, and wounded the mate with a musket ball, which broke his arm, and wounded two more of the men but killed nobody.

The mate, calling for help, rushed however into the round-house, wounded as he was, and with his pistol shot the new captain through the head, the bullet entering at his mouth, and came out again behind one of his ears, so that he never spoke a word; upon which the rest yielded, and the ship was taken effectually, without any more lives lost.

As soon as the ship was thus secured, the captain ordered seven guns to be fired, which was the signal agreed upon with me, to give me notice of his success, which you may be sure I was very glad to hear, having sat watching upon the shore for it till near two o'clock in the morning.

I Am Rescued at Last

Having thus heard the signal plainly, I laid me down; and it having been a day of great fatigue to me, I slept very sound, till I was something surprised with the noise of a gun; and presently starting up, I heard a man call me and presently I knew the captain's voice, when climbing up to the top of the hill, there he stood, and pointing to the ship, he embraced me in his arms. "My dear friend and deliverer," said he, "there's your ship, for she is all yours, and so are we and all that belong to her." I cast my eyes to the ship, and there she rode within little more than half a mile of the shore; for they had weighed her anchor as soon as they were masters of her; and the weather being fair, had brought her to an anchor just against the mouth of the little creek;

and the tide being up, the captain had brought the pinnace in near the place where I at first landed my rafts, and so landed just at my door.

I was at first ready to sink down with surprise; for I saw my deliverance indeed visibly put into my hands, all things easy, and a large ship just ready to carry me away whither I pleased to go.

At first, for some time, I was not able to answer him one word; but as he had taken me in his arms, I held fast by him, or I should have fallen to the ground.

He perceived the surprise, and immediately pulled a bottle out of his pocket, and gave me a dram of

cordial, which he had brought on purpose for me. After I had drunk it, I sat down upon the ground; and though it brought me to myself, yet it was a good while before I could speak a word to him.

We consulted what was to be done with the prisoners we had, and decided that, since we knew them to be incorrigible and refractory to the last degree, it was best to leave them on the island. I therefore let them into the story of my living there, and put them in the way of making it easy to them. In a word, I gave them every part of my own story.

When we, my man Friday and I, took leave of this island, we carried on board for relics the great goat's-skin cap I had made, my umbrella, and my parrot; also I forgot not to take the money I formerly mentioned, which had lain by me so long useless that it was grown rusty, or tarnished, and could hardly pass for silver till it had been cleaned and polished.

And thus we left the island, the nineteenth of December as I found by the ship's account, in the year 1686, after I had been upon it eight and twenty years, two months, and nineteen days.

In this vessel, after a long voyage, we arrived in England, the eleventh of June, in the year 1687.

THE ADVENTURES OF
HUCKLEBERRY FINN

Miss Watson's Jim

It was night, and the widow's house was all as still as death. I sat in my room musing on how Tom Sawyer and I, Huckleberry Finn, had found the treasure and how Judge Thatcher had invested it for us, and how the widow Douglas had said she would look after me and make her home mine also.

Things should have been well for me, but they were not. The widow's ways were not what I had been used to (too much cleanliness and religion for my liking), and when her sister Miss Watson came to live there too—it became pretty well unbearable as she constantly fussed and picked on me.

I wanted to run away, but Tom Sawyer wouldn't let me join his robber's gang unless I promised to stay. So, here I was feeling lonely and having a crafty smoke in the bedroom (for the widow didn't allow smoking) when I heard a twig snap, down in the dark amongst the trees outside—something was a-stirring. Directly I could just barely hear a 'me-yow, me-yow!' down there. That was good—says I, and I answered 'me-yow, me-yow!' as softly as I could, then put out the light and scrambled out of the window on to the shed. Then I slipped down to the ground and crawled in amongst the trees, and

sure enough, there was Tom Sawyer waiting for me.

We went tip-toeing along a path amongst the trees back towards the end of the widow's garden, stooping down so as the branches wouldn't scrape our heads. When we were passing the kitchen I fell over a root and made a noise. We scrouched down and laid still. Miss Watson's big nigger, named Jim, was sitting in the kitchen door; we could see him pretty clear, because there was a light behind him. He got up and stretched his neck out about a minute, listening. Then he says:

"Who dah?"

He listened some more; then he come tip-toeing down and stood right between us; we could a touched him, nearly. Well, likely it was minutes and minutes that there warn't a sound, and we all there so close together. There was a place on my ankle that got to itching; but I dasn't scratch it; and then my ear begun to itch; and next my back, right between my shoulders. Seemed like I'd die if I couldn't scratch. Pretty soon Jim says:

"Say—who is you? Whar is you? Dog my cats ef I didn't hear sumf'n. Well, I knows what I's gwyne to do. I's gwyne to set down here and listen till I hears it agin."

So he set down on the ground betwixt me and Tom. He leaned his back up against a tree, and stretched his legs out till one of them most touched one of mine. My nose begun to itch. It itched till the tears come into my eyes. But I dasn't scratch. I

didn't know how I was going to set still. After a while, Jim begun to breathe heavy; next he begun to snore—and then I was pretty soon comfortable again.

Tom he made a sign to me—a kind of a little noise with his mouth—and we went creeping away on our hands and knees.

Tom Sawyer's Gang

We cut along the path, around the garden fence, and by and by fetched up on the steep top of the hill the other side of the house. Well, when Tom and me got to the edge of the hill-top, we looked away down into the village and could see three or four lights twinkling.

Then we went down the hill and found Jo Harper, and Ben Rogers, and two or three more of the boys, hid in the old tanyard. So we unhitched a skiff and pulled down the river two mile and a half, to the big scar on the hill-side, and went ashore.

We went to a clump of bushes, and Tom made everybody swear to keep the secret, and then showed them a hole in the hill, right in the thickest part of the bushes. Then we lit the candles and crawled in on our hands and knees. We went about two hundred yards, and then the cave opened up. Tom poked about amongst the passages and pretty soon ducked under a wall where you wouldn't a noticed that there was a hole. We went along a narrow place and got into a kind of room, all damp and sweaty and cold, and there we stopped. Tom says:

"Now we'll start this band of robbers and call it Tom Sawyer's Gang. Everybody that wants to join has got to take an oath, and write his name in blood."

Everybody was willing. So Tom got out a sheet of paper that he had wrote the oath on, and read it. It swore every boy to stick to the band, and never tell any of the secrets; and if anybody done anything to any boy in the band, whichever boy was ordered to kill that person and his family must do it, and he mustn't eat and he mustn't sleep till he had killed them and hacked a cross in their breasts, which was the sign of the band. And nobody that didn't belong to the band could use that mark, and if he did he must be sued; and if he done it again he must be killed. And if anybody that belong to the band told the secrets, he must have his throat cut, and then have his carcass burnt up and the ashes scattered all around, and his name blotted off of the list with blood and never mentioned again by the Gang, but have a curse put on it and be forgot for ever.

Everybody said it was a real beautiful oath, and asked Tom if he got it out of his own head. He said, some of it, but the rest was out of pirate books, and robber books, and every gang that was high-toned had it.

Then they all stuck a pin in their fingers to get blood to sign with, and I made my mark on the paper.

"Now," says Ben Rogers, "what's the line of business of this Gang?"

"Nothing only robbery and murder," Tom said.

"But who are we going to rob? Houses—or cattle —or——"

"Stuff! Stealing cattle and such things ain't robbery, it's burglary," says Tom Sawyer. "We ain't burglars. That ain't no sort of style. We are highwaymen. We stop stages and carriages on the road, with masks on, and kill the people and take their watches and money."

"Must we always kill the people?"

"Oh, certainly. It's best. Some authorities think different but mostly it's considered best to kill them. Except some that you bring to the cave here and keep them till they're ransomed."

"All right. I don't mind; but I say it's a fool way, anyhow. Say—do we kill the women too?"

"Well, Ben Rogers, if I was as ignorant as you I wouldn't let on. Kill the women? No—nobody ever saw anything in the books like that. You fetch them to the cave, and you're always as polite as pie to them; and by-and-by they fall in love with you and never want to go home any more."

"Well, if that's the way, I'm agreed, but I don't

take no stock in it. Mighty soon we'll have the cave so cluttered up with women, and fellows waiting to be ransomed, that there won't be no place for the robbers. But go ahead, I ain't got nothing to say."

Little Tommy Barnes was asleep, now, and when they waked him up he was scared, and cried, and said he wanted to go home to his ma, and didn't want to be a robber any more.

So they all made fun of him, and called him cry-baby, and that made him mad, and he said he would go straight and tell all the secrets. But Tom give him five cents to keep quiet, and said we would all go home and meet next week and rob somebody and kill some people. Then we elected Tom Sawyer as first captain and Jo Harper second captain of the Gang, and so started home.

I clumb up the shed and crept into my window just before day was breaking. My new clothes was all greased up and clayey, and I was dog tired.

The Drowned Man

Well, I got a good going-over in the morning, from old Miss Watson, on account of my clothes; but the widow she didn't scold, but only cleaned off the grease and clay, and looked so sorry that I thought I would behave a while if I could.

Pap, he hadn't been seen for more than a year, and that was comfortable for me; I didn't want to see him no more. He used to always whale me when he was sober and could get his hands on me; though I used to take to the woods most of the time when he was around.

Well, about this time he was found in the river drowned, about twelve mile above the town, so people said. They judged it was him, anyway; said this drowned man was just his size, and was ragged, and had uncommon long hair—which was all like Pap—but they couldn't make nothing out of the face, because it had been in the water so long it warn't much like a face at all. They said he was floating on his back in the water. They took him and buried him on the bank. But I warn't comfortable long, because I happened to think of something. I knowed mighty well that a drowned man don't float on his back, but on his face. So I knowed, then, that this warn't Pap, but a woman dressed up in a man's clothes. So I was uncomfortable again. I judged the

324

old man would turn up again by-and-by, though I wished he wouldn't.

We played robbers now and then about a month, and then I resigned. All the boys did. We hadn't robbed nobody, we hadn't killed any people, but only just pretended. We used to hop out of the woods and go charging down on hog-drovers and women in carts taking garden stuff to market, but we never hived any of them. Tom Sawyer called the hogs 'ingots', and he called the turnips and stuff 'julery', and we would go to the cave and pow-wow over what we had done and how many people we had killed and marked. But I couldn't see no profit in it.

Well, three or four months run along, and it was well into the winter now. I had been to school most all the time and could spell and read and write just a little and could say the multiplication table up to six times.

Judge Thatcher

At first I hated the school, but by and by I got so I could stand it. Whenever I got uncommon tired I played hookey, and the hiding I got next day done me good and cheered me up. So the longer I went to school the easier it got to be. I was getting sort of used to the widow's ways too, and they warn't so raspy on me. Living in a house and sleeping in a bed pulled on me pretty tight, mostly, but before the cold weather I used to slide out and sleep in the woods as I'd been used to do. I liked the old ways best, but I was getting so I liked the new ones too, a little bit.

I went down the front garden and clumb over the stile, where you go through the high board fence. There was an inch of new snow on the ground, and I seen somebody's tracks. They had come up from the quarry and stood around the stile a while, and then went on around the garden fence. It was funny they hadn't come in, after standing around so. I couldn't make it out. It was very curious, somehow. I was going to follow around, but I stooped down to look at the tracks first. I didn't notice anything at first, but next I did. There was a cross in the left boot-heel made with big nails, to keep off the devil——it was Pap's tracks!

I was up in a second and shinning down the hill. I looked over my shoulder every now and then, but I didn't see nobody. I was at Judge Thatcher's as quick as I could get there. He said:

"Why, my boy, you are all out of breath. Did you come for your interest?"

"No, sir," says I. "Is there some for me?"

"Oh, yes, a half-yearly is in, last night. Over a hundred and fifty dollars. Quite a fortune for you. You better let me invest it along with your six thousand, because if you take it you'll spend it."

"No, sir," says I, "I don't want to spend it. I don't want it at all—nor the six thousand, nuther. I want you to take it; I want to give it to you—the six thousand and all."

He looked surprised. He says:

"Why, what can you mean, my boy?"

I says, "Don't you ask me no questions about it, please. You'll take it—won't you?"

He says:

"Well, I'm puzzled. Is something the matter?"

"Please take it," says I, "and don't ask me nothing—then I won't have to tell no lies."

He studied a while, and then he says:

"Oho-o. I think I see. You want to sell all your property to me—not give it. That's the correct idea."

Then he wrote something on a paper and read it over, and says:

"There—you see it says 'for a consideration.' That means I have bought it off you and paid you for it. Here's a dollar for you. Now, you sign it."

So I signed it, and left.

I got home later that night and when I lit my candle and went up to my room, there set Pap, his own self!

Pap Returns

I had shut the door to. Then I turned around, and there he was. I used to be scared of him all the time, he tanned me so much. I reckoned I was scared now, too; but in a minute I see I was mistaken. That is, after the first jolt, as you may say, when my breath sort of hitched—he being so unexpected; but right away after, I see I warn't scared of him worth bothering about.

He was most fifty, and he looked it. His hair was long and tangled and greasy, and hung down, and you could see his eyes shining through like he was behind vines. It was all black, no grey; so was his long, mixed up whiskers. There warn't no colour in

his face where his face showed; it was white; not like another man's white, but a white to make a body sick, a white to make a body's flesh crawl. As for his clothes—just rags, that was all. He had one ankle resting on t'other knee; the boot on that foot was busted, and two of his toes stuck through, and he worked them now and then. His hat was laying on the floor; an old black slouch with the top caved in, like a lid.

I stood a-looking at him; he set there a-looking at me, with his chair tilted back a little. I set the candle down. I noticed the window was up; so he had clumb in by the shed. He kept a-looking me all over. By-and-by he says:

"Starchy clothes—very. You think you're a good deal of a big-bug, don't you?"

"Maybe I am, maybe I ain't," I says.

"Don't you give me none o' your lip," says he. "Ain't you a sweet-scented dandy, though? A bed; and bedclothes; and a look'n-glass; and a piece of carpet on the floor—and your own father got to sleep with the hogs in the tanyard. I never seen such a son. I bet I'll take some o' these frills out o' you before I'm done with you. Why, there ain't no end to your airs—they say you're rich. Hey?—how's that?"

"They lie—that's how."

"Looky here—mind how you talk to me: I'm a-standing about all I can stand, now—so don't gimme no sass. I've been in town two days, and I heard about it down the river, too. That's why I come. You git me that money to-morrow—I want it."

"I hain't got no money."

"It's a lie. Judge Thatcher's got it. You git it. I want it."

"I hain't got no money, I tell you. You ask Judge Thatcher; he'll tell you the same."

"All right. I'll ask him; and I'll make him pungle too, or I'll know the reason why. Say—how much you got in your pocket? I want it."

"I hain't got only a dollar, and I want that too——"

"It don't make no difference what you want it for—you just shell it out."

He took it and bit it to see if it was good, and then he said he was going down town to get some whisky, said he hadn't had a drink all day. When he had got out on the shed, he put his head in again, and cussed me for putting on frills and trying to be better than him; and when I reckoned he was gone, he came back and put his head in again, and told me to mind about that school, because he was going to lay for me and lick me, if I didn't stop that.

Next day he was drunk, and he went to Judge Thatcher's and bullyragged him and tried to make him give up the money, but he couldn't, and then he swore he'd make the law force him.

The judge and the widow went to law to get the court to take me away from him and let one of them be my guardian; but it was a new judge that had just come, and he didn't know the old man; so he said courts mustn't interfere and separate families if they could help it; said he'd druther not take a child away from its father. So Judge Thatcher and the widow had to quit on the business.

That pleased the old man till he couldn't rest. He said he'd cowhide me till I was black and blue if I didn't raise some money for him. I borrowed three dollars from Judge Thatcher, and Pap took it and got drunk and went a-blowing around and cussing and whooping and carrying on; and he kept it up all over town, and next day they had him before court, and jailed him again for a week.

When he got out of jail, he got to hanging around the widow's too much, and so she told him at last, that if he didn't quit using around there she would make trouble for him. So he watched out for me one day in the spring, and catched me, and took me up the river about three mile, in a skiff, and crossed over to the Illinois shore where it was woody and there warn't no houses but an old log hut in a place where the timber was so thick you couldn't find it if you didn't know where it was.

He kept me with him all the time, and I never got a chance to run off. We lived in that old cabin, and he always locked the door and put the key under his head, nights. He had a gun which he had stole, I reckon, and we fished and hunted, and that was what we lived on. Every little while he locked me in and went down to the store, three miles to the ferry, and traded fish and game for whisky and fetched it home and got drunk and had a good time, and licked me. The widow she found out where I was and she sent a man over to try to get hold of me, but Pap drove him off with the gun, and it warn't long after that till I was used to being where I was, and liked it, all but the cowhide part.

But by-and-by Pap got too handy with his hick'ry, and I couldn't stand it. I was all over welts. He got to going away so much, too, and locking me in for two and three days at a time.

One morning when I was watching for fish on the lines for breakfast, I noticed the river was running high as the driftwood had started to float down river. Well, all at once here comes a canoe, just a beauty too, riding high like a duck. I shot head first off the bank, like a frog and struck out. It was a drift canoe, alright, and I clumb in and paddled her ashore to hide her in the willows before Pap came along. When he did come along he abused me for being slow but I told him I fell in the river. But that canoe had given me an idea that would rid me of Pap and the widow for ever.

I Make My Escape

Later that day Pap decided he'd shove right over to town to sell some driftwood he'd got hold of. So he locked me in and took the skiff and started off towing the raft about three. I waited till I reckoned he had got a good start, then I out with a rusty ol' saw I had found on a previous occasion and went to work on a crack in a log of the wall. Before he was t'other side of the river I was out of the cabin; him and his raft was just a speck on the water away off yonder.

I patched up the hole from where I had escaped and then hacked the door down with an axe. Then I took everything I could carry including all the coffee, sugar, bacon, ammunition, buckets, tin cups, an old blanket, wadding, my old saw, fish lines and matches and the gun over to my canoe. It took me

several trips but I had made no track because it was all grass clear to the canoe. All safe so far.

Then I took the gun and went up a piece into the woods and hunted about for a wild pig which I shot and took him back to the cabin. I cut his throat and laid him on the ground to bleed, whilst I took a sack, filled it with rocks and dragged it from the pig down to the river and dumped it in. This left a good clear track. I pulled out some of my hair and stuck it on the back side of the axe with blood from the pig and laid it in the corner. Then I dumped the pig in the river and finally laid a trail of meal from the cabin to a lake east of it and dropped Pap's whetstone there too. Then I took the rest of the meal to my canoe.

I decided to make for Jackson's Island, where no one ever went and just managed to start downstream in the dim light, when I heard Pap coming back in the skiff. I made two mile and a half and then got out amongst the drift wood and I laid back down in the bottom of the canoe and let her float. I laid there looking at the stars wondering if my plan would work. I figured they'd follow the track of that sack full of rocks to the shore and then drag the river for me. Then they'd follow that meal track to the lake and go browsing down the creek that leads out of it to find the robbers that killed me and took the things.

A few miles downstream I soon came to Jackson's Island. I shot past the head at a ripping rate, the current was so swift, and then I got into the dead water and landed on the side towards the Illinois shore. I hid the canoe from view and went up and sat down on a log and looked out across the big river away to the town where lights were twinkling. There was a little grey in the sky now, so I stepped into the woods and laid down for a nap before breakfast.

Next morning I was powerful lazy and comfortable—didn't want to get up and cook breakfast, when I thinks I hears a deep sound of 'Boom!' away up the river. I rouses up and rests on my elbow and listens; pretty soon I hears it again——and there was the ferry-boat full of people floating along down. I knowed what was the matter, now. 'Boom!' I see the white smoke squirt out of the ferry-boat's side. You see, they was firing cannon over the water, trying to make my carcass come to the top.

By-and-by the ferry-boat, she come along and drifted in so close that I could see most everybody that was on the boat. Pap, and Judge Thatcher, and

Bessie Thatcher, and Jo Harper, Tom Sawyer and his aunt Polly, and Sid and Mary and plenty more. Everyone was talking about the murder, but they couldn't see me laying down behind a log.

The boat floated on and went out of sight around the shoulder of the island. I could hear the booming now and then, further off, but I knowed I was all right now. Nobody else would come a-hunting after me. I got my traps out of the canoe and made me a nice camp in the thick woods. I made a kind of tent out of my blanket to put my things under so the rain couldn't get at them. I explored around a piece finding strawberries and summer grapes, then later I started my camp fire and set out a line to catch some fish for a meal.

After I had a nap it was dark and I set by my camp-fire smoking and feeling pretty satisfied; but by-and-by it got sort of lonesome, and so I went and set on the bank and listened to the currents washing along, and counted the stars and drift-logs 'til long into the night.

Jim

After four days passed, I decided to go exploring further afield. I was clipping along, and all of a sudden I bounded right on to the ashes of a camp-fire that was still smoking. I cocked my gun and slowly looked around to see a man laying on the ground. It a'most give me the fantoos. He had a blanket around his head, and his head was nearly in the fire. I set there behind a clump of bushes, in about six foot of him, and kept my eyes on him steady. Pretty soon he gapped, and stretched himself, and hove off the blanket, and it was Miss Watson's Jim! I bet I was glad to see him. I says:

"Hello, Jim!" and skipped out.

He bounced up and stared at me wild. Then he drops down on his knees, and puts his hands together and says:

"Doan' hurt me—don't! I hain't ever done no harm to a ghos'. I awluz liked dead people, en done all I could for 'em. You go en git in de river agin, whah you b'longs, en doan' do 'nuffin to Ole Jim, 'at 'uz awluz yo' fren'."

Well, I warn't long making him understand I warn't dead. I was ever so glad to see Jim. I warn't lonesome, now. I told him my plan, I told him the whole thing, and he said it was smart. He said Tom Sawyer couldn't get up no better plan than what I had. Then I says:

"How do you come to be here, Jim?"

He looked pretty uneasy, and didn't say nothing for a minute. Then he says:

"I come heah de night arter you's killed. I heard how yo' Pap come over to de town en say you's killed."

"What, all that time?"

"Yes, indeedy, I swam most of the way and laid on de drift wood."

"Well, you must be most starved, ain't you?"

"I reckon I could eat a hoss."

So we went over to where the canoe was, and while he built a fire in a grassy open place amongst the trees, I fetched meal and bacon and coffee, and coffee pot and frying pan, and sugar and tin cups and the nigger was set back considerable, because he reckoned it was all done with witchcraft. I catched a good big cat-fish too, and Jim cleaned him with his knife, and fried him. Then when we had got pretty well stuffed, we laid off and lazied, and by-and-by Jim says:

"Well, you see, it 'uz dis way. Ole Missus—dat's Miss Watson—she pecks on me all de time, en treats me pooty rough, but she awluz said she wouldn't sell me down to Orleans. But I noticed dey wuz a nigger trader roun' de place lately, en I begin to git oneasy. Well, one night I creeps to de do' pooty late, en de do' arn't quite shet, en I hear ole missus tell the widder she gwyne to sell me down to Orleans, but she didn' want to, but she could git eight hund'd dollars for me, en it 'uz sich a big stack o' money she couldn' resis'. De widder she try to git her to say she wouldn' do it, but I never waited to hear de res'. I lit out mighty quick, I tell you and I been here ever since. I 'uz powerful sorry you's killed, Huck, but I ain't no mo', now."

The next day, when Jim and I were exploring about the middle of the island, we found a good big cavern in the rock, which was as big as two or three rooms bunched together.

Jim said if we had the canoe hid in a good place and had all the traps in the cavern, we could rush there if anybody was come to the island. So we moved camp and made our new home very comfortable indeed. We fished and hunted and explored in our leisure, taking care not to be seen by any passing boats.

A few days passed and the river rose and flooded

its banks so much so the low lying parts of the island were swamped with water.

Just before daylight, we made our way up to the head of the island in the canoe to see any damage there might be. And there we saw a frame house slowly washing down on the west side. She was two-storey and tilted over. We paddled out and got aboard and looked in at an upstairs window. We could make out a bed and a table and two old chairs, and clothes hanging against the wall. There was something laying on the floor in the far corner that looked like a man. So Jim says:

"Hello, you!"

But it didn't budge. So I hollered again, and then Jim says:

"De man ain't asleep—he's dead. You hold still —I'll go en see."

He went and bent down and looked, and says:

"It's a dead man. Yes, indeedy; naked, too. He's ben shot in de back. I reck'n he's ben dead two er three days. Come in, Huck, but doan' look at his face —it's too gashly."

I didn't look at him at all. Jim throwed some old rags over him, but he needn't have done it; I didn't want to see him.

We made a good haul of all the things we could find in case they would be of use to us. These things consisted of some men's and women's clothing, an old tin lantern, a candlestick holder and a lot of tallow candles, buttons, pins, needles, a fishing line, some knives, a straw hat and a bonnet and a bottle used for a baby, an old fiddle bow, and two old empty chests to put the stuff in, but the most important find of all was a considerable amount of money that was sewn in the lining of a coat.

We loaded up the canoe and paddled ourselves over to the Illinois shore side and drifted down most a half a mile. I couldn't keep from wondering over the dead man and wanted to talk about it, but Jim warn't saying anything, so we made our way safely home in silence.

Jim Goes Missing

Time passed quite comfortably enough, until we got to thinking that sooner or later someone's gonna discover us and then it would be too late to run. So we decided to move on down river until we came to a southern state and there we would be safe.

So Jim and me got working on a new raft and Jim fixed up a kind of wigwam on it to keep things dry. When all was ready we set off, me leading the way with the canoe and Jim trailing behind.

Well, our journey certainly wasn't uneventful— firstly we nearly lost each other in a terrible fog. Then, another time we were completely overrun by

and here we stopped for some provisions and ended up with two extra passengers. These two men, nicknamed 'The Duke' and 'The King', turned out to be a couple of real swindlers and we didn't like them at all. We tried to ditch them on many occasions but it warn't no use—they latched on to us worse than leeches.

However, my chance came. I had been on shore with 'The Duke' and 'The King' and had managed to give them the slip and I ran back to the raft calling to Jim, who had stayed behind to be ready to push out quick. But when I got down to the water's edge I realised that Jim—he was gone!

Jim was gone! I set up a shout—and then another —and then another one; and run this way and that in the woods, whooping and screeching; but it warn't no use—old Jim was gone. Then I set down and cried. Pretty soon I went out on the road, trying to think what I better do, and I run across a boy walking, and asked him if he'd seen a strange nigger, dressed so and so, and he says he had.

"Whereabouts?" says I.

"Down to Silas Phelps' place, two mile below here. He's a runaway nigger, and they've got him. Was you looking for him?"

"You bet I ain't," I lied in case of trouble.

"There's two hundred dollars reward on him. It's like picking up money out'n the road."

"Yes, it is—who nailed him?"

"It was an old fellow—a stranger—and he sold out his chance in him for forty dollars, becuz he's got to go up the river and can't wait."

So I realised now it was 'The Duke' who had split on poor Jim.

I went to the raft, and set down in the wigwam to think. But I couldn't come to nothing. I thought till I wore my head sore, but I couldn't see no way out of the trouble. After all this long journey and after all we'd done for them scoundrels, here was it all come to nothing, everything all busted up and ruined, because they could have the heart to serve Jim such a trick as that, and make him a slave again all his life, and amongst strangers, too, for forty dirty dollars.

Later I took the bearings of a woody island that was down the river a piece, and as soon as it was fairly dark I crept out with my raft and went for it, and hid it there, and then turned in. I slept the night through, and got up before it was light, and had my breakfast, and put on my store clothes, and tied up

a steamboat that didn't appear to see us. We were both washed ashore to find that our raft and canoe were bobbing about on the water completely undamaged, and after getting our breath back and drying things out, we were able to carry on down river.

A mighty long way down south we came to a town

some others and one thing or another in a bundle, and took the canoe and cleared for shore. I landed below where I judged was Phelps' place, and hid my bundle in the woods, and then filled up the canoe with water, and loaded rocks into her and sunk her where I could find her again when I wanted her, about a quarter of a mile below a little steam sawmill that was on the bank.

Then I struck up the road, and when I passed the mill I see a sign on it, 'Phelps' Sawmill', and when I come to the farm houses, two or three hundred yards further along, I kept my eyes peeled but didn't see nobody around, though it was good daylight now. But I didn't mind, because I didn't want to see nobody just yet—I only wanted to get the lay of the land. According to my plan, I was going to turn up there from the village, not from below. So I just took a look, and shoved along, straight for town.

Phelps' Place

Next day I set out for Phelps' place. When I got there it was all still and Sunday-like, and hot and sunshiny —the hands was gone to the fields; and there was them kind of faint dronings of bugs and flies in the air that makes it seem so lonesome and like everybody's dead and gone; and if a breeze fans along and quivers the leaves, it makes you feel mournful, because you feel like it's spirits whispering.

Phelps' was one of those little one-horse cotton plantations; and they all look alike. A rail fence round a two acre yard; a stile, made out of logs sawed off and up-ended, in steps, like barrels of a different length, to climb over the fence with, and for the women to stand on when they are going to jump on to a horse; some sickly grass-patches in the big yard, but mostly it was bare and smooth, like an old hat with the nap rubbed off; big double log house for the white folks—hewed logs, with the chinks stopped up with mud or mortar, and these mud-stripes been whitewashed some time or another; round-log kitchen, with a big, broad, open but roofed passage joining it to the house; log smoke-house back of the kitchen; three little log nigger-cabins in a row t'other side the smoke-house; one little hut all by itself away down against the back fence; and some out-buildings down a piece the other

side; ash-hopper, and big kettle to bile soap in, by the little hut; bench by the kitchen door, with bucket of water and a gourd; hound asleep there, in the sun; more hounds asleep, round about; about three shade-trees away off in a corner; some currant bushes and gooseberry bushes in one place by the fence; outside of the fence a garden and a water-melon patch; then the cotton fields begins; and after the fields, the woods.

I went around and clumb over the back stile by the ash-hopper, and started for the kitchen. When I got a little ways, I heard the dim hum of a spinning-wheel wailing along up and sinking along down again.

I went along, not fixing up any particular plan, but just trusting to Providence to put the right words in my mouth when the time come; for I'd noticed that Providence always did put the right words in my mouth, if I left it alone.

When I got half-way, first one hound and then another got up and went for me, and of course I stopped and faced them, and kept still. And such another pow-wow as they made. In a quarter of a minute I was a kind of a hub of a wheel, as you may say—spokes made out of dogs—circle of fifteen of them packed together around me, with their necks and noses stretched up towards me, a-barking and howling; and more a-coming; you could see them sailing over fences and around corners from every-wheres.

A nigger woman come tearing out of the kitchen with a rolling-pin in her hand, singing out, "Begone! you Tige! you Spot! begone, sah!" and she fetched first one and then another of them a clip and sent him howling, and then the rest followed; and the next second, half of them come back, wagging their tails around me and making friends with me. There ain't no harm in a hound, nohow.

And behind the woman comes a little nigger girl and two little nigger boys, without anything on but tow-linen shirts, and they hung on to their mother's gown, and peeped out from behind her at me, bashful, the way they always do. And here comes the white woman running from the house, about forty-five or fifty year old, bare-headed, and her spinning-stick in her hand; and behind her comes her little white children, acting the same way the little niggers was doing. She was smiling all over so she could hardly stand—and says:

"It's you, at last!—ain't it?"

I out with a 'Yes'm,' before I thought.

She grabbed me and hugged me tight; and then gripped me by both hands and shook and shook; and the tears come in her eyes, and run down over; and she couldn't seem to hug and shake enough, and kept saying, "You don't look as much like your mother as I reckoned you would, but law sakes, I don't care for that, I'm glad to see you! Dear, dear, it does seem like I could eat you up! Children, it's your Cousin Tom!—tell him howdy."

But they ducked their heads, and put their fingers in their mouths, and hid behind her. So she run on:

"Lize, hurry up and get him a hot breakfast, right away—or did you get your breakfast on the boat?"

I said I had got it on the boat. So then she started for the house, leading me by the hand, and the children tagging after. When we got there, she set me down in a split-bottomed chair, and set herself down on a little low stool in front of me, holding both of my hands, and says:

"Now I can have a good look at you; and laws-a-me, I've been hungry for it a many and a many a time, all these long years, and it's come at last! We been expecting you a couple of days and more. What's kep' you?—boat get aground?"

"Yes'm—she——"

"Don't say yes'm—say Aunt Sally. Where'd she get aground?"

I didn't rightly know what to say, because I didn't know whether the boat would be coming up the river or down. But I go a good deal on instinct; and my instinct said she would be coming up—from down towards Orleans. That didn't help me much, though; for I didn't know the names of bars down that way. I see I'd got to invent a bar, or forget the name of the one we got aground on—or——Now I struck an idea, and fetched it out:

"It warn't the grounding—that didn't keep us back but a little. We blowed out a cylinder-head."

"Good gracious! Anybody hurt?"

"No'm. Killed a nigger."

"Well, it's lucky; because sometimes people do get hurt. Your uncle's been up to the town every day to fetch you. And he's gone again, not more'n an hour ago; he'll be back any minute, now. You must a met him on the road, didn't you?—oldish man, with a—"

"No, I didn't see nobody, Aunt Sally. The boat landed just at daylight, and I left my baggage on the wharf-boat and went looking around the town and out a piece in the country, to put in the time and not get here too soon; and so I come down the back way."

"Who'd you give the baggage to?"

"Nobody."

"Why, child, it'll be stole!"

"Not where I hid it I reckon it won't," I says.

"How'd you get your breakfast so early on the boat?"

It was kinder thin ice, but I says:

"The captain see me standing around, and told me I better have something to eat before I went ashore; so he took me in the texas to the officer's lunch, and give me all I wanted."

I was getting so uneasy I couldn't listen good. I had my mind on the children all the time; I wanted to get them out to one side, and pump them a little, and find out who I was. But I couldn't get no show, Mrs Phelps kept it up and run on so. Then she exclaimed: "Here he comes!" as Mr Phelps walked into the room. The old gentleman stared, and says:

"Why, who's that?"

"Who do you reckon 't is?"

"I hain't no idea. Who is it?"

"It's Tom Sawyer!"

By jings, I most slumped through the floor. But there warn't no time to swap knives; the old man grabbed me by the hand and shook, and kept on shaking; and all the time, how the woman did dance around and laugh and cry; and then how they both did fire off questions about Sid, and Mary, and the rest of the tribe.

But if they was joyful, it warn't nothing to what I was; for it was like being born again, I was so glad to find out who I was. Well, they froze to me for two hours; and at last when my chin was so tired it couldn't hardly go any more, I had told them more about my family—I mean the Sawyer family—than ever happened to any six Sawyer families. And I explained all about how we blowed out a cylinder-head at the mouth of White River and it took us three days to fix it. Which was all right, and worked first-rate; because they didn't know but what it would take three days to fix it. If I'd a called it a bolt-head, it would a done just as well.

Tom Sawyer Arrives

Now I was feeling pretty comfortable all down one side, and pretty uncomfortable all up the other.

Being Tom Sawyer was easy and comfortable; and it
stayed easy and comfortable till by-and-by I hear a
steamboat coughing along down the river—then I
says to myself, s'pose Tom Sawyer come down on
that boat?—and s'pose he steps in here, any minute,
and sings out my name before I can throw him a
wink to keep quiet? Well, I couldn't have it that way
—it wouldn't do at all. I must go up the road and
waylay him. So I told the folks I reckoned I would go
up to the town and fetch down my baggage. The old
gentleman was for going along with me, but I said
no, I could drive the horse myself, and I druther he
wouldn't take no trouble about me.

So I started for town, in the wagon, and when I
was halfway I see a wagon coming, and sure enough
it was Tom Sawyer, and I stopped and waited till he
come along. I says, "Hold on!" and it stopped
alongside, and his mouth opened like a trunk, and
staid so; and he swallowed two or three times like a
person that's got a dry throat, and then says:

"I hain't ever done you no harm. You know that. So, then, what you want to come back and ha'nt me for?"

I says:

"I hain't come back—I hain't been gone."

When he heard my voice, it righted him up some, but he warn't quite satisfied yet. He says:

"Don't you play nothing on me, because I wouldn't on you. Honest injun, now, you ain't a ghost?"

"Honest injun, I ain't," I says.

"Well—I—I—well, that ought to settle it, of course; but I can't somehow seem to understand it, no way. Looky here, warn't you ever murdered at all?"

"No, I warn't ever murdered at all—I played it on

them. You come and feel me if you don't believe me."

So he done it, and it satisfied him; and he was that glad to see me again, he didn't know what to do. And he wanted to know all about it right off; because it was a grand adventure, and mysterious, and so it hit him where he lived. But I said, leave it alone till by-and-by; and told his driver to wait, and we drove off a little piece, and I told him the kind of a fix I was in, and what did he reckon we better do? He said, let him alone a minute, and don't disturb him. So he thought and thought, and pretty soon he says:

"It's all right, I've got it. Take my trunk in your wagon, and let on it's your'n; and you turn back and fool along slow, so as to get to the house about the time you ought to; and I'll go towards town a piece, and take a fresh start, and get there a quarter or a half an hour after you; and you needn't let on to know me, at first."

I says:

"All right; but wait a minute. There's one more thing—a thing nobody don't know but me. And that is, there's a nigger here that I'm a–trying to steal out of slavery—and his name is Jim—old Miss Watson's Jim."

He says:

"What! Why, Jim is——"

He stopped, and went to studying. I says:

"I know what you'll say. You'll say it's dirty, low-down business; but what if it is?—I'm low-down; and I'm agoing to steal him, and I want you to keep mum and not let on. Will you?"

His eye lit up, and he says:

"I'll help you steal him!"

Well, I let go all holts then, like I was shot. It was the most astonishing speech I ever heard—and I'm bound to say Tom Sawyer fell, considerable, in my estimation. Only I couldn't believe it. Tom Sawyer a nigger stealer!

"Oh, shucks," I says, "you're joking."

"I ain't joking, either."

"Well, then," says I, "joking or not joking, if you hear anything said about a runaway nigger, don't forget to remember that you don't know nothing about him, and I don't know nothing about him."

Then we took the trunk and put it in my wagon, and he drove off his way, and I drove mine home. In about half an hour Tom's wagon drove up to the front stile, and Aunt Sally she see it through the window because it was only about fifty yards, and says:

"Why, there's somebody come! I wonder who 'tis? Why, I do believe it's a stranger. Jimmy (that's one of the children) run and tell Lize to put on another plate for dinner."

Everybody made a rush for the front door, because, of course, a stranger don't come every year. Tom was over the stile and starting for the house; the wagon was spinning up the road for the village, and we was all bunched up in the front door. Tom had his store clothes on, and an audience—and that was always nuts for Tom Sawyer. When he got afront of us, he lifts his hat ever so gracious and dainty, like it was the lid of a box that had butterflies asleep in it, and he didn't want to disturb them, and says:

"I'm Sid Sawyer——"

"My land!" says Aunt Sally, breaking in and jumping for him. She hugged him and kissed him, over and over again, and then turned him over to the old man, and he took what was left. And after they got a little quiet again, she says:

"Why, dear me, I never see such a surprise. We warn't looking for you, at all, but only Tom. Sis never wrote to me about anybody coming but him."

"It's because it warn't intended for any of us to come but Tom," he says; "but I begged and begged, and at the last minute she let me come too; so, coming down the river, me and Tom thought it would be a first-rate surprise for him to come here to the house first, and for me to by-and-by tag along and drop in after."

We had dinner out in that broad, open passage betwixt the house and the kitchen; and there was things enough on that table for seven families—and all hot too; Uncle Silas he asked a pretty long blessing over it, but it was worth it; and it didn't cool it a bit, neither, the way I've seen them kind of interruptions do, lots of times.

There was a considerable good deal of talk, all the afternoon, and me and Tom was on the look-out all the time, but it warn't no use, they didn't happen to say nothing about any runaway nigger, and we was afraid to try to work up to it.

Tom and me was to sleep in the same room and bed: so, being tired, we bid good night and went up to bed, right after supper.

Tom Makes Plans

After talking, we got to thinking. By-and-by Tom says:

"Looky here, Huck, what fools we are, to not think of it before! I bet I know where Jim is."

"No! Where?"

"In that hut down by the ash-hopper. Why, looky here. When we was at dinner, didn't you see a nigger man go in there with some vittles?"

"Yes."

"What did you think the vittles was for?"

"For a dog."

"So'd I. Well, it wasn't for a dog."

"Why?"

"Because part of it was watermelon."

"So it was—I noticed it. Well, it does beat all, that I never thought about a dog not eating watermelon. It shows how a body can see and don't see at the same time."

"Well, the nigger unlocked the padlock when he went in, and he locked it again when he come out. He fetched uncle a key, about the time we got up from table—same key, I bet. Watermelon shows man, lock shows prisoner; and it ain't likely there's two prisoners on such a little plantation, and where the people's all so kind and good. Jim's the prisoner. All right—I'm glad we found it out detective fashion; I wouldn't give shucks for any other way. Now you work your mind and study out a plan to steal Jim and I will study out one too; and we'll take the one we like the best."

What a head for just a boy to have! If I had Tom Sawyer's head, I wouldn't trade it off to be a duke, nor mate of a steamboat, nor clown in a circus, nor nothing I can think of. I went to thinking out a plan.

Next day we went down to the hut by the ash-hopper, for to examine it. We went through the yard, so as to see what the hounds would do. They knowed us, and didn't make no more noise than country dogs is always doing when anything comes by. When we got to the cabin, we took a look at the front and the two sides.

Betwixt the hut and the fence, on the back side, was a lean-to, that joined the hut at the eaves, and was made out of plank. It was as long as the hut, but narrow—only about six foot wide. The door to it was at the south end, and was padlocked. Tom he went to the soap-kettle, and searched around and fetched back the iron thing they lift the lid with; so he took it and prized out one of the staples. The chain fell down, and we opened the door and went in, and shut it, and struck a match, and see the shed was only built against the cabin and hadn't no connexion with it; and there warn't no floor to the shed, nor nothing in it but some old rusty played-out hoes, and spades, and picks, and a crippled plough. The match went out and so did we, and shoved in the staple again, and the door was locked as good as ever. Tom was joyful. He says:

"Now we're all right. We'll dig him out, at night, It'll take about a week!"

We made friends with the nigger that fed Jim—if it was Jim that was being fed. The niggers was just getting through breakfast and starting for the fields; and Jim's nigger was piling up a tin pan with bread and meat and things; and whilst the others was leaving, the key come from the house.

Tom says:

"What's the vittles for? Going to feed the dogs?"

The nigger kind of smiled around gradually over his face, like when you heave a brickbat in a mud-puddle, and he says:

"Yes, Mars Sid, a dog. Cur'us dog, too. Does you want to go en look at 'im?"

"Yes."

I hunched Tom, and whispers:

"You going, right here in the daybreak? That warn't the plan."

"No, it warn't—but it's the plan now."

So, drat him, we went along, but I didn't like it much. When we got in, we couldn't hardly see anything, it was so dark; but Jim was there, sure enough, and could see us; and he sings out:

"Why Huck! En good lan'! ain' dat Misto Tom?"

I just knowed how it would be; I just expected it. I didn't know nothing to do; and if I had, I couldn't a done it, because that nigger busted in and says:

"Why, de gracious sakes! do he know you genlmen?"

We could see pretty well, now. Tom he looked at the nigger, steady and kind of wondering, and says:

"Does who know us?"

"Why, dish-yer runaway nigger."

"I don't reckon he does; but what put that into your head?"

"What put it dar? Didn' he jis' dis minute sing out like he knowed you?"

Tom says, in a puzzled-up kind of way:

"Well, that's mighty curious. Who sung out? When did he sing out? What did he sing out?" And turns to me, perfectly calm, and says, "Did you hear anybody sing out?"

Of course there warn't nothing to be said but the one thing; so I says:

"No, I ain't heard nobody say nothing."

Then he turns to Jim, and looks him over like he never see him before; and says:

"Did you sing out?"

"No, sah," says Jim; "I hain't said nothing, sah."

"Not a word?"

"No, sah, I hain't said a word."

"Did you ever see us before?"

"No, sah; not as I knows on."

So Tom turns to the nigger, which was looking wild and distressed, and says, kind of severe:

"What do you reckon's the matter with you, anyway? What made you think somebody sung out?"

"Oh, it's de dad-blame witches, sah, dey's awluz pesterin' and makin' me see and hear all sort o' things, en I wisht I was dead, I do. Dey's awluz at it, sah, en dey do mos' kill me, dey sk'yers me so. Please to don't tell nobody 'bout it, sah, er ole Mars Silas he'll scole me; 'kase he says dey ain't no witches. I jis' wish to goodness he was heah now—den what would he say! I jis' bet he couldn' fine no way to git aroun' it dis time. But it's awluz jis' so; people dat's sot, stays sot; dey won't look into nothin' en fine it out f'r deyselves, en when you fine it out en tell um 'bout it, dey doan' b'lieve you."

Tom give him a dime, and said we wouldn't tell nobody; and then looks at Jim and says:

"I wonder if Uncle Silas is going to hang this nigger. If I was to catch a nigger that was ungrateful enough to run away, I wouldn't give him up, I'd hang him." And whilst the nigger stepped to the door to look at the dime and bite it to see if it was good, he whispers to Jim, and says:

"Don't ever let on to know us. And if you hear any digging going on nights, it's us: we're going to set you free."

Jim only had time to grab us by the hand and squeeze it, then the nigger come back, and we said we'd come again some time if the nigger wanted us to; and he said he would, more particular if it was dark, because the witches went for him mostly in the dark, and it was good to have folks around then.

We left and struck down into the woods. Tom said we got to have some light to see how to dig by, and a lantern makes too much, and might get us into trouble; what we must have was a lot of them rotten chunks that's called fox-fire and just makes a soft kind of a glow when you lay them in a dark place. We fetched an armful and hid it in the weeds, and set down to rest.

The Right Tools!

In the morning we waited till everybody was settled down to business, and nobody in sight around the yard; then Tom went to check over the hut whilst I kept watch. By-and-by he come out and we went and set down on the wood pile to talk. He says:

"Everything's all right, now, except tools; and that's easy fixed."

"Tools?" I says.

"Yes."

"Tools for what?"

"Why, to dig with. We ain't agoing to gnaw him out, are we?"

"Ain't them old crippled picks and things in there good enough to dig a nigger out with?" I says.

He turns to me looking pitying enough to make a body cry, and says:

"Huck Finn, did you ever hear of a prisoner having picks and shovels, and all the modern conveniences in his wardrobe to dig himself out with? Now I want to ask you—if you got any reasonableness in you at all—what kind of a show would that give him to be a hero? Why, they might as well lend him the key, and done with it. Picks and shovels—why, they wouldn't furnish 'em to a king."

"Well, then," I says, "if we don't want the picks and shovels, what do we want?"

"A couple of case-knives."

"To dig the foundations out from under that cabin with?"

"Yes."

"Confound it, it's foolish, Tom."

"It don't make no difference how foolish it is, it's the right way—and it's the regular way. And there ain't no other way, that ever I heard of, and I've read all the books that gives any information about these things. They always dig out with a case-knife —and not through dirt, mind you; generly it's through solid rock. And it takes them weeks and weeks and weeks, and for ever and ever."

"How long will it take, Tom?"

"Well, we can't resk being as long as we ought to, because it mayn't take very long for Uncle Silas to hear from down there by New Orleans. He'll hear Jim ain't from there. Then his next move will be to advertise Jim, or something like that. So we can't resk being as long digging him out as we ought to. Things being so uncertain, what I recommend is this: that we really dig right in, as quick as we can.

Then we can snatch him out and rush him away the first time there's an alarm. Yes, I reckon that'll be the best way."

"Now, there's sense in that," I says. "It wouldn't strain me none, after I got my hand in. So I'll mosey along now, and smouch a couple of case-knives."

"Smouch three," he says; "we want one to make a saw out of."

"Tom, if it ain't unregular and irreligious to sejest it," I says, "there's an old rusty saw-blade around yonder sticking under the weatherboarding behind the smoke-house."

He looked kind of weary and discouraged-like, and says:

"It ain't no use to try to learn you nothing, Huck. Run along and smouch the knives—three of them." So I done it.

Tom's Principles

As soon as we reckoned everybody was asleep, that night, we went down the lightning-rod, and shut ourselves up in the lean-to and got out our pile of fox-fire, and went to work. We cleared everything out of the way, about four or five foot along the middle of the bottom log. Tom said he was right behind Jim's bed now, and we'd dig in under it, and when we got through there couldn't nobody in the cabin ever know there was any hole there, because Jim's counterpane hung down most to the ground, and you'd have to raise it up and look under to see the hole. So we dug and dug, with the case-knives, till most midnight; and then we was dog-tired, and our hands was blistered, and yet you couldn't see we'd done anything, hardly. At last I says:

"This'll take a lifetime, like this."

He never said nothing. But he sighed, and pretty soon he stopped digging, and then for a good little while I knowed he was thinking. Then he says:

"It ain't no use, Huck, it ain't agoing to work. If we was prisoners it would, because then we'd have as many years as we wanted, and no hurry; and we wouldn't get but a few minutes to dig, every day, while they was changing watches, and so our hands wouldn't get blistered, and we could keep it up right along, year in year out, and do it right, and the way it ought to be done. But we can't fool along, we got to rush; we ain't got no time to spare. If we was to put in another night this way, we'd have to knock off

for a week to let our hands get well—couldn't touch a case-knife with them sooner."

"Well, then, what we going to do, Tom?"

"I'll tell you. It ain't right, and it ain't moral, and I wouldn't like it to get out—but there ain't only just the one way; we got to dig him out with the picks, and let on it's case-knives."

"Now you're talking!" I says; "your head gets leveller and leveller all the time, Tom Sawyer," I says. "Picks is the thing, moral or no moral; and as for me, I don't care shucks for the morality of it, nohow. When I start in to steal a nigger, or a watermelon, or a Sunday-school book, I ain't no ways particular how it's done so it's done. What I want is my nigger; or what I want is my watermelon; or what I want is my Sunday-school book; and if a pick's the handiest thing, that's the thing I'm agoing to dig that nigger out with; and I don't give a dead rat what the authorities thinks about it nuther."

"Well," he says, "there's excuse for picks and letting-on in a case like this; if it warn't so, I wouldn't approve of it, nor I wouldn't stand by and see the rules broke—because right is right, and wrong is wrong, and a body ain't got no business doing wrong when he ain't ignorant and knows better. It might answer for you to dig Jim out with a pick, without any letting-on, because you don't know no better; but it wouldn't for me, because I do know better. Gimme a case-knife."

He had his own by him, but I handed him mine. He flung it down, and says:

"Gimme a case-knife."

I didn't know what to do—but then I thought. I scratched around amongst the old tools, and got a pick-axe and give it to him, and he took it and went to work, and never said a word.

He was always just that particular. Full of principle.

So then I got a shovel, and then we picked and shovelled, turn about, and made the fur fly. We stuck to it about a half an hour, which was as long as we could stand up; but we had a good deal of a hole to show for it. When I got upstairs, I looked out at the window and see Tom doing his level best with

the lightning-rod, but he couldn't come it, his hands was so sore. At last he says:

"It ain't no use, it can't be done. What you reckon I better do? Can't you think up no way?"

"Yes," I says. "Come up the stairs, and let on it's a lightning-rod."

The next night we went down the lightning-rod a little after ten, and took one of the candles along, and listened under the window hole, and heard Jim snoring; we didn't wake him. Then we whirled in with the pick and shovel, and in about two hours and a half the job was done. We crept in under Jim's bed and into the cabin, and pawed around and found the candle and lit it, and stood over Jim awhile, and found him looking hearty and healthy, and then we woke him up gentle and gradual. He was so glad to see us he most cried; and called us honey, and all the pet-names he could think of; and was for having us hunt up a cold chisel to cut the chain off his leg with, right away, and clearing out without losing any time. But Tom showed him how unregular it would be, and set down and told him all about our plans, and how we could alter them in a minute any time there was an alarm; and not to be the least afraid, because we would see he got away, sure. So Jim he said it was all right, and we set there and talked over old times awhile, and then Tom asked a lot of questions, and when Jim told him Uncle Silas come in every day or two to pray with him, and Aunt Sally come in to see if he was comfortable and had plenty

to eat, and both of them was kind as they could be, Tom was satisfied.

Jim had plenty corn-cob pipes and tobacco; so we had a right-down good sociable time; then we crawled out through the hole, and so home to bed, with hands that looked like they'd been chawed. Tom was in high spirits. He said it was the best fun he ever had in his life, and the most intellectural.

Anonymous Letters

Three weeks went by without us having a chance to get Jim away in complete safety. We kept telling him to be patient and to wait until the time was really right and until we'd got things ready. We used to smuggle ourselves in after dark to keep him company and take him special treats to keep him cheerful.

Tom seemed in no hurry for our plans to progress. He seemed to enjoy looking after Jim as a prisoner. Tom could have gone on like this for years—the secrecy and excitement of it was a constant fascination to him. He said that when the time came for us to steal Jim away, it would have to be a spectacular feat with plenty of excitement and he wouldn't have it any other way.

Then we heard that the old man had wrote a couple of times to the plantation below Orleans to come and get their runaway nigger, but hadn't got no answer, because there warn't no such plantation; so he allowed he would advertise Jim in the St Louis and New Orleans papers, and when he mentioned the St Louis ones it give me the cold shivers, and I see we hadn't no time to lose. So Tom said, now for the nonnamous letters.

"What's them?" I says.

"Warnings to the people that something is up. Sometimes it's done one way, sometimes another. But there's always somebody spying around, that gives notice to the governor of the castle. When Louis XVI was going to light out of the Tooleries, a servant girl done it. It's a very good way, and so is the nonnamous letters. We'll use them both. And it's usual for the prisoner's mother to change clothes with him, and she stays in, and he slides out in her clothes. We'll do that too."

"But looky here, Tom, what do we want to warn anybody for, that something's up? Let them find out for themselves—it's their look-out."

"Yes, I know; but you can't depend on them. It's the way they've acted from the very start—left us to do everything. They're so confiding and mullet-headed they don't take notice of nothing at all. So if we don't give them notice, there won't be nobody nor nothing to interfere with us, and so after all our hard work and trouble this escape'll go off perfectly flat; won't amount to nothing—won't be nothing to it."

"Well, as for me, Tom, that's the way I'd like."

"Shucks," he says, and looked disgusted. So I says:

"But I ain't going to make no complaint. Anyway what suits you suits me. What you going to do about the servant-girl?"

"You'll be her. You slide in, in the middle of the night, and hook that yaller girl's frock."

"Why, Tom, that'll make trouble next morning; because of course she prob'ly hain't got any but that one."

"I know; but you don't want it but fifteen minutes, to carry the nonnamous letter and shove it under the front door."

"All right, then, I'll do it; but I could carry it just as handy in my own togs."

"You wouldn't look like a servant-girl, then, would you?"

"No, but there won't be nobody to see what I look like, anyway."

"That ain't got nothing to do with it. The thing for us to do, is just to do our duty, and not worry about whether anybody sees us do it or not. Hain't you got no principle at all?"

"All right, I ain't saying nothing; I'm the servant-girl. Who's Jim's mother?"

"I'm his mother. I'll hook a gown from Aunt Sally."

"Well, then, you'll have to stay in the cabin when me and Jim leaves."

"Not much. I'll stuff Jim's clothes full of straw and lay it on his bed to represent his mother in disguise, and Jim'll take the nigger woman's gown off of me and wear it, and we'll all evade together. When a prisoner of style escapes, it's called an evasion. It's always so called when a king escapes, f'rinstance. And the same with a king's son; it don't make no difference whether he's a natural one or an unnatural one."

So Tom he wrote the nonnamous letter, and I smouched the yaller wench's frock, that night, and put it on, and shoved the letter under the front door, the way Tom told me to. It said:

"Beware. Trouble is brewing. Keep a sharp lookout."

UNKNOWN FRIEND

Next night we stuck a picture which Tom drawed in blood, of a skull and crossbones, on the front door; and next night another one of a coffin, on the back door. I never see a family in such a sweat. They couldn't a been worse scared if the place had a been full of ghosts laying for them behind everything and under the beds and shivering through the air. If a door banged, Aunt Sally she jumped, and said "ouch!" If anything fell, she jumped, and said "ouch!" If you happened to touch her, when she warn't noticing, she done the same; she couldn't face noway and be satisfied, because she allowed there was something behind her every time—so she was always a-whirling around, sudden, and saying "ouch!" and before she'd get two-thirds around, she d whirl back again, and say it again; and she was afraid to go to bed, but she dasn't set up. So the thing was working very well, Tom said; he said he never see a thing work more satisfactory. He said it showed it was done right.

So he said, now for the grand bulge! So the very next morning at the streak of dawn we got another letter ready, and was wondering what we better do with it, because we heard them say at supper they was going to have a nigger on watch at both doors all night. Tom he went down the lightning-rod to spy around; and the nigger at the back door was asleep, and he stuck it in the back of his neck and come back. This letter said:

"Don't betray me, I wish to be your friend. There is a desperate gang of cut-throats from over in the Ingean Territory going to steal your runaway nigger to-night, and they have been trying to scare you so as you will stay in the house and not bother them. I am one of the gang, but have got religion and wish to quit it and lead an honest life again, and will betray the hellish design. They will sneak down from northwards, along the fence, at midnight exact, with a false key, and go in the nigger's cabin to get him. I am to be off a piece and blow a tin horn if I see any danger; but stead of that, I will baa like a sheep soon as they get in and not blow at all; then whilst they are getting his chains loose, you slip there and lock them in, and can kill them at your leisure. Don't do anything but just the way I am telling you, if you do they will suspicion something and raise whoop-jamboreehoo. I do not wish any reward but to know I have done the right thing."

UNKNOWN FRIEND

Preparations for Jim's Escape

We was feeling pretty good, after breakfast, and took my canoe and went over the river a-fishing, with a lunch, and had a good time, and took a look at the raft and found her all right, and got home late to supper, and found them in such a sweat and worry they didn't know which end they was standing on, and made us go right off to bed the minute we was done supper, and wouldn't tell us what the trouble was, and never let on a word about the new letter, but didn't need to, because we knowed as much about it as anybody did, and as soon as we was half upstairs and her back was turned, we slid for the cellar cupboard and loaded up a good lunch and took it up to our room and went to bed, and got up about half past eleven, and Tom put on Aunt Sally's dress that he stole and was going to start with the lunch, but says:

"Where's the butter?"

"I laid out a hunk of it," I says, "on a piece of a corn-pone."

"Well, you left it laid out, then—it ain't here."

"We can get along without it," I says.

"We can get along with it, too," he says, "just you slide down cellar and fetch it. And then mosey right down the lightning-rod and come along. I'll go an stuff the straw into Jim's clothes to represent his mother in disguise, and be ready to baa like a sheep and shove soon as you get there."

So out he went, and down cellar went I. The hunk of butter big as a person's fist was where I had left it, so I took up the slab of corn-pone with it on, and blowed out my light, and started upstairs, very stealthy, and got up to the main floor all right, but here comes Aunt Sally with a candle, and I clapped the truck in my hat, and clapped my hat on my head, and the next second she see me; and she says:

"You been down cellar?"

"Yes'm."

"What you been doing down there?"

"Noth'n."

"Noth'n!"

"No'm."

"Well, then what possessed you to go down there, this time of night?"

"I don't know'm."

"You don't know? Don't answer me that way, Tom, I want to know what you been doing down there?"

"I hain't been doing a single thing, Aunt Sally, I hope to gracious if I have."

I reckoned she'd let me go, now, and as a general thing she would; but I s'pose there was so many strange things going on she was just in a sweat about every little thing that warn't yard-stick straight; so she says, very decided:

"You just march into that setting-room and stay there till I come. You been up to something you no business to, and I lay I'll find out what it is before I'm done with you."

So she went away as I opened the door and walked into the setting-room. My, but there was a crowd there! Fifteen farmers, and every one of them had a gun. I was most powerful sick, and slunk to a chair and set down. They was setting around, some of them talking a little, in a low voice, and all of them fidgety and uneasy, but trying to look like they warn't; but I knowed they was, because they was always taking off their hats, and putting them on, and scratching their heads, and changing their seats, and fumbling with their buttons. I warn't easy myself, but I didn't take off my hat, all the same.

I did wish Aunt Sally would come, and get done with me and lick me, if she wanted to, and let me get away and tell Tom how we'd overdone this thing, and what a thundering hornet's nest we'd got ourselves into, so we could stop fooling around, straight off, and clear out with Jim before these rips got out of patience and come for us.

At last she come, and begun to ask me questions, but I couldn't answer them straight, I didn't know

which end of me was up; because these men was in such a fidget now, that some was wanting to start right now and lay for them desperadoes, and saying it warn't but a few minutes to midnight; and others was trying to get them to hold on and wait for the sheep-signal; and here was Aunty pegging away at the questions, and me a-shaking all over and ready to sink down in my tracks I was that scared; and the place getting hotter and hotter, and the butter beginning to melt and run down my neck and behind my ears; and pretty soon, when one of them says, "I'm for going and getting in the cabin first, and right now, and catching them when they come," I most dropped; and a streak of butter came a-trickling down my forehead, and Aunt Sally she see it, and turns white as a sheet, and says:

"For the land's sake what is the matter with the child!—He's got the brain-fever as shore as you're born, and they're oozing out!"

And everybody runs to see, and she snatches off my hat, and out comes the bread, and what was left of the butter, and she grabbed me, and hugged me, and says:

"Oh, what a turn you did give me! and how glad and grateful I am it ain't no worse; for luck's against us, and it never rains but it pours, and when I see that truck I thought we'd lost you, for I knowed by the colour and all, it was just like your brains would be if—Dear, dear, whydn't you tell me that was what you'd been down there for, I wouldn't a cared. Now cler out to bed, and don't lemme see no more of you till morning!"

Escape!

I was upstairs in a second, and down the lightning-rod in another one, and shinning through the dark for the lean-to. I couldn't hardly get my words out, I was so anxious; but I told Tom as quick as I could, we must jump for it, now, and not a minute to lose —the house full of men, yonder, with guns!

His eyes just blazed; and he says:

"No!—is that so? Ain't it bully! Why, Huck, if it was to do over again, I bet I could fetch two hundred! If we could put it off till——"

"Hurry! hurry!" I says. "Where's Jim?"

"Right at your elbow; if you reach out your arm you can touch him. He's dressed, and everything's

ready. Now we'll slide out and give the sheep-signal."

But then we heard the tramp of men, coming to the door, and heard them begin to fumble with the padlock; and heard a man say:

"I told you we'd be too soon; they haven't come —the door is locked. Here, I'll lock some of you into the cabin and lay for 'em in the dark and kill 'em when they come; and the rest scatter around a piece, and listen if you can hear 'em coming."

So in they come, but couldn't see us in the dark,

and most trod on us whilst we was hustling to get under the bed. But we got under all right, and out through the hole, swift but soft—Jim first, me next, and Tom last, which was according to Tom's orders. Now we was in the lean-to, and heard trampings close by outside. So we crept to the door, and Tom stopped us there and put his eye to the crack, but couldn't make out nothing, it was so dark; and then Tom whispered and said he would listen for the steps to get further, and when he nudged us Jim must glide out first, and him last. So he set his ear to the crack and listened, and listened, and listened, and the steps a-scraping around, out there, all the time; and at last he nudged us, and we slid out, and stooped down, not breathing, and not making the least noise, and slipped stealthy towards the fence, in Injun file, and got to it, all right, and me and Jim over it; but Tom's britches catched fast on a splinter on the top rail, and then he heard the steps coming, so he had to pull loose, which snapped the splinter and made a noise; and as he dropped in our tracks and started, somebody sings out:

"Who's that? Answer, or I'll shoot!"

But we didn't answer; we just unfurled our heels and shoved. Then there was a rush, and a bang, bang, bang! and the bullets fairly whizzed around us! We heard them sing out:

"Here they are! They've broke for the river! After 'em, boys! And turn loose the dogs!"

So here they come, full tilt. We could hear them, because they wore boots, and yelled, but we didn't wear no boots, and didn't yell. We was in the path to the mill; and when they got pretty close on to us, we dodged into the bush and let them go by, and then dropped in behind them. They'd had all the dogs shut up, so they wouldn't scare off the robbers; but by this time somebody had let them loose, and here they come, making pow-wow enough for a million; but they was our dogs; so we stopped in our tracks till they catched up; and when they see it warn't nobody but us, and no excitement to offer them, they only just said howdy, and tore right ahead towards the shouting and clattering; and then we up steam again and whizzed along after them till we was nearly to the mill, and then struck up through the bush to where my canoe was tied, and hopped in and pulled for dear life towards the middle of the river, but didn't make no more noise than we was obleeged to. Then we struck out, easy and comfortable, for the island where my raft was; and we could hear them yelling and barking at each other all up and down the bank, till we was so far away the sounds got dim and died out. And when we stepped on to the raft, I says:

"Now, old Jim, you're a free man again, and I bet you won't ever be a slave no more."

"En a mighty good job it wuz, too, Huck. It 'uz planned beautiful, en it 'uz done beautiful; en dey ain't nobody kin git up a plan dat's mo' mixed-up en splendid den what dat one wuz."

We was all as glad as we could be, but Tom was the gladdest of all, because he had a bullet in the calf of his leg.

When me and Jim heard that, we didn't feel so brash as what we did before. It was hurting him considerable, and bleeding; so we laid him in the wigwam and tore up one of our shirts for to bandage him, but he says:

"Gimme the rags, I can do it myself. Don't stop, now; don't fool around here, and the evasion booming along so handsome; man the sweeps, and set her loose! Boys, we done it elegant!—'deed we did. I wish we'd a had the handling of Louis XVI, there wouldn't a been no 'Son of Saint Louis, ascend to heaven!' wrote down in his biography: no, sir, we'd a whooped him over the border—that's what we'd a done with him—and done it just as slick as nothing at all, too. Man the sweeps—man the sweeps!"

But me and Jim was consulting—and thinking. And after we'd thought a minute, I says:

"Say it, Jim."

So he says:

"Well, den, dis is de way it look to me, Huck. Ef it wuz him dat 'uz bein' set free, en one er de boys wuz to git shot, would he say, 'Go on en save me, nemmine 'bout a doctor f'r to save dis one'? Is dat like Mars Tom Sawyer? Would he say dat? You bet he wouldn't! Well, den, is Jim gwyne to say it? No, sah—ah doan' budge a step out'n dis place, 'dout a doctor; not if it's forty year!"

I knowed he was white inside, and I reckoned he'd say what he did say—so it was all right, now, and I told Tom I was agoing for a doctor. He raised considerable row about it, but me and Jim stuck to it and wouldn't budge; so he was for crawling out and setting the raft loose himself; but we wouldn't let him. Then he give us a piece of his mind—but it didn't do no good.

So when he sees me getting the canoe ready, he says:

"Well, then, if you're bound to go, I'll tell you the way to do, when you get to the village. Shut the door, and blindfold the doctor tight and fast, and make him swear to be silent as the grave, and put a purse full of gold in his hand, and then take and lead him all around the back alleys and everywheres, in the dark, and then fetch him here in the canoe, in a roundabout way amongst the islands, and search him, and take his chalk away from him, and don't give it back to him till you get him back to the village, or else he will chalk this raft so he can find it again. It's the way they all do."

So I said I would, and left, and Jim was to hide in the woods when he see the doctor coming, till he was gone again.

I Fetch the Doctor

The doctor was an old man; a very nice, kind-looking old man, when I got him up. I told him me and my brother was over on Spanish Island hunting, yesterday afternoon, and camped on a piece of a raft we found, and about midnight he must a kicked his gun in his dreams, for it went off and shot him in the leg, and we wanted him to go over there and fix it and not say nothing about it, nor let anybody know, because we wanted to come home this evening, and surprise the folks.

"Who is your folks?" he says.

"The Phelpses, down yonder."

"Oh," he says. And after a minute, he says: "How'd you say he got shot?"

"He had a dream," I says, "and it shot him."

"Singular dream," he says.

So he lit up his lantern, and got his saddle-bags, and we started. But when he see the canoe, he didn't like the look of her——said she was big enough for one, but didn't look pretty safe for two. I says:

"Oh, you needn't be afeard, sir, she carried the three of us, easy enough."

"What three?"

"Why, me and Sid, and——and——and the guns; that's what I mean."

"Oh," he says.

But he put his foot on the gunnel, and rocked her; and shook his head, and said he reckoned he'd look around for a bigger one. But they was all locked and chained; so he took my canoe, and said for me to wait till he come back, or I could hunt around further or maybe I better go down home and get them ready for the surprise, if I wanted to. But I said I didn't; so I told him just how to find the raft, and then he started.

I struck an idea, pretty soon. I says to myself, spos'n he can't fix that leg jest in three shakes of a sheep's tail, as the saying is? spos'n it takes him three or four days? What are we going to do?—lay around there till he lets the cat out of the bag? No, sir, I know what I'll do. I'll wait, and when he comes back, if he says he's got to go any more, I'll get down there, too, if I swim; and we'll take and tie him, and keep him, and shove out down the river; and when Tom's done with him, we'll give him what it's worth, or all we got, and then let him get ashore.

So then I crept into a lumber pile to get some sleep; and next time I waked up the sun was away up over my head! I shot out and went for the doctor's house, but they told me he'd gone away in the night, some time or other, and warn't back yet. Well,

thinks I, that looks powerful bad for Tom, and I'll dig out for the island, right off. So away I shoved, and turned the corner, and nearly rammed my head into Uncle Silas's stomach! He says:

"Why, Tom! Where you been, all this time, you rascal?"

"I hain't been nowheres," I says, "only just hunting for the runaway nigger——me and Sid."

"Why, where ever did you go?" he says. "Your aunt's been mighty uneasy."

"She needn't," I says, "because we was all right. We followed the men and the dogs, but they outrun us, and we lost them; but we thought we heard them on the water, so we got a canoe and took out after them, and crossed over but couldn't find nothing of them; so we cruised along up-shore till we got tired and beat out; and tied up the canoe and went to sleep, and never waked up till about an hour ago; then we paddled over here to hear the news, and Sid's at the post office to see what he can hear, and I'm branching out to get something to eat for us, and then we're going home."

So then we went to the post office to get 'Sid'; but just as I suspicioned, he warn't there; so the old man he got a letter out of the office, and we waited a while longer but Sid didn't come; so the old man said come along, let Sid foot it home, or canoe it, when he got done fooling around—but we would ride. I couldn't get him to let me stay and wait for Sid; and he said there warn't no use in it, and I must come along, and let Aunt Sally see we was all right.

When we got home, Aunt Sally was that glad to see me she laughed and cried both, and hugged me, and give me one of them lickings of her'n that don't amount to shucks, and said she'd serve Sid the same when he come.

And the place was plumb full of farmers and farmers' wives, to dinner; and such another clack a body never heard—all jabbering about the incident at the same time.

When it was late in the day, the people all went. Pretty soon Aunt Sally jumps up, and says:

"Why, lawsamercy, it's most night, and Sid not come yet! What has become of that boy?"

I see my chance; so I skips up and says:

"I'll run right up to town and get him," I says.

"No, you won't," she says. "You'll stay right wher' you are; one's enough to be lost at a time. If he ain't here to supper, your uncle'll go."

Well, he warn't there to supper; so right after

supper uncle went.

He come back about ten, a little bit uneasy; hadn't run across Tom's track. Aunt Sally was a good deal uneasy; but Uncle Silas he said there warn't no occasion to be—boys will be boys, he said, and you'll see this one turn up in the morning, all sound and right. So she had to be satisfied. But she said she'd set up for him awhile, anyway, and keep a light burning, so he could see it.

And then when I went up to bed she come up with me and fetched her candle, and tucked me in, and mothered me so good I felt mean, and like I couldn't look her in the face; and she set down on the bed and talked with me a long time, and said what a splendid boy Sid was, and didn't seem to want to ever stop talking about him; and kept asking me every now and then if I reckoned he could a got lost, or hurt, or maybe drownded, and might be laying at this minute, somewheres, suffering or dead, and she not by him to help him, and so the tears would drip down, silent, and I would tell her that Sid was all right, and would be home in the morning, sure; and she would squeeze my hand, or maybe kiss me, and tell me to say it again, and keep on saying it, because it done her good, and she was in so much trouble. And when she was going away, she looked down in my eyes, so steady and gentle, and says:

"The door ain't going to be locked, Tom; and there's the window and the rod; but you'll be good, won't you? And you won't go? For my sake."

Laws knows I wanted to go, bad enough, to see about Tom, and was all intending to go; but after that, I wouldn't a went, not for kingdoms.

But she was on my mind, and Tom was on my mind; so I slept very restless. And twice I went down the rod, away in the night, and slipped around front, and see her setting there by her candle in the window with her eyes towards the road and the tears in them; and I wished I could do something for her, but I couldn't, only to swear that I wouldn't never do nothing to grieve her any more. And the third time, I waked up at dawn, and slid down, and she was there yet, and her candle was most out, and her old grey head was resting on her hand, and she was asleep.

Jim Returns

The old man was up town again, before breakfast, but couldn't get no track of Tom; and both of them set at the table, thinking, and not saying nothing, and looking mournful, and their coffee getting cold, and not eating anything. And by-and-by the old man says:

"Did I give you the letter?"

"What letter?"

"The one I got yesterday out of the post office?"

"No, you didn't give me no letter."

"Well, I must a forgot it."

So he rummaged his pockets, and then went off somewheres where he had laid it down, and fetched it, and give it to her. She says:

"Why, it's from St Petersburg—it's from Sis."

I allowed another walk would do me good; but I couldn't stir. But before she could break it open, she dropped it and run—for she see something. And so did I. It was Tom Sawyer on a mattress; and that old doctor; and Jim, in her calico dress, with his hands tied behind him; and a lot of people. I hid the letter behind the first thing that come handy, and rushed. She flung herself at Tom, crying, and says:

"Oh, he's dead, he's dead, I know he's dead!"

And Tom he turned his head a little, and muttered something or other, which showed he warn't in his right mind; then she flung up her hands, and says:

"He's alive, thank God! And that's enough!" and she snatched a kiss of him, and flew for the house to get the bed ready, and scattering orders right and left at the niggers and everybody else, as fast as her tongue could go, every jump of the way.

I followed the men to see what they was going to do with Jim; and the old doctor and Uncle Silas followed after Tom into the house. The men was very huffy, and some of them wanted to hang Jim, for an example to all the other niggers around there, so they wouldn't be trying to run away, like Jim done, and making such a raft of trouble, and keeping a whole family scared most to death for days and nights. But the others said, don't do it, it wouldn't answer at all, he ain't our nigger, and his owner would turn up and make us pay for him, sure. So that cooled them down a little, because the people that's always the most anxious for to hang a nigger that hain't done just right, is always the very ones that ain't the most anxious to pay for him when they've got their satisfaction out of him.

They cussed Jim considerable, though, and give him a cuff or two, side the head, once in a while, but Jim never said nothing, and he never let on to know me; and they took him to the same cabin, and put his own clothes on him, and chained him again, and not to no bed-leg this time, but to a big staple drove into the bottom log, and chained his hands, too, and both legs, and said he warn't to have nothing but bread and water to eat, after this, till his owner come or he was sold at auction, because he didn't come in a certain length of time; and filled up our hole, and said a couple of farmers with guns must stand watch around about the cabin every night, and a bulldog tied to the door in the daytime; and about this time they was through with the job and was tapering off with a kind of general good-bye cussing, and then the old doctor comes and takes a look, and says:

"Don't be no rougher on him than you're obleeged to, because he ain't a bad nigger. When I got to where I found the boy, I see I couldn't cut the bullet out without some help, and he warn't in no condition for me to leave, to go and get help; and he got a little worse and a little worse, and after a long time he went out of his head, and wouldn't let me come anigh him, any more, and said if I chalked his raft he'd kill me, and no end of wild foolishness like

that, and I see I couldn't do anything at all with him;
so I says, I got to have help, somehow; and the
minute I says it, out crawls this nigger from
somewheres, and says he'll help, and he done it, too,
and done it very well. Of course I judged he must be
a runaway nigger, and there I was! and there I had
to stick, right straight along all the rest of the day,
and all night. It was a fix, I tell you! I had a couple
of patients with the chills, and of course I'd of liked
to run up to town and see them, but I dasn't, because
the nigger might get away, and then I'd be to blame;
and yet never a skiff come close enough for me to
hail. So there I had to stick, plumb till daylight this
morning; and I never see a nigger that was a better
nuss or faithfuller, and yet he was resking his
freedom to do it, and was all tired out, too, and I see
plain enough he'd been worked main hard, lately. I
liked the nigger for that; I tell you, gentlemen, a
nigger like that is worth a thousand dollars—and
kind treatment, too. I had everything I needed, and
the boy was doing as well there as he would a done
at home—better, maybe, because it was so quiet; but
there I was, with both of 'm on my hands; and there
I had to stick, till about dawn this morning; then
some men in a skiff come by, and as good luck would
have it, the nigger was setting by the pallet with his
head propped on his knees, sound asleep; so I
motioned them in, quiet, and they slipped up on him
and grabbed him and tied him before he knowed
what he was about, and we never had no trouble.
And the boy being in a kind of a flighty sleep, too, we
muffled the oars and hitched the raft on, and towed
her over very nice and quiet, and the nigger never
made the least row nor said a word, from the start.
He ain't no bad nigger, gentlemen; that's what I
think about him."

Somebody says:

"Well, it sounds very good, doctor, I'm obleeged to
say."

Then the others softened up a little too, and I was
mighty thankful to that old doctor for doing Jim that
good turn; and I was glad it was according to my
judgement of him, too; because I thought he had a
good heart in him and was a good man, the first time
I see him. Then they all agreed that Jim had acted
very well, and was deserving to have some notice
took of it, and reward. So every one of them
promised, right out and hearty, that they wouldn't
cuss him no more.

Tom Recovers

Next morning I heard Tom was a good deal better, and they said Aunt Sally was gone to get a nap. So I slips to the sickroom, and if I found him awake I reckoned we could put up a yarn for the family that would wash. But he was sleeping, and sleeping very peaceful, too; and pale, not fire-faced the way he was when he come. So I set down and laid for him to wake. In about a half an hour, Aunt Sally comes gliding in, and there I was, up a stump again! She motioned me to be still, and set down by me, and begun to whisper and said we could all be joyful now, because all the symptoms was first-rate, and he'd been sleeping like that for ever so long, and looking better and peacefuller all the time, and ten to one he'd wake up in his right mind.

So we set there watching and by-and-by he stirs a bit, and opened his eyes very natural, and takes a look, and says:

"Hello, why I'm at home! How's that? Where's the raft?"

"It's all right," I says.

"And Jim!"

"The same," I says, but couldn't say it pretty brash. But he never noticed, but says:

"Good! Splendid! Now we're all right and safe! Did you tell Aunty?"

I was going to say yes; but she chipped in and says:

"About what, Sid?"

"Why, about the way the whole thing was done."

"What whole thing?"

"Why, the whole thing. There ain't but one; how we set the runaway nigger free—me and Tom."

"Good land! Set the run—— What is the child talking about! Dear, dear, out of his head again!"

"No, I ain't out of my head; I know all what I'm talking about. We did set him free—me and Tom. We laid out to do it, and we done it. And we done it elegant, too." He'd got a start, and she never checked him up, just set and stared and stared, and let him clip along, and I see it warn't no use for me to put in. "Why, Aunty, it cost us a power of work —weeks of it—hours and hours, every night, whilst you was all asleep."

"Mercy sakes!"

"We had to get up and down the lightning-rod, and dig the hole into the cabin, and when you kept Tom here so long with the butter in his hat, you come near spoiling the whole business, because the men come before we was out of the cabin, and we had to rush, and they heard us and let drive at us, and I got my share, and we dodged out of the path and let them go by, and when the dogs come they warn't interested in us, but went for the most noise, and we got our canoe, and made for the raft, and was all safe, and Jim was a free man, and we done it all by ourselves, and wasn't it bully, Aunty!"

"Well, I never heard the likes of it in all my born days! So it was you, you little rapscallions, that's been making all this trouble, and turned everybody's wits clean inside out and scared us all most to death. I've as good a notion as ever I had in my life to take it out o' you this very minute. To think, here I've been, night after night, a—you just get well once, you young scamp, and I lay I'll tan the Old Harry out o' both o' ye!"

But Tom, he was so proud and joyful, he just couldn't hold in, and his tongue just went it—she a-chipping in, and spitting fire all along, and both of them going it at once, and she says:

"Well, you get all the enjoyment you can out of it now, for mind I tell you if I catch you meddling with him again——"

"Meddling with who?" Tom says, dropping his smile, and looking surprised.

"With who? Why, the runaway nigger, of course. Who'd you reckon?"

Tom looks at me very grave, and says:

"Tom, didn't you just tell me he was all right? Hasn't he got away?"

"Him?" says Aunt Sally; "the runaway nigger? 'Deed he hasn't. They've got him back, safe and sound, and he's in that cabin again, on bread and water, and loaded down with chains, till he's claimed or sold!"

Tom rose square up in bed, with his eye hot, and his nostrils opening and shutting like gills, and sings out to me:

"They hain't no right to shut him up! Shove— and don't you lose a minute. Turn him loose! He ain't no slave; he's as free as any cretur that walks this earth!"

"What does the child mean?"

"I mean every word I say, Aunt Sally, and if somebody don't go, I'll go. I've knowed him all his life, and so has Tom, there. Old Miss Watson died two months ago, and she was ashamed she ever was going to sell him down the river, and said so; and she set him free in her will."

"Then what on earth did you want to set him free for, seeing he was already free?"

"Well, that is a question, I must say; and just like women! Why, I wanted the adventure of it; and I'd a waded neck-deep in blood to—goodness alive— AUNT POLLY!"

Aunt Polly

If she warn't standing right there, just inside the door, looking as sweet and contented as an angel half full of pie, I wish I may never!

Aunt Sally jumped for her, and most hugged the head off of her, and cried over her, and I found a good enough place for me under the bed, for it was getting pretty sultry for us, seemed to me. And I peeped out, and in a little while Tom's Aunt Polly shook herself loose and stood there looking across at Tom over her spectacles—kind of grinding him into the earth, you know. And then she says:

"Yes, you better turn y'r head away—I would if I was you, Tom."

"Oh, deary me!" says Aunt Sally; "is he changed so? Why, that ain't Tom, it's Sid; Tom's—Tom's—why, where is Tom? He was here a minute ago."

"You mean where's Huck Finn—that's what you mean! I reckon I hain't raised such a scamp as my Tom all these years, not to know him when I see him. That would be a pretty howdydo. Come out from under that bed, Huck Finn!"

So I done it. But not feeling brash.

Aunt Sally she was one of the mixed-upest-looking persons I ever see; except one, and that was Uncle Silas, when he come in, and they told it all to him. It kind of made him drunk, as you may say, and he didn't know nothing at all the rest of the day, and preached a prayer-meeting sermon that night that give him a rattling reputation, because the oldest man in the world couldn't a understood it. So Tom's Aunt Polly, she told all about who I was, and what; and I had to up and tell how I was in such a tight place that when Mrs Phelps took me for Tom Sawyer—she chipped in and says, "Oh, go on and call me Aunt Sally, I'm used to it, now, and 'tain't no need to change"—that when Aunt Sally took me for Tom Sawyer, I had to stand it—there warn't no other way, and I knowed he wouldn't mind, because it would be nuts for him, being a mystery, and he'd make an adventure out of it and be perfectly satisfied. And so it turned out, and he let on to be Sid, and made things as soft as he could for me.

And his Aunt Polly she said Tom was right about old Miss Watson setting Jim free in her will; and so, sure enough, Tom Sawyer had gone and took all that trouble and bother to set a free nigger free! and I couldn't ever understand before, until that minute and that talk, how he could help a body set a nigger free, with his bringing-up.

Well, Aunt Polly she said that when Aunt Sally wrote to her that Tom and Sid had come, all right and safe, she says to herself:

"Look at that, now! I might have expected it, letting him go off that way without anybody to watch him. So now I got to go and traipse all the way down river, and find out what that creetur's up to, this time; as long as I couldn't seem to get any answer out of you about it."

"Why, I never heard nothing from you," says Aunt Sally.

"Well, I wonder? Why, I wrote to you twice, to ask you what you could mean by Sid being here."

"Well, I never got 'em Sis."

Aunt Polly, she turns around slow and severe, and says:

"You, Tom!"

"Well—what?" he says, kind of pettish.

"Don't you what me, you impudent thing—hand out them letters."

"What letters?"

"Them letters. I be bound, if I have to take a holt of you I'll———"

"They're in the trunk. There, now. And they're just the same as they was when I got them out of the office. I hain't looked into them, I hain't touched them. But I knowed they'd make trouble, and I thought if you warn't in no hurry, I'd———"

"Well, you do need skinning, there ain't no mistake about it. And I wrote another one to tell you I was coming; and I s'pose he———"

"No, it come yesterday; I hain't read it yet, but it's all right, I've got that one."

I wanted to offer to bet two dollars she hadn't, but I reckoned maybe it was just as safe to not to. So I never said nothing.

Tom Is a Hero

The first time I catched Tom, private, I asked him what was his idea, time of the evasion?—what it was he'd planned to do if the evasion worked all right and he managed to set a nigger free that was already free before? And he said, what he had planned in his head, from the start, if we got Jim out all safe, was for us to run him down river, on the raft, and have adventures plumb to the mouth of the river, and then tell him about his being free, and take him back up home on a steamboat, in style, and pay him for his lost time, and write word ahead and get out all the niggers around, and have them waltz him into town with a torchlight procession and a brass band, and then he would be a hero, and so would we. But I reckoned it was about as well the way it was.

We had Jim out of the chains in no time, and when Aunt Polly and Uncle Silas and Aunt Sally found out how good he helped the doctor nurse Tom, they made a heap of fuss over him, and fixed him up

And then Tom he talked along, and talked along, and says, let's all three slide out of here, one of these nights, and get an outfit, and go for howling adventures amongst the Injuns, over in the Territory, for a couple of weeks or so; and I says, all right, that suits me, but I ain't got no money for to buy the outfit, and I reckon I couldn't get none from home, because it's likely Pap's been back before now, and got it all away from Judge Thatcher and spent it all on whisky.

"No, he hain't," Tom says; "it's all there yet—six thousand dollars and more; and your pap hain't ever been back since. Hadn't when I come away, anyhow."

Jim says, kind of solemn:

"He ain't a-comin' back no mo', Huck."

I says:

"Why, Jim?"

"Nemmine why, Huck—but he ain't comin' back no mo'."

But I kept at him; so at last he says:

"Doan' you 'member de house dat was float'n down de river, en dey wuz a man in dah, kivered up, en I went in en unkivered him and didn' let you come in? Well, den, you k'n git yo' money when you wants it; kase dat wuz him."

Tom's most well, now, and got his bullet around his neck on a watchguard for a watch, and is always seeing what time it is. But I reckon I got to light out for the Territory ahead of the rest, because Aunt Sally she's going to adopt me and sivilize me, and I can't stand it. I been there before.

prime, and give him all he wanted to eat and a good time, and nothing to do. And we had him up to the sick-room; and had a high talk; and Tom give Jim forty dollars for being prisoner for us so patient, and doing it up so good, and Jim was pleased most to death, and busted out, and says:

"Dah, now, Huck, what I tell you?—what I tell you up dah on Jackson islan'? I tole you I got a hairy breas', en what's de sign un it; en I tole you I ben rich wunst, en gwineter be rich agin; en it's come true, en heah she is! Dah, now! doan' talk to me—signs is signs, mine I tell you; en I knowed jis' 's well 'at I 'uz gwineter be rich agin as I's a stannin' heah dis minute!"

BLACK BEAUTY

My Early Home

The first place that I can remember was a large pleasant meadow with a pond of clear water in it. Some trees overshadowed the pond, and rushes and water-lilies grew at the deep end. Over the hedge on one side we looked into a ploughed field; and on the other, we looked over a gate at our master's house which stood by the roadside. At the top of the meadow was a plantation of fir-trees; and at the bottom, a running brook overhung by a steep bank.

Whilst I was young I lived upon my mother's milk, as I could not eat grass. In the daytime I ran by her side, and at night I lay down close by her. When it was hot, we used to stand by the pond in the shade of the trees; and when it was cold, we had a nice warm shed near the plantation.

There were six young colts in the meadow besides me. They were older than I was; some were nearly as large as grown-up horses. I used to run with them, and have great fun. We used to gallop all together round and round the field, as hard as we could go.

Mother had the sweetest temper of any horse I ever knew, and I think I have never seen her kick or bite.

"I hope you will grow up gentle and good, and never learn bad ways," she said to me one day. "Do your work with a good will; lift up your feet well when you trot, and never bite or kick even in play." I have never forgotten my mother's advice; I knew she was a wise old horse, and our master thought a great deal of her. Her name was Duchess, but he often called her Pet.

Old Daniel, the man who looked after the horses, was just as gentle as our master, so we were well off.

The Hunt

Before I was two years old, something happened which I have never forgotten.

The other colts and I were feeding in the lower part of the field when we heard, quite in the distance, what sounded like the cry of dogs.

"They are the hounds. They have found a hare," said my mother, "and if they come this way, we shall see the hunt. Look, there she is;" and just then a hare, wild with fright, rushed by, and made for the road.

Alas! it was too late; the dogs were upon her with their wild cries. We heard one shriek, and that was the end of her.

By the brook, two fine horses were down; one was struggling in the stream, and the other was groaning on the grass. One of the riders, covered with mud, was getting out of the water; the other lay quite still.

"His neck is broken," said my mother.

Many of the riders had gone to the young man; but my master, who had been watching what was going on, was the first to raise him. His head fell back and his arms hung down, and everyone looked very serious.

There was no noise now; even the dogs were quiet, and seemed to know that something was wrong.

When Mr Bond, the farrier, came to look at the black horse that lay groaning on the grass, he felt him all over and shook his head; one of the horse's legs was broken. Then some one ran to our master's house and came back with a gun. Presently there was a loud bang and a dreadful shriek, and then all was still; the black horse moved no more.

My mother seemed much troubled. She said she had known that horse for years. His name was Rob Roy; a good bold horse with no vice in him. Afterwards she never would go to that part of the field.

Not many days after, we heard the church bell tolling for a long time; and looking over the gate we saw a long, strange, black coach covered with black cloth and drawn by black horses. After that came another, and another, and another; and all were black. Meanwhile the bell kept tolling, tolling. They were carrying young George Gordon, the Squire's only son, to the churchyard to bury him. He would never ride again, 'twas all for one little hare.

My Breaking In

I was now beginning to grow handsome; my coat had grown fine and soft, and was glossy black. I had one white foot, and a pretty white star on my forehead. People thought me very handsome.

When I was four years old, Squire Gordon came to look at me. He examined my eyes and my mouth, and felt my legs all down. Then I had to walk, trot, and gallop before him. He seemed to like me, and said, "When he has been well broken in, he will do very well." My master promised to break me in himself as he would not like me to be frightened or hurt; and he lost no time about it, for the next day the breaking in began.

Of course I had long been used to a halter and a headstall, and to be led about in the fields and lanes quietly, but now I was to have a bit and a bridle. What a nasty thing the bit was! Those who have

never had one in their mouth cannot think how bad it feels. A great piece of cold, hard steel as thick as a man's finger is pushed between your teeth and over your tongue, with the ends coming out at the corners of your mouth, and is held fast there by straps over your head, under your throat, round your nose, and under your chin; so that no way in the world can you get rid of the nasty hard thing. Yes, very bad! At least, I thought so; but I knew my mother always wore one when she went out, and that all horses did when they were grown up. And so, what with the nice oats, and what with my master's pats, kind words, and gentle ways, I got to wear my bit and bridle.

Next came the saddle, but that was not nearly so bad, and within a few days I had grown quite used to it.

At length, one morning my master got on my back and rode me round the meadow on the soft grass. It certainly did feel queer; but I must say I felt rather

proud to carry my master; and, as he continued to ride me a little every day, I soon became accustomed to it.

The next unpleasant business was putting on the iron shoes; that too was very hard at first. My master went with me to the smith's forge to see that I was not hurt or frightened.

I must not forget to mention one part of my training which I have always considered a very great advantage. My master sent me for a fortnight to a neighbouring farmer who had a meadow which was skirted on one side by the railway. Here were some sheep and cows, and I was turned in amongst them.

I shall never forget the first train that ran by. I was feeding quietly near the pales which separated the meadow from the railway, when I heard a strange sound at a distance; and before I knew whence it came—with a rush and a clatter, and a puffing out of smoke—a long black trail of something flew by, and was gone almost before I could draw my breath. I turned, and galloped to the further side of the meadow as fast as I could go; and there I stood snorting with astonishment and fear.

I soon found that this terrible creature never came into the field nor did me any harm, so I began to disregard it; and very soon I cared as little about the passing of a train as the cows and sheep did.

My master often drove me in double harness with my mother because she was steady, and could teach me how to go better than a strange horse. She told me the better I behaved, the better I should be treated, and that it was wisest always to do my best to please my master.

"Do your best wherever you are, and keep up your good name."

Birtwick Park

At this time I used to stand in the stable, and my coat was brushed every day till it shone like a rook's wing. Early in May there came a man from Squire Gordon's, who took me away to the Hall. My master said, "Goodbye, Darkie; be a good horse, and always do your best." I could not say "Goodbye," so I put my nose into his hand; he patted me kindly, and then I left my first home.

Squire Gordon's park skirted the village of Birtwick. It was entered by a large iron gate, at which stood the first lodge; and then you trotted along on a smooth road between clumps of large old trees. Soon you passed another lodge and another gate, which brought you to the house and the gardens. Beyond this lay the home paddock, the old orchard and the stables. The stable into which I was taken was very roomy, with four good stalls. A large swinging window opened into the yard; this made it pleasant and airy.

When I had eaten my corn, I looked round. In the stall next to mine stood a little fat pony, with a thick mane and tail, a very pretty head, and a pert little nose.

Putting my head up to the iron rails at the top of my box, I said, "How do you do? What is your name?"

He turned round as far as his halter would allow, held up his head, and said: "My name is Merrylegs. I am very handsome. I carry the young ladies on my back, and sometimes I take our mistress out in the low chair. They think a great deal of me, and so does James. Are you going to live next door to me in the box?"

"Yes," I replied.

The horse in the stable beyond looked ill-tempered; her ears were laid back. She was a tall chestnut mare, with a long, handsome neck.

"The thing is this," said Merrylegs. "Ginger has a bad habit of biting and snapping: that is why she is called Ginger. When she was in the loose box, she used to snap very much. One day she bit James in the arm and made it bleed, and so Miss Flora and Miss Jessie, who are very fond of me, were afraid to go into the stable. They used to bring me nice things to eat—an apple, or a carrot, or a piece of bread; but after Ginger stood in that box, they dared not come, and I miss them very much. I hope, if you do not bite or snap, that they will now come again."

I told him I never bit anything but grass, hay and corn, and could not think what pleasure Ginger found in it.

A Fair Start

The name of the coachman was John Manly. The next morning he took me into the yard and gave me a good grooming. Just as I was going into my box with my coat soft and bright, the Squire came in to look at me, and seemed pleased.

After breakfast John came and fitted me with a bridle. He was very particular in letting out and taking in the straps, to fit my head comfortably. Then he brought the saddle, which fitted nicely. He rode me at first slowly, then at a trot, and afterwards at a canter; and when we were on the common he gave me a light touch with his whip, and we had a splendid gallop.

As we came back through the park, we met the Squire and Mrs Gordon walking. They stopped, and John jumped off.

"Well, John, how does he go?"

"First-rate, sir," answered John. "He is as fleet as a deer."

"That's well," said the Squire. "I will try him myself tomorrow."

The next day I was brought up for my master. I remembered my mother's counsel and my good old master's, and I tried to do exactly what the Squire wanted me to do. I found he was a very good rider, and thoughtful for his horse, too. When we came home, the lady was at the Hall door as he rode up.

"Well, my dear," she said, "how do you like him?"

"He is exactly what John said, my dear. A pleasanter creature I never wish to mount. What shall we call him?"

"Would you like Ebony?" said she; "He is as black as ebony."

"No, not Ebony."

"Will you call him Blackbird, like your uncle's old horse?"

"No; he is far handsomer than old Blackbird ever was."

"Yes," she said, "he really is quite a beauty, and he has such a sweet, good-tempered face and such a fine, intelligent eye—what do you say to calling him Black Beauty?"

"Black Beauty—why, yes, I think that is a very good name. If you like, it shall be so," and that is how I got my name.

A few days after this I had to go in the carriage with Ginger. I wondered how we should get on together; but except laying her ears back when I was led up to her, she behaved very well. She did her work honestly, and did her full share; and I never wish to have a better partner in double harness.

As for Merrylegs, he and I soon became great friends. He was such a cheerful, plucky, good-tempered little fellow that he was a favourite with everyone, and especially with Miss Jessie and Flora, who used to ride him about in the orchard and have fine games with him and their little dog Frisky.

Liberty

I was quite happy in my new place, and if there was one thing that I missed, it must not be thought I was discontented. All who had to do with me were good, and I had a light, airy stable and the best of food.

What more could I want? Why, liberty! For three years and a half of my life I had had all the liberty I could wish for; but now, week after week, month after month, and no doubt year after year, I must stand up in a stable night and day except when I am wanted; and then I must be just as steady and quiet as any old horse who has worked twenty years. I must wear straps here and straps there, a bit in my mouth, and blinkers over my eyes.

I ought to say that sometimes we had our liberty for a few hours; this used to be on fine Sundays in the summertime. The carriage never went out on Sundays, because the church was not far off.

It was a great treat to us to be turned out into the home paddock or the old orchard; the grass was so cool and soft to our feet; the air was so sweet, and the freedom to do as we liked— to gallop, lie down, roll over on our backs, or nibble the sweet grass— was so pleasant. Then, as we stood together under the shade of the large chestnut-tree, it was a very good time for talking.

Ginger

One day, when Ginger and I were standing alone in the shade, we had a long talk. She wanted to know all about my bringing up and breaking in; so I told her.

"Well," said she, "if I had had your bringing up I might have as good a temper as you; but now I don't believe I ever shall."

"Why not?" I said.

"Because it has been all so different with me," she replied. "I never had any one, horse or man, that was kind to me, or that I cared to please; for in the first place I was taken from my mother as soon as I was weaned, and put with a lot of other young colts; none of them cared for me, and I cared for none of

them. But when it came to breaking in, that was a bad time for me. Several men came to catch me; and when at last they closed me in at one corner of the field, one caught me by the forelock, another took me by the nose, holding it so tight I could hardly draw my breath, and a third, grasping my under jaw in his hard hand, wrenched my mouth open; and so by force they got on the halter and put the bar into my mouth. Samson, my master, used to boast that he

had never found a horse that could throw him. There was no gentleness in him as there was in his father, the old master, but only hardness: a hard voice, a hard eye and a hard hand. I felt from the first that what he wanted was to wear all the spirit out of me, and just make me into a quiet, humble, obedient piece of horse-flesh. 'Horse-flesh!' Yes, that is all that he thought about!" and Ginger stamped her foot as if the very thought of him made her angry.

"I felt my whole spirit set against him, and I began to kick, and plunge, and rear as I had never done before; we had a regular fight. For a long time he stuck to the saddle and punished me cruelly with his whip and spurs; but my blood was thoroughly up, and I cared for nothing he could do if only I could get him off.

"At last, after a terrible struggle, I threw him off backwards. I heard him fall heavily upon the turf, and without looking behind me, galloped off to the other end of the field; there I turned round and saw my persecutor slowly rise from the ground and go into the stable. I stood under an oak-tree and

watched, but no one came to catch me. Later, hungry and thirsty, I walked towards the stable. Mr Ryder—the old master—met me at the door.

"The skin was so broken at the corners of my mouth that I could not eat the hay, for the stalks hurt me. He looked closely at my mouth, shook his head, and told the man to fetch me a good bran mash and put some meal into it. How good that mash was, so soft and healing to my mouth. He stood by, stroking me and talking to the man all the time I was eating. 'If a high-mettled creature like this,' said he, 'can't be broken in by fair means, she never will be good for anything.'

"After that he often came to see me, and when my mouth was healed, the other breaker, Job, went on training me. As he was steady and thoughtful, I soon learned what he wanted."

Ginger's Story Continued

The next time that Ginger and I were together in the paddock, she told me about her first place.

"After my breaking in," she said, "I was bought by a dealer to match another chestnut horse. For some weeks he drove us together, and then we were sold to a gentleman, and were sent up to London."

"Did your new master take any thought for you?" I said.

"No," said she, "he cared only to have a stylish turnout, as they call it. I think he knew very little about horses; he left that to his coachman, who told him that I was of an irritable temper, and that I had not been well broken to the bearing rein, but that I should soon get used to it.

"However, he was not the man to do it; for when I was in the stable, miserable and angry, instead of being soothed and quieted by kindness, I only got a surly word or a blow. If he had been civil, I would have tried to bear it. I was willing to work and ready to work hard too; but to be tormented for nothing but their fancies angered me. What right had they to make me suffer like that? Besides the soreness in my mouth and the pain in my neck, the bearing rein always made my windpipe feel bad; and if I had stopped there long, I know it would have spoiled my breathing.

"I grew more and more restless and irritable; I could not help it. Then I began to snap and kick when anyone came to harness me, and for this the groom beat me. One day, as they had just buckled us into the carriage and were straining my head up with that rein, I began to plunge and kick with all my might. I soon broke a lot of harness, and kicked myself clear; so my stay there was ended.

"Soon I was sent to Tattersall's to be sold. Of course I could not be warranted free from vice; so nothing was said about that. The dealer said he thought he knew a place where I should do well, and the end of it was that I came here not long before you did. I had now made up my mind that men were my natural enemies, and that I must defend myself. Of course it is very different here; but who knows how long it will last? I wish I could think about things as you do; but I can't after all I have gone through."

But Ginger began to improve. Master noticed the change too, and one day when he got out of the carriage and came to speak to us as he often did, he stroked her beautiful neck. "Well, my pretty one, how do things go with you now? You are a good bit happier than when you came to us, I think."

She put her nose up to him in a friendly, trustful way, while he rubbed it gently.

"We shall make a cure of her, John," he said.

"Yes, sir, she's wonderfully improved; she's not the same creature that she was. It's the Birtwick balls, sir," said John, laughing.

This was a little joke of John's; he used to say that a course of the Birtwick horse-balls would cure almost any vicious horse. These balls, he said, were made up of patience and gentleness, firmness and petting: one pound of each to be mixed with half a pint of common-sense, and given to the horse every day.

Merrylegs

Mr Blomefield, the Vicar, had a large family of boys and girls, who sometimes came to play with Miss Jessie and Flora. One of the girls was as old as Miss Jessie; two of the boys were older, and there were several little ones. When they came, there was plenty of work for Merrylegs, for nothing pleased them so much as getting on him in turn, and riding him all about the orchard and the home paddock by the hour together.

One afternoon he had been out with them a long time, and when James brought him in and put on his halter, he said:

"There, you rogue, mind how you behave yourself, or we shall get into trouble."

"What have you been doing, Merrylegs?" I asked.

"Oh!" said he, tossing his little head, "I have only been giving these young people a lesson. They did not know when they had had enough, nor when I had had enough; so I just pitched them off backwards: that was the only thing they could understand."

"What?" said I, "you threw the children off? I thought you knew better than that! Did you throw Miss Jessie or Miss Flora?"

He looked very much offended, and said:

"Of course not; I would not do such a thing for the best oats that ever came into the stable. Why, I am as careful of our young ladies as the master could be; and as for the little ones, it is I who teach them to ride. When they seem frightened or a little unsteady on my back, I go as smoothly and as quietly as old pussy when she is after a bird; and when they are all right, I go on again faster, just to use them to it. So don't you trouble yourself preaching to me; I am the best friend and riding master those children have.

"It is not they; it is the boys. Boys," said he, shaking his mane, "are quite different; they must be broken in, as we were broken in when we were colts, and must just be taught what's what.

"The other children had ridden me about for nearly two hours, and then the boys thought it was their turn; and so it was, and I was quite agreeable. They rode me in turn, and I galloped them about, up and down the fields and all about the orchard for a good hour.

"They had each cut a great hazel stick for a riding whip, and laid it on a little too hard; but I took it in good part, till at last I thought we had had enough; so I stopped two or three times by way of a hint. Boys, you see, think a horse or pony is like a steam engine or threshing machine, that can go on as long and as fast as they please. They never think that a pony can get tired, or have any feelings; so as the one whipping me could not understand, I just rose up on my hind legs and let him slip off behind – that was all."

A Talk in the Orchard

Ginger and I were not of the regular tall, carriage-horse breed; we had more of the racing blood in us. We stood about fifteen and a half hands high, and were therefore just as good for riding as for driving. Our master used to say that he disliked either horse or man that could do but one thing; and as he did not want to show off in London parks, he preferred a more active and useful kind of horse.

As for us, our greatest pleasure was when we were saddled for a riding party – the master on Ginger, the mistress on me, and the young ladies on Sir Oliver and Merrylegs. It was so cheerful to be trotting and cantering all together that it always put us in high spirits. I had the best of it, for I always carried the mistress. Her weight was little, her voice sweet, and her hand so light on the rein that I was guided almost without feeling it.

I had often wondered how it was that Sir Oliver, another of our master's horses, had such a very short tail; it really was only six or seven inches long, with a tassel of hair hanging from it; and on one of our holidays in the orchard, I ventured to ask him by what accident he had lost his tail.

"Accident!" he snorted, with a fierce look, "it was no accident! It was a cruel, shameful, cold-blooded act! When I was young I was taken to a place where these cruel things were done. I was tied up, and made fast so that I could not stir; and then they came and cut my long, beautiful tail through the flesh and through the bone, and took it away."

"How dreadful!" I exclaimed.

"Dreadful! Ah, it was dreadful, but it was not only the pain, though that was terrible and lasted a long time; it was not only the indignity of having my best ornament taken from me, though that was bad; but it was this – how could I ever again brush the flies off my sides and off my hind legs? You who have tails just whisk the flies off without thinking about it; and you can't tell what a torment it is to have them settle upon you, and sting and sting, and yet have nothing in the world with which to lash them off. I tell you it is a lifelong wrong, and a lifelong loss. But, thank Heaven! men don't do it now."

"What did they do it for then?" said Ginger.

"For fashion!" said the old horse, with a stamp of his foot. "For fashion! if you know what that means. There was not a well-bred young horse in my time that had not his tail docked in that shameful way, just as if the good God that made us did not know what we wanted and what looked best."

"I suppose it is fashion that makes them strap our

heads up with those horrid bits that I was tortured with in London," said Ginger.

"Of course it is," said he. "To my mind, fashion is one of the most wicked things in the world. What right have they to torment and disfigure God's creatures?"

Sir Oliver, though he was so gentle, was a fiery old fellow; and what he said was all so new to me and so dreadful, that I found a bitter feeling toward men that I had never had before rise up in my mind. Of course, Ginger was much excited. With flashing eyes and distended nostrils, she flung up her head, declaring that men were both brutes and blockheads.

"Can any one tell me the use of blinkers?"

"No!" said Sir Oliver, shortly, "because they are no use."

"They are supposed," said Justice, our master's only other horse, "to prevent horses from shying and starting, and getting so frightened as to cause accidents."

"Then what is the reason they do not put them on riding horses, especially on ladies' horses?" said I.

"There is no reason at all," he said quietly, "except the fashion. Some years ago, I remember, there was a hearse with two horses returning one dark night, and just by Farmer Sparrow's house where the pond is close to the road, the wheels went too near the edge, and the hearse was overturned into the water. Both the horses were drowned, and the driver hardly escaped. Of course after this accident, a stout white rail was put up that might easily be seen; but if those horses had not been partly blinded, they would of themselves have kept farther from the edge, and no accident would have happened.

"When our master's carriage was overturned, before you came here, it was said that if the lamp on the left side had not gone out, John would have seen the great hole that the road-makers had left; and so he might. But if old Colin had not had blinkers on, he would have seen it, lamp or no lamp, for he was far too knowing an old horse to run into danger. As it was, he was very much hurt, the carriage was broken, and how John escaped nobody knew."

"The master," put in Merrylegs, "said that if horses had been used to them, it might be dangerous in some cases to leave them off; and John said he thought it would be a good thing if all colts were broken in without blinkers, as was done in some foreign countries; so let us cheer up and have a run

to the other end of the orchard. I believe the wind has blown down some apples, and we may just as well eat them ourselves as leave them for the slugs to have them all."

Merrylegs' suggestions could not be resisted; so we broke off our long conversation and got up our spirits by munching some very sweet apples which lay scattered on the grass.

A Stormy Day

One day, late in the autumn, my master had a long journey to go on business. I was put into the dog-cart, and John went with his master. I always liked to go in the dog-cart, it was so light, and the high wheels ran along so pleasantly. There had been a great deal of rain, and now the wind was very high

and blew the dry leaves across the road in a shower. We went merrily along till we came to the toll-bar and the low wooden bridge. The river banks were rather high and the bridge, instead of rising, went across just level, so that in the middle, if the river was full, the water would be nearly up to the woodwork and planks; but as there were good substantial rails on each side, people did not mind it.

The man at the gate said the river was rising fast, and he feared it would be a bad night. Many of the meadows were under water, and in one low part of the road the water was half-way up to my knees; the bottom was good, and master drove gently, so it was no matter.

When we got to the town, of course I had a good bait; but as the master's business engaged him a long time, we did not start for home till rather late in the afternoon. The wind was then much higher, and I heard the master say to John he had never been out in such a storm; and so I thought, as we went along the skirts of a wood, where the great branches were swaying about like twigs, and the rushing sound of the wind through the trees was terrible.

"I wish we were well out of this wood," said my master.

"Yes, sir," said John, "it would be rather awkward if one of these branches came down upon us."

The words were scarcely out of his mouth, when there was a groan, a crack, and a splitting sound, and tearing, crashing down amongst the other trees, came an oak, torn up by the roots, which fell right across the road just before us. I will never say I was not frightened, for I was. I stopped still, and I believe I trembled. Of course, I did not turn round or run away; I was not brought up to do that. John jumped out and in a moment was at my head.

"That was a very near touch," said my master. "What's to be done now?"

"Well, sir, we can't drive over that tree nor yet get round it; there will be nothing for it but to go back to the four cross-ways, and that will be a good six miles before we get round to the wooden bridge again. It will make us late, but the horse is fresh."

So back we went, and round by the cross roads; but by the time we got to the bridge, it was very nearly dark, and we could just see that the water was over the middle of it; but as that happened sometimes when the floods were out, master did not stop.

We were going along at a good pace, but the moment my feet touched the first part of the bridge, I felt sure there was something wrong. I dare not go forward, and so I made a dead stop. "Go on Beauty," said my master, giving me a touch with the whip; but I dare not stir. He gave me a sharp cut; I jumped, but I dared not go forward.

"There's something wrong, sir," said John; and he sprang out of the dog-cart and came to my head and looked all about. He tried to lead me forward. "Come on, Beauty, what's the matter?" Of course I could not tell him, but I knew very well that the bridge was not safe.

Just then the man at the toll-gate on the other side ran out of the house, tossing a torch about like one mad.

"Hoy, hoy, hoy, halloo, stop!" he cried.

"What's the matter?" shouted my master.

"The bridge is broken in the middle, and part of it is carried away; if you come on you'll be into the river."

"Thank God!" said my master. "You Beauty!" said John; and taking the bridle he gently turned me round to the right-hand road by the river side. The sun had set some time, the wind seemed to have lulled off after that furious blast which tore up the tree. It grew darker and darker, and more and more still. I trotted quietly along, the wheels hardly making a sound on the soft road.

James Howard

One morning, early in December, John had just led me into my box after my daily exercise, and was strapping my cloth on. James was coming in from the corn-chamber with some oats, when the master came into the stable. He looked rather serious, and held an open letter in his hand. John fastened the door of my box, touched his cap, and waited for orders.

"Good morning, John," said the master; "I want to know if you have any complaint to make of James?"

"Complaint, sir? No, sir."

"Is he industrious at his work and respectful to you?"

"Yes, sir, always."

"You never find he slights his work when your back is turned?"

"Never, sir."

"James, my lad," said the master, "set down the oats and come here. I am very glad to find that John's opinion of your character agrees so exactly with my own. John is a cautious man," he said, with a droll smile, "and it is not always easy to get his opinion about people; so I thought if I beat the bush on this side, the birds would fly out, and I should learn what I wanted to know quickly; so now we will come to business.

"I have a letter from my brother-in-law, Sir Clifford Williams of Clifford Hall. He wants me to find him a trustworthy young groom, about twenty or twenty-one, who knows his business.

"How old are you, James?" said master.

"Nineteen next May, sir."

"That's young. What do you think, John?"

"Well, sir, it is young; but he is as steady as a man, strong, and well grown; and though he has not had much experience in driving, he has a light, firm hand, a quick eye, and is very careful. I am quite sure no horse of his will be ruined for want of having his feet and shoes looked after."

In a few days after this conversation, it was fully settled that James should go to Clifford Hall in a month or six weeks as it best suited his master, and in the meantime he was to get all the practice in driving that could be given him.

I never knew the carriage go out so often before. When the mistress did not go out, the master usually drove himself in the two-wheeled chaise; but now, whether it was master or the young ladies who wanted to go out, or whether it was only an errand had to be done, Ginger and I were put into the carriage and James drove us. At first, John rode with him on the box, telling him this and that, and afterwards James drove alone.

The Old Ostler

My master and mistress decided to pay a visit to some friends who lived about forty-six miles from our home, and James was to drive them. The first day we travelled thirty-two miles; there were some long, heavy hills, but James drove so carefully and thoughtfully that we were not at all harassed. He never forgot to put on the drag as we went downhill, nor to take it off at the right place. He kept our feet on the smoothest part of the road; and if the uphill was very long, he set the wheels a little across the road so that the carriage should not run back, and gave us breathing time.

We stopped once or twice on the road; and just as the sun was going down, we reached the town where we were to spend the night. We stopped at the principal hotel, a very large one in the Market Place. We drove under an archway into a long yard, at the further end of which were the stables and coach-houses. Two ostlers came to take us out. The head ostler was a pleasant, active little man, with a crooked leg and a yellow striped waistcoat. I never saw a man unbuckle harness so quickly as he did; and then with a pat and a good word he led me to a long stable with six or eight stalls in it and two or three horses. The other man brought Ginger—

James stood by whilst we were rubbed down and cleaned.

I never was cleaned so lightly and quickly as by that little old man. When he had done, James stepped up and felt me over, as if he thought I could not be thoroughly done; but he found my coat as clean and smooth as silk.

"Well," he said, "I thought I was pretty quick, and our John quicker still, but you do beat all I ever saw for being quick and thorough at the same time."

"Practice makes perfect," said the crooked little ostler, "and 'twould be a pity if it didn't. Forty years' practice, and not perfect! Ha! ha! that would be a pity. As to being quick, why, bless you, that is only a matter of habit. If you get into the habit of being quick, it is just as easy as being slow—easier I should say. In fact, it does not agree with my health to be hulking about over a job twice as long as it need take. Bless you! I couldn't whistle if I crawled over my work as some folks do.

"You see, I have been about horses ever since I was twelve years old, in hunting stables and racing stables. Being small, you see, I was a jockey for several years; but at the Goodwood the turf was very slippery and my poor Larkspur got a fall, and I broke my knee; and so of course I was of no more use there.

"But I could not live without horses, of course I couldn't, so I took to the hotels; and I can tell you it is a downright pleasure to handle an animal like this; well-bred, well mannered, well-cared-for. Bless you! I can tell how a horse is treated. Give me the handling of a horse for twenty minutes, and I'll tell you what sort of a groom he has had.

"Look at this one, pleasant, quiet, turns about just as you want him to do, holds up his feet to be cleaned out, or anything else you please to wish. Then you'll find another, fidgety, fretful, won't move the right way, or starts across the stall, tosses up his head as soon as you come near him, lays back his ears, and seems afraid of you, or else squares about at you with his heels.

"Poor things! I know what sort of treatment they have had. If they are timid, the treatment makes them vicious or dangerous; their tempers are mostly made when they are young. Bless you! They are like children; train 'em up in the way they should go, as the good Book says, and when they are old they will not depart from it—if they have a chance, that is."

The Fire

Later on in the evening, a traveller's horse was
brought in by the second ostler, and whilst he was
cleaning him, a young man with a pipe in his mouth
lounged into the stable to gossip.

"I say, Towler," said the ostler to him, "just run
up the ladder into the loft and bring down some hay
into this horse's rack, will you? Only first lay down
your pipe."

"All right," said the other, and went up through
the trap door; and I heard him step across the floor
overhead and put down the hay. James came in to
look at us the last thing, and then the door was
locked.

I cannot say how long I had slept, nor what time in the night it was, but I woke up feeling very uncomfortable, though I hardly knew why. I got up: the air seemed all thick and choking. I heard Ginger coughing, and one of the other horses moved about restlessly. It was quite dark, and I could see nothing; but the stable was full of smoke, and I hardly knew how to breathe.

The trap door had been left open, and I thought that was the place from which the smoke came. I listened and heard a soft, rushing sort of noise, and a low crackling and snapping. I did not know what it was, but there was something in the sound so strange that it made me tremble all over. The other horses were now all awake; some were pulling at their halters, others were stamping.

At last I heard steps outside, and the ostler who had put up the traveller's horse burst into the stable with a lantern, and began to untie the horses, and try to lead them out; but he seemed in such a hurry, and was so frightened himself, that he frightened me still more. The first horse would not go with him; he tried the second and third, but they too would not stir. He came to me next and tried to drag me out of the stall by force; of course that was no use. He tried us all by turns and then left the stable.

No doubt we were very foolish, but danger seemed to be all round; there was nobody whom we knew to trust in, and all was strange and uncertain. The fresh air that had come in through the open door made it easier to breathe, but the rushing sound overhead grew louder, and as I looked upward, through the bars of my empty rack, I saw a red light flickering on the wall. Then I heard a cry of "Fire!" outside, and the old ostler came quietly and quickly in. He got one horse out, and went to another; but the flames were playing round the trap door, and the roaring overhead was dreadful.

The next thing I heard was James's voice, quiet and cheery, as it always was.

"Come, my beauties, it is time for us to be off, so wake up and come along." I stood nearest the door, so he came to me first, patting me as he came in.

"Come, Beauty, on with your bridle, my boy, we'll soon be out of this smother." It was on in no time; then he took the scarf off his neck, and tied it lightly over my eyes and, patting and coaxing, he led me out of the stable. Safe in the yard, he slipped the scarf off my eyes, and shouted, "Here, somebody! Take this horse while I go back for the other."

A tall, broad man stepped forward and took me, and James darted back into the stable. I set up a shrill whinny as I saw him go. Ginger told me afterwards that whinny was the best thing I could have done for her, for had she not heard me outside, she would never have had courage to come out.

At first no one could guess how the fire had been caused; but at last a man said he saw Dick Towler go into the stable with a pipe in his mouth, and when he came out he had not one, and went to the tap for another.

James said the roof and floor had all fallen in, and that only the black walls were standing. The two poor horses that could not be got out were buried under the burnt rafters and tiles.

John Manly's Talk

The rest of our journey was very easy, and a little after sunset we reached the house of my master's friend. We were taken into a clean, snug stable, where there was a kind coachman, who made us very comfortable. He seemed to think a great deal of James when he heard about the fire.

"There is one thing quite clear, young man," he said. "Your horses know whom they can trust. It is one of the hardest things in the world to get horses out of a stable when there is either fire or flood. I don't know why they won't come out, but they won't —not one in twenty."

We stopped two or three days at this place and then returned home. All went well on the journey: we were glad to be in our own stable again, and John was equally glad to see us.

Before James and he left us for the night, James said, "I wonder who is coming in my place."

"Little Joe Green at the Lodge," said John.

"Little Joe Green! Why, he's a child!"

The next day Joe came to the stables to learn all he could before James left. He learned to sweep the stable, to bring in the straw and hay, and began to clean the harness, and help to wash the carriage. As he was quite too short to do anything in the way of grooming Ginger and me, James taught him upon Merrylegs, for, under John, he was to have full charge of the pony. He was a nice little bright fellow, and always came whistling to his work.

Merrylegs was a good deal put out at being "mauled about," as he said, "by a boy who knew nothing"; but towards the end of the second week he told me confidentially that he thought the boy would turn out well.

At last the day came when James had to leave us; cheerful as he always was, he looked quite down-hearted that morning.

"You see," he said to John, "I am leaving a great deal behind—my mother and Betsy, you, a good master and mistress, and the horses and my old Merrylegs. At the new place there will not be a soul I shall know. If it were not that I shall get a higher place, and be able to help my mother better, I don't think I should have made up my mind to it; it is a real pinch, John."

"Ay, James, lad, so it is, but I should not think much of you if you could leave your home for the first time and not feel it. Cheer up! you'll make friends there, and if you get on well—as I am sure you will—it will be a fine thing for your mother, and she will be proud enough that you have got into such a good place as that."

So John cheered him up, but everyone was sorry to lose James. As for Merrylegs, he pined after James for several days, and went quite off his appetite. So when he exercised me, John took him out several mornings with a leading rein, and trotting and galloping by my side he got up the little fellow's spirits again, and Merrylegs was soon all right.

Joe's father, Thomas, would often come in and give a little help, as he understood the work, and Joe took a great deal of pains to learn, and John was quite encouraged about him.

Going for the Doctor

One night, a few days after James had left, I had eaten my hay and was lying down in my straw fast asleep, when I was suddenly awakened by the stable bell ringing very loudly. I heard the door of John's house opened and his feet running up to the Hall. He was back again in no time. He unlocked the stable door and came in, calling out, "Wake up, Beauty, you must go well now, if ever you did!" and almost before I could think, he had placed the saddle on my back and the bridle on my head. He just ran round for his coat, and then took me at a quick trot up to the Hall door. The Squire stood there with the lamp in his hand.

"Now, John," he said, "ride for your life—that is,

for your mistress's life; there is not a moment to lose. Give this note to Doctor White. Give your horse a rest at the inn, and be back as soon as you can."

John said, "Yes, sir," and was on my back in a minute.

There was before us a long piece of level road by the riverside. John said to me, "Now, Beauty, do your best," and so I did; I wanted neither whip nor spur, and for two miles I galloped as fast as I could lay feet to the ground.

The air was frosty, the moon bright, and it was very pleasant. We went through a village, through a dark wood, then uphill, then downhill, till after an eight miles' run we came to the town. On through the streets we went and into the Market Place. All was quite still except for the clatter of my feet on the stones—everybody was asleep. The church clock struck three as we drew up at Doctor White's door.

John rang the bell twice, and then knocked at the door like thunder. A window was thrown up, and Doctor White, in his nightcap, put his head out and said, "What do you want?"

"Mrs Gordon is very ill, sir; master wants you to come at once; he thinks she will die if you cannot get there—here is a note."

"Wait," he said, "I will come."

He shut the window and was soon at the door.

"The worst of it is," he said, "that my horse has been out all day and is quite done up; my son has just been sent for and he has taken the other. What is to be done? Can I have your horse?"

"He has come at a gallop nearly all the way, sir, and I was to give him a rest here, but I think my master would not be against it if you think fit, sir."

"All right," he said, "I will soon be ready."

I will not describe our way back; the doctor was a heavier man than John, and not so good a rider; however, I did my best.

I was glad to get home; my legs shook under me, and I could only stand and pant. I had not a dry hair on my body, the water ran down my legs, and I steamed all over—Joe used to say, like a pot on the fire. Poor Joe! he was young and small, and as yet he knew very little, and his father, who would have helped him, had been sent to the next village; but I am sure he did the very best he knew.

He rubbed my legs and my chest, but he did not put my warm cloth on me; he thought I was so hot I should not like it. Then he gave me a pailful of water to drink. It was cold, and very good, and I drank it all; then he gave me some hay and some corn, and thinking he had done right, he went away.

Soon I began to shake and tremble, and turned deadly cold; my legs, loins and chest ached, and I felt sore all over. Oh! how I wished for my warm, thick cloth as I stood and trembled. I wished for John, but he had eight miles to walk, so I lay down in my straw and tried to go to sleep.

After a long while I heard John at the door; I gave a low moan, for I was in great pain. He was at my side in a moment, stooping down by me. I could not tell him how ill I felt; but he seemed to know it all. He covered me up with two or three warm cloths, and then ran to the house for some hot water; then

he made me some warm gruel, which I drank; then, I think I went to sleep.

I was now very ill; a strong inflammation had attacked my lungs, and I could not draw my breath without pain. John nursed me night and day. He would get up two or three times in the night to come to me; my master, too, often came to see me. "My poor Beauty," he said one day, "my good horse, you saved your mistress's life! Yes, you saved her life."

Only Ignorance

I do not know how long I was ill. Mr Bond, the horse doctor, came every day. One day he bled me, and John held a pail for the blood. I felt very faint after it, and thought I should die. I believe they all thought so, too.

Ginger and Merrylegs had been moved into the other stable, so that I might be quiet, for the fever made me very quick of hearing; any little noise seemed quite loud, and I could tell everyone's footstep going to and from the house. I knew all that was going on. One night John had to give me a draught; Thomas Green came in to help him.

After I had taken it and John had made me as comfortable as he could, he said he should stay half an hour to see how the medicine settled. Thomas said he would stay with him, so they went and sat down on a bench that had been brought into Merrylegs' stall, and put down the lantern at their feet that I might not be disturbed with the light.

For a while both men sat silent, and then Tom Green said in a low voice:

"I wish, John, you'd say a bit of a kind word to my poor son Joe; the boy is quite broken-hearted; he can't eat his meals, and he can't smile. He says he knows it was all his fault, though he is sure he did the best he knew; and he says, if Beauty dies, no one will ever speak to him again. It goes to my heart to

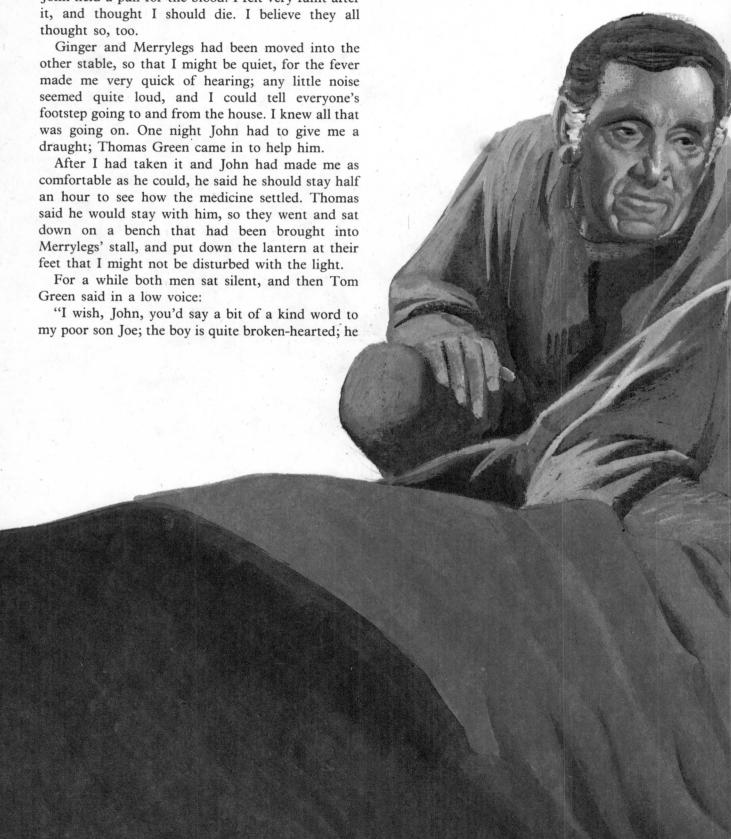

hear him; I think you might give him just a word, he is not a bad boy."

After a short pause, John said slowly: "You must not be too hard upon me, Tom. I know he meant no harm; I never said he did. I know he is not a bad boy, but you see I am sore myself. That horse is the pride of my heart, to say nothing of his being such a favourite with the master and mistress; and to think that his life may be flung away in this manner is more than I can bear. But if you think I am hard on the boy, I will try to give him a good word tomorrow —that is, I mean, if Beauty is better."

"Well, John! thank you, I knew you did not wish to be too hard, and I am glad you see it was only ignorance."

John's voice almost startled me as he answered, "Only ignorance! Only ignorance! How can you talk about only ignorance? Don't you know that ignorance is the worst thing in the world, next to wickedness?—and which does the most mischief Heaven only knows. If people can say, 'Oh! I did not know, I did not mean any harm,' they think it is all right."

I heard no more of this conversation, for the medicine took effect and sent me to sleep, and in the morning I felt much better; but I often thought of John's words when I came to know more of the world.

Joe Green

Joe Green went on very well; he learned quickly, and was so attentive and careful that John began to trust him in many things; but, as I have said, he was small for his age, and it was seldom that he was allowed to exercise either Ginger or me. But it so happened one morning that John was out with Justice in the luggage cart, and the master wanted a note to be taken immediately to a gentleman's house about three miles distant, and sent his orders for Joe to saddle me and take it, adding the caution that he was to ride carefully.

The note was delivered, and we were quietly returning till we came to the brickfield. Here we saw a cart heavily laden with bricks. The wheels had stuck fast in the stiff mud of some deep ruts; and the carter was shouting and flogging the two horses unmercifully. Joe pulled up. It was a sad sight. There were the two horses straining and struggling with all their might to drag the cart out, but they could not move it. The sweat streamed from their legs and flanks, their sides heaved, and every muscle was strained, whilst the man, fiercely pulling at the head of the forehorse, swore and lashed most brutally.

"Hold hard," said Joe, "don't go on flogging the horses like that; the wheels are so stuck that they cannot move the cart." The man took no heed, but continued to lash his horses.

"Stop! pray stop," said Joe; "I'll help you to lighten the cart, they can't move it now."

"Mind your own business, you impudent young rascal, and I'll mind mine." The man was in a towering passion and the worse for drink; and so he laid on the whip again. Helplessly, Joe galloped back home.

"Why, what's the matter with you, Joe? You look angry all over," said John, as the boy flung himself from the saddle.

"I am angry all over, I can tell you," said the boy, and then in hurried excited words he told all that had happened. Joe was usually so quiet and gentle that it was wonderful to see him so roused.

They were just going home to dinner when the footman came down to the stable to say that Joe was wanted directly in master's private room; there was a man brought up for ill-using horses, and Joe's evidence was wanted. The boy flushed up to his forehead, and his eyes sparkled. "They shall have it," said he.

It was wonderful what a change had come over Joe. John laughed, and said he had grown taller in that week; and I believe he had. He was just as kind and gentle as before, but there was more purpose and determination in all that he did—as if he had jumped at once from a boy into a man.

The Parting

I had now lived in this happy place three years, but sad changes were about to come over us. We heard from time to time that our mistress was ill. The Doctor was often at the house, and the master looked grave and anxious. Then we heard that she must leave her home at once and go to a warm country for two or three years. The news fell upon the household like the tolling of a death-bell. Everybody was sorry; but the master began directly to make arrangements for breaking up his establishment and leaving England. We used to hear it talked about in our stable; indeed, nothing else was talked about.

John went about his work silent and sad, and Joe scarcely whistled. There was a great deal of coming and going; Ginger and I had full work.

The first to go were Miss Jessie and Miss Flora with their governess. They came to bid us goodbye. They hugged poor Merrylegs like an old friend, and so indeed he was. Then we heard what had been been arranged for us. Master had sold Ginger and me to his old friend the Earl of W———, for he thought we should have a good place there. Merrylegs he had given to the Vicar, who was wanting a pony for Mrs Blomefield; but it was on the condition that he should never be sold, and that when he was past work he should be shot and buried.

Joe was engaged to take care of him and to help in the house; so I thought that Merrylegs was well off. John had the offer of several good places, but he said he should wait a little and look round.

Earlshall

The next morning after breakfast, Joe put Merrylegs into the mistress's low chaise to take him to the Vicarage. He came first and said goodbye to us, and Merrylegs neighed to us from the yard. Then John put the saddle on Ginger and the leading rein on me, and rode us across the country about fifteen miles to Earlshall Park, where the Earl of W——— lived.

We went into the yard through a stone gateway, and John asked for Mr York. It was some time before he came. He was a fine-looking, middle-aged man, and his voice said at once that he expected to be obeyed. He was very friendly and polite to John; and after giving us a slight look, he called a groom to take us to our boxes, and invited John to take some refreshment.

We were taken to a light, airy stable and placed in

boxes adjoining each other, where we were rubbed down and fed. In about half an hour John and Mr York, who was to be our new coachman, came in to see us.

Afterwards John came to say goodbye. He came round to each of us to pat and speak to us for the last time; his voice sounded very sad.

I held my face close to him, as that was all I could do to say goodbye; and then he was gone, and I have never seen him since.

The next day Lord W——— came to look at us; he seemed pleased with our appearance.

"I have great confidence in these horses," he said, "from the character my friend Mr Gordon has given me of them. Of course, they are not a match in colour, but my idea is that they will do very well for the carriage whilst we are in the country. Before we go to London I must try to match Baron; the black horse, I believe, is perfect for riding."

At three o'clock we were at the door. We heard the silk dress rustle as the lady came down the steps, and in an imperious voice she said, "York, you must put those horses' heads higher; they are not fit to be seen."

York got down and said very respectfully, "I beg your pardon, my lady, but these horses have not been reined up for three years, and my lord said it would be safer to bring them to it by degrees; but if your ladyship pleases, I can take them up a little more."

"Do so," she said.

York came round to our heads and shortened the rein one hole, I think; every little makes a difference, be it for better or worse, and that day we had a steep hill to go up. Then I began to understand what I had heard. Of course, I wanted to put my head forward and take the carriage up with a will, as we had been used to do; but no, I had now to pull with my head up, and that took all the spirit out of me, and brought the strain on my back and legs.

Day by day, hole by hole, our bearing reins were shortened, and instead of looking forward with pleasure to having my harness put on as I used to do, I began to dread it. Ginger, too, seemed restless, though she said very little. At last I thought the worst was over; for several days there had been no more shortening, and I determined to make the best of it and to do my duty, though now going out was a constant harass instead of a pleasure; but the worst was yet to come.

A Strike for Liberty

One day my lady came down later than usual, and the silk rustled more than ever.

"Drive to the Duchess of B———'s," she said. Then, after a pause, she added, "Are you never going to get those horses' heads up, York? Raise them at once, and let us have no more of this humouring nonsense."

York came to me first, whilst the groom stood at Ginger's head. He drew my head back and fixed the rein so tight that it was almost intolerable; then he went to Ginger, who was impatiently jerking her head up and down against the bit, as was her way now. She had a good idea of what was coming, and the moment York took the rein off the terret in order to shorten it, she took her opportunity and reared up so suddenly that York had his nose roughly hit and his hat knocked off, and the groom was nearly thrown off his legs.

At once they both flew to her head, but she was a match for them, and went on plunging, rearing and kicking in a most desperate manner. At last she kicked right over the carriage pole and fell down, after giving me a severe blow on my near quarter.

There is no knowing what further mischief she may have done had not York promptly sat himself down flat on her head to prevent her struggling, at the same time calling out, "Unbuckle the black horse! Run for the winch and unscrew the carriage pole; and somebody cut the trace if you can't unhitch it."

One of the footmen ran for the winch, and another brought a knife from the house. The groom set me free from Ginger and the carriage, and led me to my box. He just turned me in as I was, and ran back to York.

Before long, however, Ginger was led in by two grooms, a good deal knocked about and bruised. York came with her and gave his orders, and then came to look at me. In a moment he let down my head.

"Confound these bearing reins!" he said to himself. "I thought we should have some mischief soon."

Ginger was never put into the carriage again, but when her bruises were healed, one of Lord W———'s younger sons said he should like to have her; he was sure she would make a good hunter. As for me, I was obliged still to go in the carriage, and had a fresh partner, called Max, who had always been used to the tight rein. I asked him how it was he bore it.

"Well," he said, "I bear it because I must, but it is shortening my life, and it will shorten yours too if you have to stick to it."

What I suffered for four long months with that rein it would be hard to describe; but I am quite sure that, had it lasted much longer, either my health or my temper would have given way. Before that, I never knew what it was to foam at the mouth; but now the action of the sharp bit on my tongue and jaw, and the constrained position of my head and throat, always caused me to froth more or less at the mouth.

In my old home I always knew that John and my master were my friends; but here, although in many ways I was well treated, I had no friend. York might have known, and very likely did know, how that rein harassed me; but I suppose he took it as a matter of course that could not be helped; at any rate, nothing was done to relieve me.

Reuben Smith

I must now say a little about Reuben Smith, the other coachman, who was left in charge of the stables when York went to London. No one more thoroughly understood his business than he did, and when he was all right, there could not be a more faithful or valuable man. He was gentle and very clever in his management of horses, and could doctor them almost as well as a farrier, for he had lived two years with a veterinary surgeon. He was a first-rate driver, and could take a four-in-hand, or a tandem, as easily as a pair.

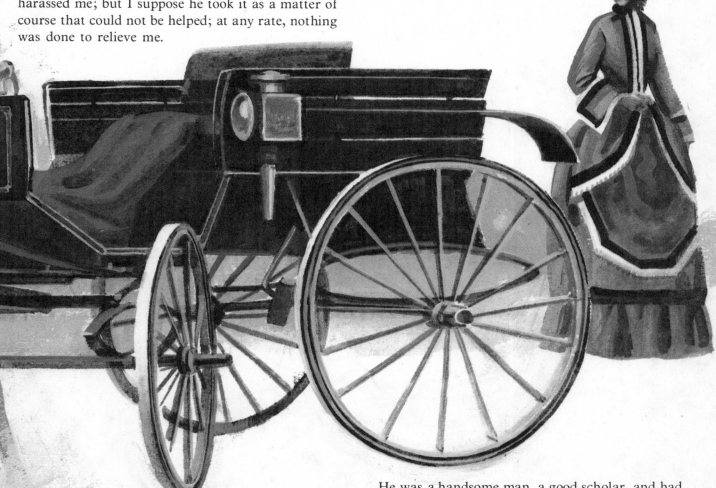

He was a handsome man, a good scholar, and had very pleasant manners. I believe everybody liked him; certainly the horses did. The only wonder was that he should be in an under situation, and not in the place of a head coachman like York: but he had one great fault—the love of drink. He was not like some men, always at it; he used to keep steady for weeks or months together; but then he would break out and have a "bout" of it, as York called it, and be a disgrace to himself, a terror to his wife, and a nuisance to all that had to do with him. He was, however, so useful that two or three times York had hushed the matter up and kept it from the Earl's knowledge.

It was now early in April, and the family was expected home some time in May. The light brougham was to be fresh done up, and as Colonel Blantyre, a cousin who had been staying at the Hall, was obliged to return to his regiment, it was arranged that Smith should drive him to the town in it, and then ride back; for this purpose he took the saddle with him, and I was chosen for the journey.

At the station the Colonel put some money into Smith's hand and bade him goodbye.

We left the carriage at the maker's, and Smith drove me to the 'White Lion', and ordered the ostler to feed me well and have me ready for him at four o'clock. A nail in one of my front shoes had loosened as I came along, but the ostler did not notice it till just about four o'clock. Smith did not come into the yard till five, and then he said he should not leave till six, as he had met with some old friends. The man then told him of the nail, and asked if he should have the shoe looked to.

"No," said Smith, "that will be all right till we get home."

He spoke in a very loud, offhand way, and I thought it was very unlike him not to see about the shoe, as he was generally wonderfully particular about loose nails in our shoes. He came neither at six, seven, nor eight, and it was nearly nine o'clock before he called me; and then it was with a loud, rough voice. He seemed in a very bad temper and abused the ostler, though I could not tell what for.

If Smith had been in his right senses, he would have been sensible of something wrong in my pace; but he was too madly drunk to notice that I had lost one of my shoes.

Beyond the turnpike was a long piece of road, upon which some fresh stones had just been laid—large, sharp stones, over which no horse could be

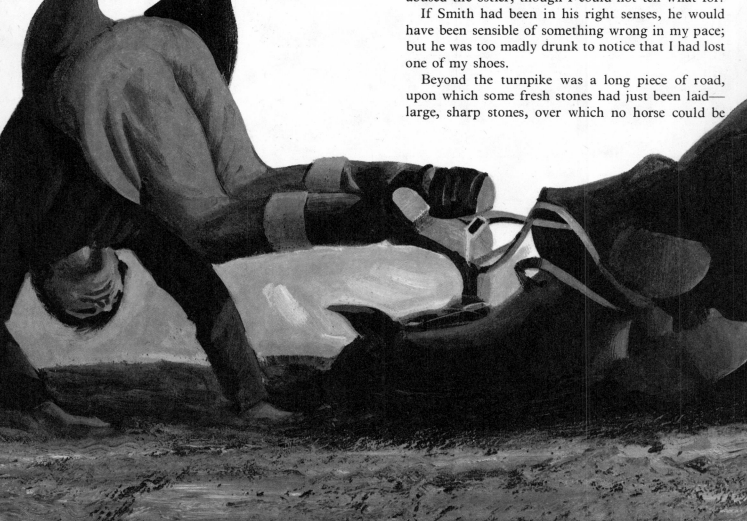

driven quickly without risk of danger. Over this road, with one shoe gone, I was forced to gallop at my utmost speed, my rider meanwhile cutting into me with his whip, and with wild curses urging me to go still faster. Of course my shoeless foot suffered dreadfully; the hoof was broken and split down to the quick, and the inside was terribly cut by the sharpness of the stones.

This could not go on; no horse could keep his footing under such circumstances as the pain was too great. I stumbled, and fell with violence on both my knees. Smith was flung off by my fall and, owing to the speed at which I was going, he must have fallen with great force. I soon recovered my feet and limped to the side of the road, where it was free from stones.

The moon had just risen above the hedge, and by its light I could see Smith lying a few yards beyond me. After making one slight effort to rise, there was a heavy groan. He did not move. I could have groaned too, for I was suffering intense pain both from my foot and knees; but horses are used to bear their pain in silence. I uttered no sound, but stood there and listened.

How It Ended

It must have been nearly midnight when I heard at a great distance the sound of a horse's feet. Sometimes the sound died away, then it grew clearer again and nearer. The road to Earlshall led through plantations that belonged to the Earl; the sound came in that direction, and I hoped it might be someone coming in search of us. As the sound came nearer and nearer, I was almost sure I could distinguish Ginger's step; a little nearer still, and I could tell she was in the dog-cart. I neighed loudly, and was overjoyed to hear an answering neigh from Ginger and men's voices. They came slowly over the stones, and stopped at the dark figure that lay upon the ground.

One of the men jumped out, and stooped down over it. "It is Reuben!" he said, "and he does not stir."

The other man followed and bent over him. "He's dead," he said; "feel how cold his hands are."

They raised him up, but there was no life, and his hair was soaked with blood. Laying him down again, they came and looked at me and saw my cut knees.

"Hallo! he's bad in his foot as well as his knees. Look here—his hoof is cut all to pieces; he might well come down, poor fellow! I tell you what, Ned, I'm afraid it hasn't been all right with Reuben! Just think of him riding a horse over these stones without a shoe! Why, if he had been in his right senses, he would just as soon have tried to ride him over the moon. I'm afraid it has been the old thing over again."

At last I reached my own box and had some corn; and after Robert had wrapped up my knees in wet cloths, he tied up my foot in a bran poultice to draw out the heat, and to cleanse it before the horse doctor saw it in the morning. Then I managed to get myself down on the straw and slept in spite of the pain.

As Smith's death had been so sudden, and no one was there to see it, there was an inquest held. The landlord and ostler at the 'White Lion', with several other people, gave evidence that he was intoxicated when he started from the inn; the keeper of the toll-gate said he rode at a hard gallop through the gate; and my shoe was picked up amongst the stones; so the case was quite plain to them, and I was cleared of all blame.

Ruined, and Going Downhill

As soon as my knees were sufficiently healed, I was turned into a small meadow for a month or two. No other creature was there, and though I enjoyed the liberty and the sweet grass, yet I had been so long used to society that I felt very lonely. Ginger and I had become fast friends, and now I missed her company extremely.

I often neighed when I heard horses' feet passing in the road, but seldom got an answer; till one morning the gate was opened, and who should come in but poor old Ginger! The man slipped off her halter and left her there. With a joyful whinny I trotted up to her; we were both glad to meet, but I soon found that it was not for our pleasure that she was brought to be with me. Her story would be too long to tell, but the end of it was that she had been ruined by hard riding, and was now turned off to see what rest would do.

"And so," she said, "here we are, ruined in the prime of our youth and strength—you by a drunkard, and I by a fool; it is very hard."

One day we saw the Earl come into the meadow, and York was with him. Seeing who it was, we stood still under our lime-tree, and let them come up to us. They examined us carefully. The Earl seemed much annoyed.

"There is three hundred pounds flung away for no earthly use," said he; "but what I care most for is, that these horses of my old friend, who thought they would find a good home with me, are ruined. The mare shall have a twelve month's run, and we shall see what it will do for her; but the black one must be sold: 'tis a great pity, but I could not have knees like these in my stables."

Through the recommendation of York, I was bought by the master of the livery stables. I had to go by train, a new experience to me, requiring a good deal of courage the first time; but as I found the puffing, rushing, whistling, and more than all, the trembling of the horse-box in which I stood did me no real harm, I soon took it quietly.

When I reached the end of my journey, I found myself in a tolerably comfortable stable and well attended to. I was well fed and well cleaned and, on the whole, I think our master took as much care of us as he could. He kept a good many horses and carriages of different kinds, for hire. Sometimes his own men drove them; at others the horse and chaise were let to gentlemen or ladies who drove themselves.

I did not stay here long, but was soon taken to the horse fair to be sold again.

A Horse Fair

No doubt a horse fair is a very amusing place to those who have nothing to lose; at any rate, there is plenty to see—long strings of young horses out of the country, fresh from the marshes; droves of shaggy little Welsh ponies, no higher than Merrylegs; hundreds of cart horses of all sorts, some of them with their long tails braided up and tied with scarlet cord; and a good many, like myself, handsome and high-bred, but fallen into the middle class through some accident or blemish, unsoundness of wind, or some other complaint.

There were some splendid animals quite in their prime and fit for anything, who were throwing out their legs and showing off their paces in high style as they were trotted out with a leading rein, the groom running by the side. But round in the background were a number of poor things, sadly broken down with hard work, their knees knuckling over, and their hind legs swinging out at every step; some were very dejected-looking old horses, with the upper lip hanging down and the ears lying back heavily, as if there was no pleasure in life and no more hope; again, some were so thin you could see all their ribs; and some had old sores on their backs and hips. These were sad sights for a horse who knows not but that he may come to the same sad state.

There was a great deal of bargaining, running up and beating down; and if a horse may speak his mind so far as he understands, I should say there were more lies told and more trickery carried on at that horse fair than a clever man could give account of.

There was one man of whom I thought that if he would buy me I should be happy. He was not a gentleman, nor yet one of the loud, flashy sort that called themselves so. He was a rather small man, but well made, and quick in all his motions. I knew in a moment by the way he handled me that he was used to horses; he spoke gently, and his grey eye had a kindly, cheery look in it. It may seem strange—but it is true all the same—that the clean, fresh smell there was about him made me take to him. There was no smell of old beer and tobacco, which I hated, but a fresh smell as if he had come out of a hay-loft.

He offered twenty-three pounds for me; but that was refused.

"Well, old chap," he said, "I think we should suit each other. I'll give twenty-four for him."

"Say twenty-five and you shall have him."

"Twenty-four ten," said my friend, in a very decided tone, "and not another sixpence—yes or no?"

"Done," said the salesman, "and you may depend upon it there's a monstrous deal of quality in that horse, and if you want him for cab work, he's a bargain."

The money was paid on the spot, and my new master took my halter and led me out of the fair to an inn, where he had a saddle and bridle ready. He gave me a good feed of oats, and stood by whilst I ate it, talking to himself and talking to me. Half an hour after we were on our way to London. We reached the great city at twilight and soon turned up one of the side streets. About half-way up we turned again into a very narrow one, with rather poor-looking houses on one side and what seemed to be coach-houses and stables on the other.

My owner pulled up at one of the houses and whistled. The door flew open, and a young woman, followed by a little girl and boy, ran out. There was a very lively greeting as my rider dismounted.

"Now then, Harry, my boy, open the gates, and mother will bring us the lantern."

The next minute they were all standing round me in a small stable yard.

"Is he gentle, father?"

"Yes, Dolly, as gentle as your own kitten; come and pat him. We'll call him Jack, after the old one, shall we, Dolly?"

At once the little hand was patting about fearlessly all over my shoulder. How good it felt!

"Let me get him a bran mash while you rub him down," said the mother.

"Do, Polly, it's just what he wants, and I know you've got a beautiful mash ready for me."

"Sausage dumpling and apple turnover," shouted the boy: this set them all laughing. I was led into a comfortable, clean-smelling stall with plenty of dry straw and, after a capital supper, I lay down, thinking I was going to be happy.

A London Cab Horse

My new master's name was Jeremiah Barker, but as every one called him Jerry, I shall do the same.

Jerry had a cab of his own and two horses, which he drove and attended to himself. His other horse was a tall, white, rather large-boned animal, called Captain. He was fairly old now, but when he was young he must have been splendid; there was still the proud way of holding his head and arching his neck; in fact, he was a high-bred, fine mannered, noble old horse, every bit of him. He told me that in his early youth he went to the Crimean War, for he belonged to an officer in the cavalry, and used to lead the regiment. He said he quite enjoyed the training with all the other horses—trotting together, turning together to the right hand or the left, halting at the word of command, or dashing forward at full speed at the sound of the trumpet or signal of the officer.

When young, he was a dark, dappled iron grey, and was considered very handsome. His master, a young, high-spirited gentleman, was very fond of him, and from the first treated him with the greatest care and kindness. He told me he thought the life of an army horse was very pleasant; but when it came to being sent abroad in a great ship over the sea, he almost changed his mind.

"But what about the fighting?" said I; "was not that worse than anything else?"

"Well," said he, "I hardly know. We always liked to hear the trumpet sound, and to be called out, and were impatient to start off, though sometimes we had to stand for hours, waiting for the word of command. But when the word was given, we used to spring forward as gaily and eagerly as if there were no cannon-balls, bayonets or bullets. I believe so long as we felt our rider firm in the saddle, and his hand steady on the bridle, not one of us gave way to fear, not even when the terrible bombshells whirled through the air and burst into a thousand pieces.

"With my master, I went into many actions without a wound; and though I saw horses shot down with bullets, others pierced through with lances or gashed with fearful sabre-cuts, though I left them dead on the field, or dying in the agony of their wounds, I don't think I feared for myself. My master's cheery voice as he encouraged his men made me feel as if he and I could not be killed. I had such perfect trust in him that whilst he was guiding me, I was ready to charge up to the very cannon's mouth.

"Do you know what they fought about?" said I.

"No," said he, "that is more than a horse can understand; but the enemy must have been awfully wicked people if it was right to go all the way over the sea on purpose to kill them."

Jerry Barker

I never knew a better man than my new master —
kind and good, as strong for the right as John
Manly, and so good-tempered and merry that very
few people could pick a quarrel with him. He was
very fond of making little songs, which he would sing
to himself. His favourite was this:

"Come, father and mother,
And sister and brother,
Come, all of you, turn to
And help one another."

And so they did; Harry was as clever at stable-
work as a much older boy, and always wanted to do
what he could. Then Polly and Dolly used to come in
the morning to help with the cab—to brush and beat
the cushions and rub the glass, while Jerry was
giving us a cleaning in the yard and Harry was
cleaning the harness. There used to be a great deal
of laughing and fun between them, and it put
Captain and me in much better spirits than if we had
heard scolding and hard words.

Although Jerry was steadfastly set against hard
driving to please careless people, he always went at
a good fair pace, and was not against putting on the
steam, as he said, if only he knew why.

Poor Ginger

One day, whilst our cab and many others were waiting outside one of the parks where a band was playing, a shabby old cab drove up beside ours. The horse was an old worn out chestnut with an ill-kept coat, and with bones that showed plainly through it. The knees knuckled over, and the forelegs were very unsteady.

I had been eating some hay, and the wind rolling a little lock of it that way, the poor creature put out her long, thin neck and picked it up, and then turned round and looked about for more. There was a hopeless look in the dull eye that I could not help noticing; and then, as I was thinking where I had seen that horse before, she looked full at me and said, "Black Beauty, is that you?"

It was Ginger – but how changed! The beautifully arched and glossy neck was now straight, lank and fallen in; the clean, straight legs and delicate fetlocks were swollen; the joints were grown out of shape with hard work; the face that was once so full of spirit and life was now full of suffering; and I could tell by the heaving of her sides and by her frequent cough how bad her breath was.

Our drivers were standing together a little way off, so I sidled up to her a step or two that we might have a little quiet talk. It was a sad tale that she had to tell.

After a twelve month's run off at Earlshall, she was considered to be fit for work again, and was sold to a gentleman. For a little while she got on very well, but after a longer gallop than usual, the old strain returned and, after being rested and doctored, she was again sold. In this way she changed hands several times, but always getting lower down.

"And so at last," said she, "I was bought by a man who keeps a number of cabs and horses, and lets them out. You look well off, and I am glad of it; but I cannot tell you what my life has been. When they found out my weakness, they said I was not worth what they gave for me, and that I must go into one of the low cabs and just be used up; that is what they are doing – whipping and working me, with never one thought of what I suffer. They paid for me, and must get the money out of me, they say. The man who hires me now pays a deal of money to the owner every day, and so he has to get it out of me first; and so it goes on all the weeks round, with never a Sunday rest."

I said, "You used to stand up for yourself if you were ill-used."

"Ah!" she said, "I did once, but it's no use; men are stronger, and if they are cruel and have no feeling, there is nothing that we can do but just bear it – bear it on and on to the end. I wish the end was come; I wish I was dead. I have seen dead horses, and I am sure they do not suffer pain; I hope I may drop down dead at my work, and not be sent off to the knacker's."

I was very much troubled, and I put my nose up

to hers, but I could say nothing to comfort her. I think she was pleased to see me, for she said, "You are the only friend I ever had."

Just then her driver came up, and with a tug at her mouth backed her out of the line and drove off, leaving me very sad indeed.

A short time after this, a cart with a dead horse in it passed our cab-stand. The head hung out of the cart tail, the lifeless tongue was slowly dripping blood; and the sunken eyes! – but I can't speak of them, the sight was too dreadful. It was a chestnut horse with a long, thin neck. I saw a white streak down the forehead. I believe it was Ginger; I hoped it was, for then her troubles would be over. Oh! if men were more merciful, they would shoot us before we come to such misery.

Jerry's New Year

Christmas and the New Year are very merry times for some people; but for cabmen and cabmen's horses these times are no holiday, though they may be a harvest. There are so many parties, balls and places of amusement open that the work is hard and often late. Sometimes driver and horse, shivering with cold, have to wait for hours in the rain or frost, whilst the merry people within are dancing to the music. I wonder if the beautiful ladies ever think of the weary cabman waiting on his box, and of his patient beast standing till his legs get stiff with cold!

We had a great deal of late work in the Christmas week, and Jerry had a bad cough but, however late we were, Polly sat up for him and, looking anxious and troubled, she came out with the lantern to meet him.

On the evening of the New Year we had to take two gentlemen to a house in one of the West End squares. We set them down at nine o'clock and were told to come again at eleven. "But," said one of them, "as it is a card party, you may have to wait a few minutes, but don't be late."

As the clock struck eleven we were at the door, for Jerry was always punctual. The clock chimed the quarters – one, two, three, and then struck twelve; but the door did not open.

The wind had been very changeable, with squalls of rain during the day, but now it came on sharp, driving sleet, which seemed to come all the way round one; it was very cold, and there was no shelter. Jerry got off his box and came and pulled one of my cloths a little more over my neck; then, stamping his feet, he took a turn or two up and down; then, he began to beat his arms, but that set him on coughing; so he opened the cab door and sat at the bottom with his feet on the pavement, and was thus a little sheltered. Still the clock chimed the quarters, but no one came. At half past twelve he rang the bell, and asked the servant if he would be wanted that night.

"Oh! yes, you'll be wanted safe enough," said the man; "you must not go, it will soon be over." And again Jerry sat down, but his voice was so hoarse I could hardly hear him.

At a quarter past one the door opened, and the two gentlemen came out; they got into the cab without a word, and told Jerry where to drive; it was nearly two miles away. My legs were numb with cold, and I thought I should have stumbled. When the men got out, they never said they were sorry to have kept us waiting so long, but were angry at the charge. However, as Jerry never charged more than was his due, he never took less, and so they had to pay for the two hours and a quarter waiting; but it was hard-earned money to Jerry.

At last we got home. He could hardly speak, and his cough was dreadful. Polly asked no questions, but opened the door and held the lantern for him.

"Can't I do something?" she said.

"Yes; get Jack something warm, and then boil me some gruel."

This was said in a hoarse whisper. He could hardly get his breath, but he gave me a rub down as usual, and even went up into the hay-loft for an extra bundle of straw for my bed. Polly brought me a warm mash that made me comfortable; and then they locked the door.

It was late the next morning before any one came, and then it was only Harry. He cleaned and fed us, and swept out the stalls; then he put the straw back again as if it was Sunday. He was very still, and neither whistled nor sang. At noon he came again and gave us our food and water: this time Dolly came with him. She was crying, and I could gather from what they said that Jerry was dangerously ill, and the doctor said it was a bad case. So two days passed, and there was great trouble indoors. We saw only Harry and sometimes Dolly. I think she came for company, for Polly was always with Jerry, who had to be kept very quiet.

On the third day, whilst Harry was in the stable, a tap came at the door, and kindly Governor Grant came in.

He was a prosperous cab-owner who had a great many horses which were hired out to drivers for so much money per day.

"I wouldn't go to the house, my boy," he said, "but I want to know how your father is."

"He is very bad," said Harry, "he can't be much worse. They call it bronchitis, and the doctor thinks it will turn one way or another tonight."

"That's bad, very bad," said Governor Grant, shaking his head. "I know two men who died of that last week. It takes 'em off in no time; but whilst there's life there's hope, so you must keep up your spirits."

"Yes," said Harry quickly, "and the doctor said that father had a better chance than most men, because he didn't drink. He said yesterday the fever was so high that if father had been a drinking man, it would have burnt him up like a piece of paper; but I believe he thinks he will get over it; don't you think he will, Mr Grant?"

The Governor looked puzzled.

"If there's any rule that good men should get over these things, I am sure he will, my boy. He's the best man I know. I'll look in early tomorrow."

Early next morning, he was there.

"Well?" said he.

"Father is better," said Harry. "Mother hopes he will get over it."

Governor Grant

"Thank God!" said the Governor; "and now you must keep him warm, and keep his mind easy. And that brings me to the horses. You see, Jack will be all the better for the rest of a week or two in a warm stable, and you can easily take him a turn up and down the street to stretch his legs; but this young one, if he does not get work, will soon be all up on end as you may say, and will be rather too much for you; and when he does go out, there'll be an accident."

"He is like that now," said Harry; "I've kept him short of corn, but he's so full of spirit I don't know what to do with him."

"Just so," said Governor Grant. "Now look here. Will you tell your mother that, if she is agreeable, I will come for him every day till something is arranged, and take him for a good spell of work; and whatever he earns, I'll bring your mother half of it, and that will help with the horses' feed. Your father is in a good club, I know, but that won't keep the horses, and they'll be eating their heads off all this time: I'll come at noon to hear what she says"; and without waiting for Harry's thanks, he picked up his coat and was gone.

At noon I think he went and saw Polly, for Harry and he came to the stable together, harnessed Captain, and took him out.

For a week or more he came for Captain, and when Harry thanked him or said anything about his kindness, he laughed it off, saying, it was all good luck for him, for his horses were wanting a little rest which they could not otherwise have had.

Jerry steadily grew better, but the doctor said that he must never go back to the cab-work again if he wished to be an old man. The children had many consultations together about what father and mother would do, and how they could help to earn money to keep the horses.

One afternoon Captain was brought in very wet and dirty.

"The streets are nothing but slush," said the Governor; "it will give you a good warming, my boy, to get him clean and dry."

"All right, Governor," said Harry, "I shall not leave him till he is; you know I have been trained by my father."

"I wish all the boys had been trained like you," said the Governor.

On the Move Again

While Harry was sponging off the mud from Captain's body and legs, Dolly came in, looking very full of something.

"Who lives at Fairstowe, Harry? Mother has got a letter from Fairstowe; she seemed so glad, and ran upstairs to father with it."

"Don't you know? Why, it is the name of Mrs Fowler's place – mother's old mistress, you know – the lady that father met last summer; who sent you and me five shillings each."

"Oh! Mrs Fowler; of course I know all about her. I wonder what on earth she can be writing to mother about."

"Mother wrote to her last week," said Harry. "You know she told father if ever he gave up the cab-work, she would like to know. I wonder what she says; run in and see, Dolly."

Harry scrubbed away at Captain with a "Huish! huish!" like any old ostler.

In a few minutes, Dolly came dancing into the stable.

"Oh, Harry! was there ever anything so beautiful? Mrs Fowler says we are all to go and live near her. There is a cottage now empty that will just suit us, with a garden, a hen-house, apple trees, and everything! Her coachman is going away in the spring, and then she will want father to look after the horses in his place. And there are good families round, where you can get a place in the garden or stable, or as a page-boy; and there's a good school for me. Mother is laughing and crying by turns, and father does look so happy!"

"That's uncommon jolly," said Harry, "and just

the right thing, I should say. It will suit father and mother both; but I don't intend to be a page-boy with tight clothes and rows of buttons. I'll be a groom or a gardener."

It was quickly settled that, as soon as Jerry was well enough, they should remove to the country, and that the cab and horses should be sold as soon as possible.

This was heavy news for me, for I was not young now, and could not look for any improvement in my condition. Since I left Birtwick I had never been so happy as with my dear master, Jerry; but three years of cab-work, even under the best conditions, will tell on one's strength, and I felt that I was not the horse I had been.

Governor Grant said at once that he would take Captain. There were men in the stand who would have bought me; but Jerry said I should not go to cab-work again with just anybody, and the Governor promised to find a place for me where I should be comfortable.

The day came for going away. Jerry had not been allowed to go out yet, and I never saw him after that New Year's Eve. Polly and the children came to bid me goodbye. "Poor old Jack! dear old Jack! I wish we could take you with us," she said; and then, laying her hand on my mane, she put her face close to my neck and kissed me. Dolly was crying and she kissed me, too. Harry stroked me a great deal, but said nothing, only he seemed very sad; and so I was led away to my new place.

Hard Times

I shall never forget my new master. Skinner had a low set of cabs and a low set of drivers; he was hard on the men, and the men were hard on the horses.

My driver was just as hard as his master. My life now was so utterly wretched that I wished I might, like Ginger, drop down dead at my work, and so be out of my misery; and one day my wish very nearly came to pass.

I went on the stand at eight in the morning, and had done a good share of work when we had to take a fare to the railway. A long train was just expected in, so my driver pulled up at the back of some of the outside cabs to take the chance of a return fare. It was a very heavy train, and as all the cabs were soon engaged, ours was called for.

There was a party of four: a noisy, blustering man with a lady, a little boy, a young girl, and a great deal of luggage. The lady and the boy got into the cab, and while the man ordered about the luggage, the young girl came and looked at me.

"Papa," she said, "I am sure this poor horse cannot take us and all our luggage so far; he is so very weak and worn out; do look at him."

'Oh! he's all right, miss," said my driver, "he's strong enough."

The porter, who was pulling about some heavy boxes, suggested to the gentleman that, as there was so much luggage, he should take a second cab.

"Can your horse do it, or can't he?" said the blustering man.

"Oh! he can do it all right, sir. Send up the boxes, porter; he can take more than that." Saying this, he helped to haul up a box so heavy that I could feel the springs go down.

"Papa, papa, do take a second cab," said the young girl in a beseeching tone; "I am sure we are wrong; I am sure it is cruel."

"Nonsense, Grace, get in at once, and don't make all this fuss; a pretty thing it would be if a man of business had to examine every cab-horse before he hired it—the man knows his own business of course: there, get in and hold your tongue!"

My gentle friend had to obey; and box after box was dragged up and lodged on the top of the cab, or settled by the side of the driver. At last all was ready, and with his usual jerk of the rein and slash of the whip, he drove out of the station. I got along fairly till we came to Ludgate Hill; but there, the heavy load and my own exhaustion were too much. I was struggling to keep on, goaded by constant chucks of the rein and use of the whip, when, in a single moment—I cannot tell how—my feet slipped from under me, and I fell heavily to the ground on my side. The suddenness and the force with which I fell seemed to beat all the breath out of my body.

I lay perfectly still; indeed, I had no power to move, and I thought now I was going to die.

Someone came and loosened the throat strap of my bridle, and undid the traces which kept the collar so tight upon me. Someone said, "He's dead, he'll never get up again."

I cannot tell how long I lay there, but I found my life coming back, and a kind-voiced man was patting me and encouraging me to rise. After some cordial had been given me, and after one or two attempts, I staggered to my feet, and was gently led to some stables which were close by. Here I was put into a well-littered stall, and some warm gruel was brought to me: this I drank thankfully.

In the evening I was sufficiently recovered to be led back to Skinner's stables, where I think they did the best for me they could. In the morning Skinner came with a farrier to look at me. He examined me very closely, and said:

"This is a case of overwork more than disease, and if you could give him a run off for six months, he would be able to work again; but now there is not an ounce of strength in him."

"Then he must go to the dogs," said Skinner. "I have no meadows to nurse sick horses in."

"If he was broken-winded," said the farrier, "you had better have had him killed out of hand, but he is not; there is a sale of horses coming off in about ten days; if you rest him and feed him up, he may pick up, and you may at any rate get more than his skin is worth."

Upon this advice Skinner, rather unwillingly, I think, gave orders that I should be well fed and cared for; and the stableman, happily for me, carried out the orders with a much better will than his master had shown in giving them.

Ten days of perfect rest, plenty of good oats, hay, and bran mashes with boiled linseed mixed in them, did more to get up my condition than anything else could have done. Those linseed mashes were delicious, and I began to think that after all it might be better to live than go to the dogs. When the twelfth day after the accident came, I was taken to the sale, a few miles out of London. I felt that any change from my present place must be an improvement; so I held up my head, and hoped for the best.

Farmer Thoroughgood and His Grandson Willie

At this sale, of course, I found myself in company with the old broken-down horses—some lame, some broken-winded, some old, and some that I am sure it would have been merciful to shoot.

Coming from the better part of the fair, I noticed a man who looked a gentleman farmer, with a young boy by his side. He had a broad back and round shoulders, a kind, ruddy face, and he wore a broad-brimmed hat. When he came up to me and my companions, he stood still and gave a pitiful look round upon us. I saw his eye rest on me; I had still a good mane and tail, which did something for my appearance. I pricked my ears and looked at him.

"There's a horse that has known better days."

"Poor old fellow!" said the boy. "Do you think, grandpapa, he was ever a carriage horse?"

"Oh, yes, my boy," said the farmer, coming closer, "He might have been anything when he was young. Look at his nostrils and his ears, and the shape of his neck and shoulders; there's a deal of breeding about that horse." He put out his hand and gave me a kind pat on the neck. I put out my nose in answer to his kindness, and the boy stroked my face.

"Poor old fellow! See, grandpapa, how well he understands kindness. Could you not buy him and make him young again, as you did Ladybird?"

The farmer slowly felt my legs, which were much swollen and strained; then he looked at my mouth— "Thirteen or fourteen, I should say. Just trot him out, will you?"

I arched my poor thin neck, raised my tail a little, and threw out my legs as well as I could, for they were very stiff.

"What is the lowest you will take for him?" said the farmer as I came back.

"Five pounds, sir; that was the lowest price my master set."

I was bought and taken to a large meadow. Perfect rest, good food, soft turf and gentle exercise soon began to tell on my condition and my spirits. I had a good constitution from my mother, and I was never strained when I was young, so that I had a better chance than many horses who have been worked before they came to their full strength.

"He's growing young, Willie; we must give him a little gentle work now, and by midsummer he will be

as good as Ladybird; he has a beautiful mouth and good paces; these could not be better."

"Oh, grandpapa, how glad I am you bought him!"

"So am I, my boy, but he has to thank you more than me. We must now be looking out for a quiet, genteel place for him where he will be valued."

My Last Home

One day during this summer the groom cleaned and dressed me with such extraordinary care that I thought some new change must be at hand. He trimmed my fetlocks and legs, passed the tarbrush over my hoofs, and even parted my forelock. I think the harness also had an extra polish. Willie seemed half anxious, half merry, and he got into the chaise with his grandfather.

"If the ladies take to him," said the old gentleman, "they'll be suited, and he'll be suited: we can but try."

At the distance of a mile or two from the village we came to a pretty, low house with a lawn and shrubbery at the front and a drive up to the door.

"You see, ladies," said Mr Thoroughgood, when they appeared, "many first rate horses have had their knees broken through the carelessness of their drivers, without any fault of their own; and from what I see of this horse, I should say that is his case: but of course I do not wish to influence you. If you wish, you can have him on trial, and then your coachman will see what he thinks of him."

"You have always been such a good adviser to us about our horses," said the stately lady, "that your recommendation would go a long way with me, and if my sister Lavinia sees no objection, we will accept with thanks your offer of a trial."

It was then arranged that I should be sent for the next day.

In the morning a smart-looking young man came for me. At first he looked pleased, but when he saw my knees, he said in a disappointed voice, "I didn't think, sir, you would have recommended my ladies a blemished horse like this."

"Handsome is that handsome does," said my master. "You are only taking him on trial, and I am sure you will do fairly by him, young man; and if he is not as safe as any horse you ever drove, send him back."

I was led home, placed in a comfortable stable, fed

and left to myself. The next day, when my new groom was cleaning my face, he said, "That is just like the star that Black Beauty had, and he is much the same height too; I wonder where he is now?"

A little farther on he came to the place in my neck where I was bled, and where a little knot was left in the skin. He almost started, and began to look me over carefully, talking to himself.

"White star in the forehead, one white foot on the off side, this little knot just in that place;" then, looking at the middle of my back—"and as I am alive, there is that little patch of white hair that John used to call 'Beauty's threepenny-bit.' It must be Black Beauty! Why, Beauty! Beauty! do you know me, little Joe Green that almost killed you?"

And he began patting me and patting me as if he was quite overjoyed.

I could not say that I remembered him, for now he was a fine grown young fellow with black whiskers and a man's voice, but I was sure he knew me, and that he was Joe Green; so I was very glad. I put my nose up to him, and tried to say that we were friends. I never saw a man so pleased.

"Give him a fair trial! I should think so indeed! I wonder who the rascal was that broke your knees, my old Beauty! You must have been really badly served out somewhere. Well, well, it won't be my fault if you haven't good times of it now. I wish John Manly were here to see you."

I have now lived in this happy place a whole year. Joe is the best and kindest of grooms. My work is easy and pleasant, and I feel my strength and spirits all coming back again. Mr Thoroughgood said to Joe the other day, "In your place he will last till he is twenty years old—perhaps more."

Willie always speaks to me when he can, and treats me as his special friend. My ladies have promised that I shall never be sold, and so I have nothing to fear; and here my story ends. My troubles are all over and I am at home; and often before I am quite awake, I fancy I am still in the orchard at Birtwick, standing with my old friends under the apple trees.